THE BOOK OF G

LILY ARCHER

THE BOOK OF G

Lily Archer
Copyright © 2023 Lily Archer

Editing: Spell Bound

Cover: Perfect Pear

Illustrations: Zakuga Art

THE BOOK OF G

A classic villain tells his own story.

I have a glorious past full of achievement and renown. I mean, I feel like I must, right? The problem is, I can't remember it. I can't even remember my own name. I was found in a river, body mangled and face scarred, with nothing to identify me besides a single embroidered letter.

My memory is a murky blur, but I have a quest, one that will give me back everything I've lost. The voice in the water told me so. But the voice seemed to miss a few important highlights—namely the woman who challenges me at every twist and turn of my journey. The woman who tells me I'm a villain. The woman who never misses an opportunity to throw an insult my way. The woman who becomes every fervent whisper of my heart, and every last thought in my head.

If I can complete my quest and recover what I've lost, she'll see we're meant to be. But villains don't get happy endings. *Do they?*

ONE

Pain. Not the kind you get when you stub a toe or bust your knee. This is searing and all-consuming, like lightning streaking off in all directions and wrapping your body in agony. And it's cold. So fucking cold that for a brief moment I wonder why I hurt so much. Why can I still feel it?

It's dark here. Not a light or a fire or even a star. Or perhaps I simply can't see.

Where am I?

I don't remember. I don't *know*.

I can't breathe. Or, I can, but it burns. So I try not to. I hold my breath until the darkness becomes new and velvety, until I can imagine it's warm. But then I scrape against something hard and sharp, sending a new streak of pain running through me until I scream, the sound distant and garbled. And then I breathe.

I repeat this process again and again until I wish it was over. I wish I was over right along with it.

How did I get here?

My mind can only process the running thread of my suffering. There is *nothing* else. When I try to think, to actually *think*, the hurt brings me right back to the cold dark, to the lightning that flashes over and over again, lighting me up in bright agony until I choke, sinking down, down, down.

I hold my breath.

Hold.

Hold.

Hold.

Hold.

Burn.

Burn.

Burn.

When I finally give in and take a breath, the burning increases a hundred-fold. My lungs are encased in flames as I scrape against the edges of the blackness that surrounds me. The sharpness of the dark cuts away my flesh, flaying me as I drown. I convulse.

This is the end. I welcome it. I want oblivion. I want anything except the agony of existing. If I could pray for death, I would. But my mind can't go there, can't stray too far away from the torment that obscures all other thought.

"*Not yet.*" A voice, one that wraps around me like silky vines.

I feel myself drifting away. I *want* to drift away. This has to be over. I can't stand it anymore.

"*Not yet.*" The voice is more forceful this time.

Fuck off! I take another agonizing breath, my lungs heavy and singed.

The coldness changes. Still icy, but somehow no longer weighing me down. I cough, water spewing from my mouth. Again and again I heave, the lightning pain growing sharper each time, reminding me that I'm caught in some sort of hell.

When I'm empty, when I breathe in gulps of traitorous air. Light sparks. A slight glow, a mirage behind my eyelids. My eyes are closed.

The darkness was so complete only a moment ago. But the light grows until it pierces me, lances thrown through my eyes and crashing through the back of my head. I'm pinned in place like a bug.

I yell, the sound ripped apart and guttural. Deep, gurgling, *wrong*.

Someone tsks. "A long fall."

A long fall? I try to pull apart my memories, to find one of falling. But once again, the deep ache rushes up and stills my mind, shattering the whispers before they can create a thought.

"Mortally wounded. You won't last but a few moments more." A woman's voice I realize, smooth and melodic.

"Just let me go," I say. But I say nothing at all. My mouth doesn't move. No sound leaves.

"I should let you go." She touches my forehead, warmth in her fingertips.

I don't want warmth. I want death! I can't stand her touch, can't bear the ribbons of sensation that wrap around my head and suffocate me. It hurts, doesn't she realize that?

She ignores my plea, her fingers still teasing me with feeling, with life. "A bargain of sorts. Your wickedness has known no bounds. You have not earned a quick death. But perhaps you can earn something more."

What is she saying? Wickedness? I don't know. I can't remember. But I want this to end. All of it.

"You would refuse my gift?" She sounds surprised.

Fuck your gift right in its arse! If I could get to my feet, I would run you through! Leave me be. Let me die. I can't ... I can't suffer any longer.

She sighs. "You can, and you will." Her light fades, and she's rising above me, a star that mocks and eludes. "If you would recover what you've lost, you will travel to the Wood of Mist and find the Graven Phylactery before the end of the Fallen Moon. Fail in this task and you will live a long life, forever cursed with what you lack."

"No!" I can't make the word. Only a grunt rises from me, a jagged denial. What the hell even is a phylactery?

The light disappears, and once again I'm floating, sinking, impaled on spikes and stripped of my skin. I am nothing but raw nerve endings grated over a burning pit.

"*You deserve no less*," she whispers.

"I will fucking gut you and hang you up for the wild hogs to chew and tear!" This time I don't grunt. I don't make a sound. My agony is complete, the dark streaked with razors that spin ever faster, bleeding me but leaving me awake to feel.

Every.

Last.

Slice.

TWO

S omething shuffles around near me, waking me from some hellish nightmare. The sound is distorted. I can't open my eyes.

When I try to speak, the glaring pain of the nightmare returns, streaking across my face.

"Lie still." A harsh voice, cracked with age. "I've already wasted four coppers on you. I won't call the butcher to bandage you again. Not worth it. Not in this sorry state."

"He still sleeping when he should be working, Madge?" Someone else, farther away.

"You still running your mouth when you ought to be mucking stalls, lad?" The woman—Madge, I suppose —retorts.

A grumble answers, then silence.

I open my mouth again, but the agony forces me to lie still as Madge instructed. Madge—who the hell is she? And why am I here? I can't remember.

"Just look at the state of you." She shuffles closer. "I should've left you in the river. Maybe drowned you and sold your body to the butcher so he could use you to teach his apprentice." She clucks her tongue.

My mind starts to haze over again, and I feel myself being dragged down, as if dozens of clawing hands are pulling me into darkness.

"But I don't know if he'd take you. Not when you're already so torn to shreds." More tongue clucking.

I want to fight the pull of the skeletal hands, but I can't. Not when I can't see, can't move. I'm helpless, and I don't like it. I *hate* it. Before, I wasn't helpless. Before, I was … I was … Who was I? A flash goes off in my mind— like the way the sun can hit a glass just right and bounce the glare into your eyes. I see a target ahead of me, and I'm nocking an arrow. I fire, and I hit the target dead center. No, I wasn't helpless. The flash fades, and the cold, hard hands are pulling at me again, sinking me into the caustic blackness that holds nightmares.

"How's he still alive?"

"I don't know, Charles. Monsieur Messier is just as surprised as you are. Same as me." It's Madge. Her voice is brittle. I've come to recognize it over the past few days. I'm finally awake more than I'm asleep, though I still haven't spoken a word. It hurts too much. So does moving. I've managed to wiggle my fingers and move my right arm a slight bit. My legs burn and sting far too much to do anything with them, and I can't decide if I can feel all my toes or only some. Lying still hurts in other ways—my back aches and a distinct claustrophobia comes over me here and there, perhaps because I can't open my eyes. The only thing I've managed to do is part my lips enough for Madge to spoon feed me some water and a horrible-tasting broth.

"He looks like he'd keel over if he tried to stand," says Charles, the stable boy, who comes by on a too-frequent basis to comment on my appearance and how I'm taking up bed space.

Madge grunts right beside me. "I was supposed to take these off two days ago, but I couldn't bring myself to do it."

"I don't blame you." Charles is closer now. "If he looks like this with the bandage on, imagine how bad it must be under there."

"Shush now. Shouldn't you be gathering the firewood like Louis told you?"

Charles groans. "Just let me take a look, then I'll go."

"Suit yourself." The bed shifts, and I get the distinct scent of armpit musk and garlic. "Now, if you can hear me, don't you move. Don't do anything at all. I'm taking off the bandage on your face, then the ones on your chest, then the ones on your legs. I'll put on a poultice the butcher left."

Why is she speaking as if I'm deaf? I can hear her fine. Smell her, too. 'Just get it over with!' is what I want to say, but those words aren't coming, so I simply breathe out.

She takes that as acquiescence, because I feel her hand easing behind my head.

A rusty groan comes from me as she places one hand between the back of my head and the bed and uses her other to unwrap the bandage. It covers my eyes, most of my nose, is open at the mouth, and then wraps around my chin.

She's not gentle. The bandage comes loose but seems to be stuck to me in places, pulling my skin off with it. I should be used to suffering by now, but the torture still hurts, and I still resent every fucking moment of pain.

"My god." Charles sounds stricken. "How did he get like this? Mauled by a bear?"

"No idea. I told you I found him in the river. Nothing on him except some torn clothes. But he'll be up and about soon, so he can tell us himself what the hell happened."

What happened? I've been trying to remember that for all my waking moments. How did I get in a river? Why am I in this state? Whose voice did I hear when I was in the river? What the hell is a Graven Phylactery? And the biggest question of all, who the fuck am I?

"You really think he'll survive?" Charles dry heaves.

"He'd better. I hate doing all this work for nothing." Madge harrumphs.

When the weight lifts from my eyes, I open them. The light stings, so I clench them shut again and wait, shuddering as Madge removes the bandages from my chest. I open them a tiny fraction, then more, then more. I can finally see, dimly.

Madge, a white-haired woman with a dingy shawl around her shoulders, bends over my middle.

I blink, my eyes watering from disuse.

I'm in a tiny cottage, the rafters close overhead and the roof thatch rotting in places.

When she reaches my legs, her touch is rough and sends bursts of fire rushing along my calves and thighs. I groan again, my head thumping, my body protesting.

"Charles, get me the pot from the stove."

"I don't know if I should be—"

"It wasn't a question, boy!" Madge snaps.

"Shit. Fine. All right."

"Damned useless shit mucker." Madge mutters then stands straight—well as straight as she gets, I suppose—holding brown bandages in her hands. Or is that my dried blood?

"There you are." She peers at me.

I stare at her.

She smiles, her missing teeth making my empty stomach turn. "You're a sight. But at least some of you is intact." She gives a pointed look at my crotch.

Something foul hits my nose, worse than Madge's scent. It's sulfur and rotten mud with a hint of dead skunk.

A shadow appears in the doorway. "Here. The poultices."

"Come in and hold them."

"They smell horrible. I should probably—"

"What's your problem, boy? Scared of a little blood? Afraid of wounds? Or is it his cock? You jealous your tiny prick can't compete?"

Charles makes a pfft noise. "Mine can compete any day of the week, Madge."

"Full of piss and vinegar, but too delicate to help an old woman." Madge spits on the floor right beside the bed.

"I'm here." Charles steps closer, his silhouette marking him as a boy no older than fifteen or so.

"Won't take but a minute." Madge grabs more bandages from the pot, but these are steeped in some sort of green gunk.

"No," I say, but the only sound that comes out is 'nnnnn'.

"Pish posh. This'll put hair on your chest." Madge cocks her head at me. "Not that you need any extra." She lays the strip of foul shit on my chest, and it burns so bad I grunt. "This'll get you better faster." She continues wrapping me in filth, and even puts one of the horrific strips along my forehead and on one cheek.

I think I might pass out from the smell.

"Look here." Madge points at my face. "What's left of him isn't so bad looking."

Charles leans over, his blue eyes taking me in. "What's left of him isn't enough to fill a thimble."

Madge clucks her tongue. "We'll see. Now get to your chores. He needs to soak for a while."

THREE

"Fallen Moon?" Madge's voice. "What are you on about in your sleep?"

Was I asleep? I can't tell waking from dreaming. Both are a nightmare.

"I'm reading here," Charles grumbles.

"What's a fallen moon anyway?" Madge asks. "He keeps mumbling about it whenever he's almost awake, almost asleep."

"It's when the moon goes black in the sky; like a shadow crosses it, then clears."

"Oh, I've seen that. Puts a fright in me when it happens." *Clack-clack*.

"Sasha says another one is coming in five months' time."

"And the villagers try to call *me* a witch!" Madge chuckles. "I'm not out here claiming I have the power to black out the moon." *Clack-clack.*

"I don't think it works that way, Madge."

"Pah, keep reading." The fire burns low, and Madge is sitting on the edge of her bed as she knits some sort of ugly gray hat.

Charles sighs. "Where was I? Oh, I see—*but the girl cried and threw herself on her bed, her wicked stepsisters having torn her dress to pieces and ruined any chance she had of attending the ball.*" Charles turns the page of a small book, his voice lulling me back to sleep, back to the abyss where I swear I can hear distant echoes of the voice from the water.

"Seems to me the girl should've slit her stepsisters' throats a long time before it got to this," Madge grumbles as her gnarled fingers work with yarn, her needles making a *clack-clack* sound in rhythmic succession.

"It's not that sort of story." Charles shakes his head and continues reading.

I don't know how long I've been here, how many nights I've fallen asleep to Charles reading a story and Madge's constant *clack-clack.* I can move now, can speak, but I still haven't fully risen from this bed. My body is broken, and I fear what I'll see if I ever look into a glass.

"—*her fairy godmother appeared and used her magic to recover what Cinderella had lost. A new dress—one that sparkled with the light of ten thousand fireflies—adorned her body*—"

I groan and try to sit up.

The *clack-clack* of the wooden needles stops. "What are you about, young man?" Madge asks.

"Do you think he might finally keel over so I can get the bed back?" Charles asks hopefully.

Madge waves a needle at him. "You're a young lad, still a boy. Your back can handle a straw bed by the fire."

I groan again, desperate to ask about this fairy godmother who promises to recover what's lost. Is that what I have? My mind swims, delirium creeping in as I struggle to sit up, the image of a black moon haunting my thoughts.

"Hush now." Madge hovers over me and draws a blanket up to my chin. "You aren't ready for that yet."

"Lost." I push the word out from between my cracked lips.

"Lost?" She backs up a few paces and sits on her narrow bed.

"Of course he's lost. He wound up here." Charles closes the book and lays back on his pile of straw.

That's not what I mean. Tell me more about the fairy godmother! The one in the water! I yell, but it's only a grunt.

Before long, Charles is snoring lightly, the *clack-clack* starts up again, and I'm lost in drowning dreams.

"I SENT FOR FIREWOOD AN HOUR AGO." Louis, the baker, gawks at me as I drop two split logs beside his potbelly stove.

I turn to leave, though I eye the fresh bread he has cooling on the front rack.

"You aren't worth the trouble Madge wasted on you." He steps behind me, and then I feel a hard kick that sends me to the floor, my body aching at the impact. "Get out of here, monster."

I turn over and scowl up at him. My hands itch to go around his throat, to choke the life out of him, to crack his neck.

"Goddamn freak." He kicks at my feet as I turn over and get to my knees, then grab the doorframe to pull myself up.

I'm covered in sweat from the effort, my dirty clothes hanging loosely on my bony frame. My breathing is labored as I leave the bakery, my body already on the verge of breaking. A chilly wind whips through the center of the small town, whistling along crooked eaves and turning my sweat clammy and cold.

Stumbling across the muddy road, I lean on Madge's fence, catching my breath as her sheep eye me cautiously. I need to feed them, then clean out the pigpen, and then feed the chickens.

I've been here a month, but I still can't remember where I came from or who I am. Madge calls me G—she said the letter was embroidered on one of the scraps of clothing that landed on the riverbank with me. It could be me, or it could just be a piece of trash that coincidentally washed up at the same time. Not that it matters. The people of Sac à Puces call me many names, none of them kind. Some of them avoid me altogether, crossing themselves when they get even a glimpse of my scarred face. I hate them all, and every night I pray for the strength to kill them with my bare hands. Everyone except Madge. And Charles. The stable boy doesn't get as much abuse as I do, but he's an outsider, too, one who doesn't make my life harder like the others do.

When I've finally managed to catch my breath, I walk along the sheep enclosure until I come to the small lean-to beside the stables. Here I sit in the shade and stack wood, forcing my body to labor and stretch and loosen the scars that mar so much of my flesh. Some of them still bleed here and there, but the ones that aren't as deep are smooth scar tissue. My face—at least half of it's a ruin. But I don't know what I should mourn. I have no memory of what my face should look like, so the gashes and scars there don't cause more hurt than the others that litter my body.

'*If you would recover what you've lost, you will travel to the Wood of Mist and find the Graven Phylactery before the end of the Fallen Moon.*' The words from a dark dream haunt me. I know what I've lost—everything—my face, my body, my memory. Do I have a family? Is someone out there looking for me?

But the woman in the water also said I was wicked. Now I *know* that was a mistake. I'm certainly not wicked. At least, I don't feel like the wicked sort. Not at all. I'm not bad. The people here are bad. If I *were* to crack their necks, they'd deserve it.

"And what in the holy fuck is a phylactery?" I toss a piece of wood onto the pile.

"It's where a sorcerer stores his soul." Charles leads Monsieur Bernard's mare from the stables. "Like a vial or something he can hide so it will never be destroyed and he can live forever."

"Didn't see you there. So, a phylactery, where could I find one?"

Charles shrugs, the sleeves of his threadbare blue jacket barely reaching his thin wrists. "No idea."

I lift a particularly heavy log and toss it onto the stack.

"Why do you keep moving the wood from one pile to another?" He runs his hands down the horse's neck.

"I need to get strong so I can follow the river, figure out where I came from."

"What's that got to do with a phylactery?" He swats the roan mare away when it tries to grab the cap off his head. "Belinda, keep your teeth to yourself."

"The phylactery is something else. Something I heard about in a dream."

Charles pauses in his reprimand of the mischievous mare. "A dream?"

"When I was in the river." I reach for another piece of wood. "Doesn't matter."

"Well, the nearest town upriver is Martinton, but you can't fight the current to get to it. You have to go over land, and the way is uphill, stony, and particularly difficult." Charles sorts the saddle and buckles it in place.

I eye the mare. Monsieur Bernard is the richest man in town—which isn't saying much—but he does have a few nice horses to choose from. Even if the path to Martinton is rough, a mare like Belinda would still be able to get me there.

"Before you came, Madge let *me* sleep in that bed." Charles grabs the bridle. "So by all means, you should go." He leads the horse toward Monsieur Bernard's cottage, dozens of pigs in the rich man's side pasture squealing with glee and wagging their tails as the stable boy and horse pass by. The sun finally frees itself from the clouds and shines down on the dumpy homes and businesses that line the only cobblestone street in town. Just the look of it disgusts me. I don't belong here.

But where am I supposed to be? My hand strays to my face, and I feel the eerily smooth skin than lines my right cheek and streaks to my forehead. If I do find my home and return to it looking like this, would they even want me?

"If you would recover what you've lost..." The melodic voice, one that is etched into my mind, haunts me again. All I have to do is find one little thing, and I'll be whole again, I'll have my memory. I won't have to search from town to town, won't have to let anyone see what's become of me in this sorry state.

I grab another chunk of wood and ignore the fatigue and aches that punish me. I have a plan now.

I'll find the phylactery and regain what I've lost. Then I'll return to wherever my home is, to people who no doubt love me, and I'll do it without pain, without scars, and without the nagging sensation of unbearable loss.

CHAPTER
FOUR

I unload the wood beside the bakery oven, the smell of bread pleasant in my nose.

"About time." Louis leans against the counter, his arms crossed over his chest.

"You have a complaint, then see Madge." I stride to him. "Now pay me."

He looks up at me, derision mixing with fear as he digs in his apron pocket and hands me two coppers.

I close them in my fist, then turn on my heel and walk away.

"Doesn't matter that you've healed. You're still garbage that washed up in the river," he calls.

I hesitate at the doorway, ire rising inside me like a whorl of winter wind. Anger trickles down my spine and pools in my gut, and I've realized over the past three months that my temper is always near the surface. But today is not the day for this, not when my plan is already laid out for tonight. I only have a month left before the Fallen Moon, one month to find the Graven Phylactery and recover everything I've lost.

I've been getting stronger, my body finally healed and strong enough to withstand a journey. The only problem is that I still don't know where to start. No one in this shithole town even knows what a phylactery is. Only Charles, and he just shrugged and walked away when I questioned him further about it.

With a deep breath, I stride out of the bakery and into the cold twilight, the thin cloak Madge made for me doing little to fight off the chill. I continue down the road, a few townspeople watching me with distrust.

Ahead, a young woman leaves the tailor's shop, her dark hair blowing in the wind. Eloisa Bernard, daughter of the man who owns the stable.

She bundles up and turns toward me, her eyes downcast as she searches her pockets for something, perhaps gloves. I keep going, my thoughts twisting and turning as I try to form a plan to find the Wood of Mist. I've never heard of it, but then again, I can't remember what I *have* heard of. There's an old woman who lives at the other end of the village who I've heard used to travel the world —others say she's a witch. I don't care what she is as long as she has maps or some way for me to find what

I'm looking for. She only arrived in Sac à Puces two days ago, back from some journey to the west, Madge said.

A gasp pulls me from my imaginings, and I find Eloisa staring up at me, her face stricken and pale. She's beautiful, easily the loveliest in the village. Her beauty sparks something in me, but I don't know what. Not lust or longing or even attraction—it's more a wistfulness. I glance my fingers along the ruined side of my face. Was I handsome once? I had to be.

"Don't touch me." She steps back.

"I wasn't—"

"You there!" The bald, portly tailor rushes from his shop. "Leave her alone!"

"I'm just walking." I sidestep her.

She screams. "Help, he's trying to touch me!"

I recognize the feeling she evokes now. It's disgust. Why should she be beautiful while I'm stuck like this? "Get the fuck out of my way." I push past her.

She screams again, making a scene as I hurry away. I don't get far before the tailor rushes me, swinging his pudgy fist at my face.

With an easy dodge, I turn away from him. He slams against the stone wall of the butcher shop and grunts from the pain.

"Fuck." I pick up my pace and keep my head down as more people come out into the street. They yell for me, and when I glance back, the girl is leaning heavily on Louis as he glares after me. Charles is jogging to her, his gaze on me as he quirks his head to the side in question. It's not like I'm going back to explain, so I keep walking.

I turn the next corner and hurry past the ramshackle homes and overgrown gardens until I come to the house with the small, pointed roof over its front stoop. A half-moon is carved into the door, and the garden beside the house has been freshly weeded.

With a harsh knock, I stand back and look behind me, waiting for someone to come after me. That stupid girl overreacted, and now I'm going to have to explain it all to Madge. She's a kind woman, if rough around the edges, and she's given me the benefit of the doubt. This time, though, I don't know if she'll side with me.

I catch movement from the corner of my eye, and when I turn, I find the old woman standing right beside me, her eyes fixed to the same spot as mine were.

"You see something?" She squints.

"No, not … No."

She turns to me, her dark eyebrows rising. "What do you want?"

"I need a map."

"Do I look like a mapmaker to you?" She puts her hands on her hips.

Shouts punctuate the air, and I glance down the alley.

"Can I come in?"

She scratches her cheek, her brown skin wrinkled and pocked in places. "I suppose so. Beats you getting the noose." She glances at the main road and grabs my arm, pulling me into her house and slamming the door behind us.

The home is slightly bigger than Madge's, but the main difference is that every inch of wall is covered in some sort of artifact or art or shelves with books or jars on them.

"I figured you'd stop by sometime." She gives me a long once-over, then swings her gray braids over her shoulder and turns to march toward one shelf in particular.

I follow her, then jump back when a black cat lunges at my feet.

"Scamper, you little shit." She cackles and bends over to grab him.

He tries to push away from her, but she presses kisses to his whiskers before turning him loose.

"He's high spirited." She watches as he hides in one of her cupboards. "And he bites."

"Do you like animals?" She turns back to her shelves, her crooked fingers slipping along the book spines.

"I've never thought about liking animals, I suppose. Some of them are useful. Some of them taste good." I shrug.

She sniffs. "A lout. That's what you are. Blackhearted, too, aren't you? My, my, a blackhearted lout coming to me for maps." She shakes her head, some of the wooden beads at the end of her braids clicking with the movement. "Didn't foresee all that, no I certainly didn't." She laughs a little, her fingers still running across book after book.

I'm not sure if I'm supposed to respond to her assessment, and I don't even know what to say. Maybe she's right. All these books are nothing short of daunting, so maybe I *am* a lout. The blackhearted part—I don't think so. I think I must've been a leader or someone others trusted. Definitely not wicked or blackhearted. They probably only say that about me because I'm scarred and ugly. I wince as I think that word about myself. I'm *ugly*. It sends a shiver through me.

"Stop thinking so hard, young man, you'll only hurt yourself." She snickers and pulls a tall and wide book from the bottommost shelf, then swipes some crumbs of bread from her small round table before laying it down and opening it to a map.

"Here we are." She taps her finger on the first page. "Now, tell me where you want to go, and I can tell you how you can get there from here."

"I need to get to the Wood of Mist before the Fallen Moon."

She slaps the book closed and returns it to the shelf.

"Hey." I shake my head. "Wasn't that the map?"

"It was." She pulls out a rough-hewn chair and sits in it, sighing with age as she does it. "But not one that will help you."

"You don't know where the Wood of Mist is?"

She reaches toward the hearth where a low fire burns and grabs a pipe. "I didn't say I didn't know where it was. But it doesn't matter either way, because you can't get there."

I step to her bookcase and grab the book again, laying it out on the table. "You just said I could tell you where I wanted to go, and then you could use this book to show me how to get there." I shove it toward her then sit, the chair creaking perilously beneath me. "So show me."

She presses some dried leaves into the pipe and uses a stick from the fire to light it, then she puffs for a while before settling back in her seat. "The Wood of Mist isn't on that map. Have a look for yourself." She points with her pipe.

I drag it over to me and look. Mountains and rivers, and on the far side an ocean. Things are labeled, and I lean closer, so close my nose almost touches the page, yet I still can't make out the place names. There are letters, but they don't make sense.

"This is gibberish." I give up and run a hand through my hair, the black locks growing long and in need of a wash.

"Eh?" She looks down at the book. "Makes sense to me." She points. "Here we are in Sac à Puces. Just west of here is Martinton, farther than that are several towns here and there along the river. Here, Paris."

I stare where she's pointing, but the letters don't spell 'Paris'. "That's a-r-p-i-s."

She raises one brow. "Are you touched, young man. Is that your problem?"

"Touched?"

She reaches up and taps the good side of my forehead. "In there." Then she cackles. "I'm just kidding. I know you aren't touched. Just can't read too well."

"I can read." I cross my arms and lean over the map again, doing my best to make the words come into focus, but the more I try, the more they seem to rearrange into nonsense.

"No matter." She swats me away. "There's no Wood of Mist on these pages."

Worry creeps across my skin like black, prickly spiders. If I can't do what the lady in the water told me, then I'll never remember who the hell I am. I'll be stuck like this —a hideous monster that makes young ladies scream at the sight of me. "It has to be somewhere." I flip some pages, but none of them are familiar, the landscapes just different assortments of similar features.

"The Wood of Mist is in the fae lands." She stills my hand. "No map exists for where you have to go."

I pinch the bridge of my nose. "The *fae* lands? You jest. Those are places from children's tales and make believe. The Wood of Mist *has* to be a real place, not some made-up nonsense."

"Is that so?" She takes a few puffs from her pipe. "Tell me, G, where did you hear about the Wood of Mist?"

I push up from the table and stand, then hit one of her low rafters. "Ouch." I rub my head. "Why does that matter?"

"Matters enough that you darkened my doorstep to ask me for a map leading to it. So tell me."

I stare at the books against the wall and try to make out their writing. "I heard it."

"From who?" she goads.

I sigh and hang my head. "From a woman in the water."

"Oh, ho ho! A strange woman in the water somehow managed to give you a quest to the fae lands, yet you say the fae lands are make-believe." She grins, her eyes bright with mirth. "Did you get a look at her?"

"No." I scrub a hand down my face and realize she has a point. The woman in the water—I have to believe she was real, no matter how improbable, or I have to believe I imagined it. There's no other explanation. And if some magical water woman is real, is it so far-fetched to believe the fae lands truly exist? "She was just a light. I was delirious. In pain. Then it was like she lifted me from the water and said ..."

"Go on, boy." She blows a smoke ring into the rafters where herbs are bunched and hung to dry.

"She said to go to the Wood of Mist and find the Graven Phylactery if I—"

She whistles. "That's a tall order. A mighty tall order, indeed."

I whirl on her. "You know what that is—the Graven Phylactery?"

"Of course I do. Even the village idiot—" she points her damned pipe at me again "—knows I'm a witch, one who's well acquainted with the fae."

Arguing against her charge of 'village idiot' will only waste time, so I take my seat again and lean forward on my elbows. "Tell me everything you know."

"Here." She flips through the book to a flap at the back and pulls out a map. "You can take this one, though I'd like it returned to me. I'd hate to have to go out and find your corpse to get it back." She takes a spent bit of coal from the hearth and marks an X in a valley between two mountains. "This is Finnraven Hill, the only way a mortal like you can access the fae lands, but you can't do it alone."

"Sure I can."

"Humans aren't allowed to pass through Finnraven Hill without leave from the fae king, which I'm certain you've not secured."

I shrug. "I'll get through."

"Not to mention, the way is dangerous, and if you make it to the fae lands, more dangerous still." She marks a dotted line from our village that winds through woods and hills, then writes a date. "The Fallen Moon is coming on this night."

"How do you know?"

She gives me a wry look. "Doubt me if you like."

"Never mind. Tell me what sort of danger you were talking about."

"Just take anything you can imagine and make it ten times more deadly—then you'd be halfway there." She cackles and hands the map to me. "Don't follow voices or lights in the trees, make no bargains with hags, do not eat or drink of fae food, and if you hear a mighty howl that shakes the leaves and the air, you may as well bend over and kiss your ass goodbye because the Beast of Gevaudan is coming for you." She eyes the map in my hands. "On second thought, perhaps I should keep that here—"

A bang on the door cuts through her voice, but she doesn't jump.

"Are you expecting someone?"

"Not as such, no. But the ones on my stoop aren't going to wait for an invitation." She stands and grabs my elbow. "This way or they'll string you up right outside my door. I don't need that smell wafting through my rooms."

"We know he's in there!" Louis, the baker, yells. "Send him out. He has to answer for what he's done."

She pauses and looks up at me. "He's right about that last part, you know. We all have to answer in one way or another." With that, she pulls aside a tapestry of a black, wizened tree and opens the door hidden behind it. "Go. Don't let them catch you."

I step out, my boots landing in some disgusting sort of muck, and she slams the door in my face before I can say anything akin to a thank you. Though, given her warnings, I can't say I'm particularly grateful for the path I'm about to tread.

With a little luck, I'll be able to evade the townsfolk and sneak out once everyone's abed. I ease through her garden and duck behind another house as torches and yells light up the main road.

Creeping from building to building, I quietly make my way back to Madge's house.

I'm almost there when I hear a hiss: "What the fuck are you doing, you bleeding idiot!"

A hand shoots out from the narrow alley between two houses and grabs my arm. "Get in here!"

"Charles?" I glance around.

"What the hell were you thinking? You threatened *Eloisa*? She's not for the likes of—"

"Shh!" I clap my hand over his mouth and push him against the cottage wall. "Keep your voice down."

He glares up at me, his blue eyes glinting in the faint light. Voices carry as more villagers rush along the main road, all of them looking for me.

Charles struggles against me, but he's too small to get anywhere. And he's soft, and warm, and—I turn back to Charles. "Why do you smell like ... like something swe—Ow!"

He pinches the meat of my palm between his front teeth. I draw my hand away. "Fuck," I say quietly through gritted teeth.

"Keep your hands off me." He yanks his lapels and rolls his shoulders. "I was trying to *help* you, you buffoon."

"You smell like a fruit jam or a sweetcake." I peer at him as he grips his cap and pulls it down tighter.

"You smell like a pig who's been rolling around in stale shit." He steps away from me. "*Bastard*. Never put your hands on me again!" He bares his teeth, looking feral as he whispers fiercely, "I could yell out right now and bring them to you."

"Calm down." I duck as more torches pass, more villagers scouring the tiny village for me. "You'll get me hanged."

"You've done that all yourself. Fool." He edges away from me.

"Look, I like you, kid, but if you do anything stupid..."

The shouts grow louder. I creep deeper into the narrow space between the houses until I'm practically pinned between the chimney of one and the wall of the other. The gloom here is almost complete, though the heat from the chimney is nigh unbearable.

"They'll find you eventually." Charles leans against the wall across from me, his cap pulled down low over his eyes. "This town is too small for you to hide for long."

"Very helpful." I try to get a better view of the main road.

My heartbeat booms in my ears. Why the hell did Eloisa have to scream? I didn't even touch the wench. Am I really so horrible to look upon? I reach up and touch the ruined half of my face, the stretched skin unnatural under my fingertips. A monstrous beast. That's what I am, and that's what I'll stay if I don't find the Wood of Mist. If I wasn't already convinced, I am now. I have to get back what I've lost.

"Let go!" A familiar voice pierces through the dark.

"Quiet, crone!" The sound of a slap follows. "Tell me where you keep your monster."

"He's not a monster!"

My insides twist and curl as I hear Madge struggling, then see her being dragged down the street by that piece-of-shit Louis.

"You'll tell us where he is, or I'll break your worthless neck."

"Madge!" Charles hisses and slides past me.

They pass out of sight, but I hear the familiar jingle of the door to his bakery. More villagers come, their torches lighting the night.

Someone yells, "Louis got her! She'll tell us where to find him."

A cold sweat breaks out all over me despite the heat from the chimney. I'll run for it. They're all busy with Madge. It might be my only chance. I force myself out of my hiding spot and creep toward the backs of the houses.

Madge screams, the tenor of it sharp, cutting.

"Where are you going?" Charles is right behind me, his small body having an easy time of the narrow alley.

"I'm getting out of here."

"What?" He grabs my arm and yanks. "You can't just leave her!"

I pull free of his grip. "It's what she would want."

"What?" He kicks the back of my calf. "Abandoning her after everything she's done for you, after she saved your life? What is *wrong* with you?"

"Nothing." I whirl on him. "But if I try to help her, I'll get strung up in a tree. That's not in my plans."

"So you're just going to ... run away?" He gawks up at me.

I scoff. "Not in a cowardly way. I'm just being smart."

He glares. "You are going to help her or I'm going to yell right now." He puts his hands up. "Try and stop me, oaf. I'll have you on your ass!"

How hard would it be to break his scrawny neck? I eye his slight frame. Not hard at all.

Madge screams again, and then I hear her fiery curses coming in a torrent.

Charles creeps closer, his fists still at the ready. This is the choice I'm left with, either kill him or help Madge. I know what would be safer, smarter, but as I look at him, at the fierce set of his jaw, I can't bring myself to end his life. Harm him, though? Definitely.

He opens his mouth and sucks in a long breath.

"Listen." I hold my hands out, palms toward him. "I'll get Madge, but I'll need your help."

His eyes narrow in open suspicion. "What sort of help?"

THE BAKERY IS COLD, nothing in the oven as the villagers crowd inside to stare at their prisoner. I stay flattened against the wall beside the back window, hidden in the dark.

"If you want to know where he is, how about you pull my finger, and then I'll tell you?" Madge offers her hand to Louis.

As someone who's been a victim of her offer, I hope like hell Louis takes her up on it.

"Pull your finger?" His brow wrinkles. "Is that some sort of witchcraft?"

"Do it and find out." She waggles her fingers. "Or I'll never tell you a thing!"

He looks around, but the other villagers are no help. "Get on with it," one goads.

Louis swallows hard and reaches for Madge's hand. Then he makes the mistake and pulls her finger. The air she lets loose from her backside is loud enough to send several villagers running out into the main street.

She cackles, her head thrown back and her white hair streaked with red. Louis must have cracked her head. I grit my teeth and wait.

"Fucking crone!" He kicks her, knocking her chair over and sending her onto the stone floor. He rears back to kick her again when someone in the street screams.

"What is—Ach!" Louis yells when a pig shoots into the bakery, its tail waggling as it snorts and runs straight for the sacks of grain. "Out!" He reaches for it, but three more pigs run in and bowl him over. The villagers clear out of the bakery as more pigs enter.

This is it. With a leap, I jump onto the windowsill then drop inside. I narrowly miss landing on a pig, then reach between two of the beasts and grab hold of Madge's arms. With a yank, I pull her from the floor and get her to her feet.

"You all right?" I peer at the cut along her forehead.

"Did you hear that wind I ripped?" She smiles, her missing teeth fondly familiar now.

"Come on." I lift her up and help her out the window.

A hard hit lands on the back of my head, and I whirl to find Louis armed with his coal shovel. "I've got him!" he yells, but the villagers are too busy running from or chasing down dozens of snorting, rooting pigs.

I advance on him. He swings again, but I easily snatch the shovel from his grip. That's when his eyes go round with fear, and it's also the moment when I smile with pure enjoyment. With a hard swing, I crack the shovel over his head.

He falls back, barely staying upright as he tries to grab the counter.

With a quick swipe, I wrap my hand around his neck and lift him, squeezing as he kicks weakly at my knees. "You deserve worse." I stare into his eyes. "If you *ever* touch Madge again, I'll gut you and bake your innards in one of your shitty pies." I squeeze harder, then throw him backwards. He lands in the midst of Monsieur Bernard's pigs, all of them snorting and eating the grain that's now spilled all over the floor.

I snatch up half a loaf of old bread, and then with a quick maneuver, I'm out the window and skirting the backs of the houses.

"Madge?" I whisper-yell, but she's nowhere in sight.

She's free. That's all I agreed to. Now it's time for me to get the hell out of here. I creep into the back of the stables and hurry to Belinda. She snorts, but when I rip off a piece of bread and offer it to her, she comes to me.

"Good." I feed it to her, then lead her from her stall. "You and me are going on a trip." I grab the saddle and put it on her, then fasten the belts and stow the rest of the bread in a bag. "Don't be scared." Belinda nickers when I grip the saddle and start to pull myself up.

"No!" Someone yanks at my shirt.

I turn around to find Charles hanging onto me. "Get off me. I saved Madge. We're done here."

"You aren't taking Belinda!" He reaches around and snatches the reins.

Belinda nuzzles his shoulder.

"I'm not arguing with you." I reach for the reins, but he jumps back.

"You can't take her."

"Why does it matter?" I throw up my hands. "Are you afraid of Monsieur Bernard? Just tell him I stole it! He won't blame you. I'm twice your size at least. He'll know you aren't lying."

He narrows his eyes. "You would've left Madge. You aren't a good man, G. You'll do the same to Belinda, leave her somewhere to suffer, get rid of her the moment you don't need her anymore."

I want to shake him. I just might. "It's a *horse*! Get out of my way, kid!"

"No." He plants his feet. "I won't let you."

Movement behind him catches my eye, and Madge creeps into the stables.

"Thank god. Can you talk some sense into—Fuck!"

Madge swings her skillet at the back of Charles's head. The boy yelps then crumples to the ground.

"What was that for?" I shake my head quickly. "Never mind. Thank you." I reach for the saddle again, then hesitate. "You didn't kill him, did you?"

"You think I've never conked someone on the head before?" She flips the pan in the air and catches it. "Of course I didn't kill him."

"Good." I hook my foot in the stirrup.

"Take Charles with you." She points the pan at me.

"What? No." I can hear the oinks and squeals subsiding. Pretty soon the villagers will get back to looking for me. I'm running out of time.

"You will take him, or I'll brain you right here and now." She brandishes the pan. "I didn't kill Charles, but that offer doesn't stand for you."

Belinda backs up a few steps and makes a distinctly unhappy sound. When I try to reach for her reins, she pulls even farther away.

"She doesn't like you." Madge juts her chin at the horse.

No shit. "Walk away, Madge. I'm leaving. Now."

"Charles won't go willingly. He's too worried about me." Her eyes soften as she stares down at her victim. "But he won't be safe, not when the village is looking for someone to blame. If he tries to get between them and me, I couldn't bear for him to get hurt. He's a good lad, and I can take care of myself." She flips the skillet again.

"I've lived here all my life, and they haven't gotten me yet. Won't get me this time, either."

I try to ease back and grab the reins, but once again, Belinda steps away from me. If she bolts, I'm finished, and Madge is making this far more difficult than it has to be. "Look, I'm not just going to the next village, Madge. I'm going somewhere far, somewhere with lots of danger. I don't even know where, exactly. Charles should stay here with you where it's safe."

She returns her gaze to me. "You think I don't know you've been planning on leaving?" She tosses me a sack with her other hand. "Food for you and Charles. You'll find a few other useful bits in there, too. Now go." She steps past me and grabs Belinda's reins easily.

I give the beast an offended glare.

She nuzzles Madge.

"He doesn't belong here, not in this tiny town. He's meant for something better, and there's more to him than anyone knows. I can feel it in my old bones. Now get him up." She points at the boy.

The villagers start shouting again, all of them winding up like some goddamn clock.

I eye Madge, then Charles. This is a bad idea, but I don't see any other way out. I just have to leave him by the roadside a little way from the village, somewhere Madge can find him. With a heavy sigh I lean down and scoop Charles up, then drape him over the front of the saddle.

"I'll hold her." Madge keeps the reins in her hands as I climb up and situate myself behind Charles. She gives me one more hard look. "If you abandon him, G, I'll curse you. I'll curse you until you take your last breath, and then I'll follow your soul all the way to hell to curse you again."

Can she hear my thoughts? "I would never do that," I say confidently and shake my head.

She hands me the reins, then makes some symbol with her fingers. "The curse is hanging over your head, young man. Cross me and find out." She pats Charles on the head. "Safe travels. Don't be afraid. Your future is waiting."

"What about my future?" I ask.

"Your future?" She shrugs and steps back. "I suppose it depends on your choices. Make better ones." With that, she smacks Belinda on the ass, and we take off from the stables, her hooves clopping on the stones as villagers yell and raise their torches behind us.

The stones quickly run out, the ground turning into mud and then a leafy mush. The sounds of Sac à Puces fade, and in only moments it's just me, Charles, and Belinda hurtling through the starry night.

FIVE

C harles groans.

I've spent the last few miles of road trying to decide if I should risk Madge's curse and simply dump him off the horse. But every time I almost do it, I look up and wonder if the curse truly is hovering right overhead.

I *already* feel cursed. Adding another one is probably a bad idea.

"Mmmph?" Charles turns his head. "What's going on?"

I pull on Belinda's reins, stopping her, then grab Charles and help him sit upright in the saddle. That deliciously sweet scent hits my nose again. "You know, if you've been stealing pies from Louis, you could've at least shared."

"What?" He rubs his head again, then turns and looks at me, his eyes wide. "How did I get—"

"Madge made me take you with me." I sigh.

"What? To where?"

"I don't know. She said some crap about wanting to save you or something and for some reason, she thought the safest place you could be is with me, on the road, headed through every danger in the world."

He rubs the back of his head. "Madge did this?"

I pause and think. "Really, you know, you should go back. It's the smartest plan. You can go right back and help Madge. She was really torn up, scared for her life. Terrified, really. But you could go back and save her! Tell the town I've left for good. Be the hero. Calm them down. Maybe it would even get you in good with Monsieur Bernard." I lean closer to him. "Maybe you could impress Eloisa."

He scoffs.

I frown and lean back. "It's the best thing. Far safer than the road. Go back."

An owl hoots overhead, white wings swooping through the dark trees.

Charles pats Belinda on the neck, rubbing her gently. "Sure. I'll return to town. Just get off the horse."

I let my head loll back and look at the canopy of branches and leaves. "No, Charles. I'm keeping the horse. I have a long way to go. You just have to walk a few miles."

"I'm not leaving her with you." He stiffens his spine. "Not a chance."

"It's just a horse!" I put my hands near his neck and hold them there, dreaming of squeezing the life out of him.

"Try it, asshole." He pulls a knife from somewhere and holds it over my thigh.

I drop my hands.

"Give me the horse and go." He stows the knife in his tunic.

"No. *You* give *me* the horse and go."

"No."

Belinda makes a huffing noise.

"You're upsetting her." Charles strokes her neck. "Are you upset, girl?"

The horse snuffles again, clearly in agreement with the boy.

I run a hand through my hair and yank on the strands in pure frustration. "I'm not going back, and I'm not giving you the horse."

"Then we're at an impasse." He keeps stroking the horse.

It would be so easy to throw him to the ground and ride off. '*If you abandon him, G, I'll curse you.*' I grind my teeth.

Charles takes the reins and makes a clicking sound with his tongue. Belinda walks at an easy pace, no longer the thundering run from the village.

I rack my brain for some way to get the boy off the horse. "I could kill you, you know? I could just snap your neck and leave you on the side of the road. Nothing to stop me. You don't stand a chance."

He shoots me a glance over his shoulder. "Liar. If you wanted to, then you would've done it already."

My teeth go back to their grinding. "All this over a horse?" I grumble. "This can't be worth it to you. Your whole life is back in town."

He shrugs and offers no further explanation.

We travel in silence for a long while, the trees growing thicker as the air gets colder. It occurs to me that I don't even know if we're going the right way. The road through Sac à Puces only goes in two directions. I need to look at the map.

Charles shivers and pulls his hat down tighter in that way of his.

"We should stop." I point ahead to a small area between two huge trees. "Make camp there. We're far enough away from town now."

He leans down and whispers to Belinda, then pats her neck. "She's tired. All the excitement and the running."

We stop, and I drop from the horse then grab Madge's bag. "I'll start a fire."

Charles grins down at me, and then I realize the stupid mistake I made.

"Wait!" I reach for him, but he kicks Belinda in the sides.

"Charles!" I lunge for the reins, but it's too late. Belinda startles and gallops away. He turns her easily as I charge after them, and they pass me at a run, flying back toward the village and leaving me alone, horseless, and in the dark.

I CHEW on the only slightly moldy potato Madge threw in the bag for me and try to make sense of the map. The words aren't turning into anything, so I've long since stopped trying to read them. Instead, I trace the path the old witch marked for me. It winds around this way and that, but it doesn't give me any clear indication of where I am, at least not now. Once the sun is up, I should be able to tell if the mountains on the map are on my left or my right, and then I'll know if I've already fucked up.

Kicking my boots up by the small fire, I finish the potato and drink some water. As I put the skin back, something tinkles around inside the bag, and I feel around for whatever it is. I draw it out. A rusty metal spoon? Why would Madge put that in here? Daft. I toss it back into the bag and feel around more, past some crusts of bread until I feel something square.

I pull that out and stare at it. It's the little book that Charles always read to us from before we fell asleep. The cover is well worn, the edges frayed, though it still has words on it and a painting of a star. I eye the fire and think about burning it out of sheer spite, but I don't. I toss it back into the bag and feel around again. This time I brush against something smooth.

"What's this?" I pull out a piece of black leather that's been molded into sort of a semicircle. There are thin strips of leather dangling from the sides. After flipping it around a few times and even holding it up to the fire to get a better look, I'm still unsure of what the hell it is, so I toss it back in the bag and lie on my side by the fire.

Some moldy food, a little water, and pieces of junk—none of that is going to be particularly helpful. What would've been helpful? A damn horse.

Belinda was the only thing that might've made this journey at least moderately bearable, but now that she's gone, I'll have to walk for miles and miles just to get to the next town—that is if I don't die between here and there. I glance around at the woods and hope the fire will keep any hungry predators at bay. It's not as if I can fight them off with a spoon, and I don't have any other weapons. I had to leave too quickly and couldn't grab my axe like I intended. I'd even started trying to fashion a bow from some ash wood and a piece of Madge's dried pig entrails, but I didn't finish that either. My entire plan blew up the moment that spoiled brat Eloisa got a good look at me.

Again, my fingers stray to my face, and I feel all the valleys and ridges that mark my ugliness. I've been almost indifferent about it, somehow shutting out the pain it causes me while I got over the very literal pain of it healing. But now, alone in the woods with a dying fire, I let my fingers roam fully, discovering every bit of ruin, every crevice of twisted skin. I take solace in the only thing I can—the promise of the woman's voice. I'll recover what I've lost. I have to. Because if I have to live like this, I think I would've preferred to die in the water.

THE SUN HASN'T RISEN YET, but its rays are faintly peeking through the leaves. I sit up and rub my sore neck. The fire still burns low after I stoked it here and there during the night. I shiver as I stretch and get to my feet.

A light breeze kicks up as the day begins, and I'm finally able to see the mountains to my left. I'm going the right way. At least I did that right—everything else has been a disaster.

I grab Madge's bag and kick some dirt over the fire before walking out to the road. There's nothing to do except walk, so that's what I do.

My stomach grumbles after I've gone maybe a mile, but I need to conserve my food and water. The woods hem me in on either side of the road, which at this point is nothing more than two wheel-ruts almost grown over by scrubby grass and covered with leaves and pine needles. My steps are muffled in the damp ground litter, and I listen for any stray sound the forest offers. The last thing I need is for some enterprising asshole from Sac à Puces trying to come bag me for a bounty.

The brisk wind grows more cutting as the day goes on, promising me a night of misery unless I can find some shelter. But the forest road seems to go on forever, and when I stop to check my map, no big towns are marked along the way, not for a while. So, I trudge on, my body giving me only a few aches and pains as I go. Despite having been ruined in places, the skin scraped away and small bones broken, I recovered well enough under Madge's care. Whatever strength I had before the river, it seems to have returned, though not completely. I know I won't be whole until I find the Graven Phylactery, and I find myself hoping again and again that it's real, that I'm not a deluded idiot searching for something that doesn't exist.

I walk until my back aches, my knees creak, and I'm parched. The trees have thinned somewhat and given way to rocky outcrops on the left and right. Some of them shoot straight up into the air like boards of wood or horrifically long bottom teeth. The farther I walk, the more rock grows from the landscape, and my feet protest with each step on the pebbles and stone. The sun is going down again, the chilly wind growing sharper by the moment.

I don't want to stop, not when I've yet to see anything resembling a town or even a homestead, but when I hear the howl of wolves somewhere in the distance, I halt and peer at the boulders, looking for one that might give me shelter.

It takes a while, but I finally find one up a slope. A tree had grown against the side of a rock, forming itself to the harsh planes of it until it was free to stretch upward and create a canopy overhead. The wolves howl again as I make my fire and pile wood nearby so I can keep it going all night.

Madge's bag provides a meager meal of stale bread and half a carrot. Her cooking wasn't particularly skilled, but at least she managed to hide the mustiness of the ingredients beneath the mustiness of her seasoning.

Once the fire is going, I study the map again, doing my best to memorize the way the land swoops and curves or rises into unforgiving peaks. Every time, my gaze strays to the final mark, Finnraven Hill. What lies beyond it—if anything—is an even more mysterious trek. That thought alone has me folding the map and sliding it into my pocket.

I lie down again, the cold ground poking into all my tender places. Scooting closer to the fire, I silently curse Charles for ruining my chances of having an easy trip with a horse beneath me. That meddlesome boy might be the end of me. As if to punctuate the thought, the wolves yip somewhere nearby, and I peer around in the dark, trying to catch movement. Nothing strays into my vision, only the swaying branches and the first fine snowflakes that fall from a sullen sky.

"Kill what beast?"

I scramble back with a yell.

"Calm down." Charles pokes at the embers of my fire.

"Wh-what?" I blink, against the first light of day, then gape when I see Belinda pawing at the stony ground only a few feet away from me.

"You were whispering over and over in your sleep about a beast. You did that back at Madge's too. Madge thought it was because you had a fever from your wounds getting infected, but now I know you're crazy at any temperature."

"You came back." I rub my eyes to make sure I'm not hallucinating from the spoiled carrot.

"Not really." He shrugs. "I was just passing through."

I can only stare. What the hell is he talking about? "Passing through?"

"I went back to Sac à Puces and found Madge. She was in her house, cooking like always." He pulls a fresh carrot from his pocket.

I reach for it, but he feeds it to Belinda as I watch with horror.

"The villagers were just happy you were gone, so they left her alone. She scolded me to within an inch of my life and bade me move on. I didn't want to at first, but then I thought about it, and she's right. I was in Sac à Puces for longer than I intended. I guess I got comfortable." He shrugs.

"You were comfortable?" I'm not following. Then again, I think my backside froze during the night, and I'm still dazed from seeing the fresh carrot go to the horse.

"Why do you keep repeating everything I say?" He turns on his heel. "Never mind. Doesn't matter. Are you coming?" He easily mounts the horse and looks down at me.

I scramble up from the hard ground and snatch Madge's bag. When I swing myself onto Belinda, she nickers and turns her head like she's going to bite my leg.

"Hey!" I yell and reach to bat her nose away.

"Girl, no," Charles says before I can land the blow. "It's okay. I know he smells."

Belinda turns forward again, but her mane twitches. Charles's short blond hair, poking from beneath his cap, tickles my nose, and I almost sneeze.

"If anyone should be offended, it's me! You two left me. I could've died!" I scoff with indignation.

"He's so dramatic." Charles nudges Belinda forward and onto the road, a light dusting of snow all around us and glistening in the trees. "Don't act like you wouldn't have done the same to me if you had the chance."

"I *didn't* have a chance because Madge threatened to curse me if I left you. Did she mention that when she was showering you with goods? Did she threaten to curse *you* for leaving *me* and stealing my horse?"

"Oddly enough, it never came up." I can hear the smile in his voice, and for what must be the hundredth time, I think about throttling his thin neck.

The sweet scent wraps around me, taking hold in weird places and making my nose tingle. "Did you at least bring some pie for me?"

"What is this obsession with pie?" He digs around in the bag at his shoulder. "Here."

I take a piece of moderately fresh bread from him along with a hunk of cheese. "Where'd you get this?"

"Since I was leaving and Monsieur Bernard only ever paid me pauper wages, I thought it was fair to get a few parting gifts from his larder."

"Stolen?" I grin as I bite the cheese.

"Judge me if you must," he says airily.

"Not at all." The small bits of food fill my empty stomach, and horseback is a welcome change from the hard ground. I find myself unable to complain about a single thing, not as we ride at a modest pace through the stony wilderness and up a long, rolling rise.

"Are you going to let me see the map?"

I cock my head to the side. "What map?"

"The one in your coat."

"How did you—"

He holds his hand out.

"I don't know what a kid like you—how old are you, anyway?" Come to think of it, Charles is probably far too young to be out on the road like this. His voice hasn't even changed, and I don't see a single hair on his chin. He's a kid, but I'm not here to babysit anyone. I have my own problems to worry about.

He scoffs. "What does my age have to do with a map? Just let me see it."

I can't readily think of an answer, so I pull the map out and hand it to him grudgingly. "Don't tear it."

"You're the one who'd accidentally tear it. Not me." He unfolds it, then his spine goes stiff.

"What?" I look over his shoulder, his hair tickling me again. I blow it away from my face. "What's wrong?"

"Why are you going to Finnraven Hill?"

I reach for the map, suddenly feeling like I shouldn't have given it to him in the first place. "It's none of your business."

He pulls it away from me. "Tell me why."

"Are you going there?"

"No!" He clears his throat and says in a calmer tone of voice, "I mean, no, I intend to stop at Paris."

"Then it doesn't matter to you. You'll be back on the streets in no time, shoveling horse shit and taking orders." I finally manage to swipe the map back. "Let's leave it at that." It was easy enough for me to tell the witch what I needed and where I was going, but telling Charles is a different matter. I realize how insane this all sounds. The last thing I need is for Charles to get spooked and take my horse again. Speaking of: "I'm taking the horse at Paris. You won't need her anymore, and I'll still have a long way to go."

"You aren't taking Belinda."

Instead of having the same argument, I glare at the back of his head. The sun glances out from behind the clouds here and there, lighting the strands until they look almost golden. It's ... beautiful. Not that I think men are beautiful, generally speaking. But no one could deny that

Charles has nice hair. Nothing untoward in that. I reach up and pinch a lock of my own hair, the strands coal black. My skin may be ruined in places, but I still have good hair—though not as good as Charles's. Not that I'm competing. That would be silly.

"Stop staring at me and work on this." He reaches down the side of Belinda and into a long potato sack before pulling out my ash wood and pig intestine.

"You brought my bow." I take it from him.

"Such as it is. I can't imagine it'll do much damage in that state."

"What about my axe?" I ask.

"Madge needed it." He shrugs.

"I need it more."

"Everything's not about you," he shoots over his shoulder.

As much as I disagree with that statement—especially considering that I am *me*—I let it go and work on stripping the dried intestine down into a stretchy string.

We ride for another hour or so until we crest the rise and stop to take in the view, allowing Belinda to drink and have a bruised apple. A valley is laid out before us, blunt mountains hemming it in on either side, and a forest of trees gathered around a glittering river that runs along the bottom. Smoke rises from the center in white wisps, filtering through the heavy leaves and up to the sky.

"That must be Arlon." He points.

"How do you know?"

"Read it on the map."

"Right." I remember seeing the treed valley on my path to Finnraven Hill, though the name was impossible to figure. "Arlon."

"Let's go. Maybe we can find a good place to stop for the night." He clucks his tongue, and Belinda starts the journey to the trees.

"Or an inn with some food. Something hot."

"You have money?" he asks.

I grin. "No, but I have a stable boy who'll work for our food."

"You're right. I'm the only one here who's even remotely useful. Fair point."

My grin falls, and I chew over different, admittedly weak retorts until the time limit has run up for me to say anything back at all.

By the time we're under the dappled shade, I've strung my bow with a braided string. It's too thick and possibly strung too tightly, but it will have to do for now. All I need are some arrows to test it out. It's strange, but working on the bow sends familiar sensations through me. Like the tips of my fingers recognize what I'm doing even if my memory doesn't. I don't know how I know the way to assemble a bow, but I do. I'm already thinking about feathers I'll need for the arrows. But the knowledge is steeped in mystery. I must've been a hunter, but where? Was that my profession?

"Why do you have that stupid look on your face?" Charles asks, and I realize he's been looking over his shoulder at me.

"Rude." I test the bow string. It has a satisfying snap when I pull on it.

He rummages around in our bags and pulls out the water skin, then takes a swallow of water.

I reach for it, but he doesn't offer it to me and places it back in the bag. "Hey, what's this?" He pulls out the weird half-moon piece of leather.

"I don't know. I guess it goes with the spoon Madge put in there." I hang the bow on Belinda's other side.

He flips it over in his hands and pulls on the leather strips. "Oh."

"Oh, what?"

He turns to me and presses it to my face.

"What the fu—"

"It's a mask." He smiles up at me. "Covers up the ugly side." When his gaze rakes over the non-ruined half of my face, his blue eyes widen a little.

"Handsome, right?" I ask.

"No, I was just wishing she'd made a mask to cover your entire face, including a gag for your mouth."

"Fucking rude."

He grins and adjusts its placement. "Now you can just tie it. This way the townspeople won't run screaming."

I grumble some choice words under my breath and tie the mask. It's not too uncomfortable and it hides the worst of it. I don't need Charles to tell me that side of my face looks awful; I already know. But I'm not going to agonize over it when I know I'll get it back once I do what the woman in the water said. This hideous mess isn't really me. It can't be.

The road becomes clearer the deeper we get into the woods, and there are small hovels off in the trees, though they don't seem occupied. In fact, the forest is quiet. I don't even see any birds in the frosty limbs overhead. A lot of the trees also look dead, not just winter dead, but dead-dead. They're a gray color, and I feel like if I touched the bark, it would slough off in my hand.

"Something's strange here." I see more grayish plants along the road, even the pine needles that ashy gray.

Charles turns his head to the right and cues Belinda to stop.

"What?" I ask.

"Shh."

I scan the trees where he's looking, but I don't see anything. "What do you—"

"Shh!" he whispers harshly.

I can't strangle him. I can't strangle him. I can't strangle him. Wait a second. Madge only said I couldn't *abandon* him. She never said I couldn't—

"Look." Another harsh whisper as he elbows me.

I follow his line of sight again. "What?"

"The smaller tree. Watch it."

I focus on the tree I think he's talking about. Probably ten feet tall, it's a spindly tree covered with green lichen with only a few leaves at the very ends of its branches. "It's just a tree."

"Look away from it."

"But you just told me to—"

"Look away!"

With a groan, I turn my head.

"Now look."

I let out a longsuffering sigh and go back to it. "Hang on." I squint. "Did it ..."

"It moved." He grips the reins tighter. "And it's not the only one. Spriggans."

"What's a spriggan?"

Something creaks to my right, and I turn quickly. All I see are trees, but the hair on the back of my neck stands on end.

"They're all around us." Charles keeps his voice low.

Belinda snorts and paws at the ground.

"Are they dangerous?" I reach for my bow even though I have no arrows.

He clucks for Belinda to get going.

I turn the slightest bit, then hear a high-pitched shriek and feel something spray on my face.

"Belinda, go!" Charles yells.

We bolt, and I wrap one arm around Charles to keep both of us on the horse as we take off down the road.

An itch takes hold on my ear, and I reach up and unlace the mask. It dangles in my hands, and I see a yellow sappy substance on it, burning and bubbling into the leather.

"What the hell was that?" I turn back and forth, trying to keep my eye on the forest from all angles but failing.

"They spit acid to incapacitate you!" Charles yells over the wind and the thud of Belinda's hooves.

I wipe the sting from my ear and find more of the sap. With a hard flick, I fling it into the woods that are now passing by in a blur.

Then Charles cries, "Whoa!" and we stop hard, the force nearly throwing us over the front of the horse. Up ahead, two spriggans block the road.

Belinda moves back, but several more are clambering onto the path behind us.

"We have to go." I turn back toward the ones ahead of us.

"We can't."

Belinda is still backing up, taking us right to the spriggans behind us.

"We have to."

"Go, girl, go." Charles kicks her sides and makes his clucking sound.

She nickers and keeps backing up.

"Make her go!"

"She's frightened!" Charles snaps back.

"Here." I reach around him with one hand and grab the reins, then raise my other hand and bring it down painfully hard on Belinda's ass.

She takes off running. We race away, and I hear more of those shrieks as some squat buildings appear ahead. The town of Arlon. Two big fires burn on either side of the road, and a handful of men stand there waiting, each of them wielding an axe, each of them looking nothing short of murderous.

"Oh, shit. I don't think we should—"

"We have no choice!" Charles cries over the wind.

I take his point when another squirt of sap goes shooting past my shoulder. Belinda flies, pounding down the road, and she doesn't even stop when she gets near the fires. The men with the axes raise them as we pass, but they don't turn and follow us. They remain focused on the trees outside the village.

"Whoa!" Charles pulls back on the reins. "Whoa, girl. We're safe. Whoa."

Belinda slows and then stops, and I can feel her breathing hard.

Charles pats her neck. "Good girl. That's a good girl."

I take in the village, the thatched-roof huts and the stalls that stand empty. Stumps litter the area, every single tree cut down and recently, from the look of it.

"You can let go now," Charles says.

"Oh." I didn't realize I'd still been holding him tight to me. "I was just—"

"Sure." He dismounts and rolls his eyes at me. "Just so you know, I'm not interested."

"What?" I scoff. "*I'm* the one who's not interested."

He raises a brow, then yanks his cap down and pulls out some small turnips from the bag, offering them to Belinda before pouring her some water into a rough wooden bowl.

I slide off the horse and peer around, my interest mostly on the men with the axes. Two of them are striding toward us. They're thin, their clothes hanging loosely and their faces gaunt. My hope for a hot meal dwindles with each step they take.

Someone gasps, and a woman covers her daughter's eyes and rushes her into the hovel closest to me.

"It's your face," Charles offers helpfully.

I ignore him and approach the two men with the axes. "Hello, friends. I take it this is Arlon?"

They exchange a look, and one of them—a tall barrel-chested man with a scraggly beard and thinning red hair—gives me a nod. "Welcome to Arlon, such as it is. I'm Corlis, and this is Raphael."

"The spriggans—" Charles comes to my elbow. "—how long have they been here?"

The men exchange another look, this one with raised eyebrows. "So you know what they are?" Corlis scratches

70

his chin. "We didn't know what to call them. Spriggans, you say?"

Charles nods. I nod, too, and pretend I know exactly what's going on.

"They showed up two months ago. We thought at first old Claymon was going crazy, saying the trees were moving and spitting at him." Corlis grimaces. "We almost burned him at the stake for it." He chuckles, the other man joining in.

"Yes, flint, firewood, and charred bodies are such a commonplace miscalculation," Charles deadpans.

He uses such big words for his age. It must be all those books he reads. Or perhaps he's the runaway son of some lord, destined to inherit the family fortune when he comes of age. I snort at the thought of it.

He turns and gives me a sharp look, as if he's somehow guessed I'm silently mocking him.

"What?" I shrug.

"For only having half a face, you wear your thoughts quite clearly." He rolls his eyes and looks away.

I can't tell if I'm being insulted, but with Charles, I have to assume I am.

A young man marches by, his arms loaded with firewood.

The men sober. "The fire keeps them at bay. Once the sun goes down, we light them all around. They still try to get in, still pick us off here and there, but we're trying to outlast them."

"You won't." Charles leads Belinda to a low stone wall next to a blacksmith's stall and puts her water bowl on the ground. "Spriggans multiply until they take over the entire forest. They'll suck the life out of everything here, including the people of Arlon."

"How does a young pup like you know so much about this?" Corlis turns his axe in his palm, twisting it like a deadly sleight of hand.

I ease closer to Charles, my eyes on the axe. Then I whirl on Charles. "That's a good question. How do you know this?"

Charles shrugs. "I read a lot."

Corlis doesn't seem convinced, and he twists his axe faster, the wooden handle whispering against his dry palm. "You sure you aren't one of them?"

Charles rolls his eyes. "Do I like look a tree to you?"

"Not as such, no. But we have to be careful." Corlis glowers.

"If he knows what they are, maybe he knows how to get rid of them. Maybe the ugly one can help." The woman who'd hidden her child from me steps from her hovel, her hands on her hips and a particularly surly expression on her round face. "Think with your head instead of your axe, Corlis."

I know an opportunity when I see one. "Now, now." I cross my arms over my chest. "Let's not be hasty. As you know, information comes at a price—"

"There's a wood sprite controlling them. If you find her and kill her, the spriggans will die," Charles says, his tone matter-of-fact.

"Boy!" I yell, but it's too late, so all I can do is glare at him.

"What?" Unbothered, he stares right back.

"The Crone Tree," Raphael says and makes the sign of the cross.

"That has to be it." The woman nods.

"This whole time, we could've ended it!" Corlis whirls and throws his axe, embedding it in a tree just outside the ring of the village. "But now we'll never make it to the damn thing."

"What's the crone tree?" Charles asks.

"We don't care what it is." I take his arm and lead him back to Belinda. "We're only passing through." I don't have time for spriggans or sprites or whatever the hell is going on in this broken-down village. There's no hot food. No reason for us to stay.

"Passing through, eh?" The woman laughs, her yellowed teeth edged in black. "Headed east?"

"Yes." I gesture to the horse. "Come on, Charles, let's go."

"You'll have a hard time with that, lads. The crone tree is dead east on the road. Can't miss it. Looks like an old woman bent over with a cane. The way's been blocked for nearly a month. Anyone who goes down there never comes back. Now the creatures have spread all around through the forests. We're almost completely cut off."

"We'll just go around." I start feeling in my pocket for my map.

"You could." She nods. "Through the mountains where the wolves rule. It would add weeks to your journey, at the very least—that's if you survive. Do you have enough food for the trip?" Her unfortunate teeth make another appearance as she smiles.

Charles turns on his heel. "If we manage to clear the wood sprite and the spriggans, would you give us enough food and water to make it to Paris? For the two of us *and* our horse?"

"What? No. We're leaving." I try to lift him onto Belinda's back.

He elbows me hard. "Lay off."

I grunt and let him go.

Corlis turns to the woman. "Shazza?"

She stares hard at Charles. "That would be all the food we have left."

Wait. They're actually considering it? If we could get those provisions, the road to Paris would be easy.

"That's right. All the food." I station myself beside Charles, my chin high. "Take it or leave it."

Shazza wrinkles her nose, the rounded point like the end of a sausage. She considers us for a while longer, then says, "Deal."

Charles nods. "We'll need leather hides for protection, then axes, tar, and fire. Also some help getting it out to the Crone Tree."

"And arrows." I grab my bow.

"We've all that, but we aren't sacrificing any more of our people. You two go alone." Shazza motions to one of the men carrying wood around the camp. "Come, fetch me that brazier and load it with kindling and solid logs. Put it in Raphael's wheelbarrow so they can push it out to the tree. Dip some arrows in tar and pack a quiver."

The man gives her a questioning look.

"Get to it!" Shazza claps her hands as someone yells, a spriggan spitting acid toward the fires burning high along the road. "Dark will be here soon. You'd best get going." She points to the other side of the village. "Stay on the road and hurry. Once it gets dark, they're stronger."

I reach for Belinda's reins.

"No, she stays here." Charles smacks my hand and strides away.

"Hey!" I take off after him. "We need the horse. The spriggans will spit all over us just walking out there like fools. We won't even make it to the Crone Tree."

"That's what the leathers are for. We can shelter under those until we make it to the sprite."

I grab his shoulder and turn him around to face me.

"What?" he asks.

"How do you know this will work? Why are you so ... so—"

"Knowledgeable?" he fills in.

"Foolhardly," I say.

"You mean 'foolhardy'?"

"Yes, that."

His blue eyes sparkle. "I can handle myself with spriggans and a wood sprite. Worry about yourself, G." He ducks from my grip and keeps going.

"How?"

"We kill the sprite with the fire, then the spriggans will rot. That's how."

"No, how do you know all this? Just from books?" I can't imagine some paper with confusing letters shat all over it could be this helpful. It seems ... wrong. Like it's too much.

"Yeah, from books." He stops at the edge of the village near the lighted bonfires.

The woods are thicker here, the light barely penetrating to the leafy ground.

I feel an itch at the back of my mind, a sense that Charles is full of shit. But he's never been much of a liar before, not that I can recall. In fact, I always thought he was painfully honest. Why is he lying about this?

"Books?" I ask again.

He glares at me. He isn't going to give me any other answer, and I suppose I don't have much choice other than to trust him. With a resigned sigh, I move on to more important questions. "How dangerous is this? I already know about the spit, but what's the sprite like?"

"Leathers." A boy drags two pieces of rawhide over to us, one of them from some sort of deer and the other a bear.

I throw the deer over Charles's back. He makes an *oomph* sound but grabs it and pulls it around his narrow shoulders. The bear smells of mustiness and cat piss, but it's a nice thick hide. I wear it like a cape, high enough to shield my head from spriggan spit.

Another boy hands me a quiver full of arrows, and I sling it over my back beneath the bear hide.

"The sprite is dangerous. She has claws and teeth with the same venom the spriggans spit. And she'll likely be monstrously large." He pulls the hide tighter.

"This is a bad idea." I peer out into the trees ahead of us. "I don't even know if all the food and water is worth it if I die here."

"We'll be helping this whole village. Isn't that worth it?"

I simply stare at him.

He sighs. "Never mind. Let's go."

Raphael struggles toward us with his wheelbarrow loaded down with a decent fire, a clay pot of tar, and several torches with crappy fabric wrapped around the ends. Two axes lay to the side, and I grab one, testing its heft in my hand. Not bad.

Charles takes the other axe and does an experimental swing. "We just need to move as fast as we can."

"Pushing a wheelbarrow?"

"You push the wheelbarrow, I'll hack any spriggan that gets in your path."

I don't like the sound of that. "I'm better at chopping wood."

"You're also stronger, so you can move the wheelbarrow faster." He strides out ahead. "Come on."

The sky rumbles overhead, clouds obscuring the coming sunset as the cold wind picks up even more. The fire whips around in its pot as I grab the wheelbarrow and push it down the road. It moves easily, not heavy at all.

The woods encroach on either side, some of the trees gray and ashy, others with streaks of decay crawling up their trunks.

Charles hacks at a few branches, clearing little bits as we move farther into the trees, the village already obscured behind us.

I have that feeling again, of eyes on us, several of them.

"Ach!" Charles ducks as the first spray of acid comes from our left.

He speeds his pace and pulls his leather cloak up higher.

"Did it get you?" I call, then almost get squirted in the face by another one on our right.

"Watch out!" He spins, a heavy stream of spit coming from a spriggan that's moved onto the road ahead.

It's spindly, the branches poking from it covered with moss and flaky lichen. Two eyes are on mismatched bits of its trunk near the top, their green color seeming to glow in the dark. It rears back and spits again, pelting Charles with so much acid that his leather smokes and sizzles.

I grab the axe from the wheelbarrow as more streams of spit come from all sides.

"Duck!" I yell and throw the axe right over Charles's head.

He drops, and it flies past him to lodge in the spriggan's face. It lets out a rickety shriek, like a chair scraping across a splintered floor, and takes off into the woods.

"You lost your axe," Charles scolds.

"I saved your life!"

He rises and continues onward, his steps faster as we start to get pelted from either side. The entire forest is moving, the creaking wood all I can hear as we break into a near run.

"Ahead, I see the Crone Tree!" Charles yells.

We're moving so fast the fire begins to blaze wildly— almost sputtering and then springing to life again. The Crone Tree is just as the woman described, its branches twisting and forming the shape of an old woman resting on her cane.

"Wait!" Charles skids to a halt as a row of spriggans form ahead of us, a wall of acid and shrieking anger. "They know what we're doing."

"Fuck!" I pull the leather tighter as the acid rains on us from all angles, the creatures surrounding the tree. "I knew this was a bad idea!" Acid splatters onto my wrist, the burn moving me to even more urgency.

Reaching forward, I grab a torch and hold it over the flame, more spit making my fingers sting as I get it lit and swing it around, wielding it like a club against the bastards who've gotten bold.

Charles grabs one, too, and moves forward, focusing on the row of spriggans separating us from the tree. They're all different sizes. Some four feet, others over ten, all of them making an effective fence.

One screams as he presses the torch to it, the fire licking up its trunk. It takes off, moving jerkily away and spreading the flames through the forest. The gray, deadened trees spark immediately, as if their dry remains are nothing but kindling. Soon, more cries rip through the woods, the spriggans trying to escape the flames.

"We have to push!" Charles hacks at another spriggan ahead of him, his axe taking off an arm. But there are still too many lined up to block our way to the tree. At this rate, the acid will eat through to our skin before we get rid of them.

I think about using my bow, then I glance down at the wheelbarrow. An idea forms, and I yell for Charles to get back.

"Why?" He hacks at another spriggan who practically vomits acid on top of him.

"Just get behind me!"

He backs away and then runs, the spriggans moving in to close the hole he'd made.

"What are you—"

I take off at a run, the wheelbarrow ahead of me, and aim for the smallest spriggan on the line. They all focus on me, their acid splattering and burning bits of my cheek, my hands, my arms, but I simply turn the bad side of my face forward and keep going. A little more ruination won't matter at this point.

With a hard surge, I ram the small spriggan. It crumples, some of its wood splintering and flying as I wrench the wheelbarrow over its body and keep going. Another steps in my way, and I use the wheelbarrow like a weapon, shoving it forward until the spriggan stumbles back.

Something whistles past my ear, and I see Charles's axe embed in its chest. It screams and tries to pull it free, but I push the wheelbarrow into it, the flames from the brazier jumping up and latching onto its leaves. When it falls, I wrench the wheelbarrow to the side and over it, but then it stops so hard I almost impale myself on the handle.

"The wheel—you broke it!" Charles runs past me and snatches a torch, lights it and darts for the Crone Tree.

A spriggan grabs at me, yanking on my leather. I push forward and reach for a torch, then whirl with it, fighting off the monsters as they move closer, their knobby arms out as they pelt me with spit. The wheelbarrow is stuck, but I grab the edge of it and try to yank it toward the tree. It only gives the spriggans more of an opening to hit me, some of them swinging thick branches that take the wind from my lungs. I swear I hear a rib crack, pain shooting through my back. But I swing the torch some more, lighting the closest ones on fire and breaking their weaker branches as they scream.

"I need the tar!" Charles cries.

A roar follows, the sound of a thousand branches rubbing together, and I spin as a creature jumps from the top of the Crone Tree, its thunderous landing shaking the ground beneath my feet.

Charles yells and runs toward me, but a spriggan darts forward and grabs him, pulling him to its chest and squeezing.

"Shit!" I run to him and beat the spriggan with my torch. I yank Charles's axe from the smoldering spriggan and use it to hack away at the arms holding him in place.

He gasps, the monster tightening its hold as Charles swings his legs, trying to kick. Then his eyes widen. "The sprite!"

I'm knocked off my feet and slammed against the Crone Tree. For a moment, I see nothing but white, then black, and then a branch swinging toward me. I roll, scraping myself against the hard roots as the sprite tries to crush me with its massive limbs.

It roars again, the sound terrible and horrifying as spriggans pour their acid onto Charles, dousing his leather as he struggles against the one holding him.

"The tar!" he chokes out.

I jump forward, barely missing another swing from the towering creature, its eyes red as it comes for me with plodding legs, huge and unwieldy trunks. It smells of grass and leaves and earth, but the scent is fierce and stinging, as if it's an attack of its own.

With another leap, I barely dodge its clawed hand, the tips curled and wicked like giant thorns. The spriggans have closed around the wheelbarrow, the fire hidden. But I know it's still there. It has to be.

Charles is dangling now, his body nearly limp as he tries to free himself from the spriggan. Panic and worry— both unexpected—rise inside me.

But my hesitation costs me, because the sprite lands another blow, hurling me forward and into the spriggans around the wheelbarrow.

I get sprayed with more spit, and my already ruined cheek burns with it. But this is an opening. The fire is just ahead. I pull the leather over me and stay on my knees, scurrying between the tree creatures until I bump into the wheelbarrow.

When I get there, I pull myself up and grab the clay pot of tar.

With my other hand, I swing the axe, hacking away at the spriggans until enough fall so that I have a clear view of the sprite again.

Charles isn't moving anymore. Fear trickles down my spine in a cold sweat, and I steady myself on the downed spriggans, then fling the pot with all my strength. It smashes against the sprite's chest, the gooey substance rolling down its bark.

With a yank I free my bow and an arrow, then turn around to light the tip.

That's when I realize the fire's gone out.

"Fuck!"

The sprite swipes at me, not caring that it's bowling over spriggans in the process. They shriek as they splinter and fall, and I dive behind them when the sprite swings again, trying to smash me right along with her minions.

I run, acid spraying me from all directions as I try to do the only thing I can—save Charles. But then I see a flicker near the base of the Crone Tree. Charles's torch is still there, the flames licking along the dry roots and leaves.

Changing course, I catch a piece of a spriggan's gangly arm in my back, the thin limbs yanking my covering and leaving gaping holes in the leather, already weakened from the acid. I push ahead, not stopping even when it falls off and I'm left unprotected from the spriggans massed around me.

They spit.

I burn.

But I don't give up.

I hurtle toward the torch and hold my arrow out in front of me to light it. It skirts the edge of the flame, but the tar catches quickly, fire engulfing the tip and a good way up the shaft.

The sprite roars again and wheels toward me, both of its thick arms rising overhead, ready to pound me into paste.

I draw back on my bow and nock my arrow, then let it go. The bow falls apart in my hands, the gut string flinging away. The arrow flies weakly and glances off the sprite's chest.

It brings its arms down, breaking off bits of the Crone Tree as it does so. I clench my eyes shut and throw my hands up on pure instinct to defend myself from the killing blow.

But it doesn't come.

The sprite shrieks so horribly I think my ears might rupture, and when I open my eyes, it's staggering backward, its chest on fire with flames that leap and seize on its shoulder, its face, its red eyes.

The spriggans all begin to shake, their collective wails rising as the sprite falls back, the huge thud shaking the forest as the spriggans hurry to their master and climb, trying to use their own bodies to extinguish the flames.

The sprite thrashes, spreading the fire as it struggles, more piercing cries rising from all around as the fire shoots higher and higher, lighting up the rotting trees.

"Charles!" I rush to him, his form crumpled on the ground beneath his smoking leather. With a hard yank, I rip it off him, then grab his shoulders. "Charles!"

He doesn't wake, and I can't tell if he's breathing. The sprite is still screaming, the spriggans falling to pieces, their limbs shattering and turning that horrible gray color.

I scoop Charles up, and for a moment—only a moment, mind you—it occurs to me that if I leave him here, I'll have all the food and provisions for myself. My trip to Paris would be nothing but ease, and I might even have enough to get me all the way to Finnraven Hill. I wouldn't have to fight to keep Belinda, either.

I hesitate and look down at the boy, at his pale cheeks and closed eyes, at the blond hair that always seems to tickle my nose. I could leave him. My hold on the boy slackens.

The sprite lets out one last shriek, all its spriggans already rotted gray and flaking into a fine soot.

It's done. All that's left is to get paid. I pull my arms from the boy slowly, my decision creeping into a finality.

But then he moves his lips, his eyelids twitching but not opening, and he says, "G."

Just that.

A simple letter.

One that's worth nothing, that means nothing.

One that may not even apply to me.

"You did it!" Corlis cries as I run into the village, my lungs screaming and my body aching.

"I need a healer!" I rush past him, Charles cradled in my arms.

"Shazza!" Corlis bellows and follows close behind me. "What happened?"

"One of the spriggans crushed him, and the forest is on fire."

Corlis turns on his heel and yells for water and aid.

Shazza hurries to me, her eyes on Charles. Then she glances up at me and winces.

"Not me. Charles. He's hurt bad."

"Bring him in." She gestures toward her small home, and I follow her inside.

The little girl is in the bed in the corner, her eyes wide as I lay Charles on the rough-hewn table beside the hearth.

"Can you help him?" I ask Shazza.

"If you move." Shazza shoves me out of the way and leans over Charles, then presses her ear to his mouth.

I scrub a hand down my face, my skin on fire from the spots of acid.

"Is he breath—"

"Shh!" Shazza holds up her finger.

I cross my arms over my chest and force myself to stay still. The girl in the corner stares at me, her blanket drawn up to her chin.

Shazza stands. "He's alive. For now. Help me strip him so I can see his injuries."

My heart seems to loosen, the beats coming easier. I grab one of Charles's sleeves and pull, working it from his arm, and then Shazza pulls the other. His shirt underneath is stained and torn, and I pull it off over his head, his cap falling to the floor. Then I stop and point to his chest. "What's that?"

Shazza's eyes widen.

"Was he already injured? Why's he all wrapped up?" I peer at the white fabric that lays tightly against his skin all the way around his chest.

Shazza reaches behind her and grabs a knife.

"Whoa!" I yelp.

She ignores me and slides the knife beneath the fabric and pulls. It cuts cleanly and falls away.

My mouth falls open, my breath stilling in my chest. "Are those ... Why does Charles have tits?"

SEVEN

"Tits." I cradle my head in my hands as I sit beside Shazza's fire while she dabs some stinking ointment onto my burns. "This whole time. For *months*, he's had tits! Nice ones, too."

Shazza laughs, the sound coarse though her touch is gentle. "I think *she's* had them for longer than that."

Charles sleeps in the bed with the little girl, both of them on their backs, both of them snoring a little. Charles is all wrapped up again, his—I mean *her*—chest bound with different fabric to support her broken ribs. Dark bruises already mottle her sides, and she wears bandages on her chin, arms, and hands from the acid.

"Her ribs aren't broken, but they're going to hurt like hell for a while. She's lucky you were there to save her."

I sigh. "She's the only one who can read my map."

Shazza raises a brow and puts more smelly salve along my wounds from the spit. "Mmhmm. I'm certain that was the only reason." She finishes her work and stands with a groan, her back popping. "Now that the woods are clear, we'll be able to get provisions and visit our hunting grounds." She wrings her hands. "We don't ... We don't have much in the way of food right now. And while you were out fighting the spriggans, I'm afraid my daughter Nathalia—" She gestures to Charles's bag. "—she was so hungry, you see." She winces as I grab the bag and open it.

Empty. Only a few bits of the moldy food and the spoon remain.

"We haven't had anything fresh in so, so long, and she—"

"Save it." I toss the bag down and lean back in my chair, my body aching in plenty of ways that do nothing to improve my already-sour mood.

"I'll just ..." She sits by the hearth, her back to me, and fusses with the rest of the bandage material.

No food, no provisions, and my stable boy is actually a stable *girl*. My gaze strays to her again, to the steady rise and fall of her breath, to the way her golden hair—now free from the worn green cap—falls across her forehead.

My stomach rumbles as I wonder what else she hasn't told me. I think back and realize I've never really asked her about her life. She knows mine—not much to tell when I can't remember a damn thing—but she's a mystery. Did Madge know? I rub the thick stubble that grows along the good side of my face. From my experience, Madge didn't miss much at all.

I catch the scent of a particularly ripe onion and glance at the hearth. No food's in the pot. Then I raise my arm. I almost fall out of the chair.

With another rumble from my empty stomach, I rise and walk out into the cold night. Raphael and Corlis are laughing by the fire in the center of town, they and several of the menfolk sharing drinks from a large bottle of who-knows-what.

"There he is!" They raise their wooden cups to me.

"Ugly as the day is long but helped us all the same." Raphael laughs, his eyes bloodshot as he pours me a cup. "Drink up, friend!"

"Is there a stream nearby where I could—"

"Aw come on and celebrate with us." He claps me on the back, sending a wave of pain through my cracked rib, then shoves the cup into my hand.

"I suppose it couldn't hurt." If anything, it'll take the edge off from finding out my stable boy is a stable girl. Then it dawns on me—all the times I took a piss along the road. Charles kept going behind a tree, but I thought it was because he was intimidated, what with having a boy-sized penis and all.

"You all right? The good side of your face seems paler all of a sudden." Corlis leans closer.

"I'm fine." I down the contents of the cup, the burn slithering down my throat and into my gut, then hold up my cup. "Another."

The men cheer, the fire burning bright as I drink until the world makes more sense, until I almost feel complete, until it's fine that I can't read, that my stable boy is a girl, that I have no past, and that I'm a ruined wreck on the outside—and maybe the inside, too.

So I drink and discover I don't just like nearly-curdled wine. I *love* it. And I *excel* at drinking it. Finally, something I'm truly skilled at.

SOMETHING POKES me in the side.

I grunt and roll over, my body aching, especially on the right side of my chest.

"Up, G. We're wasting daylight."

I know that voice. Charles. But he's not really Charles, is he? I blink my eyes open, the sun burning into my brain as I try to look up at the shadow standing over me.

"What's your real name?"

Not-Charles cocks her head to the side, her green cap back in place. "What? Did the wine make your tongue three sizes too big?"

"Huh?"

"Get up. We need to get going. There's no food here, and Belinda's already hungry."

Belinda's hungry? I can feel the yawning pit of my stomach as I labor to my elbow, and then to a sitting position, my head pounding. My insides lurch, and I let out a robust belch.

Charles steps away and crosses her arms over her chest. "Belinda and I could leave you here."

I glare up at her. "You aren't going to mention all the lies?"

She shrugs. "There's nothing to talk about. You know the truth." Color rises in her cheeks.

"Your 'truths' practically poked me in the eyeballs."

I take a fraction of satisfaction when her cheeks turn even redder.

She clears her throat. "That doesn't change the fact that I'm going to Paris and you're going to your death somewhere along the road."

I get onto my knees, then force myself to my feet. "I'm going to Finnraven Hill."

"Like I said, going to your death." She turns to Belinda, adjusting the saddle as the little girl peeks out from Shazza's house.

"Are you leaving?" The child's voice trembles as she glances from me to Charles.

Charles stops fussing with the horse and goes over to her, dropping down to her haunches in front of her. "We have to go, but I know you can take care of Arlon while we're gone, right?"

The girl shakes her head and keeps sending me worried looks.

I throw up my hands and turn around, giving her what Madge often referred to as my 'good side.'

"Don't go with him," the girl whispers, almost too low for me to hear. "He's a monster."

I grind my teeth. Yes, I look like a monster, but it's not real. I want to tell her it's just on the outside. On the inside I'm ... I'm ... really handso—I lean over and dry heave, then wipe my mouth with my sleeve. What's left of the wine sits precariously in my gut.

"—can handle him. Don't you worry," Charles says. "He's not as bad as he looks."

My handsome heart sings. Finally, vindicated. Was that so hard?

"Sometimes he's worse," Charles whispers conspiratorially, and the girl giggles.

"Ah fuck." I stand straight and look over my shoulder. "Can we go now, not-Charles?"

"You take care, little one." She kisses the waif's forehead and stands. Charles's ass rounds out her pants nicely. How had I never noticed that before?

"We collected what little we have, true to our bargain." Corlis offers me a small burlap sack, his eyes on the packed dirt at his feet.

I snatch it and greedily look inside. A few pieces of cured meat and some fat mushrooms—it's not much, but it'll do.

Charles steps to my elbow. "G."

I don't like her tone. I don't like it one bit. My grip tightens on the bag. "What?"

"They won't be able to find good hunting until they get past the areas of the sprite's devastation and the burned spots. That could be days or weeks before any fresh food is brought back here." She tries to pull the bag from me.

I don't let go.

"G." She looks up at me, her eyes especially bright this morning. "Come on."

"Come on what? We had a deal."

"He's right, young miss." Corlis bows his head even farther.

"See?" I yank it toward me, but she winces. Her ribs must be killing her. I relinquish the bag with a slew of curses.

She digs through it and pulls out a fat radish, then hands the rest of it back to Corlis.

"What are you doing? We need that for the journey." I grab her arm.

"G, they need it more. We'll find more for ourselves on the road." She feeds the radish to Belinda, and I swear the horse gives me a smug look as she chews it. "Just look at Nathalia. She's skin and bones." She juts her chin toward the little girl.

"*I'm* skin and bones!" I look down at myself for emphasis.

She rolls her eyes. "You'll live. Come on. The sooner we get going, the sooner we'll find food. There should be a vineyard once we get past Arlon."

How does she know—"The map?" I ask.

"Yes, it's marked on the map." She grabs the saddle and starts to pull herself up, then lets out a yelp and drops to her feet.

"You're hurt. Maybe we—"

"I said you could stay longer." Shazza hurries out to us. "Those injuries are going to take a while to heal." She looks up at the cloudy sky. "And I think the weather's going to turn colder. Maybe quite a bit colder."

"I'll be fine." Charles waves her concern away like it's a biting fly. "I heal quickly, and we can make a fire anywhere. We'll be safe."

Shazza frowns. "I know, but that doesn't mean you shouldn't go easy, at least for a few days."

Charles persists. "The faster I get to Paris, the faster I can start over again. I'm kind of looking forward to it this time."

"This time? How many fake lives have you had?" I ask.

She tries to pull herself up onto Belinda again, and again she yelps and drops back to her feet.

I smirk. "Allow me." I grab her waist and lift her easily.

"G, put me down!" She squirms.

"Spread your legs and get on the damn horse." I hold her up, a groan escaping me as my chest screams in pain. "Go!"

She grabs the saddle and swings her leg over. I set her down and then pull myself up beside her, my cracked rib sending shooting pain through my side.

"Wait!" One of the younger men comes running, my bow in his hands. "A gift. I repaired the string and tightened it up, and I refashioned one of my old quivers and filled it." He holds the bow and arrows up to me.

I take them and test the string. It's my materials, but the string is taut and sings when I pluck it. It's not the flimsy mess it was last night.

"Well done, son." Corlis beams and claps the boy on the back.

"Thank you, sir." He watches as I test the bow then examine the fletching on the arrows. I don't know how I know, but I'm certain the arrows are made well, the feathers cut right to send the bolts with speed and accuracy.

"And for you." Shazza hands Charles an axe, the light wood of the handle darkened from use. "It's my favorite one. Has the best bite."

"I don't think I can take—"

I lean down and snatch the axe from her hand. "Take it." I shove it into Charles's palm.

She gives me a rude look over her shoulder, then turns back to a grinning Shazza. "Thank you. That's very generous."

"Not at all. You've given us our lives back, and for that, we'll be forever grateful. If either of you ever venture back this way, you're welcome to stay. By then, god be merciful, we'll be back to good times."

"I'd love to." Charles takes the reins and guides Belinda to the road.

"May the light of your king lead you to the safest roads and greenest vales." Shazza gives her a little bow.

Charles stiffens.

Shazza stands tall again and winks at her. "You aren't the first to visit us, but it has been ages. We take it as a sign of luck." She taps the side of her nose.

Is Shazza having some sort of fit? "Huh? What was that?"

"Doesn't matter. Let's go."

"What king? Who's she talking about?"

"Drop it, G." Charles says, her words tight.

"More secrets." I sit back and cross my arms over my chest. "Typical. Fine." I stare daggers at her beautiful hair.

The rest of the villagers come out to see us off, some of them waving, some of them clearly in the middle of gearing up for a trip to hunt or find food.

My stomach grumbles. "You hear that? That's your doing."

Charles sighs and gestures around at the grubby villagers who wave at us. "Isn't this enough?"

"*Enough?*"

She doesn't elaborate. "Never mind. We'll be out of these woods in a day, maybe a little more."

I settle myself more in the saddle, and that's when I become aware of how close we are. We're touching. My hips are pressing against her ass. Before, I didn't care. In fact, sometimes I'd lean against her as obnoxiously as I could, just for a little fun. But now. Now I'm keenly aware that this isn't Charles, it's not-Charles, and not-Charles has the most perfect set of tits I've ever seen. Her hips are rounded, and so is her ass. And her waist is warm and soft. So where do I put my hands?

"Stop," she snaps.

"What?"

"You're being weird."

"*I'm* being weird? I didn't even say anything, and I'm not the liar of the two of us."

"Does it really matter that much to you that I'm not a man?"

I sputter. "Of course it does!"

"Why? I can fight. I can ride. I can read your map."

"Yes, but women are ... they're not supposed to—"

"Be very careful with what comes out of your mouth next unless you want *both* sides of your face torn off."

"Low blow." I peer ahead as the Crone Tree comes back into view. Sun dapples its pale bark, the fire only damaging it a little on one side. It'll survive.

"Look, we're on the same journey. Nothing's changed. Nothing has to change. Just be your usual grumpy, self-involved, oafish self, and we'll be fine."

I let the insults roll off, because I notice the word 'liar' wasn't included. I puff my chest with my own superiority. It feels right. "Is Charles even your real name?"

"No." She guides the horse around the tree, and I keep my head on a swivel looking for any more sprites or spriggans, but the woods are calm now. No one's spitting at us, at least not at the moment, and I can hear birdsong for the first time.

"What is it?"

"There's power in names, G."

"What's that supposed to mean?"

"Exactly what I said. How does it feel not to know your name?"

"It doesn't matter. I *will* know my name once I get to the Wood of Mist."

"You really believe you'll make it and somehow magically get your memory back?" She glances over her shoulder.

"Yes. I'll get my memory, my face, everything back. That's what the woman in the water promised me."

"Mmhmm." She doesn't sound convinced. "You know you should never trust the Sidh, right? Not the fae folk or the folk of the wood, the folk under the hill, or the folk of the air. Not the fairies or pixies or the wandering boggans."

"A load of nonsense, and you're just trying to dodge telling me your name."

She snorts a small laugh. "I'm not going to tell you."

"Why not?"

"Because you've known me as Charles this whole time, and that's been enough for you. You've never even asked me my last name or where I'm from. Why does it matter so much now?"

I scoff. "That's not true. I'm sure I have." I think back, trying to remember so I can prove her wrong.

"You can't be serious. Ever since Madge dragged your torn body out of the river, you've only thought about yourself. Did you even thank Madge for saving you? Hmm? I bet you didn't. After all, you were happy to leave her there to suffer for your mistake."

I bristle. "Walking down the street wasn't a mistake."

"It is if you look the way you do." She makes an exasperated noise in her throat. "And you know it. Your injuries may not be your fault—hell, they may be, I don't know— but you have to know how to work with what you've been given."

"By concealing it the way you do?" I snap back.

"Sometimes." She pats the saddle bag. "Why do you think Madge made you this mask? You have to work with your limitations—even if they aren't fair or if they're placed on you by someone else."

My hand strays to my face, to the roads and curves of ruined skin. How could this possibly be my fault? It couldn't... Could it? If only I could remember how I got into the river, but I can't. No matter how hard I try, it's as if my past is wrapped in a shroud of thick fog that nothing can penetrate. But maybe Charles is right. The way I look is a limitation—a harsh one. There's no point thinking otherwise, at least not until I get it all fixed in the Wood of Mist. Only temporary, that's all it is.

"I'm not trying to make you feel bad, G. I'm only trying to help." Her tone softens. "And I know you saved me when you could've left me."

Why does that hit me in the gut? I could tell her that I thought about it for too long, that I almost left her for the spriggans. But I don't. She probably already knows, given her assessment of me.

"Thank you," she says, her tone still soft like the edge of a rose.

"You're the only one who can read the map."

Her shoulders tighten. "Ugh! I was trying to have a moment and—"

"It's still a moment." I smirk.

"Asshole!" She kicks my foot with her heel. "Look, you can call me Charlie, all right? That's not my full name, but it's closer to it than Charles, if that makes you feel any better."

"It doesn't make me feel better." And I still can't figure out what to do with my hands.

"Relax. We have a long ride. Stop being ridiculous about me being a woman."

I suck on a tooth. "Did Madge know you were lying?"

She makes a disgusted sound. "I didn't *lie*. It's not like I ever said 'Hi, G, I'm a man.' And yes, Madge knew. She busted me pretty early on. Too smart for her own good." She sighs, and I get the sense that she misses the old woman. When I think back to how much kindness she showed me when she didn't have to, I almost miss her, too.

"So, ah, where are you from?" I ask.

She guffaws. "It's too late now. Just enjoy the scenery. Sheesh." Then she grabs my hands and puts them on her hips, the same way we rode before I knew she was a woman. But this time, my heart seems to kick up its pace, and when I lean closer and inhale, I once again catch the scent of ripe berries and sweetness. That's when I realize she isn't a pie addict, after all. She's Charlie.

EIGHT

The fire crackles as I hold a juicy pheasant over the flames. Snow falls all around us, though we're sheltered somewhat by the trees overhead. After a day's ride, we're at the edge of the woods and far beyond where the sprite sucked the landscape dry.

Charlie huddles close to the fire, her gaze on the sizzling bird as she makes a stack of its best feathers.

"Just think, we could've had a nice little bit of roasted mushroom to go with it." I turn the bird as bits of fat sizzle onto the fire below. "But you had to be oh-so-malignant."

"*Magnanimous*," she mumbles and scoots closer.

"What?"

"Never mind. Is it ready yet?" she warms her hands at the fire.

"Soon. If we eat it before it's done, we'll be vomiting it up in no time."

She nods, as if she already knew the answer to her question.

Belinda snores nearby, having eaten plenty of vegetation along the road, though Charlie was very particular about what she could and could not munch. At least half of everything in the world is poison—that's what I've learned.

"How are your ribs?" I ask.

"Better." She shrugs her shoulders back, swinging her arms a little. "Like I said, I heal fast."

"I don't. The side of my chest feels like there's a fire inside it."

Her eyes snap up. "You don't seem feverish."

"I'm not. It's just normal pain. Nothing I haven't felt before."

Her eyes stray to my ruined face. Before, when she was Charles, I didn't care, but now I find an uncomfortable feeling lurking inside me when she looks at my ugliness. It's not exactly that I'm self-conscious, it's more that I find myself wishing things could be different, that *I* could be different. I've been pondering all day what she said about me only being interested in myself. The uncomfortable feeling springs from that, too, as if I'm afraid she's right.

"Now?" she edges around the fire until she's sitting beside me.

"Just a little while longer."

A sharp wind gusts past, sending the flames dancing wildly and snow swirling around us. It's going to be a frigid night.

"Maybe the snow will keep the wolves away."

She looks around into the deep gloom that lurks beyond the firelight. "There are worse things in these woods than wolves."

"Worse than acid-spitting tree assholes?"

She nods. "Definitely."

"You're superstitious." I turn the bird one more time.

"What?"

"All that talk about fairies and boggies. You really think there are dangerous monsters everywhere."

She looks at me pointedly. "And you don't?"

I shrug. "Now that we have a bow and an axe, I'm not worried."

"Well, you know what they say, 'ignorance is bliss.'" She grins, her face looking even more youthful.

"How old are you?" I ask.

"How old are you?" she retorts.

I shrug. "How should I know? Madge said she thinks I'm about twenty-five. Sounds good to me."

"I'm older."

I almost drop the bird. "No, you aren't."

"I am. And I'm starving. Is it done?"

I grumble and pull the bird from the flames and set it on the wooden plate from Charlie's bag. "You're twenty at most."

"No, I just have great skin." She reaches for the bird.

I grab her slender wrist. "Don't. You'll get burned."

She pulls back, a sheepish look on her face.

"Healing makes you hungry." I stretch my right arm, my rib aching. "And we would've had more food if you—"

"Drop it, G. The food is where it belongs." She clasps her hands together, as if to keep herself from reaching for the bird again. "Besides, I have you to hunt for me now."

Damn, that sounds good. I can provide. She relies on me. I could beat my chest and whoop right now if it wouldn't hurt so damn bad.

She rolls her eyes. "Don't let it go to your head."

When the bird finally cools down enough, I break it apart with my hands—but only after Charlie rinses them with water while saying, "are you always so filthy?"

We eat until there's nothing left but tiny bones, and even those I break in half in hopes of finding marrow. But they're hollow, so we toss them into the fire and sit there for a long while, just watching the flames burn against the inky blackness of the night.

When we finally settle down to sleep, she uses the saddle as a pillow, and I lie down close by the fire.

We watch each other through the flames and listen to the sounds of the forest, the wind in the trees, and the scamper of small creatures in the underbrush.

Sleep comes quickly, and it feels like I just closed my eyes when I feel a hand on my arm shaking me awake.

"Time to go." Charlie rubs her arms, the snow falling even heavier now. The ground is blanketed with it, and only the fire kept it from covering us overnight. "We have to get to the vineyards before the rest of this storm hits." She looks at the sky. "Tonight is going to be a killing kind of cold. We'll need real shelter to survive it."

I would ask how the hell she knows that, but the breeze that blows by is all the convincing I need. It cuts like tiny knives all over my exposed skin, and even where I'm facing the fire, I can still feel the wind's bite.

I help her onto Belinda, then climb up behind her. This time I don't hesitate to pull her back against me. She shivers, and I wrap my arms around her as she urges Belinda to get going.

We finally leave the woods after an hour of riding, but the wind cuts even deeper once we're away from the shelter of the trees. The snow falls in fat flakes that build up as we go, the entire world covered in white.

Her shivers grow more frequent, and she pulls her hat down even tighter. My back feels raw from the constant attack of the cold, and I can barely feel my toes.

"We can't stay out in this," she yells over the howl of the wind.

It can't be much past midday, but the sky is dark, the clouds so thick it coats the landscape in a false twilight.

Belinda has been slowing, but she hasn't faltered, not even when we encounter drifts that she has to plow through. Ice has formed along her nostrils, and she keeps her head down against the onslaught. We need a break, some sort of a letup, but it never comes. The snow falls faster, and we can only see a short distance ahead of us. Everything else is a wall of white.

Short rows of vines appear along the road. The vineyard, everything dead for the winter, but the farmer still has to be here somewhere. At least that sounds right. But even if there were a welcoming home somewhere ahead, we'd never see it in this endless white onslaught.

Charlie leans forward and rubs Belinda's icy mane.

"Your hands." I reach out and pull them back. Her skin is red and angry, maybe already at the frostbite stage. Covering them with mine, I keep her tightly to me and take the reins.

Belinda moves a little faster, her entire body shuddering at intervals.

We won't last much longer out here. I grit my chattering teeth and peer through the endless storm, looking for something, anything that could be shelter. If I can't find anything, we'll have to stop and try to make a fire with the wood I packed from the forest. But it isn't likely. The snow is too heavy for me to have a chance to light it.

"Belinda, sniff it out! There has to be something nearby!" Charlie yells and pulls her hands free, putting both of them on the mare's neck.

Belinda stops, a shiver tearing through her.

"Don't stop!" I wrap my arm around Charlie's waist and use my other hand to smack Belinda's ass. "Go!"

But the horse simply nickers and turns to one side.

She's lost the trail.

"I have to start a fire." I move to climb off.

"Wait!" Charlie shakes her head vehemently, her hands still on the horse's neck. "Just wait!"

"We'll die if we wait!" I shout back.

"Come on, girl."

Belinda fights the reins for a moment, then turns again and begins to trudge through the suffocating snow. She walks between tall posts, the only markers remaining over the frozen grape vines.

"She's lost!" I yank on the reins.

Belinda doesn't change her course.

"We have to stay on the road." I pull again, but Belinda plods ahead, the brittle edges of the hidden vines plucking at my pants and scratching along her legs.

"There!" Charlie yells and points.

Ahead, barely visible through the falling snow, is a small barn.

I'm off the horse before she can say another word, and I grab her, pulling her down with me. "Get inside!"

"We can't leave Belinda!" she cries.

I take the bridle and pull her along to the building. It's squat, barely high enough for the horse to walk inside. If she doesn't fit, then she'll have to stay out in the cold.

I yank the door open and push Charlie. "Get in."

"I won't leave her!" She tries to snatch the bridle from my grip.

"In!" I yell and fist the back of her jacket, then shove her inside.

"Come on, girl." I lead Belinda in, and just manage to close the door behind her rump. That was close.

Charlie pets the horse's icy face, and both of them shiver together.

The barn is small and freezing, but there's enough room for us and a fire. I quickly unload the firewood and kindling, then squat down in the center of the room and make a flame. My red hands shake, and I can't feel my fingertips, but I manage to get it started.

Belinda drops to her knees, and then all the way to the floor with a hard exhale, her legs folded beneath her.

"It's okay." Charlie coos to her.

"Sit right up against her. We need all our heat." I let the fire get going and grab some straw from one corner along with some coarse blankets and burlap sacks.

Once Charlie is down, I lie beside her and cover both of us with everything I found.

"Come here." I pull her to me, resting her on my chest as I scoot closer to Belinda.

Charlie tenses but doesn't fight me. Somehow, I know she wants to. We all shiver together and pray the fire doesn't go out. The smoke swirls around and flows out the small glassless window along the front of the building. I need to cover it with something, but for now, I'm not moving until the fire is burning high.

Charlie shivers again and again, and I do too. I rub her arms vigorously, then her back to try and warm us both.

Despite the cold, I don't miss the way her breasts press against me, or the way she's trying desperately to stay rigid so she doesn't straddle me.

"S-s-top s-s-smirking," she says through chattering teeth, then burrows her face into my neck, her frigid nose sending an extra chill through me.

We lie there for a long time, the wind howling outside and blowing snow through the window. But the fire picks up and sends glorious heat wafting over us.

When we finally stop shivering, my muscles slowly relax. Feeling returns to my fingers and toes, and I keep my arms wrapped around Charlie.

Belinda's snores begin to fill up the small space, and when I shift a little to stop a piece of straw from stabbing into my ass, Charlie snuggles closer to me, her body heat like a warm blanket. That's when I realize she's asleep, her breathing low and slow. Exhausted from the cold.

My toes tingle and my fingers sting, but at least I can feel. That has to be a good sign.

When she lets out a long exhale, she relaxes completely, her legs no longer tense as they spread and her warmth surrounds my hips.

I swallow thickly, my eyelids drooping as I feel her breathing, her heat, her golden hair tickling my nose as usual. I close my eyes and soak her in, taking her with me to dreams of curses, castles, and monsters.

CHARLIE SHIFTS ON ME, her eyelids fluttering against my throat. I've been awake for a while, just listening to the storm die down. It's right before dawn, the outside world eerily still as our fire crackles and Belinda snores as she sleeps on her feet, having tired of our company on the ground.

The strangest thing—even on this hard earthen floor that smells at best of horse piss—I slept better than I ever have. My dreams were so wildly implausible that I felt like a spectator at a puppet show, and then I faded into a deep, easy slumber.

We made a comfortable den out of what can't be more than an old shed. Tools hang from the back wall, and there is only one stall, likely for a small mule, by the looks of it.

"Mmph." Charlie turns her head, her lips gently pressed against my neck.

That does things to me. Very obvious things that I have no doubt she'll feel the moment she wakes. But perhaps it's better if I feign innocence despite the deeply un-innocent thoughts I've been having for the past hour. For longer than that, if I'm being honest—which never seems like a good idea. I close my eyes and pretend to sleep as she moves again, then lifts her head to look at me.

I feel her stare for long moments as I keep my breathing deep and even. Then I feel the softest touch of her fingers, traveling along the spider web of scars on my face, across my widow's peak, then higher into my hair. When she lifts her other hand and presses her palm to the good cheek, her warmth seems to seep into my skin, heating me from the inside out.

"I know you're awake." She pulls her hand back.

"How do you know?" I whisper.

She snorts a laugh, then sits up. "Maybe from the erection that's trying to impale me." Easing off me, she plops onto the floor by the fire.

I have half a mind to pull her back to me so I can have the chance to inspect her as thoroughly as she did to me, but Belinda chuffs loudly from where she's standing against the back wall.

Charlie turns toward her. "She's going to wet the floor if we don't take her outside in the next few minutes."

"I've never met a horse that knows to piss outside." I groan and stand, my body sore and my rib sending those vicious stabs of sensation through my side.

She gives me a wry look. "Belinda's been trained by the best."

"Mmhmm." I raise a brow at her. "Come on, girl." I grab Belinda's bridle and help her turn around, though Charlie has to move to the other side of the fire to avoid being trampled.

I force the door open, the snow drift outside of it almost as tall as I am. The wind is gone, and the world is at a snowy standstill, the cold still brutal enough to kill. If it doesn't warm up more during the day, we'll be stuck here for another night. Without food. I groan at the thought.

"Hurry up and close the door," Charlie fusses. "You're letting the chill in."

The sun is just rising over a hill to my right, and a bell begins to ring from that direction. A town. It has to be. I squint and see low buildings and plumes of smoke on the hilltop, though they're all ghostly and distant in the low light.

Belinda halts at the doorway, no doubt wary of pushing her way through the snow.

"Look, you aren't pissing in the shed." I kick through the snow drifts closest to me, then pull her through the path

I made and into the vineyard. I can't tell where the plants are, so I just stomp ahead, cracking grapevines beneath my heel as I go. Once I've made a good enough path, I clear more snow to make a clearer area for Belinda, then leave her to do her business.

Hurrying back to the shelter, I close the door and huddle next to the fire, my toes already going tingly.

"You're wet." Charlie looks me over as she collects some old straw for Belinda. "You're going to freeze."

"I'm fine. The fire will dry me."

"Take off your shirt." She stands and looks around the small space. "And your pants."

"If you plan to ravage me, I must protest." I don't protest at all, but she doesn't need to know that.

"Idiot," she murmurs and pulls a few short planks of wood from the stall, then lays them out beside the fire. "Here, hand them to me." She turns her head away.

"Wait, you're serious?" I cock my head.

"Yes, I'm serious. You can't just sit around in wet clothes when it's freezing. It won't take long for them to dry. Stop being a baby, and take off your clothes."

"I'm not being a baby." Maybe I'm being a little bit of a baby. My body is strong and muscled, but it's marred by scars, some of them deep and jagged, as if the river rocks took bites out of me as I floated past. But she's right, and she's seen it all before. Madge didn't give a damn about my modesty when she was helping me heal. That seems even more egregious now that I know she was aware Charles was a woman. With a sigh, I yank my shirt over my head and toss it to her.

Her eyes roam my torso, and I wonder if she's inspecting my scars. Her face gives nothing away as she carries the shirt to the stall, wrings it out, then lays it over her boards. When her gaze returns to me, I could swear I see more color in her cheeks. Pride swells inside me.

"I think you just wanted me out of my clothes."

"Get over yourself." She blows a blonde lock of hair from her face and stares at the wall.

Once I shuck my pants, I hand those over. This time, she avoids looking any lower than my chin, her posture tight as she takes the pants and wrings them out.

"Now it's your turn." I grin at her.

She harrumphs. "I think you've seen enough."

"Oh, I have to disagree there, Charlie. I haven't seen nearly enough."

"Ugh, you are by far the worst—"

Belinda bumps against the door, so I rise and let her back in. She takes her same spot at the back of the small shed, happy to be out of the cold as I shove the door shut again. Charlie watches me, her eyes raking over my torso. I'm ruined all over and my side is bruised, but something about the way she stares strokes pride in my breast.

"Go on." I sit beside the fire again, the flames feeling wonderful against my bare skin. Steam is already rising from the wet clothes. "I'm by far the worst what?"

"There are a million different words that would fit perfectly in that sentence," she simpers.

"Rude." But my lips still twitch a slight smile at her insult.

"Are you going to tell me where you're from?" I lean against the chilly wall, my now-dry clothes doing little to temper the cold. We've been in here for hours, our bodies recovering from the hard road as our stomachs grumble. Even if the freezing temperatures don't let up, we'll have to move soon.

Charlie looks up from the fire. "Why does it matter?"

"Just making conversation."

"Sure you are." She gives me a wry look.

"What?" I give an offended huff. "I can't do that?"

"You can, but you never have. Not even in Sac à Puces. In the village, I felt like I was one wrong step away from you kicking me in the ass and laughing as I splatted in the mud."

"That mental image does bring a sense of amusement. I won't deny it. But I'd much rather have you in other compromising positions."

"Admitting that you're awful is a good step in the right direction. Keep it up."

"I didn't say that. I simply agreed that watching you flail in fresh mud would be entertaining, but watching you beneath me would be even better."

She grabs the small bowl we filled with snow, now melted, and takes a drink. "You're not getting into my pants, G. No matter how much conversation you try to make. Just go back to pretending I'm a boy."

"Can't do that."

"You can."

"No, I think ... I think maybe some part of me knew there was something special about you. Otherwise, I would've already ditched you."

"You were just afraid of Madge's curse." She shakes her head.

"Maybe. But maybe I wanted to keep you, and I just needed a reason. Maybe Madge knew that too."

She rolls her eyes. "I'm still not interested."

"Why not?" I grab a fallen branch from our dwindling pile and snap it in half.

"Do you *really* want me to recite all the reasons why you and I will never be more than travelling companions, and barely that?" She scowls at me through the flames.

"I mean, when you put it that way, no." I try to glower at her, but I know it turns into a smirk. I can't help it. When she's cross, it somehow amuses me more. Just seeing the way her cheeks heat and how her clever mouth is at the ready to hurl an insult sends a tingle down my spine in the best of ways.

"Stop looking at me like that." She crosses her arms. Then her stomach growls.

Fuck, she's got to be starving. We'd shared the bird, but that feels like forever ago.

"What are you doing?" she asks as I get to my feet.

"I'm going to go out and see if I can find some food." I grab my bow and arrows.

"There's nothing out there, G." She stands, too, her head shaking. "It's too cold for you to go wandering."

"I'll be fine. Just stay by the fire. Hopefully, I'll scare up some rabbits, maybe a huge stag." I give her a grin and throw a burlap sack around my shoulders.

She frowns and steps around the fire to block my way. "This is stupid, even for you."

"You wound me, Charlie." I clasp a hand over my heart.

"I'm serious. You can't go out in this. Nothing's thawed."

"You're so concerned." I step closer to her. "I guess you don't really think I'm the worst after all?"

"Did you hear the part where I called you stupid?" She glares up at me.

"I won't go far." I grip her upper arms lightly, fully expecting her to shrug away from my touch. But she doesn't. Instead, she chews her bottom lip for a moment.

"Just don't do anything reckless. I'd hate to have to ride away from here with Belinda while you cried because you were stuck down a well."

I scoff. "I'd never fit down a well."

She smacks my chest. "Oaf." But then she backs away, silently giving me permission.

"I'll be back in no time. Sit tight." I brace myself against the door and shove. This time it opens a little easier, the snow cleared somewhat from my earlier efforts.

The sun is nothing short of blinding as it reflects off the fresh snow. I push into the drift, forcing my legs to move as I climb a little, then sink down again. It's powdery and loose, never giving me a decent footing. My bones ache as I struggle forward, pushing and pretty much falling forward to make progress away from the shed.

When I finally make it to what I think is the road, I stop and catch my breath, then scan the blue sky for any hint of a bird. Nothing. I then try my best to scour the land-scape, but the brightness from the snow hurts my eyes. Still, I look for any sign of animals. When I come back empty again, I look up at the town in the distance.

It's small. Very few houses sit atop the rise. But there will be food. I try to get a good idea of the distance, then decide it doesn't matter. We can survive another night out here, but Charlie is still injured. She needs some-where to recover, and that includes somewhere she can fill her stomach with something other than snow water.

Turning, I work my way back to the shed.

When I walk in, Charlie looks at my hands, and her face falls almost imperceptibly.

"We're leaving." I lean down and grab the saddle, then settle it on Belinda's back.

"What?" Charlie's on her feet.

"The town I told you about. We have to get there. I think we can make it. The snow is still powder. The horse can manage it." I stand in front of the fire and warm myself, steam rising where the snow soaked me through.

"She could manage it, but not in this state. She's hungry too. Weak." Charlie places her hand on Belinda's neck. "She won't eat the straw anymore. Not even if I soak it in water."

"She'll only get weaker. We have to go before the top layer of snow turns to ice. If we wait, that could happen as soon as this afternoon with the sun out like it is. She won't be able to forge through it, not without getting cut up." I glance at Belinda. "And though roast horse sounds pretty good right now—"

"Don't you dare!" Charlie tries to cover the creature's ears.

"—we'll be better off with her alive," I finish. Once my fingers are warmed, I get back to buckling the saddle in place. "Let's get going. I want to be there before night-fall." I hold my hand out to Charlie.

"This is a terrible idea."

I take her hand, then grab her waist and lift her onto the horse, my ribs aching. "You always say that." I turn Belinda, taking care she doesn't stomp through the low fire, then lead her from the shed as Charlie ducks beneath the door frame.

With her bridle in my hand, I lead her down the same route I took until my path ends on the road. Then I climb up behind Charlie.

She leans over and presses a kiss to Belinda's neck, whispering to her so softly I can't hear. When she sits back up, Belinda begins walking steadily into the snow, little shivers racing through her as the crystalline air assaults us from all directions. At least there's no wind. Only stillness and invading chill.

When I wrap my arms around Charlie, she leans back, sharing what little warmth we have as Belinda moves us through the snow.

Her gaze lifts to the town. "Will they help us?"

I hunch down so I can rest my chin on her shoulder. "Maybe if you show them that perfect pair of ti— oomph!" I grunt as she kicks me.

"You're so good at foreplay." I grin.

"Ugh." She shakes her head. "See? That's why I pretended to be a boy."

"Because you were afraid of how attracted you were to me?"

"That doesn't even make sense. I was a boy before you ever washed up."

"So you don't deny that you're attracted to me?"

"You know? Maybe this was a good idea. This way I can freeze to death so I don't have to hear any more of your ridiculous arrogance."

I press my lips to her ear and enjoy the shiver I feel coursing through her. "I think you like my arrogance."

"If you want to stay on this horse, you'll keep your mouth to yourself." She turns and glares at me, our lips only a whisper away.

I want to kiss her, to see what she tastes like, but I'm pretty sure she'd find some way to knock me off the horse and take off to town without me.

She turns forward again, her hair tickling my nose as usual. More often than not, she's wanted to get rid of me on this journey. She even managed it once. But, of course, she realized how great I am and came back.

It doesn't make sense that I want her, that she makes me feel things that seem utterly foreign to me. I have no doubt that I would've left anyone else with the spriggans. Even though I don't know who the fuck I am, I know I'm more interested in survival than being a hero. I would've taken the reward and left Arlon with no regrets. It was the smartest thing to do, a decision that would've ensured my survival. But her—even before I knew she was a her—I couldn't let her go.

"Will you tell me where you're from now?" I ask.

"No," she snaps.

I sigh.

We ride for a little while in silence, Belinda struggling but making it through the snow, the town looming closer with each passing second. The hill is higher than I thought, and I have serious doubts we'll be able to make it all the way to the village on top before the sun goes down, but we can't stop now.

"Could you at least tell me why you always have to wear this old hat?" I tap the top of her head.

Charlie turns and looks at me out of the corner of her eye. "You don't like my hat?"

"I didn't say I didn't like it. I just want to know why you're so attached to it."

"Maybe I'm a hat person."

"What?"

"Some people are hat people, and some people have no taste." Her lips curl at the corner.

"Insulting me again?" I can't help the amusement it gives me.

"Not at all," she says airily. "Just stating facts."

"Okay, if you have such wonderful taste, then why do you insist on wearing this grubby hat?" I reach up and snatch it off her head.

"Hey!" She spins. "Give it back!"

I hold it out so she can't reach it. "Tell me why you love it so much."

"I don't love it. It's just a hat!" She slaps my arm and tries to lean out to grab it, but I keep my other arm wrapped firmly around her.

"If you keep squirming like this, you're running the risk of impalement again."

This earns me a scalding look as she snatches for the hat again.

The movement sends her hair into even more disarray, and that's when I notice her ears.

"What the—"

She yanks the hat from where my arm's gone lax and pulls it onto her head and over her ears. Her very *pointed* ears.

CHAPTER

NINE

"You saw nothing." Charlie shivers as Belinda carries us slowly the last of the way into the town.

"Maybe, but I'm pretty sure your ears—"

"Drop it!"

I've tried to address the ear situation several different ways on the trip through the high snow. Each one has ended with Charlie almost chucking me from the horse.

The sun has fallen now, only a few rays poking over the snowy peaks. We had a slight respite from the painful chill when the sun was out, but now that it's gone, the temperature is dropping rapidly.

"Almost there, girl." Charlie's been encouraging Belinda, but the beast's steps have slowed more and more. She's worn out.

When I catch a whiff of woodsmoke, a spark of hope lights inside me. We're almost there.

Belinda takes a faltering step, barely managing to stay upright.

"Fuck." I lift up and slide off her back.

"What are you—"

"Give me the reins." I reach up and take them from Charlie, then hand her the burlap sack from my back. "Put it on." Gripping the bridle, I lead Belinda up the hill, doing my best to avoid icy patches as we move along.

The trees on either side of us are hunched over like beggars, their limbs covered with snow and ice. Up ahead, a low wall marks the edge of the village, and the road clears the closer we get.

"That's it." I lead Belinda, hoping she won't give out right here. I need her to get to Finnraven Hill. "Good girl."

"Don't patronize her," Charlie says through chattering teeth.

"Okay, bad girl. You're doing terrible." I shake my head.

"That's not what I meant!" Charlie snaps.

I chuckle and keep pulling Belinda onward until the ground finally levels out and buildings rise around us. Not tall, nothing fancy, though the icicles hanging from them make them look particularly picturesque.

The houses are lit from the inside, smoke floating from their chimneys. Up ahead, a few people stand in front of the tallest building in the village—the church. I slow our pace, then turn and see a stables to our right.

I guide Belinda to it and open the doors to lead her inside.

"We don't even know who owns this place," Charlie hisses.

"It doesn't matter." I point. "There's fresh hay and thawed water." I lead Belinda to the water trough where she drops her head to drink.

"Come on." I hold my hands up to Charlie.

She throws her leg over and drops to the ground by herself, though she sways a little. I catch her shoulders and keep her upright as she shudders, the cold bone-deep for both of us.

My fingers ache as I unfasten the saddle and pull it off. Belinda makes a sound that edges on relief, then moves a few steps to the side and munches from the pile of fresh hay.

One of the horses down the row snorts, and another nickers in worry.

"Here." I take Belinda's bridle and lead her to the closest empty stall. "You'll be safe in here. If someone asks you about who's going to pay for the accommodations, we don't know each other. Got it?"

Charlie snorts a laugh as I grab the wooden pitchfork and toss the fresh hay into Belinda's stall. Once there's plenty, I grab up the bigger saddle bag. Charlie already has the smaller one slung across her back.

"You all right?" I ask.

She nods, her face reddened from the sun and the cold. We're both beat to hell at this point.

"Maybe there's an inn or something. I can do farrier work on all the animals in exchange for lodging," she says.

I remember the way her sides looked, the ugly bruises left by the spriggans. She needs rest, not work. "I'll chop wood or woo a wealthy old lady." I grin.

She digs in her bag and pulls out the mask. "Here. Put this on. Not that I think it'll help with the elderly women you intend to bed. All it would take is for you to open your mouth and—"

"You only wish you knew all the ways I can use this mouth. And it doesn't have to be just on rich matrons." I stare down at her.

She shoves the mask into my hands. "Your come-ons stink almost as bad as your armpits. *Almost.*"

I fasten the mask onto my face, then look to her.

She nods. "Let's go."

"Let me do the talking. I have a way with people. I think you've probably noticed it." I open the stables' door, and she gives me a nasty look as she walks out. Again, I can't help but get a little thrill when she does it. Maybe the cold has driven me insane.

We walk down the narrow lane until the buildings move back from the road, the entire town opening to the church at the center.

The people we saw from a distance are still standing around the frozen fountain, smoking pipes and talking quietly. They go silent as we walk up.

I give my best winning smile and open my mouth to greet them.

"What's wrong with your face?" The closest one points his pipe at me.

Charlie steps in front of me. "We come from the village of Arlon."

"Arlon's been shut these many months. No one goes in or out." An older man, his eyes squinted, steps toward us and stares at me.

"Not anymore," Charlie says. "We took care of the spriggans and the wood sprite. The path is clear. I expect some of the village folk will be visiting or passing through as soon as the snow melts."

"A young lad like you did all that?" The older man laughs. "Do I look like I just fell off the turnip cart?"

The men around him chuckle.

They think Charlie's a silly boy. Idiots. I realize I thought the same for quite some time, but now, everything about her is so ... appealing. Smart, clever, beautiful. Even the odd ears that she's refused to so much as joke about.

"Not alone." She hitches her thumb over her shoulder. "With him."

"Aye, he's a strapping lad, but what's wrong with his face?" The first man asks again.

"Injured fighting off a boggan of the swamp."

"You jest, young man." One of the others puffs on his pipe.

I stay silent, wondering where the hell this is going to go.

"Not at all. We're traveling warriors." She bows. "I'm his apprentice, of course. G here has slain many a witch and boggan. But this sort of skill comes at a great price. He's suffered great injuries physically and—" she taps her temple "—here as well. On top of that, he's gone mute."

It takes every shred of self-control I have, which isn't much I admit, to keep myself from both protesting loudly and grabbing hold of Charlie.

"You don't say?" The oldest man peers at me even harder.

Charlie waves a dismissive hand. "But enough of my boring explanations. We got caught in the storm and are very weary. Is there an inn?" she asks.

"No." The one who is still staring at my face shakes his head. "Don't have one of those. But that'd be nice."

"All right, is there a home where we could have a room for the night? We could chop wood in the morning, and I'm quite good at farrier work if you have the tools and a smithy." A chill goes through her as the night gets that crystalline coldness to it.

"No room here, but if you walk past the church on this side to the last house on the right——" the old man points ——"Widow Valor has a spare room. She won't say no to you young men." One of them guffaws.

"Thank you. We'll head there now." Charlie leads me around the fountain, the men there eying me warily.

I don't know why they're worried. Apparently, I'm an addled, mutilated mute.

As soon as we pass by the church and the men can no longer see us, I grab her arm and whirl her around to me. "What the hell was that?"

"Keep your voice down." She glances around. "It's the safest option."

"The safest option is for me to be a silent monster?" I ask.

"Yes. It got us pity—not fear—which led us to a room for the night."

"But the mute part?" I move closer to her, pulling her to me until we're touching. "Was that necessary?"

"I thought it was funny." She shrugs, a gleam in her eye as the moon rises.

"I told you to let *me* do the talking."

"I heard you, but I didn't think it was a good idea." She puts her hands on her hips. "Now do you want to stand here arguing or find the widow's warm house?"

I sigh. "Let's go."

She nods and turns, her steps faster now that relief is in sight.

The last house on the right is silvery in the moonlight, the front shutters dark and a light through the window. The chimney belches smoke into the air and promises much-needed heat.

Charlie strides right up and knocks on the door. "Shh." She reminds me with a look out of the corner of her eye.

I want to scold her for being so cheeky for someone who'd be dead if it weren't for me, but since I'm a goddamn mute, that's not an option.

The door swings open, and a woman peers at us. She has dark hair falling in ringlets to her waist, dark eyes, and pale skin. She holds a wine goblet in her hand. How is she already a widow? She can't be much older than I am.

"Madame Valor." Charlie bows. "The men in the village suggested we come to you for a room for the night. We've been on the road for—"

"Come in." The woman turns on her heel and marches away. "And they all call me Widow Valor. You can too."

Charlie and I share a surprised look, but the heat pouring into the night lures us inside without another word.

"You're hungry, I take it?" She walks to her kitchen, one far larger and nicer than those in Sac à Puces. "I have old baguette. Nothing fresh till morning." She sets out the bread along with a jar of jam and a generous hunk of cheese. Then she pours us two cups of wine before sitting down at her round kitchen table, her drink in hand. "Sit and eat."

We need no further invitation. Charlie plops down and grabs the cup of wine, slaking her thirst noisily before reaching for the baguette.

I down my wine as well, and Widow Valor pours us more. Suspicion tries to creep into my mind. "*Why would she be so kind?*" I wonder as I devour cheese and jam, then lick the leftovers from my fingers. But it's not as if I'm going to stop eating the food. She could tell us it's poisoned at this point, and I doubt we'd mind.

Once the food is gone and the wine bottle is empty, she rises from her seat and winds her way down the hall, her body swaying in a happily inebriated fashion.

Charlie stands, her eyelids already looking heavy. Exhaustion has snuck up on both of us—and with the warmth of the fire and the food in our bellies, we won't last much longer.

She opens a door and stands beside it. "In here. Leave the door open so the heat from the fire makes it in." With a jut of her chin, she points to the door across the short hall. "That's my room. Don't knock. Don't bother me. If you want more food in the morning—" She digs in the pocket of her dress and pulls out some coins, letting them drop on the floor. "Get whatever you like, but don't come back without two more bottles of what we were drinking tonight." She lifts her cup and downs it, then opens her bedroom door and walks in, a fireplace crackling happily in one corner.

She shuts the door as Charlie yanks on my sleeve. "G, look." Her voice is coated in sleepy glee.

Inside the room is a bed with quilts atop it. One big enough for the both of us.

I follow her inside, the room still warm despite its lack of a fire. It's like a small island of heaven.

"You can take the floor." She sits on the bed, bouncing a little. "This is mine. I mean, she's weird. She's weird, right? But I'm not going to pass this up. Even if she tries to kill me in my sleep, at least it'll be a *warm* sleep in an *actual* bed."

I pull my mask off, then kick off my boots.

She drops her bag beside the bed and pulls her shoes off, then buries herself under the covers. Her moan of pleasure sends heat shooting along my body and straight to my cock.

I pull my shirt over my head and toss it aside, then crawl into the bed beside her.

"Hey!" She shoves at me as I pull the blankets over us both and settle down at her back. "You're supposed to be on the floor."

I don't say anything, just breathe in and out deeply.

She yanks the blankets up to her chin. "You can't wear a shirt to bed? Are you using your chest hair as a widow lure or something?"

Silence.

"Don't get any ideas." She rolls over and faces me, her eyes burning in the dark. "Ugh, did you hear me?"

I nod.

A sigh leaves her, and she pushes her hair from her face. "Is this ... Is this because of the mute thing?"

I smirk.

She smacks my arm. "I should've been honest with them and said you were an asshole, a talking one."

The smirk turns into a grin. I want to kiss her on the forehead, to just brush my lips against her skin as a reassurance to both of us that this is real, that we're safe and warm. I know I shouldn't. But slowly, I move closer to her and do just that, pressing my lips against her soft skin.

Her breath hitches.

I draw back and close my eyes, wondering if she's about to slap me across the face or knee me in the crotch. When she does neither, it warms me even more than the food and the fire.

CHAPTER
TEN

T he sun is out, the sound of dripping water tapping all around the widow's cottage as I stumble to the hearth. Two bottles of wine, two loaves of baguette, and some fresh meats and cheese sit perched on the kitchen table.

I sit heavily and rub my eyes.

Where the fuck is Charlie? I lean over and look out toward the village. The sun is high overhead. Shit, I overslept and then some.

Stretching, I yawn and make myself a small breakfast as I glance around the house. In the daylight, it's quite homey. There's a sitting area with rough wood furniture covered with handmade pillows, and different pieces of art line the walls. Some are done with needle and thread, others in paint. The widow or her late husband must be an artist.

Her door is still closed, and I wonder if she's sleeping off last night, too.

When I'm done with breakfast, I step outside to relieve myself. The sun hits me, its rays melting away the lingering ice and snow and bouncing off the white land-scape on the valley floor far below. The vineyards will be thawed soon—maybe this afternoon, maybe tomorrow. After the road is clear, we can get on our way.

Widow Valor is at the kitchen table when I walk back inside.

Her head pops up, her eyes widening as she looks at me.

Fuck, my mask. I'd forgotten all about it.

"What the hell happened to you?" She makes the sign of the cross, then grabs a wine bottle, pulling the cork with her teeth.

I open my mouth to speak, then remember I'm a goddamn mute, so I clack my teeth together.

She takes a long swig from the bottle and wipes her mouth with the back of her sleeve. "What's the matter with you?"

God, this is impossible. I point to my mouth and shake my head.

"Oh, you're a mute?"

I nod.

"Probably for the best. I don't need any more lies from a man. Had enough of that." She takes another swig, and I retreat to my room and don my mask.

When I return, she looks me up and down. "You're big, but you might fit into some of my husband's old clothes. Come with me." She stands and makes her way down the hall, her long hair swaying with her uncertain steps.

I follow her into her bedroom, and she points to a small wardrobe. "Help yourself. He isn't coming back."

The wardrobe creaks as I open its doors, the clothes inside dusty but in good repair. I pull out a shirt with elbow patches, the fabric thicker than what I have on. It's on the small side, but I'll take the warmth over the proper cut.

I look at her over my shoulder. She doesn't make any move to leave.

"Go ahead. Try it on."

Of *course* she wants me for my body. How could she not? I strip my shirt off, then pull on the new one. It's tight across my chest, and the sleeves are ridiculously short, but I can make it work.

"There. Much better." She's closer now.

I stiffen when she presses her cheek to my back. "Just like my old man." She wraps her arms around my waist. "And even better, you don't talk."

This is an opportunity. I could bed the widow. It's a sure way for her to continue being generous with us—maybe she'll even give us all the supplies we need for the road ahead. Even as I think it, Charlie's bright blue eyes flit through my vision.

No. But I'd be doing this for her. A sacrifice. I would give the widow the most pleasure she's ever experienced because I'm doing what's best for Charlie and me. It makes total sense. It really does. Except ... I'm cold. Not like I was out in the snow. It's a different kind of cold, one that eats away at me. The widow's touch makes my skin crawl, and I realize I don't want her hands on me. If anyone is going to touch me like that, I want it to be ... It has to be Charlie.

I turn in the widow's embrace and hold my hands up, then try to crabwalk sideways toward the door.

Her grip tightens. "Just stay with me for a little while, stranger." She looks up at me, her dark eyes half-lidded. "I know I'm beautiful. The bloom may be off the rose, but I'm still just as sweet as I was back then."

I shake my head and back toward her door and out into the hall.

She finally lets go, then reaches up to grab onto my neck, hanging on me as she turns her mouth up to mine. "Just a kiss. You'll see how sweet I am."

I keep backing up until I hit the wall.

A door creaks, and when I turn my head toward the sound, Charlie stands in the doorway, some sort of muslin in her hands, her gaze on me.

Her mouth drops open, and I don't miss the hurt in her eyes as she spins and marches away.

"Fuck!" I pull the widow's hands off me.

"You can talk?" she asks.

I ignore her and run out the door after Charlie, but she's nowhere to be found. She can't have gone far. I race to the plaza in front of the church. The group of men is there again, some of them the same, some different from last night.

I'm frantic, but I'm also a mute. Fuck!

I put my hands over my eyes like I'm scanning the horizon, then I hunch down like I'm short, then I put my hands out beside me palms up. That has to translate for '*I'm looking for my short traveling companion. Where is she?*'

One of the men bites a piece of jerky and chews thoughtfully while another whacks a piece of ice from the fountain, making it splash into the water below.

"Reckon what's wrong with him?" One of the young men stares up at me.

I do the pantomime again and glare at him.

"Is he having some sort of a fit?" He's gawking now, his mouth hanging open.

"The boy said he's been touched by a boggan and some other such creatures. Took parts of his mind."

"I can see that." The young man chuckles. "And his face too." He reaches for my mask. "I want to see what's under there."

I smack his hand away, an inhuman growl in my throat.

He steps back quickly, his face going pale. "He's off, for certain."

I don't have time for this.

"Where is sh-he? The stable boy?" I ask.

The oldest man from last night raises his bushy brows. "He speaks!"

"Where'd he go?" I spin, looking for the gleam of her golden hair. "Tell me. He had to have just come through here."

"That boy is a godsend. He shoed all the horses this morning. Did the best work we've seen around here in a long time. He even trimmed up the donkeys and took a look at the milk cows. They've never been treated so well, and their hooves are shining like a—"

"Where is he?" I bellow, my voice ricocheting off the church.

He jumps, his bushy brows drawing together in irritation. "The hot springs." He juts his chin toward the narrow lane that leads farther up the hill. "That way."

I take off, my chest still aching from my injured rib with each footfall. When I see the haze of moisture in the air, I know I must be getting close. The houses up here are sparse, some of them abandoned and falling in. There's a stone bathhouse to my left with a sign over the door that I can't read. I dart past it and into the building, which is empty save for a few towels on hooks along the wall. The water that runs along the floor into shallow pools is all frozen.

When I exit into the sunlight on the other side, I find the hot springs. Two round pools steam in the cold air, one of them higher than the other and feeding it with a waterfall.

"Charlie?" I call.

Movement at the upper basin catches my eye, and I climb the steep stairs carved into the stone until I reach it.

"This is the women's section." Her pale hand pokes out of the thick fog and points to the sign at the back of the pool. Not that I can read it, which she *knows*.

Then I freeze. "Are you naked?" I ask, trying to glimpse her through the swirling mist.

"Generally, that *is* the way to take a bath, yes. What are you doing here, anyway? Don't you have a widow to woo?"

Her jealousy sends desire spiraling through me. "No." I strip off my boots and socks. Then I engage in a short battle with the too-small shirt, but I get it and my old one off.

When I reach for my pants, she says, "Don't you dare!"

"I dare quite a lot when it comes to you." I shuck my pants, then toss my mask onto the pile and climb down the steps into the warm water. I don't stop, dunking all the way under and holding my breath for as long as I can. I open my eyes for only a moment, catching a glimpse of her fair skin, her ribs no longer black and blue. What? There's no way she could've healed already.

When I pop back up, Charlie is pressed against the far side of the pool, her wet hair doing nothing to hide her delicately pointed ears.

"You aren't supposed to be here." She blinks. "And especially not *naked*."

I shrug and move closer to her, the water tickling at chest level. She's submerged up to her neck, and I suspect she's covering herself with her hands beneath the water.

"I can't see anything, Charlie. Relax." I wave a hand through the mist rising from the water's surface.

"I saw plenty," she mumbles and pins me with a glare.

"I know. There's a lot to look at. Prodigalous, some might say."

"You mean prodigious?" she asks.

"Oh, so you *did* see it." I smirk.

"Ugh!" She splashes water on me.

I creep closer. "I wasn't going to woo the widow, Charlie. She threw herself at me, obviously. How could she not?"

Another splash.

"But I didn't want her." I pin her with a stare. "I want someone else."

She rolls her eyes. "You don't even know me."

"What? I've known you for months."

"Yeah, and the whole time you thought I was a boy." She crosses her arms beneath the water.

"So?"

"So, all of a sudden you find out I'm a woman and now everything has changed? Please. I'd be a fool to fall for that."

"No, I always liked you when I thought you were a boy. You know that's true."

She wrinkles her nose.

I edge even closer, my skin on fire as if the water between us is super-heated. "Remember that time the Crane boys threw rocks at one of the horses, and you got mad and threatened them?"

Her face sobers. "Yes, I remember them knocking me into the mud and kicking me."

"I came to your rescue." I tap my chest. Her eyes follow the movement, and I catch the way her tongue darts out and licks her lips.

Damn, she's setting me on fire even though we're drifting in a pool.

She arches a brow. "My rescue? You said, and I quote 'get off him. Leave some of the little twat for me.' And then you kicked me in the stomach."

"No. I *pretended* to kick you in the stomach while I started spitting and trying to foam at the mouth."

She laughs, the sound so free and beautiful. "Yes, they ran away screaming that you were possessed."

"I almost got strung up that day, but Madge spoke for me."

"She really was the only thing between you and a noose," she says wistfully, though I don't know if she's reminiscing fondly about Madge or my frequently-impending doom.

"Sometimes I wonder if she was always meant to find me in the river. Maybe the voice from the water set it up that way so I might have a chance of finishing her quest. I never gave her enough credit—not Madge or the water lady."

"You can't trust voices in rivers, G." She sighs. "You should know that by now."

"What she said was true." I'm not giving up on that, on my only chance at redemption. "I can trust her."

"You trust *everything* she said, then?"

Sensing some sort of a trap, I give her a wary look. But there's no denying the belief I have for the voice in the water. It's the whole reason I'm out on this damn road. "Yes. Everything."

The corner of her mouth turns up, a cocky look if ever there was one. "If you recall, she also said you were wicked."

"How do you know that?"

She shrugs. "You talk in your sleep."

I'm so close now I can see the glistening tips of her ears, and I have the impulse to run my tongue along them.

"Does that really apply to me, though? I mean, if I was wicked before—in a life I don't even remember—that doesn't make me wicked now."

She purses her lips in disapproval. "G, I hate to break it to you, but you have a streak of wicked wider than the Pyrenees."

I clutch my chest over my heart. "Why do you insist on wounding me, Charlie? Is it because you're trying to break the tension between us?"

"What tension?" She kicks her chin up.

"Oh, you don't feel it?" I lower myself in the water until we're at eye level.

"No. Stop being silly." She tries to back up, but she's already at the pool's edge.

"If you don't believe we have any tension, then you won't mind if I touch your face?"

"W-what?" She swallows thickly.

I lift a hand toward her. "I just want to touch you. That's all."

"You're being weird."

"No, I'm just proving a point. If you're right, then me touching your face won't amount to anything. Right?"

"It won't." The stubborn tone of her voice does things to me. "And this is stupid."

"If you're so confident, then why not prove yourself correct?" I gesture toward her blushed cheek.

Her eyes narrow. "Just my face?"

"I *want* to touch you everywhere, but for this exercise, I'll only touch your face. But, if you feel like that'll create too much tension—"

"Fine." She presses her lips together.

That's all I needed. I close the distance, my palm sliding against her cheek as I cup her face.

Her breath catches, but then she releases it slowly, clearly fighting whatever she's feeling.

"How's the tension?" I ask and bring my other hand up, caressing her cheek.

"What tension?" she retorts, more color rising in her neck.

I move closer, our bodies almost touching, my hard cock straining toward her, though I keep my hips back.

"This tension." I lean forward, my lips brushing over hers.

She jolts, and her hands come up to my wrists. "You said just my face."

"This *is* your face." I kiss her. At first, she flinches, her eyes wide open as she glares at me. Then I angle my head and run my tongue along the seam of her lips.

She opens and pins my bottom lip between her teeth, biting until she draws blood. I don't let her go, not even when I taste copper as I delve my tongue into her mouth, finally tasting her.

A moan escapes her, the sound sending a blast of heat through me, and I deepen the kiss, my tongue laving hers as she answers, her body floating to me, her skin pressing against mine in the most maddening way.

I run one hand through her wet hair and pull the strands, positioning her head so I can tongue her wickedly, stoking my own desire with each moment that we tangle together. When she wraps her legs around my waist, I groan and push her against the side of the pool, my body covering hers as I feast on her lips, her tongue, every bit of her breath.

She tangles her fingers in my hair then runs her hands to my shoulders, her nails digging in as I pin her to the wall, feeling her breasts, her hard nipples against my chest as my cock presses between us. When I feel the heat between her thighs, I think I might lose my mind from the sheer wanting of her.

Wrapping one arm around her, I hold her tight, needing more and more and more until I'm on the verge of fucking combusting or dying from the lack of her.

She pulls away and gasps in air as I kiss to her throat, sucking her soft skin between my teeth and biting down, leaving small marks along her neck as I kiss to her shoulder.

A sound behind me is the only thing that breaks my concentration on her, and I turn to look over my shoulder.

A man from the village stands at the edge of the pool, a towel wrapped around his waist.

"Well, the ah, you see, ah, the men's pool is ... " His voice trails off as if he can't find whatever words he was about to say. "I'll just leave you boys to it." He turns and disappears into the mist, and then I hear him splash into the lower pool.

Charlie presses her forehead to my shoulder, her body shaking with quiet laughter.

I release her, the magic broken, though the moment I let her go, I want her back again. I want her in all the ways a man can want a woman, no matter what the old man next door might think.

She floats back against the wall, her glassy eyes on me. "That wasn't just my face."

I grin. "You already knew I was wicked."

She splashes me again, her laughter bright and wonderful, a sound that no truly wicked thing could ever elicit from a woman like Charlie.

CHAPTER

ELEVEN

T he small mountain of wood I've chopped leans precariously as I put the final piece at the top. Widow Valor will have plenty to last her through the winter.

I wipe my brow and curse the stupid mask. It's itchy where it rests against my sweaty skin. Pulling it off, I wipe it dry as my skin relishes the cold air. Once I've recovered, I replace it, tying it into place behind my head. It's been of great use in this village, and I give Madge a silent thanks for making it for me. I've realized I almost like it. It gives me a chance to hide my ugliness, to present a decent—if odd—face for people. There's still fear, but not the open loathing I've become used to. Madge never treated me any differently, though. Neither did Charlie.

I lean on the axe and look up through the clear night. The moon is between half and a crescent, which means I have about three weeks left before the Fallen Moon. A chill goes through me, my sweat now cold along my brow. The deadline looms large, and I still have quite a way to go after we leave this village. But Charlie needed the rest, and so did Belinda.

Paris is our next stop, a thought that sits heavy in my gut. It's where Charlie wants to part ways. With each piece of wood I chopped, my mind was working through that puzzle. How can I convince her to come with me past Paris? She already questions the reality of my quest—not that I can blame her—but I want her with me. All the way to Finnraven Hill and whatever lies beyond it.

When I realize no solution is going to make itself known in either the pile of firewood or the moon, I heave the axe into a stump and head to the door.

I walk in, shaking off the cold, and stop when I see Widow Valor and Charlie in the hallway.

"I could make you a man. Don't you want that?" Widow Valor is too drunk to even notice that I'm here.

"I'd prefer not to be, if that's all right." Charlie ducks under her arm and edges toward me. "I'm sorry, Vivian."

"But you're a young lad. Young, dumb, and full of—"

"Come now, Widow Valor. Leave my poor stable boy alone." I wink at Charlie.

Widow Valor turns to me, her eyes bloodshot, then stumbles down the hallway and sits heavily in front of a canvas. "I was just trying to show him a good time. That's all."

Charlie smooths the front of her shirt while she shakes her head in what seems like disbelief.

"I'm lonely," Widow Valor wails as she picks up her paintbrush and makes a few strokes of dark gray on her canvas.

Charlie moves nearer to her, though she's careful to stay out of grabbing range. "It's all right. I understand."

"I don't think you do." She drops her brush and leans back, draping one arm over her eyes. "I've been alone in this house for a year. The town shuns me because of my husband. Because of how he died."

"Oh." Charlie tangles her fingers together while I pour myself a cup of wine. I'd tease her about being on a first-name basis with the handsy widow, but for once I read the room and stay silent.

Widow Valor lifts her glass to me, and I refill it for her.

"Do you want to talk about it?" Charlie asks.

"No." Widow Valor sniffles.

I cut a piece of bread and layer some prosciutto and gruyere on top of it. Charlie waves it away when I offer it to her and glares at me before motioning toward the widow.

I shrug and devour it, then make another.

Charlie gives me an exasperated look—one that I've come to enjoy—and sits in a chair at Widow Valor's side. "I'm sorry I couldn't—"

"It's fine." Widow Valor turns her head away from Charlie with dramatic flair.

Charlie sighs, her face twisted in concentration.

"*Just leave her alone,*" I mouth around my food.

That earns me a glower. It warms my heart.

"Henri wasn't a smart man." The Widow Valor reaches blindly for her wine cup.

Charlie puts it in her hand. "All right."

"He wasn't known for his way with words or his skill at hunting or tending the grapes. He was, by all counts, useless. But I married him for a reason. A distant cousin of the Dauphine, he had a nice inheritance. But even that wasn't enough to convince me."

"No?" Charlie maintains a sympathetic tone.

The widow finally drops her arms from her eyes and looks at Charlie. "No, he had the most wondrous cock."

I snort a laugh. Charlie gives me a death glare.

"He had a talent. The way that man made me scream." Widow Valor falls into more sniffles. "I miss him. I miss him so much."

"There there." Charlie pats her hand awkwardly.

"But he's gone. I'm alone. I've already been through all the men in Loudin. Not a single man in this cursed village came even close to what my Henri could do with a single thrust." Her tears fall, dropping into her dark curls as she swigs her wine.

"What, um, what happened to Henri, if you don't mind me asking?" Charlie's voice is gentle, coaxing.

"The Beast of Gevaudon," the widow says sadly. "Ripped him to pieces just outside of Jouarre last spring. I asked his hunting partners, when they returned, if there was anything left, but alas. No. It ate every last scrap of him, cock included."

I want to laugh so badly that I almost spit out my mouthful of Gruyere. Sputtering, I drink more wine to wash it down.

The widow finishes her cup and holds it up. I refill it as she continues, "Lord LaMarque invited Henri to his hunting party, likely because LaMarque thought it might curry favor with the Dauphine. They travelled beyond Paris to the east, where the beast was last sighted. I told my Henri to stay in the carriage, not to go riding into danger. He didn't listen. Ripped to pieces." She wails again, then goes silent as she downs her wine. "Gone. And the village blames me for letting him go. They think the beast has cursed my name, marked me."

"That's ridiculous." Charlie stands, her hands on her hips as she starts pacing. "They can't blame you for what happened to him."

"But they do. They'll warm my bed for a night, but that's all. And it doesn't matter, not a one of them has half of what my beautiful Henri had." She wipes her nose. "But maybe you do?" She looks at Charlie hopefully.

"I'm afraid I'd leave you unsatisfied, Madame." Charlie shakes her head.

"You then?" The widow asks me. "You're so big. It only makes sense that—"

"He's a eunuch." Charlie cuts in. "Lovely singing voice. Like an angel, truly."

I choke on my wine, coughing as my eyes water and Charlie gives me a self-satisfied look.

The widow collapses into a pile of self-pity yet again. "They'll never stop shunning me. Not until the beast is dead. I'll die here alone."

"Why don't you leave?" I ask once I can catch my breath.

"And go where?" She meets my gaze, her eyes red-rimmed. "I'm *marked*. My name is cursed. All families whose kin have been victims of the beast share the same fate." She reaches to her wrist and rolls up her sleeve.

Charlie kneels and takes her arm in her hands to get a better look at the black mark on the widow's wrist. "Who did this to you?"

"All of the bastards. The village. Everyone gets this mark if they're cursed by the beast. Whole families have been run out of villages, their homes burned. Loudin lets me stay because of my money. That's all. As soon as it runs out, they'll burn me out too."

"That's awful." Charlie holds her hand. "I'm sorry."

"I miss him. I miss having a life outside this damned cottage." She weeps, her sobs growing snottier by the moment.

"We could kill it." Charlie points at me and then back to herself.

"No we can't." I gawk at her. "Not a chance."

"We can."

The widow shakes her head sadly, speaking between sobs. "There have been reports here and there that someone—has killed it, but it always turns out to be a bear or—something like that. The beast itself supposedly resembles a huge bear—and wolf mixed. Matted black hair, long poison claws, sharp fangs—" She puts the back of her hand to her forehead. "I can't speak of it more. It makes me feel faint."

"We can help. Right, G?" Charlie gives me a pleading look.

"Charlie, a word?" I stride down the hall to our room.

She follows. "Look, I know what you're going to say—"

"That my time is running out, that I have to get to Finnraven Hill and find the Wood of Mist before the Fallen Moon, that I *don't* have time to hunt some mythical beast that I don't even know how to kill?" I run a hand through my hair, yanking at the strands.

"Calm down."

"I'm calm." I throw my hands up.

"Mmhmm, sure." She walks past me and sits on the bed. "Look, that woman is miserable. We could help her."

"Why?" I shake my head. "There's absolutely *nothing* in it for me to help her. It's a detour I can't afford." I don't understand her. Why would she volunteer to fight a bloodthirsty beast that's already killed dozens if not more? It's a fool's errand, and Charlie is many things, but a fool isn't one of them.

"It wouldn't only help *her*. Think of all the people who were already victimized by the beast! Entire families. Children! We could free them of this ridiculous—*man-made*—curse." An idea starts to form. "It would only take a few extra days. Once we get to Paris, we can keep an ear out for reports of where it was seen last. Then—"

"You'll come with me after Paris?" Fuck, I shouldn't have blurted that. I need to play this carefully, to lead her right into my trap before I spring it shut.

She nibbles her bottom lip, that clever mind of hers working in a whirl of cogs and springs. "I'll stay with you until we kill the beast. After that, I'll return to Paris. I'm *not* going to Finnraven Hill."

The vehemence in her voice surprises me. "Why not? Is this because of our kiss?"

She sputters. "I—you—don't flatter yourself!"

I will absolutely continue to flatter myself, but I put that aside for later. "All right, if our passionate, extremely hot kiss isn't the reason, then tell me why."

"Because I'm *not* going." She crosses her arms in that stubborn way of hers.

"Then I'm not hunting some poison-clawed beast." I sit beside her and cross my own damn arms.

She turns to look at me, her blue eyes so beautiful in the soft light of the fire. "G, we can help so many people. Don't you want that?"

I give her the only answer that makes any sense. "Not unless they're going to help me back."

Her face falls. "You know, I don't put a lot of stock in your 'lady in the water', but she sure as hell was telling the truth about your wickedness," she spits.

"Do you have any idea what those words do to me?" I run my hands down my thighs to keep myself from grabbing her. I want to turn her over my knee. The mental image of spanking her round ass is almost too much to bear. I don't know where these ideas come from, but I rather like it.

Her eyes go to the bulge in my pants. "Oh, god, G! What the hell?" She jumps up and takes a few steps away from me, but not before I see the color in her cheeks.

"You do this to me. Only you. I can't fucking explain it. Ever since I saw you, I mean *really* saw you as you are, not as you pretended to be—"

"You mean when you saw my tits?" she interjects.

"No, though that was quite nice."

"Asshole." She crosses her arms over her chest, her back tense as I stare at her.

"Not then. When I saw you fighting against spriggans and sprites and god knows what else without giving up, all because you wanted to help the people of Arlon. When I saw you sticking by Madge when I wanted to run. When I saw you always choose kindness when I barely even knew what it was. When you never, not once, said anything about *this*." I hold my hand up to the ruined side of my face, to the piece of me that's missing, the piece I pretend doesn't hurt. "When I saw *you*." I can admit I'm not good with words, but I don't think I could convey what I'm feeling even if I were. It's too big, too damn much for me to ever say.

She lets her head loll back, and she sighs. "You don't even know me. If you did, you wouldn't—" she cuts herself off, shaking her head as she does so.

"You keep saying that, and you're wrong. I don't even know who the hell I am, but I know *you*. If I could explain it, I would. But I suspect you realize that, and I suspect you know me better than you want to admit."

She stands, her back still to me, and stews. After a short while, she says, "What do you want in exchange for hunting the beast? Money? I'll get a job as soon as I land in Paris. I can guarantee you a share of my wages. Hell, I bet Widow Valor will fund our expedition and maybe even pay us a bonus for killing the monster. I'll give you my cut. How about that?"

"All that sounds nice." I let my gaze follow the curve of her neck, the way her shoulders round and flow into her arms, the way her waist narrows and her hips flare.

"But?"

"Hmm?" I glance back up, and she's looking at me over her shoulder. "Oh, yes. All that sounds nice, but it's not what I want."

"Then what do you want?" she says slowly through clenched teeth.

"You come with me to—"

"I'm not going with you to Finnraven Hill!" She stomps her foot, hands on hips. Damn adorable is what she is.

"That's my price. I'll slay this beast, but I need your promise that you will finish this journey with me. All the way to the Wood of Mist and the Graven Phylactery. To the very end."

She makes a sound of deep, thorough frustration, then kicks the wall.

"I love it when you get emotional." I sigh.

She roars this time, the sound loud and full of so much irritation that it only makes me smirk more.

"So that's a yes, then?" I ask.

With a frustrated groan, she storms past me. "Yes. We'll leave tomorrow." Then she slams the door to our room and says a litany of curses so vile that my lips turn up in a grin as I listen to every last one and memorize a few for later use.

TWELVE

"Comfortable?" I ask as we ride out of Loudin, our new cloaks warm on our backs as the sun shines and melts the rest of the snow.

She wiggles forward, rubbing maddeningly against me as she does it. "If you could give me more room, then I'd be comfortable," she snaps.

"Still mad about our deal?"

"Shut up, G."

"You didn't seem mad last night when you cuddled up close to me and—"

"*Shut up*, G!"

I chuckle quietly as she guides Belinda into an easy walk down the hill, carefully leading her away from any patches of ice.

The day is cold, our breath coming out in puffs, but it's nothing compared to the storm. With the sun on our backs, the weather seems almost mild, the world fresh and new from its coat of snow.

I pull out the map and study it again, my finger tracing the route from Loudin to Paris. From the looks of it, the journey will take us three days of travel if we're making decent time, and I intend to do just that.

We settle in, our stomachs full and our bodies rested. Even the pain in my rib has receded, the dull ache only making itself known if I twist the wrong way.

Once we're in the valley again, the horse making easy progress between the dormant vines, Charlie pulls a book from her pocket and flips it open.

I look at it over her shoulder. "What's that?"

"A book." She flips to the first page full of text. No pictures at all. I frown.

"I know it's a book, but what for?"

"It's a small collection of various writings on creatures and monsters in and around this region. I found it in Loudin's library."

"There was a library?"

"Yes." She shakes her head. "Whenever I arrive in a town, it's one of the first things I check for. I suppose I should've known Sac à Puces wasn't the town for me when I discovered there was no library, though Sasha's small collection held me over for a short while."

"Sasha?" I ask.

"Sorry, I was speaking in terms of mutual respect, which are foreign to you. As you knew her, she was the witch at the edge of town. The one who gave you the map in your pocket."

"Oh, *that* witch. Yeah, she did have a lot of books." I agree.

"There's that sharp intellect," she deadpans.

"Have I mentioned what your meanness does to me?" I grip her waist and pull her tightly against me.

"Fool!" She laughs and wriggles away but not far. "Let me read."

"Fine." I stay silent for a while, but eventually I can't help myself. "What's the story about? Are there swordfights or something interesting?"

"Ugh, I knew you were just bursting to interrupt. No sword fights—well, it's not really a fight. There's blood, though. This one's about a family of redcaps that settled near a sheep farmer. It didn't turn out well."

"What's a redcap?"

"A fae known for its love of fighting and gore. It wears a white cap—"

"But then why—"

"At first." She holds up a finger. "At *first* the cap is white when it's gifted from a parent or a relative. But with each fight the redcap wins, it dips it in its victim's blood until it turns—"

"Red."

"Very clever indeed, G." She glances at me over her shoulder, her eyes sparking in the sunlight. I realize at that moment I've never seen a prettier shade of blue.

"The book told you all that?"

"And more." She flips some pages, then pauses. "Ah, this is the part about the beast. Says it's a firsthand account from one Lord Battenbaum of the Plains."

"Someone saw it up close and survived to write about it?" I stare at the words, trying to force them into submission, but it doesn't work. They're still gibberish, no matter if I cross my eyes or concentrate hard.

"Yes. Here, I'll read to you."

Generally, I don't care for books, especially given the fact I can't read them, but her voice will go a long way toward making this part of the ride enjoyable.

"'*On the morning of July 20, I hosted a hunting party with the honorable goal of defeating the fearsome, monstrous, and bloodthirsty Beast of Gevaudon. Armed with nothing more than my crossbow, my attendants, several men from the local village, and a small accompaniment of soldiers, I intended to best the beast and save the country from its violent scourge.*' July 20—it's dated last summer. It must've happened after Henri's ill-fated trip. Good information, but ugh, this guy is so pompous. Let me skip to the good parts."

"He didn't seem so bad to me."

"To you? Of course he didn't." She flips some pages. "Okay, this part is better. '*After a grueling morning wherein my carriage struck a rock on our journey to Mount-faucon—the last town where the beast was sighted—and I had to wait half an hour for my men to repair it, I joined the hunt proper. My hounds had already caught the monster's scent and chased it into a nearby wood. I mounted my thoroughbred steed Barnabus and rode valiantly at the front of the contingent, with only two lines of soldiers ahead of me.'*" She groans. "This guy. Sheesh. '*We rode for hours, and I suffered for this quest, the pain in my spine very great for I chose to use the saddle gifted to me by His Majesty the King rather than my usual—*' blah blah blah— '*the beast was cornered against a steep cliff, the rock far too sheer to climb. Behind it yawned a dark cave, the entrance littered with mounds of bones. The soldiers approached in strong formation as the beast gnashed its teeth, the things like great daggers in two rows inside its gaping mouth. Covered in black fur, it had long claws tipped with a viscous green substance. It killed the hounds with it, their bodies steaming and rotting at the creature's feet. Huge eyes bulged from its head, but they were like no animal I'd ever seen. Instead, they were like a man's, if man was borne of the devil. Man after man approached it, raining down arrows and trying to find a way to attack. Some arrows struck true, but the beast simply grabbed them between its massive teeth and pulled them free as if they were nothing more than toothpicks. It crushed men in its great jaws, breaking their bodies and throwing them through the trees. A barbed tail whipped behind it, skewering anyone who attempted a flanking maneuver. The soldiers and the hunters fell until I, in yet another great act of sacrifice, sent my servants out to try to incapacitate the great beast so I could strike the killing blow. But they succumbed, their bodies steaming with poison as the beast reared its head and roared, the forest shaking and even the sun hiding its face from the terror of it. Routed, I made the informed decision to retreat, and I galloped from that den of death, my life saved by Almighty God for some greater purpose. Perhaps I am meant to be pope, or crowned*—Okay, that's enough." She closes the book.

"It was just getting good," I tease.

"G, you're the worst."

"So you keep telling me."

"Though, to be honest, Lord Battenbaum is some steep competition for that title."

"He'll never unseat me." I shrug. "I would've turned tail far sooner."

She stows the book and looks out at the vineyards, her gaze thoughtful. "The beast has a thick hide, one that arrows barely penetrate. I'd heard about the poison claws, but the steaming and rotting is ... illustrative. And we also know that it uses its tail as a weapon, same as its claws and teeth. We also know it has a den—all those piles of bones aren't coincidence. That's where it takes its victims."

"Sure, but none of that gets us any closer to how to kill it." I *knew* books were useless.

"No, but now we know brute force isn't going to work." She pats my hand with a patronizing touch. "That means you'll need to sit this one out and let me think."

"You know, I'm beginning to think you get off on being rude to me." I put my hands on her shoulders and run them down her arms to her wrists. "I certainly do."

"That's what you call 'thinking'?"

I bark a laugh and pull her wrists inward, wrapping her up in my arms. "See what I mean? You can't help yourself. It's practically foreplay."

She shakes her head. "I'm not playing this game with you."

"What game?" I feather my lips along her exposed neck. "Like the one we played in the pool?"

"G, that was—" Her breath hitches as I nuzzle her earlobe, her cap the only thing stopping me from going higher and kissing the pointed tip. "That was a mistake."

"I don't think so. I think the mistake was when I didn't take it any further. We could've solved this little riddle right there in the water."

"There is no riddle."

"There is. It's the riddle of 'how much of me can you take before you feel like you'll split apart'?"

"Get over yourself," she says, but I feel the tremble in her, the one she desperately wants to hide.

"Some day soon, you're going to tell me you want me. And when that time comes, I won't hold back, Charlie. Not for a single second." Fuck, I want her to tell me right now. I'd do viciously depraved things just to hear those words fall from her lips.

Her golden hair tickles along my cheek. "As if you'd know what to do with a woman."

"I know what I'd do with you." I drop my palms to her thighs and let them rest there. "I've thought about it quite a bit. First, I'd get a taste of you, every bit of you. I want to inhale it, lick it, fucking bask in it. I think about how you'll feel on my tongue, and I already know it's sweet. It's that scent I catch every now and again, the one I thought was pie." I chuckle, the sound raspy and low in my throat. "It's you, and I want to gorge myself on nothing but you."

"G, don't." Her voice is breathy.

"I'd worship those perfect tits of yours, and I'd definitely leave a bite mark on your round ass. I'd kiss your ears, especially the points—the ones you pretend don't exist."

She shivers, her breath coming out in a harsh whoosh.

"And then I'd bury myself inside you and fuck you until you couldn't think straight, couldn't do anything except take what I'm giving." My hands drift higher on her spread thighs. "All you have to do is ask. Just say the words, and I'll make good on everything I've said. It's a promise."

"You'll never hear that from me." Her voice trembles. "Never." She pulls my hands away.

"All right." I sit back and watch the vein thrumming at her neck. Her heart is beating just as fast as mine, and I felt the heat of her, the way her thighs warmed under my touch. "We'll see."

As if sensing my stare, she pulls her cape higher, hiding herself from me as best she can.

The tension fades eventually, and we fall into a comfortable silence as we wind our way out of the vineyards and into fields left barren for the winter. When the day begins to fade, I look behind us, but the rolling hills hide any view of Loudin. We're back into the wilderness, only a mish mosh of small towns between us and Paris. After that, all I'll have to do is kill a monster, and then I'll be on my way to Finnraven Hill with plenty of time before the Fallen Moon. The Graven Phylactery will be mine in two weeks, maybe less.

"What's a Graven Phylactery look like anyway?"

Charlie jumps at the suddenness of my question.

"On edge? I told you I could help with that."

"Shut it." She rolls her shoulders as if they ache. I'd offer to rub them for her, but I'm pretty sure she'd bite one of my fingers off if I tried it.

"It's a small ... You know, a small thing." She holds up her thumb and forefinger with perhaps two inches between them. "A vial, usually glass, with what looks like liquid inside, but it's a soul."

"Souls aren't liquid?"

"No one knows what they are." She shrugs.

I scratch my nose. "The lady in the water never said what I was supposed to do with the phylactery. I think once I get it, maybe she'll just *poof* appear and fix me."

"Nothing is just *poof* and fixed. Not that I've ever seen."

"For being a ray of sunshine who loves to help others for no good reason, you sure are a pessimist."

"I'm a realist," she corrects, then glances up toward the rising crescent moon. "We need to find a safe spot to stop."

"I saw a patch of trees ahead. I figured that would be a good place. Plenty of firewood so we don't have to use what we brought."

She nods. "Sounds good."

We reach the small copse of trees between fields and make camp for the night. The food Widow Valor gave us provides a nice meal, so we sit and eat, chatting easily about the road to Paris. Charlie does her best to avoid touching me, and she makes her bedding pallet across the fire from where I'm sitting.

"Now that the snow's let up, you have no use for me anymore?" I ask.

She has her back to me, her arm curled under her for her pillow. "I think it's best if we sleep separate from now on."

"Why is that?" I ask.

Charlie turns onto her back and looks at me through the flames. "You know why."

"Afraid you'll jump on my cock and ravage me in my sleep?" I waggle my good eyebrow.

"What's it like to have the self-confidence of a man at least twice as intelligent and good looking as you? Seems like it would be jarring."

Belinda gets to her feet, her ears flattening back against her head.

"It's quite nice, actually." I lean back and lace my fingers behind my head as I watch the horse. "Never having to doubt yourself. You should—"

"Hello?" a voice calls from the dark trees to my left.

Belinda nickers, her eyes on the gloomy woods.

I'm up immediately, an axe in my hand as I step forward. "Who's there?"

"Hello? Please help me." The voice warbles, seeming neither near nor far.

The hackles on the back of my neck rise. "Show yourself!"

"Don't talk to it!" Charlie hisses and grabs my elbow, yanking me back toward the light of the fire.

I shoot her a confused look. "You, of all people, don't want to help whoev—"

"Please, come quickly." The voice moves to our left, and I turn with it. "Help me. What's your name?"

"It's not a person." She holds my elbow in a death grip. "Don't listen to it."

"That's kind of difficult when it's calling out to me."

Her eyes are huge as she stares into the dark. "Do *not* engage with it. You'll only draw it to us," she whispers.

"What is *it*?"

"I need help. Please. I know you're there. What's your name?" It's to our right now, and I turn, raising my axe to strike.

"Nothing good. Nothing we want to invite to our campfire."

"I'll tell it to go away."

"No!" She squeezes so hard her nails dig into me. "Do not address it at all."

A vicious cackle cuts through the stillness. "I know you're there. I can smell you. Don't ignore me." The voice changes back into a mournful tone. "I need help. I'm hurt. I have children here. They're injured." Suddenly, a cacophony of crying voices rises all around us, children yelling and screaming in anguish.

"Fucking hell." I grip the axe tighter and keep my eyes trained on the trees.

"It won't come near the fire," Charlie whispers. "It can't stand the light."

"I'm waiting here in the dark for you. I'm so scared. It's cold. Please help me." A child's voice, one whose tone is just a little off, just a little ... sour. "What's your name?"

Charlie raises her finger to her lips and shakes her head, her grip still fierce on my arm.

"Tell me your name, friend, and I'll tell you mine." I jerk my head to the left and just catch a set of deathly white claws disappearing around a tree trunk, leaving gouges in their wake.

"Turn your back on it." Charlie tries to pull me around to the fire.

Everything inside me screams to *absolutely not* turn my back on the creature in the woods.

"You *must* ignore it."

"Just tell me your name, traveler. Tell me your name and help me. If you do, I'll lead you to a great treasure, to your heart's desire. All you have to do is tell me your name."

I meet Charlie's gaze.

"Tell me your name, and your troubles will be over. I know what you seek. I know, I know, I know. I heard it on the wind," it singsongs, the voice coming from everywhere and nowhere all at once. "The Graven Phylactery. It can be yours."

My skin crawls at the glee in its words.

"Don't," Charlie whispers.

"All I need is your name. Please share it with me, friend. Help me. That's all I need. Then I'll give you what you desire." It wheedles and sighs, always hiding itself in the trees.

I lean down to Charlie's ear. "What exactly are we dealing with here? Something I can kill, right? Why don't I just play its game, then when it comes out—"

"No." Her vehemence blazes in her eyes. "Don't you dare. It's an Eater," she says darkly, as if I have any idea what she's talking about.

"A what?"

The thing continues its cajoling, sometimes with many voices, sometimes with one.

She gives me an incredulous look, then presses her lips to my ear and whispers earnestly. Fuck me, I can't think, can't focus on anything except the way she feels, the heat from her mouth against my skin. It's heaven, but it's hell because it can't go any further, no matter how badly I want to simply turn my head and take her mouth again. I won't. Not until she asks. Not until she *breaks* for me. Perhaps the most wicked part of all—I want to hear her begging for me, her mind destroyed with need for *me*. Only me.

"—that's why you can't engage it." She pulls back, her warmth gone, and my mind clears a little.

"Could you, um, do that again?" I ask. "I seem to have missed everything you said."

That earns me a smack on the arm.

"Or tell me hers. Tell me the pretty one's name." The monster has taken a different tack, but it's call is just as incessant.

"It can die, yes?" I ask. "All I have to do is tell it my name?"

"Yes!" the creature cries through the trees.

"No!" Charlie steps in front of me. "That's stupid. Even for you!"

"But what if it's telling the truth? We won't have to go to Finnraven Hill."

She shakes her head, firelight bouncing off her shiny strands. "It's a liar. It only wants your name so it can have *you*. The Eater devours everyone who gives in. All those voices you hear?" She points to the trees. "Those are its victims. It will add your voice to them if you tell it anything." She reaches up and puts her hands on my shoulders. "Believe me, I don't want to go to Finnraven Hill, but bargaining with the Eater is *not* the answer."

"What about you, little one? Little pretty thing. Doesn't your father miss you?"

Charlie freezes, her hands falling to her sides.

"He does. He misses you so, little lost lamb. Searches. Even asked me about you. I'd never tell. No, no, no. I'd never tell. Not even him. I'd never tell him where you went. But tell me your name, little lost one. He wouldn't tell me, but I know who you are. I knew his name, but I couldn't eat him. No, not strong enough. But if I had you here with me, we could eat whoever we wanted! I just need a name. Please—" The voice changes again, this time to a woman's. "Please, help me. Please, just tell me your name." It giggles, the sound vibrating through the air like a swarm of hornets. "We could be the best of friends. You know what it is to consume, to rend and tear, to destroy. We could eat our fill. Never go hungry. Never, never, never."

Charlie puts her hands to her ears, pressing hard, distress all over her face.

"We aren't telling you shit!" I yell and pull Charlie against me.

She trembles, her body rigid in my embrace.

Movement catches my eye, and the creature moves from tree to tree, closer now. Firelight flickers across it as it moves, revealing horror after horror. It's nothing but pieces; bits of bodies stuck into a trunk of skin. Eyes poking out, elbows, feet, hands, dozens of them, all roiling in a mass of flesh.

"Tell me your name." A mouth near the bottom cries before disappearing again, another mouth taking its place. "Please, help."

Charlie doesn't move, barely breathes.

The more I look at the creature stalking us, the angrier I become. It's abhorrent, and it's upsetting Charlie. She's so unbothered all the time. To see her shaken like this, it breeds violence in my blood. I step back from Charlie and lift my axe.

"Yes, yes, come to me. Strike me down. Come, come, come! Or you, little one. Oh, how sad your father was. How his heart is broken from your absence."

"Don't." She clings to me, her hands fisting my cloak, her eyes shimmering with tears. "Please don't."

I lower my arm and use my other hand to wipe away the tears that trace down her cheeks. The fire crackles behind her, the wood I found in the trees at dusk dry enough to burn without too much urging despite the snow.

"Stay here." I kiss her forehead. "I'm going to pack up."

She stands close by the fire as I gather her bedroll and mine. The creature jabbers the entire time, goading me to enter the small grove of trees, desperate for my name.

Once I've gotten the spooked Belinda saddled and ready, I take Charlie's hand and lead her to the horse. She mounts it quickly and keeps her gaze glued to the fire.

I grab the bridle and lead Belinda away from the trees and into the fallow field on the other side of the road. When I step back, Charlie's eyes widen.

"What are you doing?" Her knuckles are white as she grips the saddle horn.

The creature rails against us in a multitude of voices, all of them demanding we come back.

"I'm not doing anything stupid." I hand her the reins. "Wait here for me."

"No!" She reaches for me, missing me as I jump back.

"Can you trust me?" I ask. "Just this once?"

"The Eater is dangerous. It's ancient. You can't beat it. You won't survive if you try to play its game." Her tone is desperate, her hands still reaching for me. "Don't do this."

"I need you to trust me. I know trust doesn't come easy for you, especially with the likes of me." I step to her again and put my hand on hers. "But will you, please?"

She takes a deep breath, her nostrils flaring as she exhales. "Promise me you won't do anything stupid."

I smirk and squeeze her hand. "Only an oaf would do that." With that, I turn and hurry back to the fire, grabbing up bits of fallen limbs and somewhat sturdy sticks as I go.

Once I put them all in to catch the flame, I wait while the creature stalks me.

"I could tell you about her." A meek little girl's voice. "Do you know who she is? I could tell you all her dark secrets. Wouldn't you like to know? You don't know, do you? But I do. All you have to do is—"

"Tell you my name. I get it. Now be quiet. Daddy's trying to concentrate." I use my axe to wrench a large smoldering log from the fire and heave it away. It rolls closer to the trees. I walk up behind it and give it a hard kick, sending it sparking and sizzling through the undergrowth until it comes to rest against a sapling.

"What're you doing? I need help." The creature oozes to my left. I back away from the trees and get another log, sending it into the woods in the other direction.

"Stop!" It's close now, roiling behind a tree that's far too small to hide it.

I grab the burning limbs and heave them into the woods at intervals, then use the axe to scoop the burning coals and sprinkle them along the leaves and pine needles at the edge of our camp.

"Stop right now!" A child's voice screeches.

My eyes on the creature, I stay beside what's left of the fire and wait, axe in hand. The Eater comes closer, only a tree between it and me. It's mass of body parts roils more quickly, voices calling and changing, one mouth dying as another surges to the surface.

The logs begin to crackle, finding kindling beneath them as they burn, and at least half of the limbs I threw are starting to catch.

"It won't be long now." I grip up on my axe and watch the monster. It watches me back with untold eyes, all different shapes, all gleaming at me in the growing light of flames.

"You could've had anything you wanted." It screeches. "Anything!"

"Okay, sure. Tell me how many deals you've closed."

It moves closer, smoke and flames beginning to creep up behind it.

"What?"

"Tell me how many of these deals you've actually closed. How many times have you given people what they asked for?"

"Just tell me your name." A gruff man's voice. "Tell me."

"See, that's what I thought. You always win, don't you? It's a fool's game."

"Tell me your name!" it wails.

I laugh and watch as it creeps closer, all its eyes focused on me. "That's the thing, Eater, I don't *know* my name."

It collectively blinks.

"I couldn't play your game if I wanted to. Joke's on you, asshole." I point my axe toward the flames jumping up behind it, licking along the trunk of an old, dead tree.

The eyes disappear, and in their places are mouths. Dozens, maybe hundreds, and they all cry out with utter rage, shaking the forest with the sound and making me wince from the pain in my ears.

Then it rushes me, rolling forward in a gelatinous muck.

I hurl my axe, burying it in the monster's center. It shrieks and slows, but it's still coming. Waiting for it, I bend my knees, getting low. When I feel its putrid breath and see the bone and sinew that connects its parts, I use all my force to spring up and back, jumping the fire as it lunges at me. It lands right on the flames, its putrid flesh sizzling as it screams, so many mouths of all different sizes bubbling to its surface and falling back again and again.

Scrambling away, I get to my feet as it lunges again, the long arm with the horrible claws reaching for me.

A yell rips from me when it slashes my leg. It reaches again as I fall, the flames engulfing its mass as the clawed hand seeks me out.

It almost has me when an arrow whistles past my ear and embeds in it. Then another, and another shoot past until the hand retracts back into the boiling mass, flames racing over its surface as it screams and shudders.

I get to my feet and limp away, the forest blazing at my back as Charlie sits astride Belinda, an arrow nocked as she aims past me.

"I didn't know you could shoot like that."

"You said you wouldn't do anything stupid," she says tightly.

"No, I said only an oaf would do something stupid." I reach up and grab the saddle, then lift myself to sit behind Charlie. My leg burns, the scratches deep. I'll deal with it when we stop again.

We watch as the woods burn, the creature's screams dying away, the voices no longer luring or begging.

She lowers the bow and lets out a shaking breath. "What were you thinking?"

"I wasn't." I keep my eyes on the woods, making sure the Eater doesn't slink out or come after us. I want it dead.

"At least you're honest."

"Only with you." I wrap my arm around her waist and press her against me, just feeling her heartbeat enough to ease the racing pace of my own.

"You killed it." She watches the flames, the orange light dancing in her eyes as wonder tinges her voice. "You really killed the Eater." She shakes her head, her usually scolding tone returning. "But you shouldn't have risked it. Why would you do that? We could've just left."

I adjust my leg, wincing as I move. "It made you cry."

She turns her head sharply. "What?"

"I wanted to kill it, so I did."

"Because it made me cry?" The word flabbergasted has never really occurred to me as one I could use, but as I look at her now, I know it must be the one that fits.

I shrug.

She turns back around quickly and clicks her tongue for Belinda to get going. But I hear her muttering, the words 'oaf', 'dense', 'idiot', and 'sweet' all making an appearance. I only focus on the last one. The others are just flirting.

THIRTEEN

"Quit flinching, you big baby." Charlie re-wraps the cuts on my leg.

"You're just so rough. Violent, really. Your feelings for me are—Ow!" I yelp when she cinches the last bit of fabric.

"There." She pulls my pantleg down and hands me my boot. "We should make it to Paris before I have to check them again."

"Thank god." I pull my leg away and stuff my foot into my boot. "You're so vicious when you're in need."

"I'm *not* in need of anything." She stands and pulls her hat down tight on her head. "Let's go. We can get a few more miles before the sun sets."

"Fine." I clamber to my feet and offer to help her onto Belinda, but she pulls herself up without me.

We've been riding for two days since the Eater, and for two days and nights, Charlie's words have been clipped as she's refused all my extremely smooth attempts at making conversation.

With a sigh, I climb up behind her, and we set off again, a small village up ahead.

"Your mask." She digs around in the saddle bag, then hands it to me.

I put it on, securing it with the leather laces as we maintain our easy pace. Only a few villagers sit in front of their homes, some of them smoking and others talking. They all look at us suspiciously as we pass. It's a small town, only about a dozen houses around the lane, likely farmers who take care of the nearby fields.

"Maybe we could find a place here to stay for the night?" I suggest.

"No, I'd rather keep moving."

"I'm the one with the deadline. Why are you so antsy to get to Paris?"

She doesn't answer.

I don't understand her. After the Eater, she seemed almost happy for a while. But then she became distant and silent. I don't know what's changed, but I'm going to find out.

Something tickles my nose, and for a moment I think it's Charlie's sweet scent. But as I look ahead, I see a small house with a baker's windowsill, and sitting on it is a steaming pie. My mouth waters.

Glancing around, I slip from the horse.

"What are you doing?" Charlie glares down at me. "Get back up here."

"Just keep going." I point down the road, then turn around and stroll back toward town where the villagers have stopped chatting. Charlie grumbles but clucks her tongue and trots away on Belinda.

"Who goes there?" one calls.

"Just a weary traveler." I sidle up to the small group who have a decent view of my pie. "Say, I was wondering if there's a doctor in town."

"No, just a midwife. We get the doctor from Lyonne if there's a need. Why?"

I lean against the wall and sigh deeply, blowing my breath over the nearest villagers. "No reason, really. I mean, I'm perfectly fit and—"

"Your face doesn't look so fit." An older woman squints up at me. "Give us a look."

"Oh this?" I wave a hand at the mask. "It's just a remnant from the plague."

They all lean back. "Plague?"

"Yes, I had it a while ago, but I'm cured. It's gone. No need to worry. None at all." I unlace the mask and pull it off.

The old woman gasps, and one of the villagers recoils so hard he almost falls from his chair.

"As I said, all healed." I grin.

"Jesus, Mary, and Joseph." The old woman clutches the cross at her throat. "That you survived such a thing is a miracle."

"I couldn't agree more." I replace the mask.

The villager who almost fell on his ass visibly shudders, then asks, "If you're cured, then why would you need a doctor?"

I laugh. The old lady starts to smile a little with me. "I was only asking because my friend—" I hitch a thumb over my shoulder in the direction Charlie went. "—he's eat up with the plague. And had leprosy to start. Skin rotting to pieces." I point to my cloak and bend closer to the old lady. "Look here, I believe that's a piece of his ear. Can you believe that?"

The shriek that comes from her raises my hackles, and she jumps up spryly for a woman her age.

"Get out of here!" one of the men bellows as they all scatter, running for their homes and slamming their doors behind them. Not a soul is left on the street, and no one even looks at me through a window.

"No doctor, then?" I say to no one in particular. "That's a shame." Then I straighten up and stride away down the lane, grabbing my pie as I go.

"THEY REALLY JUST GAVE YOU that pie?" Charlie finishes her last bite and rubs her stomach, contentment written on her face.

"Why wouldn't they?" I offer her the final bit of crust from the bottom of the pan, but she waves me away.

"I can't eat another bite, and you didn't answer my question."

"Does it matter how I got it?" I chew the crust and swallow, my stomach full and warm.

She lies back, her skin luminous in the firelight. "I suppose not. As long as no one is following us and demanding their pie back."

I chuckle and lie down, too. "Oh, trust me. No one is coming anywhere near us."

She makes an irritated noise but decides against asking more questions.

We both stare up at the starlit night, only whisps of clouds passing quickly over a sliver moon. My time is ticking away. I feel it, as if my breaths are getting shorter, my steps shorter, my life ... shorter. I swallow hard and push down my fears. It's funny, not knowing who I am has given me this strange ability to assess myself in ways I don't think regular people can. It's almost as if I'm on the outside looking in. And this outside version of me, he can ignore fear and pain and the horror of this face, but he can't avoid the ever-ticking clock. I try not to think about it. But when Charlie is off to dreamland and it's only me and the cold, I can feel my time growing thin.

"What are you thinking about?" she asks.

"Time."

"Hmm." She turns over and looks at me.

After the Eater, she agreed to sleep beside me, but refuses to sleep with me—a distinction I do not care for, not one bit. She lies next to the fire, and I lie beside her, hemming her in should anything else decide to call out to us from the dark.

"What?" I ask.

"Nothing. I'm just counting. If we can slay the beast in say, three days—"

"Three days?" I scoff. "I'll only need one day to track it, then—" I drag my thumb across my throat. "We're done and can head to Finnraven Hill."

"Don't underestimate this thing, G. It's killed countless people."

"If Lord ButtBalm survived it, so can I."

"Lord *Battenbaum* sacrificed dozens of men—many of them trained soldiers—to make his escape."

"We won't have that luxury." I nod.

"That's one way to put it." She shakes her head. "We have to be smarter than this creature. Lead it into a trap or trick it in some way. Otherwise, we're done."

"We won't be done." I reach out and take her hand. To my relief, she doesn't pull away. "I mean, *I* certainly won't. If a sacrifice needs to be made, you'll be the one—"

"Ugh!" She pulls her hand away and smacks my arm. "G!"

"Kidding, only kidding."

She smacks me again. "I know." For some reason, that makes her frown, and she tucks her hand beneath her cloak.

"What's wrong?"

"Nothing," she says too quickly.

"No, it's definitely something. You've missed multiple opportunities to ridicule me for almost two days now. It's not like you. Something's bothering you. Is it what the Eater said? The part about your father?" I know I'm treading dangerously close to something she never wants to talk about—her past—but I do it anyway.

"No." She bites her bottom lip. "Yes. I don't know."

"Helpful." I prop my head up on my hand and rest on my elbow. "So it *is* about the Eater then?"

She chews her lip for a long while, long enough for me to wish I was doing it instead. But she finally says, "Some of the things the Eater said bothered me. But the way you ... " She sighs with frustration. "The reason you killed it—it sort of, I don't know." She puts one hand to her face, pressing her index finger and thumb to her temples.

"It gave you tingles?" I ask.

She smiles a little at that. "You wish."

"So that's a yes. The tingles are what's got you all quiet? That's silly. I already know you're mad for me. You don't have to be self-conscious about how much you want me. It's honestly so cute when—"

"Here we go." She drops her hand and rolls her eyes.

I settle back down, my gaze still on her. As always. "Do you want to talk about it?" I ask quietly.

She shakes her head.

"Do you want to talk about what the Eater said about your father?"

We lie there for a long while, the fire crackling as a light wind soughs through the trees on the hill behind us. She stares at the moon, her gaze thoughtful and more than a little sad. "I don't think I can. We parted on ... strange terms, to say the least. After that, I left, and I've never gone back. I think—" she presses her lips together and shakes her head, then starts again, "I think if I saw him again and we talked about everything that happened before I left ... I don't know if I could take it. Besides, maybe he doesn't want me back."

I reach out and burrow into her cloak, finding her hand and holding it. "Do you miss home?"

She closes her eyes. "Only when I dream." Then she laces her fingers through mine, her warmth seeping into my veins. "And sometimes when I wake. Whenever I see a misty morning, and when there's a red horizon just before twilight."

"Oddly specific."

She laughs. "Any thoughts I had of becoming a poet died right here and now. Thank you for that dose of stone-cold reality."

"It was my pleasure." I rub my thumb along her wrist. "You know, I don't think there's anything you could do that would make you unwelcome where you're from."

She gives me a wry look. "That's because you don't know me."

"You keep saying that, but I keep showing you it isn't true."

She smiles softly, her full lips a rosy pink in the firelight.

"You could go home, Charlie. The Eater said your father came looking for—"

"The Eater lies." Her smile is gone as soon as it arrived. "You can't believe anything it said. Just forget about it."

I know that tone, the one that says 'push any farther and I'll knife you.' So I do the only thing I can, I keep stroking her wrist, smoothing her skin beneath my calloused thumb. It seems to calm her as much as it does me, but it still takes a long while for her mind to settle, for her breath to become softer and more even.

Maybe the Eater lies plenty, but I can feel the disquiet in her. Its words hurt her, and that hurt is something I can't fully grasp, something I can't even begin to heal. Not when she insists on keeping so many secrets from me. That thought keeps me awake long after Charlie's lost in dreams of her mysterious home.

FOURTEEN

P aris is a fucking shithole. I mean that literally. We've passed at least three pairs of people fucking openly in their windows or on the street, and the gutters are full of sewage. The stench alone could kill a small child.

"You want to live *here*?"

"Yes." Charlie wrinkles her nose as we pass a woman loudly selling sucks of her breastmilk to the people passing by. A man is already attached to one of her large teats. "Okay, not in this part." She points up the hilly streets and away from the Seine. "Up there."

"Then by all means, let's head that way." I turn Belinda, and she strides through filthy streets, leaving the foul-smelling river at our backs as we climb through the haphazard streets.

"Along the Seine is the fastest way through," Charlie protests.

"Maybe so, but this way will keep Belinda free of catching the clap from the road."

Charlie turns to me. "That's possible?"

"I don't think Belinda wants to find out, do you, girl?" I pat her ass.

She doesn't try to bite me … this time. I think that she wants to get Charlie out of this mess as badly as I do.

We cut away from the river, passing through some crusty areas with half the buildings in shambles.

"What a dump." I look up at the broken windows.

A woman screams from an alley to our left. "Help!"

Charlie gasps and tries to get off Belinda.

"Nope." I hold onto her.

"Hey!" She struggles. "We have to help her."

"No way. We've done enough mercy missions."

I try to urge Belinda onward, but she stops, refusing to budge. "Hey, move!" I reach back and smack her bottom. Still, she doesn't move.

The scream comes again.

"G!" Charlie is still wriggling.

I hold her tighter. "You're not running into danger. Forget it."

"I'm warning you." She throws her head back, nailing me in the nose. It blooms with an explosion of pain.

"Dammit, Charlie!" I let her go, then follow her to the ground, rushing to get ahead of her.

Down the alley a man has a woman by the hair and is shaking the shit out of her. "Where's the money, Monique?"

"Let her go!" Charlie tries to storm past me.

I grab her shoulder and push her against the wall. "Stay put."

"But—"

I pin her with a glare. "I'll help, but only if you stay put."

Her lips form a pout, but then she says, "Fine."

I turn to the man. "What's going on here?"

"What's it to you?" he spits.

"Help me!" the woman screams again.

"Ah, shut it, Monique." He pulls her hair. "I paid her to carve my pipe, and the slag tried to run off with my money without giving me service."

I'm kind of leaning to Jean's side in this. After all, he paid up front.

"I ain't sucking you off, Jean, not after last time!" The woman shrieks.

"You leave her alone!" Charlie yells.

"Give me the money, Monique." He raises his hand to strike her.

Charlie gasps.

"Ah, fuck." I dart forward, grab his arm, then yank it behind him and shove him headfirst into the wall.

He groans and falls forward.

Monique rears back and kicks him right in the crotch. "There's your money, Jean. Right fucking there!"

He lets out a wheezing cry.

"Are you all right?" Charlie tries to get past me to Monique. "Did he hurt you?"

"No, we aren't doing this." I grab her shoulders and turn her around, then march her from the alley.

"Wait, we should check on—"

"She's fine." I lift her onto Belinda's back. "He won't be going back to her for pipe services anytime soon."

Once I climb up behind her, she sits stiffly for a moment, then gives in and takes the reins. Belinda starts walking up the narrow street again.

"You can't go running into every fight you see, Charlie. You've already volunteered us for Beast of Gevaudon duty. Isn't that enough?"

"You'd really just let him hurt her like that?" She crosses her arms over her chest. "You're that, that … *bad*?"

"If you didn't notice, she seemed to have the situation under control. She wasn't giving up that money. And I suspect if we hadn't busted into the argument, she might've shivved him and been done with it."

"I was thinking 'morally gray' but you're more like a midnight abyss." She mutters something under her breath, ending with the word 'wicked.'

I shake my head and keep her between my arms. There's no way I'm letting her go running into another fray. She could get hurt. Not on my fucking watch—which is all the time.

The farther we get from the center of town, the better the streets become. The stench finally wafts away, and businesses appear here and there amongst the homes. Boulangeries and patisseries—their windows loaded with delicious treats—beckon, and clothing stalls selling all sorts of items line the streets at intervals.

"Here." I point to a smithy banging out some metal by the roadside.

We stop, and I barter for two blades, one small and perfectly suited for Charlie, the other large and heavy, suited for me. Once the deal is struck with Widow Valor's gold, I grab the swords and look around for Charlie.

She stands in front of a shop window, her gaze on a pale blue dress with sleeves that flutter in the breeze.

I walk up behind her quietly. "You'd look like a dream in that."

She startles and turns. "No." She shakes her head. "No, that's not me. Not anymore."

"Not anymore?" I try to imagine her in a world where she wears dresses and does things like sew or play a piano—but none of that seems like her. There's too much wild in her, too much dirt and fresh air. Even so, I'd love to see her in a dress—though I might tear it off her.

A musician plays a guitar somewhere nearby, and the tart notes of a flute flutter through the air from a distance.

She takes her sword from me and holds it out, looking down its length. "Nice and straight. Good weight. I like the leather wrap." She grips it and turns it this way and that. "It'll do."

I move closer to her. "You sure you know how to —Whoa!"

She puts her sword to my throat, so close if I swallow she'd cut me.

"I can handle a sword, G." She lowers her blade.

"I see that. Are you ever going to tell me how you learned?" I hand her the scabbard for it, and she takes it and the blade to stow on Belinda. "I'm the one with the faulty memory, but your past is just as mysterious, if not more so. You know more about my short history than I know of yours."

"It's not that interesting," she says disingenuously.

"Everything about you is interesting." I fashion my sheath to sit at the center of my back and practice drawing the sword and replacing it a few times. I manage to cut my cloak in a couple of places before I get it down. I don't realize Charlie is watching me intently until I sheathe it the final time. "What?"

She blinks, then shakes her head as if to clear it. "Nothing."

"Is that a blush in your cheeks?" I stalk to her.

"No." She lets out an odd laugh, far too high and nervous for her, as she turns toward Belinda.

"If I had known that all I needed to catch your eye was a sword, I would've gotten one ages ago." I rest my hands at her waist.

She brushes a hand down Belinda's rump. "Do you hear this arrogant ass, Belinda?"

The horse snorts, giving me her usual side-eye.

"We both know you were drooling." I lift her easily onto the horse then climb up behind her.

"I was not." She takes the reins and guides Belinda through the busy street, carts and people passing with no care for getting struck or crushed.

"You were. But there's no need to argue. We're in the city of love, after all."

"Where we just bought weapons." She pats her sword.

"And you got hot watching me use mine."

"Sometimes I wonder what you were like before you lost your memory. If you were even half as full of yourself back then, I bet you were a goddamn terror to be around."

"I'm certain I was a joy. I bet everyone in my town loved me. When I disappeared, they must've had a huge mourning event for me. Think of all the young ladies who would've come and cried on my grave, sad that they missed out on bedding me."

She laughs. "You tell such funny stories. All make-believe, of course, but funny all the same."

We ride farther into the city, the rues becoming a little wider with the buildings more spread out.

"I want to live somewhere like this." Charlie looks back over the city, the filthy river at the heart of it looking shiny from here. "Somewhere with food and art and *life*."

"I think the woman selling her milk would argue she's giving plenty of life."

"Gross." She laughs.

"I could see you here, having tea and judging everyone who walks past. What would you do for money?"

"Farrier. I've always had a way with animals."

Belinda snorts, seemingly in agreement.

Charlie points at one of the tall chateaus locked behind a wrought-iron gate. "There's always rich people who keep more animals than they need for status and what-not. I'll work for them and spend my free time exploring the city."

I tighten my grip on her waist as I think about the dirty and dangerous portion we barely glimpsed. "Not alone."

She looks at me over her shoulder. "I've spent most of my life alone, G. No point stopping now."

Her usual barbs never strike their target, but for some reason, this comment—no barb embedded in it at all—slices through me and digs in. So much so that I think about her words long after she uttered them, until she finally brings Belinda to a halt and turns halfway in the saddle. "What?"

I blink. "What?"

"You've been silent for a quarter of an hour. You're never silent for that long."

"Sometimes I am."

"Never." She stares at me. "What's bothering you?"

"I'm just worried if we have enough time to—"

"Nope."

"What?" I ask.

"No, you never *worry*. Not like that. Not like someone who does a proper analysis of their situation. It was annoying at first, but now it's kind of endearing." She smiles a little, then wipes it from her face with a stern look. "Like I said, you don't worry. You're either completely oblivious or blithely optimistic—neither of those leave room for worry."

"What did you just call me?" I literally don't know.

She rolls her eyes. "Try again, but this time the truth."

God, I don't want to sound like a whiny twat, but when she stares at me like this, I can't seem to tell her anything but the truth. "I was just thinking that your plans don't seem to include ... me. Which I realize must've just been a mistake on your part, because there's no way you'd want to keep living alone now that you've met me. I know the face is a problem, don't get me wrong, but that will be all fixed and you won't have to look at—"

She presses her finger to my mouth, her eyes taking on a soft quality that I love so much. "Your face has never bothered me, G. You know that." She drops her finger. "I don't even notice it anymore, honestly. You're just … you." Her eyes search my face, skating over the mask and meeting my good eye. "And we've shared a lot, but I'm not—" She chews her lip, then continues, "I'm not who you think I am."

"I know. Your name isn't Charlie."

"You know what I mean," she says quietly as someone playing an accordion approaches from one of the side streets.

"I do, but I need more. What are you hiding? Do you think I'm going to judge you? *Me*?"

The accordion gets louder, hitting wrong notes here and there. I shoot the musician a nasty look. He hurries to the other side of the street, his eyes going wide.

Charlie opens her mouth to answer, then closes it as he passes, his accordion squeaking with each of his quick steps. After another long pause, she says, "I think you might be the only one who wouldn't judge me, but that doesn't change what I've done."

"I don't care what you've done." I reach up and cup her face. "I don't care, Charlie. You could set fire to orphans—"

She winces.

"I mean, I know you wouldn't, but my point stands. I don't care what you've done. If it makes you feel better, I'll take whatever it is and double it. Then you can judge me and feel better about yourself. Just tell me how many orphans I need to light up. We could even make a competition out of it. Take wagers and everything on who can toast the most."

She glances at my lips as she reaches up and covers my hands with hers. "Remember when I told you that your wicked streak is wider than the Pyrenees?"

"Yes."

"I was wrong. It might be wider than all of France."

"By the time we're through with this trip, you'll understand there's no amount of wickedness I wouldn't do for you."

"You're the worst." She sighs, her breath tickling my lips as she leans closer, her lashes fluttering.

"I know." I kiss her, pulling her against me as I taste her again, a groan in my throat. I want to drown in her. She clutches me tightly, her mouth opening as I slide my tongue against hers. How have I gone so long without this? It's been pure torture. Every night, I think of that kiss we shared in the pool. Every day, I want her so fucking bad it hurts. I pour all that into this embrace, into each brush of our tongues and the press of our bodies. I want her to feel what I feel, that longing that goes so deep it must be embedded in my center.

I don't know how long we're lost in each other, my body on fire for her. God, I would do absolutely filthy things to her right here, right now, if only she'd ask. Why the fuck did I give her the option? I must've been a much more reasonable man back then, because right now, I want to tear her clothes off and rut her like a goddamn animal.

She pulls back, her breath shaky as she meets my gaze. "What are you doing to me?"

"Anything you'll let me."

She swallows hard and licks her lips. "L-let's go." She turns.

I groan. "I think what you meant to say was 'take me, G, take me right here on the street while everyone watches.'"

She shivers as I press a kiss to the back of her neck. "Just tell me what you want, Charlie. Tell me and I'll burn down heaven and earth to give it to you."

Her spine straightens, and she grips the reins tightly. "We should get beyond the city before nightfall."

With that, she clucks her tongue, ordering Belinda forward.

I bite back a frustrated roar, my body on the brink of snapping. A mime climbs a rope as we pass, and I almost ask him for a length of it to hang myself.

"We need to stick to the plan." Charlie nods, likely more to herself than to me. "Nothing else."

I have to adjust myself, my cock sitting straight up against her lower back. She notices, her posture getting even more tight.

"No, Charlie." I pull her back, forcing her against me. "You should feel what you do to me. What you *keep* doing to me."

Her breathing hitches, and I swear she moves her hips, just a little, just enough to make insanity flood my mind.

"Don't do that," I grate out.

"You're the one stabbing me with your cock," she hisses.

"Now that's a pretty picture," I breathe in her ear, loving the way her skin pebbles.

"Oaf," she spits.

I smirk and wrap one arm around her waist, then grind my erection against her backside. "Tell me more. You know what your insults do to me."

"G, knock it off."

"G? Not 'oaf' or 'simpleton' or what's that one that starts with a 'd'? I really like that one."

"Dolt," she says tightly.

I groan and put my hands on her thighs as we pass a half-built cathedral. "That's the one. Drives me wild."

"Ugh. Belinda, gallop. Now!" Charlie leans forward right as Belinda takes a leap.

I yell as the horse puts on speed, and I have to reach around Charlie and grab onto the saddle's horn.

We hurtle up the hill and over the other side, buildings and people passing by in a blur as my ass takes hit after hit from the rough ride.

"Charlie!" I yell.

I swear I can hear her laugh over the pound of hooves as we speed through the edges of the city, past houses and weedy lots until she finally reins Belinda in, the horse breathing hard as I sit up and catch my breath.

"What. Was. *That*?" I grit through clenched teeth. "My ass is numb."

"Just keeping Belinda fresh. That's all," she simpers.

"I thought we weren't supposed to lie to each other." I smooth back my hair and stow my mask.

"White lies don't count."

"Look who's wicked now."

"Oh, please. It was just a quick ride. Aren't we in a hurry?"

I look behind us, the city already a memory. "I was going to steal croissants and tons of pastries."

"We don't need to steal. We have food and coin." She reaches into the saddle bag and pulls out a stale baguette. I push her hand back and shake it so she releases the old bread.

"I'm good."

"We'll get as far east as we can before nightfall. Then we can start tracking the beast." She snugs her hat onto her head in her usual fashion.

"Are we ever going to talk about your ears?"

She whips her head to the side, looking at me from the corner of her eye. "Did you just request a fast ride again?"

"No, I—"

She grins. "I think you did." With a cry of "yah!" she kicks Belinda back into a hard pace, and all I can do is hold on and hope that my ass still works once it's all over.

FIFTEEN

"I've got a lead on a hunting party." Charlie hurries across the muddy street.

The small village of Marnet looks particularly rundown in the morning light, and only a handful of people live here.

"They've seen the beast?" I feed Belinda another pear, and she takes it from me with something that approaches trust. She still prefers Charlie, but so do I. I can't hold that against her.

"Two weeks ago, a boy minding the sheep a few villages to the east said the beast tore three of them apart and dragged one away, loping across the hills until it disappeared."

"Sounds like a boy let wolves get the sheep and made up a story to keep himself from getting a whipping."

She mounts Belinda. "I don't think so. Another hunting party has already come through. They're on the same trail, and it's leading us to the woods in Battenbaum's diary."

I rub my sore cheeks, last night's ride still evident in the ache of my tail bone.

"We'll take it easier today." She offers me her hand. "Unless you start asking more questions."

I climb up and settle down behind her. There are plenty of questions I'd like to ask, but trying to get information from Charlie only makes her clam up more. Coaxing doesn't work either. She'll only tell me something when she wants to—and those times are few and far between. I sigh.

"What was that for?" She glances over her shoulder at me.

"Nothing."

She guides Belinda back onto the road as a few farmers peer from their windows, some of them gawking at my face.

I ignore them and squint against the rising sun that peeks over the hills in the distance. The vineyards here aren't quite as dire as the ones where we'd been trapped by the snow. The climate seems milder, the plants a faint green, as if they're only waiting for a whisper from Mother Nature to go into bloom.

Charlie yawns and rubs the back of her neck. "I love horses, but once we're done with this quest, I'm going to spend at least a week off of them."

"Only a week?"

She pets Belinda's neck. "I can't stay away too long. Horses are some of the most intelligent and curious creatures I've ever met."

Belinda snuffles, her ears twitching when Charlie scratches along the darker brown near her mane. I didn't know it was possible to be jealous of a horse, but here I am wondering why Charlie refuses to pet *me*.

"Don't worry, girl, we'll handle the beast and get word back to Widow Valor. Hopefully, she and all the others who bear that idiotic mark will be able to fully mourn their lost loved ones and start over."

"I can't believe we're doing this, all because of Widow Valor's favorite cock. Who knew one could cause so much trouble?"

She gives me a sober look. "You don't actually think Widow Valor only misses her husband for his cock."

I give her an 'obviously' look. "That's what she said."

"I *know* that's what she said, but that's not what she really meant."

"That ... makes no sense. She misses her husband's cock. You felt sorry for her because of it, and that's why we're going to slay the beast. That's what I heard, and that's why we're here."

"Are you always so surface on everything?" She smirks. "Yes, yes you are. I don't even know why I asked."

I scoff. "You heard her, same as me. She's sad about his cock. Anything else is just made up nonsense on your part."

"Or *maybe*, people are complex with complicated emotions. Maybe some people don't know how to express those emotions, so they sort of create these little fictions to help them get over a loss."

I think about what she's saying, then I get an idea. "You mean Henri didn't have a great cock, after all?"

"No!" She makes that frustrated sound I love. "I'm saying yes, maybe Henri had a great cock, but Widow Valor was too heartbroken to talk about all the other ways she missed her husband, so she focused on that one thing."

I nod a little, then stop. "Nope, I don't buy it. The guy was clearly hung like a horse—I can relate—and she's upset she can't ride that pony anymore."

"No, that's not why she's—" She huffs. "Why are you so, so maddening? You know what? Never mind."

"I think you're a romantic." I lean down and rest my chin on her shoulder. "That's why you're making this into something it's not. You're a romantic who can't accept all the ways a man's cock can improve your life."

She barks a laugh and shrugs me off her shoulder. "You've always thought far too much of yourself."

"No, I know my strengths." I run my hands down the outside of her thighs. "I think you know them, too."

"I know you're good at lying, stealing, obfuscating, chopping wood, making a fire, and ..." She taps her finger on her chin. "Yes, I think that's it."

I drag my nails back up her thighs, noticing the way she doesn't stop me. "You know how your insults turn me on. Why must you keep torturing me?"

She laughs, this time the sound is warm. "You'd best get used to it, G. You're not getting what you want from me."

"I don't recall hearing all that when I had my tongue in your mouth." I nip at her ear. "Twice."

She elbows me, but not hard. "Everyone makes mistakes."

"If you say so, Charlie. You can keep fighting it all you want, but you'll break. Don't worry, I'll be gentle." I lean into her ear again. "That's a lie."

Her skin pebbles. "Focus, G."

"I *am* focused." I stare at her.

"On the beast."

"The one in my pant—Ow!"

She's elbowed me even harder this time. I grin. Getting under her skin has become my favorite pastime on horseback.

We ride for another hour before I catch the sounds of a party ahead of us. I pull out my mask and fasten it on.

"It must be the hunters." Charlie gives me a look over her shoulder and increases Belinda's pace until we come upon a group of about a dozen men, all of them armed.

One at the rear notices us and rides back. "These hills are dangerous at the moment, friends. The Beast of Gevaudon is prowling." The man, likely no older than I am, pulls alongside us. "Where are you headed?"

"We're after the beast," Charlie says.

"You two?" He raises a light brown brow, a look of amusement twisting his lips. "By yourselves?"

"Is that a problem?" I sit up straighter and glare at the man.

His eyes widen and he shakes his head slowly. "No, ah, not at all."

Charlie pinches me on the leg. "Great. We'd be happy to tag along and help wherever we can. We heard from the locals in Marnet that a shepherd spotted the beast only a few days ago."

The man clears his throat. "Yes, we heard the same. We've been searching for weeks, finding signs of the beast but never encountering the monster itself." He bows his head slightly. "I'm Luc, by the way."

"I'm Charlie, and this is G. It's very nice to meet you."

"Come, I'll ask Commander Thorpe, but I'm certain he won't have a problem with more hunters in the group. We need all the help we can get to bring down the beast." He gives a two-finger wave and rides ahead.

We follow, and I watch as he speaks to the man at the head of the group.

"I don't like him." I wrinkle my nose.

"You don't like anyone."

"I like you."

"Other than me, can you honestly say you liked anyone in Sac à Puces?"

I think back over the people I knew there. "Madge."

"She doesn't count. She saved your life, and then you almost abandone—"

"Water under the bridge," I interrupt.

"Mhmm. Other than that, did you care for anyone?"

"Look, we both know the answer to that, but you think it's my fault, and I don't. Why would I like the assholes who ridiculed me before I regained my strength? Why would I care for any of those cunts?"

"Not them. But there were others in town you could've befriended. People *were* kind to you. Not everyone, of course, but there were some who pitied—"

"Ah, pity. How big of them to feel sorry for me. I suppose I should've kissed their feet and sniffed their chamber pots in equal measure."

She sighs. "No, that's not what I mean. I'm simply saying you could've had friends."

"Did you have friends?"

She stiffens. "No, but that was my choice."

"Then why can't it be my choice?"

"Because you need friends."

"And you don't?"

"I'm different."

"How?" I stroke a hand down the masked side of my face. "I'm pretty sure all the people we've met—in Sac à Puces or otherwise—noticed how *different* I was right off." I drop my voice. "Hang on, is this because of the ears?"

She cuts me a sharp look over her shoulder. "Don't talk about them."

"Why?" I throw my hands up. "I don't care that they look weird."

Her mouth drops open in indignation, and that's when I realize I've fucked up.

"*Weird*?" She glares at me.

"I mean, I think they're cute, but they don't look like normal—"

"Don't you dare say it," she hisses, her eyes flashing.

"Okay, I get it, you're sensitive about it. But I'm not normal either." I pat my mask. "See? We're the same."

Her eyes narrow. "Don't flatter yourself. We aren't even the same breed."

"Charlie." I know I'm only digging myself deeper, but I don't stop. "I think you're amazing. The most beautiful creature I've ever seen. If you—" Someone clears their throat.

I look up to find the entire group of hunters on the road just ahead of us, all of them listening while pretending to be deeply intrigued by something off in the distance.

"Fuck," Charlie growls under her breath as she turns back around.

"Lover's spat between you boys?" One of the hunters leers.

"Mind your business, Gerard." The leader rides back to us. "Welcome. I'm Commander Thorpe."

"I'm Charlie, and this is G. We're hunting the beast."

Commander Thorpe glances at our wrists. I suppose he thinks we must be marked if we're going on this suicide mission.

The commander, his face scarred and his eyes shrewd, gives us a nod. "Our tracker followed its trail into the Thorny Forest at the edge of Mountfaucon. It's not a big area, but as far as I know, only one man has gone in and managed to get out alive."

"Lord Battenbaum," Charlie says.

Commander Thorpe eyes her more closely. "So you've heard his story?"

"I read the section of his diary on the beast. We need to be clever to slay it. Brute force won't be enough."

He gives her a look that verges on respect. "Very well. Then you know everything we do. He's the only surviving eyewitness to what we believe is the beast's den. It's deep in the Thorny Forest and lies against the stone cliffs. If we make it to its lair, there is no easy escape for us. No escape at all, truth be told. We either kill it, or it drags us into the dark for good."

That doesn't sound like a good deal to me. Not at all. I whisper to her, "It's not too late to turn around—"

"Let's go." Charlie grips Belinda's reins.

Commander Thorpe nods at her. "We're going to make camp outside the forest, go over plans and strategies. At first light tomorrow, we go in." He turns his horse and leads us up the road, his other hunters falling in around us.

Charlie is silent as I inspect the men and their weapons. None of them seem particularly well equipped, at least not for killing the legendary Beast of Gevaudon. If anything, they're common men from communities nearby armed with axes, scythes, and whatever weapons they could borrow or buy. From cursory glances, I see that some of them bear the mark on their wrists. They're trying to get their own lives back, so perhaps that means they'll fight that much harder.

We make camp at the edge of the woods as Commander Thorpe said. The hunters seem to have something of a comradery among them, which I'm all too happy to avoid as Charlie and I set up our bedrolls apart from theirs but still near the fire.

Luc, the first hunter we met, motions to me.

I raise a brow.

"Go ahead. I'm good." Charlie nibbles a piece of cheese and goes back over Lord Battenbaum's diary by firelight. "But wait a second." She looks up at me.

"What?"

"I just, um, I might try something on the hunt tomorrow. Something that might seem odd, but I don't want you to worry. That's all."

I don't like the sound of that. Not at all. "Try what?"

She waves me away and goes back to her book. "Don't worry. That's all I wanted to tell you. Go have boy talk or whatever it is he wants."

"We aren't done talking about this." I point a finger at her.

"Yes, we are. Stop interrupting my reading." She eats another hunk of cheese. "Go."

I remember when I used to want to strangle her, and realize sometimes, I still do. But I also know when she isn't going to budge on something, which is most of the time. Fuck. I follow Luc outside the light of the fire. "What?" I say a little more harshly than I intended.

He peers at the dark woods. "Are you certain you want to bring the boy on this hunt?" he asks.

"Sometimes I'm not." I run a hand through my hair. "What's it to you?"

"He's so young, and our chances of success are ... slim, if I'm being honest. I wouldn't want his death on my conscious when I go to meet our Lord, you know?"

"I'll worry about Charlie." I bristle at his interest in her.

"All right." He shrugs, then reaches down and unbuttons his pants. "I was only asking because I have a brother about his age." He takes a piss, and I catch a glimpse of his monstrous cock. Not that I was looking—I fucking wasn't—but that thing is hard to miss. "I'd hate for our mother to lose us both, especially with how young he is. I meant no offense."

"You're not married, I take it?" I ask and unbutton my own breaches, taking a piss since the opportunity has presented itself. It's not because I want him to know I'm equally blessed, if not more so. That would be "childish" according to Charlie, I'm certain. So that's definitely not why.

"Married? No." He buttons himself back up. "Not yet, anyway. No one wants to marry a poor rhubarb farmer."

"I'll tell you what." I finish up. "If you live through this, I know someone who'd be very interested in meeting you."

"A woman, you mean?" he asks.

"Even better." I turn back toward the fire. "A widow."

SIXTEEN

The Thorny Forest lives up to its name. We walk into it at daybreak, the air full of mist and not a single breath of wind, and immediately run into a prickly thicket. One of the hunters runs ahead and hacks it with his axe, opening the way for us to pass through.

I keep us toward the back. No need to be an appetizer for the beast when we have a dozen tasty hunters who've already volunteered for the job.

Charlie leans to the side and tries to look ahead. "I can't see a damn thing."

"Settle down. How far in did Battenbaum say the cave was?"

"He didn't," she grumbles.

A thorny branch grabs onto her cloak. I grip it and yank it free.

"Careful." She grabs my wrist and looks at my palm. "You're bleeding."

"It's nothing." I wipe it on my own cloak. "Keep your ears and eyes open." I already have my bow in hand, my sword resting against my back as we venture deeper among the trees. After the run-in with the Eater, I'm not particularly fond of shadowy woods, but if this is what it takes to keep Charlie by my side, I'll brave it a hundred times over.

The hunters aren't quiet, their steps loud in the creeping stillness. Commander Thorpe's worn metal breastplate scrapes at intervals, and I wonder how long we have to wait before the beast is upon us.

"Amateurs," I whisper.

We continue forward for at least an hour, the men taking turns hacking our way through the thorny brambles that seem to sprout up from every bit of free terrain on the forest floor. Some of the vines are thicker than my arm and spiral up the trees, spreading from branch to branch like a huge spider web.

When the sun is finally streaming through the canopy and burning off the fog, we stop for a break. I hand Charlie our water skin and break a savory pie in half to share.

Commander Thorpe consults his map, though Charlie already got a look at it and said it wasn't a true rendering of this patch of woods. '*More a patchwork of guesses than anything else,*' she'd told me last night as we huddled together, though she was clear I was not to kiss her, hold her, or whisper anything filthy to her while we were in the company of the hunters. I abided by points one and two, but three? I whispered her a bedtime story so scandalous about two completely fictional characters named "Charlie" and "G" that I knew her cheeks were burning bright by the time I was done.

"How close do you think we are?" I chew the somewhat dry pie.

She looks up. "I can't see the cliff from here, but that doesn't mean anything. The trees are dense, the vines more so. We could be right up on it and not know it."

"Comforting." I drink some water to wash down the pie.

"It can't be far. This piece of woods isn't that deep, but it's certainly a pain to navigate." She glowers at a nearby patch of thorny brambles. "The beast is intelligent, not as much as a human, but enough that it knew to make its home somewhere that protects it from direct attack."

"We could burn the place down," I suggest.

"It would simply hide in its cave until the fire was done, then escape. Think of the damage it could do while we chased it to whatever new home it chose." She shakes her head. "We have to stop it here and now."

241

She's right, but I can't go telling her that. I'd never hear the end of it. "I wonder where it comes from. There's never been anything like it, has there? Not that I've heard of."

"I have my suspicions, but I can't say for certain."

"What's your suspicion, then?" I hand her the water. "Witches? Devils?"

She arches a brow at me. "Now you're a believer, are you?"

"Not all the way. But after the spriggans and the Eater, I'm a little more open-minded about the strange creatures we keep running into." Something prickles along the back of my mind, an instinct without a name alerting me to danger. That's when I realize the hunters have gone silent. "Charlie!" I reach for her right when one of the hunters springs at her, his blade drawn.

She drops the water and grabs for her sword, but the hunter fists her cloak and yanks her backwards into his grasp.

I rush forward, but another hunter puts his blade to my throat and drags my sword from its scabbard.

"G, don't!" Charlie yells. The bastard behind her has one arm around her neck.

I push forward, my skin stinging as blood flows from my neck. Still, I step toward her.

"Stop!" Commander Thorpe steps between us, his hands up. "We don't need to spill any blood."

"What the fuck are you doing?" I growl.

"We can't run straight at the beast. We wouldn't have a chance." He glances at Charlie. "Lad, you said yourself brute force won't be enough."

"Let him go." My skin itches from the inside as my blood runs hot. Murder is the only thing in my mind. I just need an opening.

"I have a plan." Commander Thorpe motions toward the trees. "Take him. Do what I told you. But first—" He waves the hunter and Charlie to him, then draws his blade. "Hold out his hand."

"Don't you fucking touch him!" I press forward again, the blade sinking deeper into my neck. Another hunter joins the first, his blade at my stomach.

"One wrong move, and I'll spill your guts on the ground." The hunter spits, his foul breath wafting up to me.

Luc steps forward. "Commander, this isn't—"

"Can it, Luc, unless you want to be bait right along with this boy!" The commander barks. A hunter steps to Luc, his hand on his sword.

"Hold still." The commander yanks Charlie's hand up and slices across her palm. She doesn't make a sound, though her eyes water at the deep cut.

243

"I'll kill you for that." I glare at the commander.

"That'll draw the beast out." He sheathes his knife. "Go, and make sure you tie him up well. We don't need him running and spoiling the plan."

"This is a terrible idea." Charlie tries to shove the hunter away from her, but he's too big. "It's like waving red in front of a charging bull. You're going to—"

"Gag him if you have to." Commander Thorpe turns his back on her.

"No!" she yells as she's dragged away, and I swear a piece of my insides is torn apart at the fear in her tone.

The commander glances at my throat. "Let the big one go, boys. We need him intact for the fight."

The hunters drop their swords and back away from me quickly.

"What makes you think I'll help you now?" I stalk to the commander.

"Because if you don't, the beast will kill us all, including your lover boy."

As if on cue, a horrendous roar shakes the forest, the ground trembling from the strength of the sound.

"I could've spilled his guts for the beast." He spits. "I will if you make one wrong move."

Charlie disappears through the trees as I imagine hacking the commander's head off.

The only thing I can think of is Charlie, fear coursing through me as I spin and look for my sword. The asshole who took it still has it in his hand. I run to him, give him a hard kick in the ass that sends him sprawling, then grab my sword.

"G!" Charlie screams, the sound bloodcurdling, and I take off through the trees, thorns tearing at my skin and ripping away my mask. I hurdle a fallen tree and keep going until I see the two hunters who'd taken her away. They're running toward me, their faces pale. I have no mercy on them, not when they hurt Charlie. With a hard swing of my sword, I send one of their heads spinning into a tangle of thorns. The other one screams as I wrench the sword toward him and slice across his middle. He falls to his knees, but I don't have time to finish him, not when Charlie's in danger.

I keep going in the direction they came from, looking through the vines for any hint of Charlie.

I don't see her.

But I do see a huge shape covered in black fur crashing through the thickets, crushing them beneath its massive paws as if they were soft as down.

Its head is that of a wolf except for the two giant tusks that grow from its lower jaw and curve upward. The body is more like a gigantic bear, the fur matted and thick, likely impossible to stab through. Whipping along behind it is a barbed tail, the tip curved and topped with three barbs.

Raising its snout in the air, it sniffs deeply, then turns and bares its fangs. I know it's scented Charlie's blood. I can't let it get to her.

With a yell, I rush forward, drawing its attention as I slash the vines ahead of me and hurtle toward it. It rears back, its eyes—nearly human in their appearance—landing on me and dilating.

"I'm right here, you stinking cunt!" I keep running, then drop right before I reach its massive hind leg. Sliding along the forest floor, I slice at its paw then roll and dash out from beneath it. As I'm underneath it, I notice its belly is covered with far less fur, pale skin showing up to its rib cage. But I don't have time to capitalize. It turns quickly, its movements fluid like a cat's as it swipes at me, its claws black and coated in venom.

I barely evade it as I run, slashing through the brambles with my sword as I finally catch a glimpse of the stone cliff face. Its lair must be just ahead, which means I'm at a dead end. But I can't run back toward Charlie.

It roars again, and bits of stone rattle along the cliff and fall in puffs of dust. I scramble up the brambles, and I swear I feel the beast's hot breath on my neck as my pace slows.

"Give it all you've got, boys!" Commander Thorpe's voice bounces off the rock.

I glance behind me and see the beast whirl. Its tail comes toward me, the three tips marked by drops of yellow fluid. I fling myself to the left. The stingers come down right where I'd been climbing, then lifts again and stabs in rapid succession, as if its searching for me.

My feet lose purchase as the brambles give way, and I flip forward onto my front, my ankle trapped between the thick vines. The stingers are still stabbing, getting closer each time. I roll to my side, my ankle screaming in pain, then swipe at the beast's black tail.

It shrieks and yanks its tail away, then leaps forward. A man yells, the sound suddenly cut off. I watch as the beast throws a hunter's body into the air, then opens its mouth and swallows him whole.

"Fuck!" I reach down and grab my ankle, trying to free myself, but it's not budging. I wedge the heel of my free foot between the vines and push. It scrapes the skin off my trapped ankle, but with another push, I'm able to wrench it free, though my boot is gone.

A body flies past me and crashes into a tree behind me, then lands only a few feet away. A hunter, his face smashed into nothing and his body crumpled.

I race down the vines I'd been climbing, back toward the fray where the beast is swiping at the trees where the hunters have taken shelter. Arrows fly, some of them bouncing off the beast's thick hide and a few embedding, though not deeply enough to do any damage.

The cowards have to get closer, to hack and shoot from beneath it. I don't mind the beast killing them, not after what they did to Charlie, but if she and I are going to get out of here alive, we need them to do their goddamn part.

"Get underneath it!" I bellow. "It has a soft belly!"

The beast pays me no mind as it claws at the trees, desperate to get at the men. I circle around its back, careful to avoid the whipping tail. Once I'm out of range, I turn and search through the trees for Charlie.

I almost miss her. But the slightest glint of light off her golden hair catches my eye, and I dash across an opening the beast stomped into the thickets to get to her.

"G." She looks at me, then turns and screams. "Get down!"

I obey, dropping to my knees as the barb sweeps over my head, so close to impaling me. With a yell, I turn and find the beast's huge eyes on me, its mouth open as it snaps at me.

I drop my sword and whip my bow off my back. Nocking quickly, I send two arrows at its face. One sticks into its snout. It roars and uses its paw to snap it, then it squares up with me before lunging.

Throwing myself to the side, I barely escape its maw, then roll behind a tree, the thorns ripping into me anew.

"This ends now!" Commander Thorpe yells.

I peek out to see him rushing toward the beast, his sword high as he aims for its gut. He slashes it, drawing blood, but before he can swing again, the barb stabs him from behind and drags him from beneath the beast.

He drops his sword and reaches for the stinger protruding from his chest, his armor nothing more than tin to the power of the beast. When he touches it, his hands begin to steam, and when he opens his mouth to scream, smoke comes out. It's as if he's boiling alive from the venom.

The beast whips him off its tail, flinging him into the trees before it turns to go after him.

I take the opening and rush to Charlie, grabbing my sword from the ground as I go. "Lift your arms!" I yell.

She does, and I slice the rope binding her to the tree.

"Are you all right?" I grip her shoulder. "Are you hurt?"

"I'm good." She pulls her sword from its scabbard. "G, I need you to trust me."

More screams cut through the forest, the beast wrecking every hunter it can find.

"What? I always trust you." I turn my back to her and hold up my sword. "You should run. I'll hold it off as long as I can."

"Trust me."

I whirl and find her sprinting away from me and toward the beast. "Charlie!" I cry and follow her. "Stop!"

She bursts out of a thicket and comes face to face with the snarling monstrosity, its face drenched with the blood of its victims as it catches her in its sights.

"No!" I run, pushing my aching ankle to the brink as I jump another log and dash ahead. When I get close enough to swing at its belly, its back leg comes forward and knocks me away, sending me careening into the brambles and taking my breath away from the force of the hit.

"Charlie!" I struggle to my feet, my cloak caught in the hold of the thorns. "Don't!" My heart stalls when I see her standing in front of the beast, her hand up, her gaze locked with the monster.

She closes her fist, and the beast yelps, but it doesn't move. Its snarl is frozen, its body not moving.

"G!" Charlie cries, anguish in her voice. "I can't hold it much longer!"

I push myself forward, my cloak ripping off me as I make another run at the beast. It doesn't kick at me, even its barbed tail seems to be frozen mid-whip. With all my strength, I lift the sword high and run beneath it, my blade opening its guts. Hot blood cascades all around, and heavy entrails land on me. I keep going, running my blade the length of the beast, then turning and cutting back the way I came, releasing more and more entrails, the stench clogging my lungs as I cut and sever.

"I can't!" Charlie cries as she drops to her knees, her body listing to the side.

The beast jolts, its wide jaws bearing down, its venom dripping in long strings that fall far too closely to her.

I hack and slash and cut and tear until my arms burn, and I can barely see through the gore that coats me.

Charlie shakes, her whole body trembling and falling.

"Charlie!"

The beast moves, its body straining as it lets out a screeching sound of pain so intense it feels like a physical hit. I turn and run, barely avoiding its back paw as it spins toward me, its jaws slamming together like the sound of thunder clapping.

I clear its legs and hurtle toward a wide tree. If I can get behind it, then I—*Fuck*! I see the black blur whipping toward me, but it's too late for me to avoid it. The beast's tail hits me with full force, taking me off my feet with a crushing blow and sending me flying backwards. Thorny vines rip at me, cutting me open as I sail through them. I try to look for Charlie, but I see only branches and leaves as my body erupts in scorching agony. Then I slam against the stone cliff face and, thankfully, feel no more.

SEVENTEEN

T'm underwater. I try to inhale but can't, as if my body knows to do so is the ultimate betrayal. I thrash and claw, desperately trying to reach the surface. It never comes. I sink.

"Shhh," someone whispers to me.

Is it the lady in the water? Has she come back to promise me something else impossible?

"Lie still. You're safe."

I know that voice.

I know it like I know the sun in the sky or the glow of the moon. "Charlie?" I ask.

"It's all right."

I hear her, but is this real? Am I underwater again?

Drifting away, I can't tell if I'm drowning. I must be. Maybe I should've drowned in the river long ago, the voice never gracing my ears, my body sinking into the deep never to resurface. It's what I deserve, isn't it?

Isn't it?

I don't know.

I may *never* know.

And maybe that's a blessing.

I think it must be.

The cold water takes me, dulling the pain and easing me into oblivion.

∾

I OPEN MY EYES.

There's a ceiling above me, one with thick wooden beams that flow in clean lines back and forth. I'm in a bed, comfort all around me as I blink.

"Charlie?" My voice is rusty and barely coalesces to make a sound.

"She's out fetching breakfast." Someone moves in my peripheral vision.

When I turn my head, a dull ache rockets up my spine. "I'm fucked up."

She chuckles. "That's putting it mildly."

I hear the sound of water, and when I close my eyes, I see the rushing currents of the river. Whitecaps and rapids, all of them dragging me through gorges and over sharp rocks. They cut into me, stripping away my identity, my past, my life.

"She suspected you'd wake for good. That one knows things." She taps the side of her nose, then bends over, her prodigious behind ballooning out her gray skirt. She lifts a bucket from the fireplace and pours it into a copper tub. "She told me to draw you a bath." She looks at me, her cheeks rosy and her eyes somehow knowing. "You smell like a several days' old dead raccoon, so this is for the best."

I shift to the side, my body screaming in protest. "Charlie —wait, you know she's a she?"

She laughs and hangs another bucket of water over the fire. "I was born and raised in a brothel. A pair of breeches and a hat can't fool the likes of me."

"Huh." I try to nod, but my neck is too tight. "But she's all right? She's not hurt?"

She sighs and comes to sit at the foot of the bed. "She's fit as can be."

"How'd I get here? Where *is* here?" I look out the window and see the tops of buildings glinting in what must be morning sun.

"Paris. She and Luc brought you here three days ago. You were a sight." She shivers.

"I've been out for three days?" I try to count my time until the Fallen Moon, but even simple math isn't working out in my mind.

"Longer. They brought you from some horrible place out to the east."

"The Thorny Forest." When I blink, I see the Beast, it's snarling face so close to Charlie. It makes my stomach lurch.

"Easy now." She pats my leg gently. "Don't go getting worse on me. I don't want the reputation as the one who killed the man who slayed the Beast of Gevaudon."

"It's dead then?"

"Absolutely." She wrinkles her nose. "There's a great big paw in the room next door with Luc. He cut it free and brought it as proof that the Beast is finally dead."

"Luc?" I remember him. He's one of the hunters—he turned on us. "I'll kill him." I grit my teeth.

"I wouldn't go doing that." She rises and checks on the water over the fire. "He helped Charlie get you here."

The image of him with Charlie only adds to my discomfort. He must know she's a woman now. What if he went for her when I was out, when I couldn't protect her?

"For a man with only half a face, you certainly wear your thoughts openly. I can read you like a playbill." She pours the bucket into the tub. "Let me put your worries to rest. Charlie has been by your side these many days and nights. Never left you. Comforted you while you cried out in your sleep. I've never seen such devotion. Almost made me jealous." She smooths her skirt. "But I won't let any man get his claws into me. I'm too much of a free spirit, and I make too much coin on my back to just give it up." She winks at me. "Your bath is ready. Here, let me help you." She comes to the bed and grabs my arm.

"I can do it." I swing my legs to the floor and realize I'm wearing only a dressing gown that bears bloodstains, though I don't know if it's my blood or the beast's.

She ignores me and lifts, surprisingly strong as she helps me to my feet.

"I'm seriously fucked." I shuffle toward the tub, my body sending new sensations of stabbing and throbbing.

"The bath will help. I've added some salts and herbs to it." She keeps her grip on my arm as I climb over and settle down, the warm water bringing a sigh to my lips.

"Arms up as best you can."

My left arm obeys. My right arm twinges fiercely as I lift it, and I can't get it all the way vertical.

She pulls off the gown and bunches it up. "Just lie back and soak. Charlie will be here soon. I'll go get this into the wash with your other things." She bustles to the door. "If you need me, just yell for Bonnie."

"Um, thank you, Bonnie."

"My pleasure." She walks out, closing the door softly.

I close my eyes and let my arms float, my body warming all the way through. I don't know how long I'm in the bath, but Bonnie returns after a while and adds another bucket of hot water. It feels so good I decide I might just live in this bathtub from now on.

The door opens again, and I turn to look.

Charlie walks in, a basket in one hand. She stops and stares when she sees me.

"You're awake." She smiles so big that my eyes tear up.

Fuck, why am I being a twat all of a sudden? I wipe at my eyes, pretending to rinse them with water.

"I'm so glad you're up!" She drops the basket and hurries to me, sinking on her knees beside the tub. "Are you okay? I had the doctor here when we first arrived. He checked you over and said you might have internal bleeding. He wanted to bring leeches, but I said absolutely not. You're so bruised, and I think your right arm is dislocated, but I wanted to wait for you to wake up to make sure before I tried to put it back. And your left ankle is so swollen still. It could be—"

"Charlie." I lift my hand to her face and cup her cheek. "Thank you."

She presses against my palm, sending my heart soaring to places it has no business being. Taking a deep breath, she simply stares back at me, her beautiful eyes watering. It's a conversation without words, a comfort taken and given.

When I'm finally forced to blink, she smiles and leans backward, grabbing the basket and digging inside.

"Here." She hands me a croissant, then pulls out a small cup and pours from a silver pot into it.

"What's that?"

Her eyes glint with mischief. "A delicious drink called espresso."

"Espresso?" I take it from her and drink some.

"What do you think?" she asks.

"It's bitter, and strong, and sort of sludgy." I down the rest of the small cup. "I love it."

She laughs, the sound soothing my aches even more than the water. "I'm glad you like it." She pours me another, then moves around behind me.

I drain the cup again and put it on the floor beside me, then eat half the croissant in one bite.

"Lean forward."

I try not to groan as I do what she says, but my body does not like the change in position.

"That's good enough. Now tilt your head back." Her hand is on my shoulder, holding me steady, and then she pours warm water through my hair.

"That feels so fucking good." I chew my croissant as she pours more water, my eyes closed as I simply enjoy.

The scent of soap floats past, and then I hear her lathering her hands. When she runs them through my hair, I can't stifle a moan. And when her fingers go to work on my scalp? Fuck me, I'm in heaven.

She washes my hair, rinses it, then guides me back against the tub. "Want more croissant?" she asks.

"Not right now." I pat my stomach beneath the water. "But later, definitely."

"Here." She hands me a lathered washcloth.

I do a half ass job of rubbing it on my chest. Charlie falls into my trap, snatching the cloth from me and giving me a vigorous rub down, front and back. I keep my mouth shut, one wrong word and she might stop, though I do groan a little when she avoids touching me between my legs. I take the cloth and do that part of the job.

"Are you okay?" When she's done, she moves her stool around to the side of the tub and stares at me. "Like really okay?"

"I think so, though I may be missing some skin after that scrubbing. Are you?"

"I'm fine."

"When the beast hit you—" She shudders. "I thought you were ..." She clears her throat. "By some miracle, you were alive when I reached you."

"I bet I looked valiant, didn't I?"

"You looked like you fell off a cart, beneath a horse, down a cliff, and into a grape press."

I smirk at her vivid description.

"Luc carried you on his back all the way out of that cursed forest. Belinda was pacing when we reached her. She was worried about you."

"And the beast?" I ask.

"It fell right after it flung you. Dead on the ground, thanks to you."

"And to you. That thing you did." I let my head fall to the side and open my eyes to look at her. "The thing you did to the beast. What was that?"

She suddenly finds something interesting on the floor, her gaze glued to it.

"Hey, you can tell me." I reach for her again, and she takes my hand.

"I know." She shrugs. "I just … I just want to keep things like this between us."

"You mean you want me to stay naked?" I ask.

She smiles, her gaze meeting mine again. "Glad to see none of your arrogance was lost."

"Never." I squeeze her fingers. I want to press, to figure out exactly what the hell she'd done, but she's not ready to tell me. And maybe I'm too tired to hear it anyway. Exhaustion washes over me, and I decide falling asleep right here in the warm water is an excellent idea.

"Hey." She stands. "No drowning on my watch."

I realize I'd already drifted off.

"Come on. Back to bed." She grabs my arm and pulls.

I barely move.

"You're going to have to help," she scolds and pulls again.

With a groan, I sit forward, then bend one aching leg beneath me as I push myself to standing, water flowing off me. She looks, her eyes lingering on my hips and lower.

Pride swells in me, and I'd puff out my chest if taking a deep breath didn't hurt so much.

"Behold, the real Beast of Gevaudon." I waggle my brows.

"Ugh, you are so full of it." She steps to the edge of the tub and pulls me toward her as I step out. "Come on."

I lean on her, and she huffs as she helps me to the bed. When I sit, everything sparkles with pain, and I lie down with a hard sigh.

She grabs a strip of linen that was warming by the fire and uses it to pat my front dry, though she gives my cock a wide berth. "All done." She pulls the blanket over me.

"What about my arm?" I grit my teeth as I try to lift it over my head.

"We'll deal with it later. For now, just rest."

I yawn.

"Two espressos and you're already half asleep." She tucks the blanket in around my chin.

With my good arm, I surprise her and pull her down to me.

"G!" She presses her palms on my chest.

"Stay with me." I pull her up until we're face to face. "Read your little books or do what you like, just stay in this bed with me. Yeah?"

She stops squirming and gives me a wry expression. "Well, it's not as if you can ravish me in this state."

"Don't be so sure." I thrust my hips against her, my cock already half hard.

"G." She purses her lips and shakes her head.

I sigh. "I already told you, I can't give you what you need until you ask. I realize now that was a dumb decision on my part."

"As are most decisions on your part."

My cock goes all the way hard at her insult. "Music to my ears."

She shakes her head, and I let her roll off me, though I keep her tucked to my side.

My eyes close, and I hear her flipping pages in a book.

"I'm going to eat all your croissants while you're snoring, just so you know." Her voice is a million miles away, but it's warm and it's hers, so I wrap it around me as I go.

CHAPTER

EIGHTEEN

I spend three more days in bed, my time ticking down as the Fallen Moon approaches. Charlie could start a patisserie delivery service with how often she brings me baked goods, and Bonnie is always more than happy to pour me a bath. I'm beginning to suspect she just wants to get a look at my cock, though I don't blame her of course.

When I'm finally able to get to my feet and walk around the bedroom without wincing, I know it's time to go. My destiny is waiting at Finnraven Hill.

Stretching, I look out onto the busy street. We're in an almost posh part of town, Widow Valor's coin enough to get us lodging and food. Not to mention the baths. Carriages rumble down the street and Parisians wander in and out of shops, parcels in their hands and too-wide hats on their heads.

A knock sounds at the door, and I turn. "Come in."

Luc opens the door, his hat in his hand as he walks in. "Bonnie said you wanted to see me?"

"I do." I lean on the windowsill and fold my arms across my chest.

He takes a seat at the small table by the fire. "What can I do for you?"

"Charlie has told me—multiple times—how you carried me out of the Thorny Forest."

"I did, yes." He nods.

"You don't know Charlie like I do, but the reason she keeps mentioning that you helped me is so I don't kill you."

He swallows thickly. "Wh-what?"

"She knows that the commander conspired with his hunters—of which you were one—to tie her up and use her as bait. And she also knows that I will kill you for it."

"I didn't know." He scoots back, his chair scraping across the wood floor. "Commander Thorpe didn't tell me anything. I swear. I would never have gone along with it."

"Why should I believe you?" I stride over to the fireplace and grab my sword that's resting beside it.

"Hey, wait!" He scrambles from his chair and almost falls on his ass. "Listen, I didn't know. I tried to help, remember? They held a knife to me, same as you."

I twirl the sword's grip in my palm, the blade glinting as it spins.

"A-and I told you that you should send the boy home. I didn't think he should've been there in the first place." He backs to the wall, his hands out in front of him. "I swear I'd never harm a hair on his—I mean her—head."

I walk to him, my steps nonchalant, sword still in my grip. "That's what I'd hoped to hear from you, Luc. I'd hate to have to kill you after all we've been through together, but I would. For her, I'd do it and not blink an eye."

He turns his head and clenches his eyes shut. "On my dear mother's life, I swear I wouldn't have hurt her then, and I won't hurt her now. You have my word."

I stare at him a while longer and think about how easy it would be to cut him down. Then I back away and replace my sword in its spot by the fire.

He slowly opens his eyes and looks at me. "Holy shit." He bends over and puts his hands on his knees as he takes in deep breaths. "Holy fucking shit."

"Calm down." I go back to the window.

"Calm down?" he wheezes. "You were about to gut me!"

"Bygones." I shrug. "Now that we understand each other, we need to talk about where you go from here."

He looks up at me. "I'm going home tomorrow. Charlie said for me to take the beast's paw with me to prove that it's dead."

"You've got a new home."

"What?"

I smirk. "Remember that widow I told you about?"

CHARLIE'S familiar footsteps sound in the hall, and she bursts into the room and gives me an assessing look as I swing my sword back and forth. "How do you feel?"

"Better."

I roll my shoulder. It aches from where Charlie and Bonnie shoved it back into place, but it's usable. That's all that matters.

I stow my sword in its scabbard. "We leave for Finnraven Hill in the morning."

Her face falls, and she pulls out a baguette from her basket and nearly slams it onto the table. "You're not ready yet."

"I have to be ready. The Fallen Moon is almost here."

She shakes her head. "We still have time." With a rough movement, she drops her espresso cup on the table and barely grabs it before it falls off.

I walk up behind her and wrap my arms around her. "Hey."

She sighs and straightens, leaning against me as she lets out a long breath.

"It doesn't matter if you spill the espresso, I'm still making you come with me."

She snorts a small laugh and puts her hands on my forearms.

We stand like that for a long while, the sun going down and leaving the room in shadow.

Slowly, I turn her around to face me. "I know you're scared."

Her lips twitch like she wants to deny it, but she doesn't.

"I know you have secrets." I reach up and pluck the hat from her head, dropping it behind her and running my fingers through her golden locks. "I know there are things you're afraid to tell me, though I don't know why." I skirt my fingertips down her cheek and tilt her chin up. "It's unfair really, since you know my entire life story, at least the life that I remember."

"G ..." She bites her bottom lip.

"I want to know everything about you, down to the very last boring bit. I'll even let you tell me things you read in books or silly notions like that." I smirk. "I'll listen to whatever you say, just talk to me."

I run my thumb along her lip, freeing it from her teeth. "Talk to me," I say softly.

Her eyes water. "I can't. It's not that simple." She tries to pull away, but I don't let her. I can't. Not after everything we've been through and the danger that lies ahead.

"Charlie, there's nothing you could tell me that would change how I feel about you."

She shakes her head. "You don't know that."

"I do know that. Remember the orphans?"

She gives a pained laugh and puts a hand to her mouth.

"Look at me." I pull her closer. "Just look at me."

Reluctantly, she meets my gaze again, her eyes still glistening with unshed tears. "I love you. Don't you know that? I don't think I've ever loved anything other than myself. I don't remember how I used to be, but somehow, I know that's true. At least it was, until you. I feel like maybe I'd been empty, like whatever life I had before was only a buildup to this. To you and me. I can't explain it, but I know this is real, this is where I'm meant to be, because it's where you are. I'd follow you anywhere, Charlie. I'd do anything to keep you safe, to make you happy."

A tear spills from her eye, and I wipe it away with my thumb. "I know you could never love me. Not when I look like this. Not when I'm so fucking broken and scarred, but once I find the Graven—"

She puts her palms to my face. "G, shut up and kiss me."

I don't hesitate. With one hand, I grip her hair and angle her head, then kiss her with all the fierceness in my body. I want her to feel what I can't say, what I can't express worth a damn. It's rough, the way I press my tongue against her lips, the way I hold her against me and make her mine. But she responds, her hands going to my chest as she opens her mouth, her sweet breath mingling with mine as I kiss her like I'll never see her again.

I've wanted her so badly for so long that I can't think, can't do anything except taste and touch and revel in her. Our tongues move together, caressing and stoking the fire inside me.

Reaching down, I grip her ass and lift her, dragging her up my body until we're face to face. She wraps her legs around me, her arms twining around my neck as I turn and carry her to the bed.

I lay her down, covering her as I kiss her, as my hips wedge between her thighs, my entire body wrapped tightly, tension in every muscle.

My fingers in her hair, on her throat, and lower still. I want to touch all of her. Her lips are too much of a lure, and I can't stop kissing her. When I finally kiss down to her throat, she takes in a deep breath, her body so warm and soft as I press my lips to her neck, sucking her tender flesh between my teeth.

She moans, the sound going straight to my cock.

"Fuck." I growl against her then kiss to her collar bone.

Raising up, I take the hem of her shirt and pull it up and off. Her breasts are still bound, and I grip the fabric in each hand and rip it down the middle.

"G!" She squeals as I pounce on her, taking one of her hard nipples into my mouth and palming her other perfect breast.

I lash her nipple with my tongue, sucking and licking until she moans, her body shivering as I switch to her other breast and give it the same attention. Her hands go to my shirt, and she yanks it up. I pull back for only a second so she can pull it completely off, and then I'm kissing down her stomach, her fingers twisting in my hair as I run my tongue around her belly button, then go lower.

"Off." I get to my knees and grab the waistband of her pants right as she reaches for mine.

We're tearing each other's clothes off, revealing her beautifully smooth skin and my twisted marred flesh. But she doesn't flinch. She sits up and drops kisses on the scars along my side, her hands tracing the ones on my back as she runs her tongue up to my nipple.

I jolt when she sucks it into her mouth, her fingers straying higher and running through the dark hair at the center of my chest.

She sets me on fire, every part of her like the strike of flint against me. I push her down to the bed and bite her nipple. She arches, a cry on her lips as I drag my tongue lower until I reach her mound and kiss it, the golden curls there scented with her.

I groan as I inhale her then spread her thighs apart with my wide shoulders.

"G, what are you—Oh!" She bucks when I lick her slit, my tongue coated with her sweet nectar. I put one forearm across her hips, keeping her still as I taste her, pressing my tongue inside her as she fists the blanket and cries out.

"I've wanted this for so long." I look up at her as I swirl my tongue around her clit.

She gasps, her eyes glazed with need as she stares down at me.

"Just like this." I suck her clit between my teeth.

"G!" Her cry drives me mad, and I use the broadside of my tongue to lick her again and again, focusing on that small nub as her thighs spread wider. I give her what she needs, my tongue laving her as I press a finger inside her tightness.

Her hips lock, her body going taut, and then she lets out the sexiest, breathiest moan. I don't stop, my finger moving in time with my tongue as I wring out every bit of her pleasure, drinking it down as she comes. Her walls contract and release again and again around my finger, and I push in a second, rubbing her inside and out as her thighs shake.

When she melts into the bed, her body shuddering each time my tongue glances across her clit, I slow down and kiss her mound.

Then I climb back up her body, licking my lips clean as I go. When my cock rests against her slick flesh, I hiss.

She leans up and kisses me, softly at first, still floating on her ecstasy. I return it, sharing her taste with her as I cup her cheek then slide my hand to her delicate throat.

"So beautiful," I murmur against her lips. "So fucking perfect."

Her hands are in my hair, tangling in the strands, and I wonder if she can feel the rapid beat of my heart.

Our kiss becomes more heated, her hands more urgent, and when I move my hips against her, I groan. She opens her thighs wider, and when I press against her again, she digs her nails into my back. I thrust, coating myself in her wetness and rubbing myself all over her hot flesh.

"Please," her whispered plea is almost enough to make me come all over her.

I pull back and position myself at her entrance. "Look at me, Charlie."

She opens her eyes, and I watch her as I slide into her halfway. Her teeth sink into her bottom lip, and she throws her head back. The pressure on my cock is like nothing I've ever felt before. I'm hanging on by a fucking thread. When I pull back this time, I feel myself falling away, feel only my need to have her burning in my veins.

With a hard thrust, I seat myself deep in her wetness. She yelps, her nails digging deeper.

"Look at me." My muscles shake as I force myself to stay still.

She meets my gaze again.

"Are you all right?" I kiss her, my tongue dancing with hers. "Tell me you're all right."

I pull back and look at her, those beautiful eyes on me and her short golden hair splayed on the pillow. I've dreamed about this. About her. Maybe before I fell in the river. Maybe before any of this, she was there.

"Don't stop." She pulls me back down to her mouth.

I groan at her words and reach up to grip the headboard as I try to start a slow rhythm. But it doesn't last long, not when her nails rake down my back and my cock feels like it's in the tightest, wettest vise. I move faster, pounding deeper, feeling every bit of her as she licks my throat and moves her hips to match my pace.

Faster and harder, I give her all of me, so much so that the bed begins to creak and bang against the wall. I give up on the headboard and reach down to grab her ass with one hand, pinning her beneath me as I thrust and thrust. Leaning back, I watch as I enter her, her body taking all of me as her breasts bounce with the impacts. Her hands trace down my chest, my abs, and then she brings them to her breasts and squeezes her nipples.

"Oh, fuck! Mine." I lean down and take her hands, pinning them to the bed as I suck her nipples, one at a time, licking and biting the hard tips as she arches beneath me.

Wrapping one arm around her back, I roll over and perch her on top of me. "I want you to come. I want to feel you squeezing my cock."

She presses her palms to my chest and moves her hips, rolling them as she comes down hard on me.

I groan as I watch her, a temptress, a fucking angel working my cock with a sultry expression that has me digging my fingers into her hips, feeling every bit of her movement.

I'm so close, so fucking close that I grit my teeth, my body tight as she works me. When she bears down and grinds against me, my cock wedged deep inside her as she rubs her clit against me, I reach up and cup her breasts.

She moans and sits straight up, riding me with her head thrown back, my bites on her neck, on her breasts.

I pinch her nipples, and her hips work more erratically, her body winding tighter. When she grabs my wrists and arches, she moans low.

I let go and surge up, keeping myself deep inside her as I come. My cock kicks, spurting as the purest pleasure surges through me as I watch her shatter. A guttural roar breaks free from me, and I reach up and yank her down to me, kissing her fiercely and claiming her last moans for myself.

We kiss until there are only aftershocks and contentment, our bodies slicked with sweat, our hearts pounding together.

She lies on my chest, her cheek pressed against me, and I run my fingers up and down her back. Still inside her, I feel utterly contented in a way I've never known. Because of her.

Night falls around us, Paris coming to life in the evening as the streets get noisier and rowdier. I keep stroking her, then run my fingers through her hair, grazing one of her pointed ears.

She shivers and looks up at me, one of her eyebrows arched. "Bold of you."

I laugh. "Which part? The fucking the shit out of you part or the touching your ear part?"

She scoots up—I groan when my cock slips from her—and kisses me softly. "Both," she whispers.

"You loved it." I sigh with contentment.

She snuggles against my chest again, and I throw the blanket over us.

"Are you finally going to tell me the deal with the ears?" I ask and skirt my fingertips over one again.

"Why should I?" The playfulness in her tone sends arousing tingles to my cock.

"I've been inside you."

She scoffs, then turns and perches her chin on my chest. "The place where I'm from—everyone has ears like this."

"Where? Denmark or something?"

She snorts a laugh. "Denmark?"

I shrug, enjoying the feel of her body moving against mine. "My best guess."

"No, not Denmark. Somewhere farther away. But it's normal there. Here, people ask too many questions about them." She narrows her eyes at me. "Which is why I wear a hat."

"I thought you wore a hat because you're stylish and I'm not."

"That goes without saying." She bites my chest, which *definitely* sends heat racing through me.

"Your ears are like ..." I weigh whether this will get me slapped but decide to risk it. "They're like elf ears, you know, from stories. Are you an elf?"

"What?" She tries to push herself off me, but I wrap my arms around her back, keeping her in place.

"Oh, come on, that's a fair question."

She bites me again, harder this time.

I groan and press my hips up so she can see just what her bites do to me.

She squeals and releases me, her eyes flashing as she meets my gaze. "Elves are a completely different race. You can't go calling my people elves and expect to keep your head intact."

"Okay, okay." I smooth my hands down her back. "I apologize."

She gives me a wary look but finally relaxes, her cheek against my chest where it belongs.

"A few months ago, you could've told me about the Beast of Gevaudon and the Eater and Finnraven Hill, and I would've thought you'd gone mad. But now ... I mean it's not so far-fetched that you could be an el—" I stop myself. "I mean, that you could be magical. Like the way you held the beast in place and the way you always seem to know what Belinda needs or is feeling. What about that?"

"Ears are just ears." She avoids my gaze.

"But yours are special. Like you." I run my fingers down her spine to the rise of her ass. "Like *all* of you."

She sighs, her breath tickling along my skin. "I wish we could just stay here. Start a new life in Paris. Forget about the woman in the water and this quest to the Wood of Mist." She props her chin up again, her eyes hopeful. "What about that?"

I tuck her hair behind her cute ear. "Nope. I'm getting that phylactery. It's the only way to get back what I've lost." *It's the only way you could ever love me*, I think silently.

"You don't have to do that." She runs her fingers along my chin on the ruined side of my face. "You know that, right?"

"I do." I take her hand and kiss each of her fingertips. "And I'm running out of time."

Her eyebrows draw together. "You don't even know if the lady in the water was telling the truth."

"I have to take that chance. I can't go on like this."

She pulls her hand back. "Like what?"

"Like a freak." The word sounds harsh even to my ears.

She sits up and pulls the blanket around her. I grunt when I feel her ass pressed against my cock.

"A freak?" She shakes her head. "You're not a freak, G."

"Tell that to people who see me in the street." I wave a hand at the window. "The only thing that kept people from running away screaming was my mask, and now that's gone. I can't live like this. This isn't who I am. You'll see."

"I see you now," she says gently.

"I know, and I wish you didn't have to look at me. I wish you could see me the way I'm meant to be."

"What if this *is* the way you're meant to be?" She touches one of her pointed ears. "Like this is the way I'm meant to be."

"It's not the same." I shake my head. "I'm a monster, Charlie. I can't ever be anything more than this, not unless I get that phylactery."

"Even if it's dangerous?"

"Yes."

She clenches the blanket tighter. "Even if it's likely you'll die trying to get it?"

"Yes."

She gives a frustrated huff and climbs off me.

"Hey." I swipe for her and pull her back. "What is it?"

"You're being stubborn, and it's going to get you killed." She frowns.

I roll over and pin her beneath me. "I've always been stubborn. So have you."

"I'm not stubborn."

I laugh and nuzzle her neck. "You are nothing *but* stubborn."

She giggles and smacks my shoulders. "Oaf."

I thrust my hips against her. "Charlie, you know what that does to me."

She giggles again. "Cretin."

I groan and yank the blanket from between us, then press along her wet slit, my cock head seeking her entrance. "More."

"Dolt!" She laughs as I kiss her.

"Oh, fuck yes, that's the one." I press inside her, our bodies becoming one again as we delight in each other for the rest of the Parisian night.

NINETEEN

Running a hand down the smooth side of my face —thanks to Bonnie's razor—I hope Charlie likes the clean-shaven look. I don't think I've had anything but scruff in the time I've known her. It's ridiculous, given the state of my face, but I suddenly feel nervous. What if she hates it?

"She'd tell you to get over yourself," I grumble to myself and grab the last of my things from the bed.

Once I've checked the room, I head to the door. Once I open it, I stop dead.

"Charlie." I can't form any other words.

She's standing in front of me, a new hat on her head, and she's no longer the 'boy' Charlie. Her black tunic fits her well, and her breasts aren't bound. Dark gray pants hug her legs and disappear into a pair of black boots.

I stare.

I stare some more.

I have no idea how long I stare.

"You shaved." She gets onto her tiptoes and runs her fingers along my skin. "I like it."

"You look ..." Still, no words.

"Come on. Belinda's waiting. She's had a good rest while you recovered." She turns, and I get a view of her ass. If I thought it looked amazing before, I just didn't know how good it could get. "And, listen, after last night, I don't want you getting any ideas—"

"You know I never do that." I take her arm and drag her back to me. "I think we should stay in the room a little while longer." I kiss her, stealing her breath as I hold her close.

She melts for me, her body going lax as she digs her nails into my chest. Her tongue wars with mine, both of us vying for control. But I bend her backwards, forcing her to rely on me to stay upright. She grips my shoulders and bites my bottom lip. "We have to go."

I drop my mouth to her neck, kissing the spot beneath her ear that makes her shiver. "Surely, we can spend an hour or four—"

"No." She laughs and lifts her chin so I can kiss lower. "Unless you've given up on the phylactery?"

I sigh and put her back on her feet.

"That's what I thought." She frowns a little. "Stubborn."

"Don't start calling me names or I'll *definitely* drag you into bed."

She smirks. "Imbecile."

I grab for her, but she darts away and down the stairs to the bar below.

I follow, limping only slightly from the injury to my ankle. Catching up to her, I wrap my arm around her shoulder as we stroll up the short hill toward the stables. Plenty of people are already hustling through the lane, headed to their job or coming back from a hard night.

Someone gasps, and I hear, "Mama, his face!" said in a tone of pure terror.

Charlie puts her arm around my waist. "Ignore it."

"Always do."

We keep going, meeting a few more horrified looks and cruel whispers on our way.

"They just don't know any better." Charlie glances up at me, the brim of her hat almost hiding her eyes.

"This is why I have to get the phylactery." I shrug. "If I'm going to be walking these streets with you, I don't want you to be ashamed of me."

"Hey." She steps in front of me. "I'm not ashamed of you. I couldn't care less what these people think."

"Is that why you wear a hat?" I ask.

She puts her hands on her hips. "That's different, and you know it."

"You keep saying that, but I fail to see the difference."

"I was born this way."

"So was I. When Madge dragged me out of the water, that's what I was, a newborn. I don't remember a damn thing from before. This is my life, the only one I know."

Another gasp and a whispered "his face" from a young woman with an armful of flowers.

I put my hands on Charlie's shoulders. "This is why I have to go to Finnraven Hill."

"Don't make this about me." She shakes her head. "You're going for you."

"Yes. Is that wrong?"

Her eyes soften. "No. But I don't know if this is going to end the way you think, G."

"I know you don't trust the lady in the water, but I have to believe she was telling the truth. This is the only way to fix me." I gesture toward my face.

"Maybe it doesn't need fixing."

I scoff. "You don't believe that."

"I do."

A woman screams.

I cock my head to the side and give her a wry look. "Did you hear that?"

"Are you all right? Is he hurting you?" The woman calls from across the street. "Someone help her!"

"Miss, do you need help?" A burly man walks over to us.

"We're talking," Charlie barks. "Fuck off!"

I take her arm and keep walking her up the street. "See?"

"No. I just see a bunch of fools."

"Don't go insulting other men. I'll get jealous."

That gets a laugh from her. "You're demented."

"Charlie." I slip my hand to her ass and squeeze. "I warned you."

"Ugh, focus." She leads me to the stables.

Belinda whinnies when we approach, and Charlie strokes her muzzle. "That's a good girl."

"Did you miss me?" I put my hand out to stroke her. To my surprise, she lets me. For a moment, at least. Then she nips at me with her teeth.

"Better." Charlie smiles up at me. "She likes you, but she still isn't entirely sure about you."

"Of course she likes me. How could she not?"

Charlie rolls her eyes.

I put all our items and food into Belinda's saddle bags as Charlie feeds her some dried plums. Once we're packed, I help her onto the horse, then follow her up.

"At least my ass isn't sore anymore." I shake out my ankle that's already swelling in my boot.

"Is that a challenge?" Charlie looks over her shoulder, her mouth in a mischievous smile.

The thought whirls through my mind unbidden—"*God, I love this woman*." I don't say it aloud, though. She knows. I told her everything last night. I didn't expect her to say it back. I can't ask that of her when even now, a woman is staring up at me with a stricken look on her face as we ride by.

"How many days to Finnraven Hill?" I ask.

"Two, unless we run into trouble. Then we have a week before the Fallen Moon."

"Plenty of time." I glance up at the cloudy sky.

"You don't know that."

"I do. Finnraven Hill is the way to the Wood of Mist. Once we get to the hill, we're there."

"No, Finnraven Hill is the gateway to the fae world. A whole world, G."

"What?" I suppose I haven't thought of it like that.

"Like this world, but not." She clucks her tongue and Belinda picks up the pace a little. "It has its own mountains, rivers, forests—you name it."

"And there's no map." I don't bother grabbing the one that got us this far. It has a single notation for the hill, not that I can read it.

"Not here. No."

"You make it sound hopeless." I scrub a hand down my smooth cheek. "But it isn't. The lady in the water wouldn't have given me an impossible task."

"What would make you think that? Of *course* she would. It wouldn't be the first time someone was sent on a hopeless quest."

"That's not what this is."

"See? This is what I mean when I say you're rabidly optimistic but with absolutely zero basis for it."

"Was that an insult?" I run my teeth along her neck. "Sounded like an insult."

"More of a running commentary." She laughs and smacks my leg.

"It doesn't matter. We're going there, and I'm going to find the phylactery." I rest my hands at her waist.

She leans back against me, her hair tickling my nose as usual. "I wish I could talk you out of this." Her tone turns sad.

"Why, though?"

"Lots of reasons." She grabs my arm and wraps it around her, her fingers running up and down my skin. "It's dangerous. There's no guarantee this lady in the water will show even if you get the phylactery. And what if the phylactery itself is a curse or something? The fae lands aren't hospitable to their own kind, much less mortals who go barging in to look for relics that don't belong to them."

"You seem to know a lot about the fae realm."

She shrugs and falls silent.

"And you've made it pretty clear that you don't want to go there." I prop my chin on her head. "Is it because—"

"We both have a past, G. You don't remember yours, and I don't want to remember mine. Can we just leave it at that?"

Her walls are back up. Even after last night, she's still shutting me out of some parts of herself. I can't help but believe it's because of what I am. The same way she could never love me in this state—it affects everything. She can't open up with me. Not until I've regained everything I lost. Not until she can see me as a complete man, not some monster that makes children cry and grown men go pale.

Once I'm back to the way I'm supposed to be, things will be different. Then she'll trust me enough to tell me her story. And after that, I can only hope for her love.

TWENTY

I feed Charlie the last bit of rabbit from the skewer. We still had food from Paris, but I wanted to hunt for her. She says it's because I'm a caveman at heart. She might be correct, because seeing her lick the last of the meal from her lips makes my heart swell to a ridiculous size.

"That was delicious." She tosses the bone into the fire and licks her fingers.

A jolt of desire shoots through me, and she looks at me with a sexy expression that tells me she knows exactly what she's doing.

"Have I told you all the ways I've imagined having you?" I ask.

She smirks. "No, you've never graced my ears with such filth."

"Allow me to remedy that." I take her hand and pull it to my mouth, sucking one finger after another. "Tonight, I want you on your knees, crying out like a wild animal while I rut you from behind."

She sinks her teeth into her bottom lip.

"But that's just one scenario. There are plenty more. Your mouth around my cock, my tongue inside you, you sitting on my face while I lick you until you scream, taking your tight little asshole, marking your body with my teeth—"

She laughs. "You've put more thought into fucking me than you have into anything else, *ever*."

I shrug, not denying it.

"You haven't had any thoughts along those lines?"

Her cheeks are already pink, but they go scarlet at that question.

"Oh, you have." I grin. "Do tell."

"I'm um—" She stands. "I'm going to relieve myself." She strides off toward one of the bushes along the roadside nearby.

"Don't worry, I'll relieve you plenty soon."

"G!" she groans.

I laugh and stow everything for the night. When she returns to our little camp, I've laid out our bedrolls and pat the spot next to me.

She sinks down, and I pull her against me.

"Our last night under the stars before we get to Finnraven Hill." I hold Charlie tightly as the fire crackles into the cold night.

She sighs. "I know." Turning in my arms, she meets my eyes.

I move so she can rest her head on my bicep. "What is it?"

"The same thing. I don't want you to get your hopes up. I don't want you to go at all." She presses her lips together.

"I know. But this is what I have to do." I kiss the tip of her nose. "Even if it turns out to be lies. If I don't at least try, I'll spend the rest of my life wondering and regretting."

She runs her fingers along my throat and down along my chest. "I know what that feels like."

"How so?"

She toys with my chest hair, bringing a smile to my lips. "Where I grew up—"

"Denmark, you mean."

She laughs low in her throat. "Yes, Denmark. There, we sort of had roles that we fit into. We figured them out from an early age, and we were expected to stay in that same role for the rest of our lives."

"What was your role?"

She glances at Belinda who's snoring happily. "Animals. Creatures. I have ... a way with them."

"I've noticed."

"It's what I was meant to do, and in my home country, that's *all* I was meant to do."

"You're a lot more than an animal master."

"That's why I left. That and ..." Her gaze darkens. "Anyway, I didn't want to be that person anymore. I wanted to be more."

"So you left."

"Yes. I came here, and I started a whole new life."

"As a stable boy."

She nods. "Yes, I did that job all over, but while I was doing it, I learned so much. I read every book I could get my hands on. Practiced fighting, building things, I even tried my hand at baking." She gives a wry smile. "That didn't go so well, but at least I got to *try* it. I wasn't allowed that at home. I had my position, my role. It was like a prison."

"But now you're free. You don't have to worry about that prison anymore." I drop a kiss to her cheek, her forehead.

"I wish that were true, but you heard the Eater. My father has been searching for me. He won't stop."

"Then I'll just have to hide you away with me." I pull her on top of me, my hands at her hips. "Keep you hidden. Perhaps tied to my bed for safekeeping."

She giggles as I kiss her throat. "You don't even own a bed, G."

"I will. Widow Valor will pay handsomely the next time we see her."

"For what?" She raises a brow.

"Let's just say I performed a matchmaking service for her."

"What did you do?"

I grip her shirt and yank it over her head. "Doesn't matter." I hold her sides, then lean up and capture one of her nipples in my mouth.

She moans, the sound low and sensual. "Wicked," she scolds.

"What's wicked is hiding these from me." I suck her other nipple, tonguing the tip as she settles back onto my hips, her hot sex pressing against my cock in a maddening way.

"Less clothes." I sit up and reach for her pants as she grabs my shirt. After some wrangling, we're both naked. She's still astride me, and I have a hand tangled in her hair, keeping her mouth on mine. I can't get enough of her. Not her mouth, her body, her clever fucking mind. I can't live without her. I know that now.

She moves against me, her slick flesh against my cock. I cup her breast, kneading her as our tongues tangle and tease. She grips my shoulders as she grinds on me, her rhythm growing faster.

I let go of her mouth and pull her closer, licking her throat then biting down, leaving my mark on her fair skin. She moans, her hips still moving as she chases pleasure, but that's mine to give.

I sit up and move her beside me, close enough to stay warm by the fire. Then I prowl behind her, my cock already glistening with her arousal.

With a yank, I pull her hips back to me. "I told you, Charlie. This is what I've fantasized about." I lean over her and press kisses down her spine all the way to her ass. I bite down there and slide two fingers along her hot flesh.

A groan rips from me. "So fucking wet."

"G," she pants and turns to look at me.

I lick the spot I bit on her ass, then kiss up her back. With one hand, I reach to her front and rub her clit. She jolts, her toes curling as I use my other hand to grip her shoulder. Lining up my cock, I push forward, sliding into her tight body and grunting at the pure pleasure it sends through me.

She arches her back, and I thrust deeper, taking all of her as she moans. "Don't stop."

Pulling back, I surge inside her. Again and again, I thrust, our bodies slapping together as she pushes back against me. I move faster, my fingers playing her clit as I bend down and bite her shoulder.

She turns her face to me, and we kiss, a rough embrace as I keep pounding into her, my cock so hard it almost aches. But it's nothing but bliss. Being inside her silences my mind, and there is only this—she and I, together. I never want it to end.

When she bends her elbows and presses her face to the bedroll, I slide even deeper, my balls slapping against her as I give her every inch. I can barely hold on, my cock ready to spill inside her.

I pull my fingers away for only a moment, licking her taste off them, then I press them against her clit again, giving her pressure and rubbing her the way she needs.

Her breath hitches. "Yes," she moans. "Don't stop."

"Never." I pound her harder, my need like a whip at my back.

Her hips lock, her fingers gripping the bedroll.

"G!" she gasps.

I feel the first squeeze of her walls, and I let go. Black stars explode in my vision as I thrust, coming so hard I roar into the night. I keep stroking her, giving her what she needs as she rocks back against me, our wetness mixing as I press my forehead to her back. I take gulps of air, my body letting go of its tension.

Her legs spread even wider as she sinks down.

I kiss her shoulder blades. "Are you all right?"

"Mmmph," she says against the bedroll.

I pull out of her with a wince, then lie down beside her and nestle her against my chest. "I think that was a yes?" I swipe her sweat-slicked hair from her forehead.

"Yes," she says, her eyes closed.

"Is this the part where you tell me not to read too much into how much you enjoy my cock?"

She snorts.

"Got it." I kiss her crown. "So that was one fantasy, but I think we have time for ano—"

"G!" She smacks my chest and laughs.

I hold her close, listening as she falls asleep in my arms. I may not be whole, but in this moment, I know I will be. I *have* to be.

"THIS IS IT?" Finnraven Hill isn't what I'd imagined. I was thinking a spectacular rise with old trees and beautiful flowers, fairy dust blowing in the breeze, and the song from harps all around. Instead, it's a low hill, much like a burial cairn that's flattened over long years. When we reach it, a cold rain is falling and thunder booms in the distance. Dismal.

"Not what you thought?" Charlie reads my mind.

"No." Disappointment coats the word.

"You thought there'd be naked fairies dancing for you?"

"That'd be a start."

"Don't hold your breath." The closer we get, the stiffer Charlie becomes until she's leaning forward, her body tight.

"What is it?" I ask.

"Just keep yourself sharp." She glances around, peering into the tall, dead grass and the trees that line the valley on its far edges.

I throw my leg over and drop off Belinda's back. With my bow in hand, I slowly approach the hill. From the look of it, I'm not sure how anyone could pass through it. It only rises to my waist, the top ringed with red mushrooms.

For the first time, a sliver of doubt cuts into my heart. Was it all a lie?

The rain intensifies, the storm rolling in.

Charlie dismounts, her hand on the sword at her waist. She moves with her usual grace, but she radiates tension.

"You've been here before." It should be a question, but it isn't.

"Yes," she says through gritted teeth, her gaze darting back and forth.

"Why didn't you tell me?"

"Some secrets are mine to keep."

"That's a fucking bullshit answer, and you know it." I want to be angry, but with the way she's tighter than my bow string, her eyes darting this way and that, I'm too worried about her to be properly pissed. I load my bow and back to her. "What's coming? What is it?"

"I don't know, but I feel it." She draws her sword as the thunder rumbles closer, lightning streaking the sky.

"How do we get into the hill?" I raise my voice over the pelting rain.

"We should go back." She grips my forearm. "We shouldn't be here."

"This is the only way."

"We'll think of something else."

"There is nothing else!" A burst of lightning strikes the trees nearby, the thunder deafening.

Belinda bolts, running hard into the sheeting rain.

"Belinda!" Charlie calls and holds out her hand, her eyes closed.

"What—"

"Come." Charlie's voice cuts through the wind and rain, the sound vibrating in a way that sends goosebumps along my skin.

The horse appears, walking back to us and shaking its head.

"That's a good girl." Charlie presses her trembling hand to Belinda's snout.

The wind begins to swirl, spinning around us and flinging the rain in stinging drops.

"Charlie!" I wrap her in my arms, trying to shield her.

She shakes. "He's coming."

"Who?" I look around wildly, but the wind and rain have cut us off. It's only us and the hill.

She looks up at me, rain streaming down her face. "My father."

"Come again?"

The wind stops, the rain too. The world goes silent as if some great magician waved his wand and halted time.

"You've finally come home," a voice booms from the hill and sends suspended raindrops skittering away from us like suspended crystals.

I turn and raise my bow, stepping in front of Charlie.

A man in a purple robe threaded with gold stands atop the hill, his gaze bearing down on me like a lead weight. Golden hair, familiar blue eyes, delicate features coated in masculine strength, and a sneer—he must be Charlie's father—but without her softness or humor.

Suddenly, and perhaps far too late, I wonder what she's risked to keep this bargain with me, to return to a place she so desperately wanted to stay away from.

"What creature is here with you?" He glares at me.

I jerk my chin at Belinda. "It's a horse, obviously."

His sneer only intensifies. He's tall and has a stately air to him, one I decidedly don't like. If he's the one who stopped the rain and froze the world into silence, he's more powerful than anything we've faced.

She puts a hand on my elbow and steps beside me. "Father." She bows her head slightly. "We've come to—"

"We?" His eyes narrow, his stately head lowering as he looks at me. "Have you forgotten, dear daughter, that you are engaged to Lord Tristan Martant?"

Engaged? I tighten my grip on my bow. Somehow, he notices, his gaze flicking to my palm.

"I'm not here for that." Charlie's voice trembles. She clears her throat and continues strongly, "We only seek passage to retrieve an artifact from the Wood of Mist."

He sighs deeply, his eyes finally settling on Charlie. "Do you know how long I've searched for you?" Something like sadness tinges his voice. "You ran away. We finally beat back the Seelie Court, thanks in great part to you, and you left. Your fiancé begged me for leave to come to this uncivilized plane to search for you. I refused and searched myself, risking breaching the peace between our worlds each time I ventured here."

"I know you've been looking." She swallows thickly. "We found the Eater."

The sides of his lips tick up. "And how does our old friend fare? I let it loose for something of a holiday in the human realm."

"It's dead," I answer.

"What?" His hand strays to the sword strapped at his side, the hilt glinting gold.

"It attacked us." Charlie takes a step forward, her chin up. "It had devoured countless humans by the time we chanced upon it. G ended it, as it deserved."

"G?" He smirks. "That's this creature's name?"

"What's yours?" I shoot back.

His eyes flash. "You don't know me, boy?"

"You're a guy who popped out of a hill." I shrug. "How would I know you?"

He grips his sword but doesn't draw, though I get the keen sense he wants to, desperately. "Your kind may as well call me god," he sneers. Holding out his hand to Charlie, he says, "Come, daughter, return home where you belong."

"Not without G. And I'm *not* staying."

He tsks. "My advisors warned me not to give you too much leash, but I'm afraid that, in my old age, I've grown soft. I was too easy on you, Charlieta, and that's why you've become so willful."

Charlieta? Her name is beautiful, and even in his cutting tone, the sound of it is musical, lilting.

"Come now, no more childish rebellions. You belong safe at home."

"I'm not coming without G. I mean it, Father. You can drag me back, but I'll fight to escape, and I will. Eventually, I'll get out, and I'll run so far you'll never have a chance of finding me."

He sighs, his eyes turning tired. "Why must it be this way between us?"

She backs to my elbow.

He stares at her for long moments, the two of them engaged in a silent battle of wills. I don't know what I've walked into or what lies beyond the hill he's standing on, but I know I'm not leaving Charlie's side.

Tapping his fingers on the hilt of his sword, he shrugs. "I suppose you can bring a pet if you absolutely must. You've always been so partial to animals. Come."

"Hold on." Charlie grips my arm.

"Hold on to—" I yell when the ground drops out from beneath us.

We fall endlessly, the world going dark, then bursting in fits and starts of light. Belinda neighs, and I feel her at my back.

I try to ask Charlie what the fuck is happening, but my breath is stolen the moment I open my mouth.

Gasping for breath, all I can do is hold on tightly to her as we fall endlessly, midnight surrounding us as the earth is swallowed up, us along with it.

TWENTY-ONE

We land hard, my ankle crumpling as I fall on my ass with Charlie in my arms. Belinda thumps to the ground beside us, a sharp nicker leaving her.

"Holy fuck." I sit up and grab Charlie's shoulders. "Are you okay?"

"I'm fine. Are you?"

My stomach roils, and I sit her beside me, then take a deep breath. I refuse to vomit. My stomach disagrees, but I swallow several times as I look around. We're in a huge hall, the floor beneath us white marble with golden swirls, and above a golden ceiling with wide windows showing a bright blue sky. The size and beauty of it give me a dazed sensation, like perhaps I hit my head a little too hard.

Movement catches my eye, and I see several soldiers marching toward us, their armor gold, and golden weapons at their sides.

"Charlie!" I yell and get up, grabbing for my sword as I push her behind me.

One man strides out ahead of the others, his gait certain as he aims for us.

I pull my sword and point it at him. "Stop!"

His dark eyebrows rise as he slows. "What is this creature?"

"She's a horse. What is with you people?"

Charlie takes my arm. "Put it down."

"No way." I point my sword at the dark-haired man.

"We're safe here." She sighs.

I glance around at the two-dozen soldiers who say otherwise. "I won't let them touch you."

"Princess?" The dark-haired man, his outfit a crisp green with golden buttons down the front of his jacket, steps closer. "Are you all right?"

"Princess?" I glance at Charlie.

She pulls her hat from her head. "I'm fine. Could you take Belinda to the stables? She could use some fresh hay and a rest."

"Of course." He comes toward us.

I keep my sword at the ready. "What's going on?" I ask Charlie.

She takes my wrist and gently lowers my sword. "Come on. I guess it's time I explained." She glances toward the front of the room. There's a dais with a large golden chair in the center with a daintier replica on its left side. Another golden chair sits to its right, but there's a black sash draped across it.

"Varwin, my rooms are still the same, I take it?" she asks the man who's taken Belinda's bridle with ease. I'm offended. She used to snap at me when I did that, but she's taken to this stranger in no time.

"Of course, Princess." He gives her a bow, and I notice then that his ears are pointed like Charlie's and her father's, then leads Belinda away. I could swear the horse gives us a doleful look, but she follows the stiff-backed man, no problem.

Charlie takes my hand.

Some of the soldiers shift uncomfortably, sharing looks.

"Back the fuck off." I step toward them.

They don't move.

"Go," Charlie says sharply.

They bow, then turn and march back to whatever hole they came from.

"What the hell is happening right now?" I mumble as she pulls me to the right and through a gilded door.

"Just give me a few minutes to think."

"What's there to think about?" I follow her up a wide set of marble stairs, my limp growing more pronounced with each step. Attendants whisper in alcoves and bustle about like they're important. All with pointed ears and stares. "Just tell me where we are, and why you're a princess, and does that mean your father is a king? Is this your palace?"

She grips my fingers tighter. "How's the ankle?"

"You can't answer my question with a question."

"Why not?"

We reach a landing, and she pulls me down a long hallway decorated with huge paintings of more people with golden hair and pointed ears.

"Relatives?" I ask.

"Yes." She stops in front of a set of double doors and pushes them open, drags me inside, then shuts them behind us.

"You live here?" My mouth drops open as I take in the huge bed with the fluffiest white blanket I've ever seen. Gilded furniture is arranged in a sitting area, and sun streams in high windows with sheer curtains blowing in the breeze. I've never seen anything like this.

"Not anymore."

"Why not?" I could make camp in this room right now and never leave it. "Is there food?"

"We can get whatever you like from the kitchen, yes."

"And you *left* this?" I am, for lack of a dumber word, agog.

She walks backward, pulling me to the sitting area and plopping me down on an emerald green sofa. "Yes. I left it, and I'm glad I did." She drops to her knees and unlaces my boot, gingerly pulling it off as I continue gawking.

"It's worse off than before." She winces at my swollen, purple ankle. "I'll call for the healer." She returns to the door, cracks it open, whispers to someone, then closes it and returns to me.

"Someone's just standing out there waiting for you to need something?" *A-fucking-gog*.

She sits across from me and rubs her eyes, her mouth in a tight line.

"My father is King Finnraven of the Unseelie Court, Lord of Death and Darkness, Bringer of Oblivion and Blight, Ruler of Shadow."

"But he was so ... pretty." I stare at her. "Like you."

"Appearances aren't everything, G. You of all people should know that." She lets her head loll back, her gaze on the sunny ceiling. "I'm Princess Charlieta Finnraven, though I haven't gone by that name for a long, long time."

"Why did you leave?"

"A lot of reasons." Her head pops up when there's a soft knock at the door. "Hang on." She answers it, and a young woman enters, her dress all white and her eyes downcast. She kneels in front of me.

"What is— Ow!" I flinch when she touches my ankle. "Hands to yourself."

Charlie puts her palm on my shoulder. "She's a healer. Let her work."

"Your highness?" the girl asks, though she still doesn't look up.

"Go ahead. He's just a big baby."

She nods and touches me—more gently this time— feeling around my injury before stopping with her fingertips on my ankle.

"This may feel a little ... funny. Just go with it." Charlie squeezes my shoulder.

"What do you mean by funny?" I grunt when my ankle grows warm. "What's that?"

"Shh." Charlie stays by my side as the girl whispers something over and over.

My ankle grows warmer still, the sensation creeping up my leg as her whisper grows louder, her hands moving along my skin, touching every bit of my ankle.

When she sits back, I wiggle my foot. The pain is gone.

The girl bows low, then rises.

"Thank you, Ellian," Charlie says.

"My pleasure, your highness."

"Just call me Charlie." She opens the door for the girl, who slips out without responding. Once she's gone, Charlie closes the door and leans her forehead against it. "She's never going to call me Charlie."

I stand and put all my weight on the bad ankle. It's perfect. I don't even feel a twinge. My hand strays to my face. "Charlie, do you think ..."

She turns to me, her eyes soft. "No, G. I'm sorry. They can help hurts, but not once it's healed."

"Oh." I should've known better than to hope. The only answer for me is the phylactery, though staying in this palace definitely has its perks. "Come here." I sink onto the loveseat again, then pull Charlie into my lap.

She starts to protest, but I put a finger to her lips. "Tell me if we're in danger."

She frowns, then I move my finger, and she says, "No. Well, not in the general sense. My father isn't fond of humans, but he won't kill you. At least I don't think he will. I wouldn't let him."

"So when you said before that we're different breeds, you weren't speaking meteorically?"

"*Metaphorically*. And no, I wasn't."

"What does that mean? I mean, other than the fact that you are, as it turns out, not from Denmark."

She smiles for me, and even in this strange place surrounded by people who may or may not try to kill me, it puts me at ease. "Not from Denmark, no."

"So you really are an elf?"

Her eyes blaze for a moment. "No!" She smacks my arm. "Don't say that to anyone else here or they might gut you. We are fae. Elves are a different race entirely."

I open my mouth, but she covers it with her hand. "Don't say we're fairies either. That's not correct. We are *fae*. Some refer to us as the Folk or the Sidh, but never fairies and *never* elves."

I stare at her, my Charlie, with new eyes. She's the same to me, but she isn't. She's royalty. Fae royalty, at that. "How many more secrets do you have?" A memory flashes through my mind. "And wait, you're *engaged*?"

She runs a hand through her hair. "Look, I would've told you everything, but I was hoping we could pass through the Hill without running into my father. That's what I wanted, then you would've never found out about all this." She waves a hand at the ornate room.

Once again, she didn't say anything to hurt me, but I feel the sting all the same. "Why wouldn't you tell me?"

"It's complicated."

"It's not." I shift her off my lap. "You know who I am. I've never hidden myself from you. I can't. Why didn't you think you could trust me with this?"

"It's not about trust—"

"It is to me." I rise and pace back and forth in front of the wide fireplace.

"G, please." She gazes up at me, her eyes somehow bluer when surrounded with so much gold. "There's a lot that happened here, and not all of it good. It's why I left."

"Your father said you ran away. From what?" I spin. "From all of this?"

"He's my father, but he's also a king. It's not so simple." She clasps her hands. "I had my reasons."

"Then share them with me. I want to understand." I stop in front of her. "Help me."

She looks down. "I did things," she says softly. "Things I can't take back."

I drop to a knee and tilt her chin up so she meets my gaze. "Tell me, Charlie."

"There ... There was a war. I—"

A sharp knock at the door puts my teeth on edge.

"Charlieta?" a deep voice calls. "I just heard you've come home. May I come in?"

"No." She jumps to her feet.

"Charlieta, it's me."

"I know who it is. Go away!" She glares at the doors.

My hackles rise, and I stand with her, my hand ghosting across my sword. "Who is it?"

"Charlieta." The handle turns and the door swings open.

I'm on the man before he can step into the room. "She said go away, asshole." I press the point of my sword to his throat.

He's tall, almost as tall as I am, and with sharp features and piercing black eyes that are in contrast to his long blond hair. Even so, I can admit he's handsome in a twatty sort of way, *and* he has both sides of his face intact.

Charlie groans. "G, drop the sword."

"Are you sure?" I don't want to drop it. In fact, I want to use it. On him.

"Yes. Please."

Fuck. I lower the blade, though I don't sheathe it.

The man scowls at me. "What is this? King Finnraven mentioned you brought a pet, but your tastes have turned a bit macabre since you've been in the human world."

"I don't know what you just called me, but I'm certain I've maimed people for less." I glare back at him.

He smiles thinly. "I see why you brought it. It's quite amusing." Turning his attention to her, he says, "Now that you've returned, your father has already instructed that preparations be made for our wedding. A fortnight should be enough—"

I put the sword back to his throat. "You aren't marrying Charlie."

"G." Charlie runs her hand down my forearm. "Don't."

The asshole watches the movement, his lip curling. "Humans never have any manners."

I lean forward, the blade nicking his throat. "You're right, and I've the least of all of them."

Charlie presses her forehead to my bicep. "Let me handle this. G, please."

That word again. *Fuck.* I want to draw more blood, to make this prick squeal, but I can't say no to her. I realize I never could.

Slowly, I lower the sword, but I stare daggers instead, hoping to bleed him with them.

"Tristan, please go."

"And leave you with this monster? Absolutely not." He pulls out a dainty fucking kerchief and wipes the blood at his throat with a wince.

"I'm not asking." Charlie's voice is edged with steel. "Leave my chambers."

"We'll speak later then?"

"Like hell you will." I bare my teeth. "In case you haven't noticed, she ran away from you. She's not going to marry you, so get the fuck out."

His sneer turns into a slight smile. "Oh, now this is fun. The hideous beast has fallen in love with my beauty, is that it?" he simpers. "You think she would ever choose a repugnant monster like you over me? Just look at you and look at her. Laughable." He chuckles.

Bloodlust like I've never felt pulses through my veins. I'm going to kill him. I lift my sword again.

"G!" Charlie steps between us, her eyes on mine as she shakes her head. "Tristan, leave. Now."

With the way his eyes narrow, he doesn't like being told what to do, but he steps back through the door, his eyes on what's mine. "Charlieta, I'm honored to be your mate. You'll see what a good match we are."

I step forward, but Charlie puts her hands on my chest. "Don't," she whispers.

"Have fun with your broken toy." He smirks and turns, walking away with a goddamn jaunty step.

Charlie grabs the doors behind her and closes them, then turns the lock.

"You're not marrying him." I sheathe my sword, my mind seething. "You're not."

"Calm down." She reaches up to cup my face.

I shake her off and back away. "Tell me you're not marrying him."

A hint of hurt passes across her eyes before she steps to me again. "I'm not marrying him, G."

Just those few words soothe the anger in my breast, the jealousy that coils through my veins like snakes.

"I ran away, didn't I?" She cups my face, and this time I let her. "I refused my fate, the one my father chose for me, and I left. I went out into the human world looking for my destiny." She steps closer, her warmth like a touch. "And then I found you." On her tiptoes, she tilts my face down to hers and kisses me.

I drop my sword, grab her ass, and lift her, pinning her against the door as I take her mouth. Not slow and sweet, anything but. I need her to feel my claim, to know I'll never let that twatty ponce touch her, much less marry her.

She wraps her legs around my waist as I grip her hair, pulling roughly and angling my mouth over hers. Her moan rolls through my chest, my body still tensed, still ready to fight. I press against her and feel the curves of her breast, the heat between her thighs. She's intoxicating, the most heavenly creature I've ever come across. And she's fucking *mine*.

I pull her from the door and carry her to the bed. She gasps as I grip her pants and yank them down.

"G, we can't."

"Why not?" I'm already freeing my cock.

She licks her lips, her gaze on me as I stroke myself. "B-because—"

"That's what I thought." I strip her panties, then spread her legs. "Tell me you want me, Charlie. You want *us*." I pull up her shirt, her hard nipples taunting me as I take one in my mouth.

"I-I—" She moans as I bite down on the hard peak, my cock rubbing against her wet slit.

"Tell me."

"I want you." She buries her fingers in my hair, and I slide inside her.

"Fuck." I grunt and push the rest of the way inside, forcing her to part for me, to make way for us. "That's my girl."

She moves her hips, her body demanding more. I give it to her, thrusting hard, shaking her canopy bed and bringing obscene sounds from her mouth. She tries to be quiet, I can tell. But I don't let her. I lick my thumb and press it to her clit.

She gasps as I swirl it, teasing her, bringing her higher and higher as I give her every inch of me. Our bodies slap together, the sound ricocheting off the walls and back to me.

Leaning over her, I claim her lips again, kissing her deeply as I grind against her, giving her what she needs with each stroke.

"Like that?" I look down at her. "Tell me, Charlie. Tell me how you want my cock."

"Like that!" she cries as I take her wrists and pin them over her head.

"Take it all." I thrust harder, the bed creaking at each impact. "I love you. I'm yours." I bite the juncture of her shoulder and throat, bruising her with my mark on her skin. "You're mine."

"G!" Her back bows from the bed, taking me so deep I think I might see god, and then she comes apart, crying out my name as I push deep and let go, ecstasy pouring through me as I come inside her. I want to fill her, to leave my scent on her so that anyone who comes near her knows she's mine. It's animalistic, but that's what I am for her. A fucking beast who'll rip and tear anyone who tries to come between me and what's mine.

I can't breathe, can't do anything except watch her, be with her, exist for her. She gasps in air, her body shaking as I press kisses to her throat, her chest.

When I return to her face, her eyes are fluttering open. "Mine, Charlie." I thrust again, just so she knows I'm still here, still ready to give her pleasure.

"You're an animal." She reads my thoughts.

I nibble her chin. "Makes sense. Animals are your specialty." Her lips are swollen and soft, and I kiss her again, unable to get enough.

She turns her head and puts her hand to her forehead. "Shit. I think the whole palace heard that."

"Good." I meet her gaze.

"Not good, G." She glances at the door. "If my father didn't hear it, he's definitely heard about it by now."

"So?"

She wriggles beneath me. "So he's going to be on my ass in no—"

A hard knock at the door. "Charlieta. I need to speak with you. *Now*."

"Fuck! It's him." she hisses and pushes against my chest. "Move."

I smirk and refuse to let her up.

"G!" She fights harder, smacking my shoulders.

I give her another hard kiss, then get up.

"Go! My bathing room." She points to a doorway at the back of the room. "And stay in there." Her gaze falls to my cock right as her father knocks again. "Hurry!" She shoves me, and I almost trip with my pants around my ankles.

When I make it into the room, she closes the door so hard it smacks my ass.

I laugh, then pull my pants up and lean against the door to listen.

"Father."

"Where is he?" His tone is vicious.

"Taking a bath."

"Are you set on embarrassing me? Is that why you've returned?"

"No. I was—"

"Tristan heard everything as did I, and now what? Now you expect me to smooth this over for you?"

"No. I'm not—"

"I thought you came home for good reason. I thought you'd learned your lesson and realized that you belong here. You have *responsibilities*, Charlieta." His tone softens. "I won't be around forever, daughter. This court is yours to rule once I'm gone. I've tried to be understanding and let you explore for as long as you needed. I thought it would make you come to your senses, would instill in you a sense of duty. When I saw you at the Hill, I thought ..." He sighs. "I don't know what I thought, but I was glad to see you."

"I was glad to see you, too."

The room goes silent for a long while, then Charlie speaks, "But you know I've never wanted to rule here."

"I know you've shirked your duties whenever possible." His sharp, condescending tone is back. "And you need a strong partner to keep you on the throne where you need to be. That's why I chose Lord Martant. He's seasoned in battle and diplomacy, and he's been enamored with you for over a century."

I cock my head to the side. Surely, I misheard that last part.

"I'm not marrying Tristan, Father."

"You are. I've already summoned the nobles. This has to happen, Charlieta. One day, you'll understand."

"You're not listening to me." Her voice rises. "I didn't come here for the throne. I came here to help a friend."

He scoffs. "That foul creature listening at the door?"

I ignore his insult and focus on hers: I'm just a *friend*?

"He's not a creature. He's G, and I'm traveling with him to the Wood of Mist."

"Nonsense. The Seelie rebels run rampant there." He laughs, the sound nothing short of sinister. "They're still smarting from their defeat at your hands."

"I don't want to talk about that." Her tone turns almost brittle.

"I don't see why not. The bards have immortalized it in song, and the slaughter is the highlight of our peoples' spring festivities. You may not want to be the ruler of this land, but you are indelibly in the heart of this court, Charlieta. Far more so than I ever have been."

Silence returns, and this time it feels almost sickly. *The slaughter*? That's a word I'd never put in the same thought with my Charlie. The quiet rolls on, and I imagine the two of them in a staring contest.

King Finnraven breaks first. "I'll have a talk with Tristan. After all, we're all due our dalliances, even if they're with entirely unsuitable beasts. It's not important. The only thing that matters is you're home now where you belong."

"Father—"

"Don't thank me yet, daughter. Wait until after I've smoothed it over. Rest now. I'll have the kitchens prepare a selection for you to lunch here in your rooms. You look positively peeked. I need you perked up before we greet our nobles. But don't fret, we'll discuss the wedding arrangements tonight at dinner. Your mother was the sentimental one, as you know, but I have to say, seeing you here—even with your shorn hair and in the company of that human—warms me. It truly does."

Footsteps, and then I hear the doors close, the lock clicking over. A thumping sound follows, and I know immediately it's Charlie bouncing her head against the door.

I walk out and stride to her. She doesn't turn, but she does stop banging her forehead.

"Don't, G."

"What?"

"Just ... don't."

"Look, Charlie, as your *friend*, I think you should—"

"Ugh!" She whirls. "I don't need this right now."

"Need what?" I cross my arms over my chest. "You don't need to hear your *friend's* opinion on—"

"You're acting like a child." She stalks past me. "This isn't even about you."

"Don't be silly. Everything is about me."

"G! This isn't a joke!" She stops at the window and looks out. "I told you I never wanted to come here, but you wouldn't let me go. You made me promise. You—"

"I made you promise to stay with me, but I didn't know about any of this." I glance around the room that's coated in more wealth than I've seen in all my life. "You never told me." Her shoulders stiffen, so I change tacks. "Look, we can get what we need for the journey to the Wood of Mist and go. We don't have to stay. Once we have what we came for, we'll go to Paris, just like you said."

"You don't understand. Just being back here—I can feel all this weight on my shoulders. My father's expectations, the entire court looking at me and wondering if I'm strong enough to lead them. I don't even *want* to lead them. I want to live my own life. But my father expects me to be the princess, to follow in his footsteps, to take his throne one day. It suffocated me until I left, and now all that weight is on me again. Smothering me." She hangs her head. "Twice as heavy."

My irritation fades, concern for her welling up in its place. "Look, we can figure this out. It doesn't have to—"

"I was free of it. I was living, truly *living*, out in the human world until you dragged me back here. I should've stayed in Sac à Puces. If I had, I'd still be hidden, just a stable boy. But now ..." Another heavy sigh. "This was a mistake."

My heart speeds up, as if it's preparing me to jump a chasm or dodge a sword blow. "What exactly do you mean by 'this'?"

"I don't know. All of it. *Everything*. Everything that led me back here into this trap."

Me. She uses so many words to say it, but I hear it all the same. I'm the mistake. I'm the reason she's here. But how could I have known about all this? She's full of secrets, and I didn't force them from her. I didn't want to push her away.

"If you'd only told me—"

"Then what?" She turns, her expression dark. "If I'd told you, you would've kept on this path anyway. You're so obsessed with the phylactery—with the vague-as-fuck nonsense from some voice in the water—and like you said, *everything* is about you. It always has been from the moment I met you."

I've been kicked in the gut before. Plenty of times. But none of them ever hurt like this. "You think I would've risked you, risked *losing* you? I love—"

"Stop." Her eyes flash.

The gut punch comes again, worse this time. All I can do is look at her while an ache builds in my chest.

"G, you *can't* love me. Maybe you think you do, but—"

"Don't." I step toward her, my arms dropping to my sides. "Say what you want, convince yourself that I'm a mistake, do what you need to do to survive, to make sense of your life, but don't ever tell me what I feel for you. I know you, Charlie." I reach for her.

She swipes my hands away. "You don't even know *you*, G. You're lost, chasing a fantasy that doesn't exist." She slides the knife in with nothing more than words and the look in her eyes. Then she pushes past me and out of the room, the doors closing behind her.

I stand where she's left me, my black heart cracking as her footsteps fade.

TWENTY-TWO

I've peeked out the door about half a dozen times, but I have no clue how to find Charlie in this enormous palace. What's worse, I don't think she wants me to find her. And maybe, maybe I need some time, too. I rub my chest and think back to her scathing words. Yes, I need time.

Sitting on the sofa, I kick my feet up on her fancy coffee table and stare at the intricate beams holding up the ceiling of glass. Though I don't know if it's glass or some sort of fairy—*fae*—magic.

Her words continue to circle my mind, like dirty water in a drain. "I'm *not* chasing a fantasy." I try to say what I should've said to her before she walked out. "You're wrong. I'm going to find that phylactery, and once I'm set to rights, you'll know I wasn't being an oaf. Not this once, anyway."

I walk around the room again, then sit in front of a small writing desk and pull open a drawer. A few quills roll around inside. There's parchment and some wax. I pluck up a gold coin that's toward the back. When I flip it over in my fingers, I freeze. Charlie's face is stamped onto the coin. I'd recognize the line of her nose and the almond shape of her eyes anywhere. Here, her hair is long, flowing over her shoulders as she looks confidently ahead.

"You're on the money, Charlie. Holy shit." I stare at it.

Someone clears their throat.

I jump and reach for my sword.

"Apologies. I thought the princess was out." The fae backs away from the doors, his arms laden with trays of food.

"She is, but come in." My stomach growls at the feast he carries. I pocket the coin and close the drawer.

As he places the trays on the table, I get a good look at him. Like the other fae, his face has sharp features and no lines. It makes me wonder how old they all are. Then again, Charlie did say she was older than me. I just didn't realize she meant by centuries.

"What's your name?" I ask.

"Clotho, sir."

"You don't have to call me sir, and you can look me in the eye. I'm not one of these powdered ponies."

He nods and stands straight after adjusting the plates, then gives me a slight bow. "May the light of our king lead you to the safest roads and greenest vales. If that will be all ..." He backs away.

"No. It's not all." I lean forward, my elbows on my thighs. "I have some questions."

"I'll answer what I can, but I'm only a kitchen attendant, sir." He keeps his gaze downcast.

"I'm sure you know plenty." I take a turkey leg from the nearest tray and tear off a hunk of it, the taste rich on my tongue as I chew. "How long has Charlie—ah, I mean the *princess*—how long has she been gone?"

"I can't time it to the year, but I believe it's been about less than a century, maybe by half."

"So she's how old?"

"I'm afraid I'm not entirely certain, sir. She was born long before I came to work at the palace, but I would think she's at least two hundred perhaps more. She's still quite young."

I swallow hard then pour myself a cup of wine. "That's young? Then how old's her father?"

"King Finnraven is just shy of his three-thousandth birthday."

"Holy shit." The wine is strong and delicious. So fucking good. I drain the cup then refill it. "That's ... I can't even think about that many years all at once. Is he the oldest fae?"

"Oh, no sir." He glances up at me finally. "Not even close."

I offer the wine cup to him. He declines, not a hair of his light brown hair out of place as he shakes his head. He wears the same green as everyone else I've seen in the halls. It must be a servant color. My head goes woozy for a moment then snaps back. It must be wine on an empty stomach. Grabbing a piece of crusty bread from the tray, I tear off a chunk of it with my teeth. "What was she like?"

He glances at me and quickly looks down again. "Pardon me, sir? I don't understand."

"Charlie—err, Princess Charlieta. Before she left, what was she like?"

"I don't think I can speak to—"

"Listen, Clotho, it's just you and me. You don't have to worry. No one here cares what I think."

He purses his lips and nods, agreeing. "As a human, you do have a status that's unfortunate."

I ignore the sting to my pride. "Right, so telling me a few things won't matter."

"I suppose not." He makes a *hmm* sound. "I wasn't around her terribly much, sir. Just at dining room service or when she had something brought to her rooms."

"But you must have noticed something. Just ..." I sigh. "Was she happy?"

His shoulders rise slightly in an almost imperceptible shrug. "I think she was, in a way. The king for all his might and the terror he instills in his enemies—he always had a soft spot for her, his only child. I believe, though I'm not certain, that is because of her resemblance to our late queen in both appearance and spirit. At least, that's what I've heard. But I will also say that they had their fair share of arguments, and Her Highness did seem to ... chafe. Yes. She chafed at the confines of the palace and her role. As do we all from time to time, I suppose. But in the times before she left, we were in open war with the Seelie Court, so the princess had a constant guard and couldn't leave palace grounds."

I try to imagine her stuck in these rooms or even in this huge palace, wanting to go out and explore but not getting the chance. "What did she do to end the war? The king mentioned a slaughter."

He perks up a little, as if this is one of his favorite subjects. "She hasn't told you about it? You're her traveling companion."

"I know, but she's not big on sharing. I didn't even know she was a fae until we got here."

His eyebrows rise. "How could you not have noticed?"

I shrug. "I just thought she was from Denmark."

He gives me a quizzical look, then clears his throat. "At the end of the last great war, the vicious Seelie—"

"What's a Seelie?"

He gives me a confused look. "The Seelie fae?"

"Yeah. Are they different from the fae here?"

He scoffs. "They're not fit to kiss the boots of King Finnraven."

"So they don't have the ears?" I point to my own ear. "The pointy kind?"

He shakes his head. "Of course they have pointed ears. We are all ..." He says it grudgingly. "Fae. But that is where our similarities end. The Seelie are nothing more than sanctimonious brigands who pretend to be all that is good and right."

"Enemies. I get it."

"Enemies indeed." His tone is sour, and then he continues, "The Seelie had surrounded the palace. King Finnraven had been gravely wounded in battle, so much so that the healers could neither get him to wake, nor could they say if he would survive. We were in dire times. The Seelie had laid waste to our villages and slaughtered animals, burned crops, and committed any number of atrocities against us on their march to our king. We were under siege, and everyone from the towns near the palace had run here for safety from the advancing army. The siege lasted for weeks, and then into months. Food was running low, healers were out of supplies, and we were losing soldiers to enemy snipers set up all around the palace walls. Without the power of our king, we had only days left before starvation or the Seelie wiped us out."

The princess had been valiantly walking the walls, keeping the troops in good spirits, and visiting with the fae who'd been sheltering inside the palace gates. But she knew we were wearing thin. That night, she visited her father, sitting with him until late in the evening as reports began arriving that the Seelie intended to take the palace at daybreak the next morning. We began making preparations for the final assault and brought the elderly and children into the heart of the palace while every able-bodied fae was given a sword to fight."

When day broke over the realm, the Seelie began to surge toward the palace and used ladders and grapple hooks to scale the walls. Our forces were quickly overcome, the Seelie striking down everyone in their path. Then, the princess emerged from her father's chambers, his battle armor strapped to her body, and she hurried to where the fray was the thickest. The Seelie were coming, the fight already fading as they murdered any who stood in their way."

The princess stood against the bloody tide and raised her arms, beseeching the shadows to give her the power to vanquish the foes of her father. Dark power seeped from the earth itself, wrapping her in a vortex of doom the likes of which neither the Seelie or Unseelie have seen in many ages. The dark power of her bloodline then mixed with the calling of her heart. A mighty rumbling began to sound throughout the realm. The Unseelie heroes retreated to the palace as the roar grew and grew, the ground trembling and the skies going dark. Screams began to sound from the rear of the Seelie line, and even the Unseelie knelt and prostrated themselves before such unbridled power. The screams grew louder, the ground quaking, and then the huddling Unseelie saw the beasts of the land and the air descending on the Seelie, tearing them apart with gnashing teeth and rending claws, swooping down and carrying them away or dropping them from great heights so they splattered like overripe grapes on the stones."

He smiles wistfully. "A beautiful sight for the kingdom—the princess brought a horde of creatures to destroy the Seelie, tearing them apart and leaving their corpses for the carrion birds that remained. When the battle was done, the power seeped from her, and she dropped to her knees and looked upon the beautiful destruction she had wrought. Thousands of Seelie dead and dying—all because of her, our princess of darkest night and deepest shadow to whom we owe our allegiance and our lives." He finishes like a prayer, his voice solemn and deep.

When the room is silent again, I realize my mouth had dropped open at some point during his story, so I snap it shut. My Charlie did this? *My* Charlie who would go out of her way to save the lowliest creature on earth? I try to imagine her as a dark goddess, evil incarnate with doom shooting from her fingertips, but I can't. Even so, I believe him. Because my Charlie would absolutely do everything in her power to save the lives of innocents, even if it meant destroying herself in the process.

I let out a loud sigh. "That's going to take a while for me to digest."

He nods. "She means a lot to her people. I hope she knows that. When she left ... A lot of her subjects didn't understand why. I suppose I don't either. But we're all glad she's back here where she belongs."

But is this where she belongs? I don't know. She ran from here, after all. Or maybe—though I don't want to over-think it—maybe she was just running from herself, from what she did. I groan. The secrets she keeps are bigger than my entire life. And to think, I only kept her around because she could read the map. I snort a laugh at the ridiculousness of it all. But speaking of maps...

"Is there a library around here?"

"Sir?" His eyebrows rise.

"Don't call me sir. My name is G."

"I'm sorry, G. Yes, the largest library in all the Unseelie Court is located in the palace."

"Does it have maps?" The bread is good, too, almost a little sweet. Damn, the food alone is a hundred times better than anything I've ever tasted.

"I'm certain it does."

"Okay, I need you to get me one. I'm looking for the Wood of Mist, so make sure—"

"Oh, you don't need a map for that, sir—apologies, *G*." He strides to the window.

I follow him, my steps uneven.

"The main palace road—" he points "—see it there leading through the golden gates? It will take you north through the land and all the way to the border of the Seelie Court. The Wood of Mist lies there, straddling the line between the realms. But be warned, the Seelie roam these areas. You'll see just how foul they are if you truly intend to go to the Wood of Mist."

"I'm going, and soon. How long will it take to get there?" I lean on the wall, my entire body buzzing with warmth.

"If you ride without trouble on a decent horse, you can make it to the border in about a week, perhaps a little more."

"Fuck." I wipe a hand across my brow. "I'll need to ride through the night to make it in time." I have to leave the palace as soon as possible. I can't even wait till morning. Where is Charlie? This is her homeland. She has to know how far the Wood of Mist is and that my time is tight. Why wouldn't she have told me we need to leave as soon as possible?

He gives me a kind look, one that also has a bit of pity in it. "As I said, you can make it in a week if there is no trouble along the way. But the Seelie fae rebels have been seen at the border, and in the Wood of Mist in particular. That's not to mention the boggans, the Hag of the Bloody Stump, the imps are running riot this time of the season, kobolds, the Piper of the Shallows, the Eater—"

"Already handled that one." I raise my cup to him and drain it.

"Truly?" He laughs a little, then regains his stoic composure. "The Unseelie Court can be treacherous even for us, and we so rarely have human guests. If you venture beyond the palace, I hate to say it, but you will likely not make it through your first night in the wilds, or perhaps even in the villages."

"I'll worry about all that." I wave a hand at him, my fingers going squiggly in my blurry vision.

He gently pries the cup from my fingers, then his eyes widen in alarm. "I should've realized you ought not drink this, sir. I'm terribly sorry. Our wine is far stronger and laced with dewed honey."

"With whatsit?" The floor tilts.

Clotho catches me under one arm, and he grunts from my weight. "Oh, no." He sounds truly worried. "I wasn't thinking. My apologies." He helps me to the bed where I sprawl out, the sky above me swirling like liquid marble in hues of blue, gold, and white.

"You'll need to sleep it off. Again, I apologize. I'll bring water for you from now on."

"No." I reach up and try to grab the huge butterfly with the face of a lion that dances on the tip of my nose. "I like the wine. More wine!"

It's dark when I wake, my head pounding in steady thumps. The moon is above, mocking me in its more than half-full form.

I grunt and roll over, my mouth dry as I blink hard and sit up. There's something crinkly underneath me. I grab it and pull, then turn over on my back again. It's hard to tell in the dark, but I think it's a map. Clotho must've come through for me after all. I tuck it inside my tunic and sit up, my stomach threatening to empty all over the nice floors.

"Charlie?" My voice is hoarse, and there's no response.

The food is gone, and in its place is a large pitcher of what I hope is water. I get up, a mallet beating on the base of my skull, and stumble over to it, pouring myself a cup and gulping it down. There are fresh clothes draped over the side of the love seat, all of them in the servant green. I pluck up the cloak. It'll come in handy.

"Charlie?" I call again, even though I know she isn't here. Her warmth is missing. My chest aches again, and I rub two fingers over my heart.

She never came back. Where is she? Worry slithers along my spine, and I down another cup of water before rising. I stand still for a few moments until I know I can manage without falling on my ass. With a swipe, I grab my bow and cloak, then go to the doors and out of the room. There's no attendant out here now. I suppose that's only for when Charlie is here.

The scent of food is on the air, and my stomach churns with soured wine. I wipe my mouth with the back of my hand in case there's drool, then hurry down the stairs. One of the attendants dressed in green is standing there, gazing straight ahead.

"Where's the princess?" I ask.

"They are dining. If you'd like to dine as well, you'll need to use the staff entrance to the kitchens where—"

"Where's the dining room?" I glance around at the long hallways lit with glowing orange candles at intervals.

"Sir, you are not permitted to—Ah!"

I fist the front of his green tunic and push him against the wall. "Where is the fucking dining room?"

He juts his chin toward the main hallway, and I release him then hurry along it.

The scent of food intensifies, and I pass more statue-like servants as I catch the sound of voices. One of those is Charlie's.

I speed my steps, then stop when I come to a set of windows that are open to a courtyard. My eyes go straight to Charlie, her hand on a cup of wine as she sits beside her father.

A soldier across the way spots me and rests his hand on the hilt of his sword. If it wasn't already clear that I'm not invited, he'd certainly do the job of letting me know.

I back away a little, remaining in shadow as I watch the scene, but I can't take in any detail, not when Charlie looks the way she does. She wears a gown of light blue fabric, the shade matching her eyes and floating orbs of light glimmer over her head. A silver tiara sits atop her golden hair, jewels glistening in the ornate metalwork as her father leans closer to her and whispers something that makes her smile.

She's ... happy. Or at the very least, she's missed her father a great deal. They have a bond, one that's easy to see. The table has at least a dozen other fae sitting at it, but they're all watching her from the corners of their eyes or straining to hear whatever she and her father are discussing.

So beautiful, it's hard for me to imagine that I ever believed her to be a stable boy. She shines from every facet here, no dull clothes or a tatty hat to hide who she is.

I watch, notice the way she eats her food, the way she drinks her wine, the way she speaks to others at the table. She fits here, but she also fits with me. I *know* she does. Our time together was just as true as all this.

A door across the courtyard opens, and the fae from earlier—Tristan—strides in, his white tunic embellished with a collar of the same color as Charlie's dress. He moves straight for her, then takes the open seat at her side.

King Finnraven gives him an approving look, which I expected, and so does Charlie, which I didn't.

Tristan takes her hand and brings it to his lips. My hand is on the hilt of my sword, gripping it tightly. I want to murder him. That wicked streak is rising inside me, engulfing everything until all I can see is his severed head lying at my feet. But I don't move, don't fucking flinch. I wait.

"Throw him off, Charlie. Tell him to go fuck himself," I whisper.

But she doesn't. She smiles at him. She *smiles*.

My cracked heart begins to crumble at the edges, shards falling away and revealing the soft flesh at the center.

He's a twat. She knows he's a twat, and yet ... "*He may be a twat, but he has a whole face. He's the same breed. He's meant for her,*" my vicious mind whispers.

I step forward, my breath caught in my lungs as I watch her. "Look at me," I tell her softly. "Look at me."

He cuts a piece of meat and offers it to her on the end of his fork.

Her smile falters for only a second, but then it returns, and she opens her mouth, accepting the intimate gesture from him.

She never once glances in my direction.

The rest of the shards around my heart fall, piercing the still-beating organ and bleeding me as I step back into the shadows where I belong.

TWENTY-THREE

N o one bothers me as I leave the palace. The fae are peculiar like that. None of them gasp or gawk at my face. Instead, it's like I'm not even there. Because I'm a human, I'm about as noticeable as a fly on the wall—not that I've seen a single one of those in the palace. A couple of golden candelabras clink in my pack—I figure they might come in handy later— along with a few other shiny bits and baubles I found in the palace. No one will miss them, especially when this entire place seems to be coated in gems and precious metals.

After walking around a few courtyards covered in deep red roses and vines that wrap around arbors that rise several stories overhead, I spot a fae getting off a horse and handing the reins to an attendant. I follow the huge horse all the way to a building near one of the far walls.

It has to be the biggest stables I've ever seen, larger than the entire main street of Sac à Puces.

I sneak in, keeping my steps quiet as I ease along the stalls. The palace attendants might not ignore me if they think I'm stealing a horse, so I keep my head down and search as stealthily as I can. When I come to the end, I find an old friend munching on some hay. I grab Belinda's saddle from where it's been hung over the low wall of her stall, then walk inside.

She nuzzles me for the first time, her neck craning around and almost pinning me in a hug.

"Hey, girl." I return her embrace, then throw on her saddle and belt it into place. "Ready for another ride?"

She nuzzles me again, her face on my back, as if she knows I'm mortally wounded on the inside. I always thought I'd die before she ever showed me real affection. Turns out I was half right.

"Don't worry. I've got tons of provisions this time. Food, water, you name it. We're going to have an easy time of it." I run a hand down her mane, then take her bridle and lead her out of the stables.

The green-clad attendant doesn't look at us as we pass by, though I suppose he's not terribly impressed with us. From what I saw, the fae horses are far bigger than Belinda, but I wouldn't trade her. She's carried me this far.

Once we're out, I lead her away from the palace.

When we near the edge of the grounds, she slows, then stops, planting her hooves.

"What?" I turn to face her.

She turns to look behind her.

I sigh. "Listen, Charlie's not coming."

She nickers.

"I know. I thought she'd be here with us. With me." I scrub a hand down my face. "But she's where she belongs."

Belinda gives me a hard look.

"I want her here, too. I love her. I think you already know that." I look up at the sky, the stars here so much brighter than the ones I'm used to. "But she doesn't love me." Fuck. Why does saying it out loud gut me? I stand silent for a long time just trying to gather what's left of me. "She said some things that I thought she didn't mean. But then …"

Belinda puts her chin on my shoulder.

I pet her cheek. "I thought if I could fix my face, she'd be able to love me, you know? But I don't think it'll be enough. *I'm* not enough. Because I'm broken and an oaf and wicked—everything she's ever accused me of. She was right. You should've seen her at the palace." I sigh more deeply than I ever have in my life. "It's like … it's like we never happened. Maybe I was just a pet, like her father said. And now she's tired of me. She's moved on." I swallow thickly. "Even though I never will."

A huff of breath, and she presses herself against me harder in another hug.

"I want her, but I don't want to get in the way of her being happy." The hurt goes even deeper, all the way to my center. "I want to be selfish and march in there, slay that Tristan the Twat, and throw her over my shoulder. I think ... I think that's what the old me would do. I wouldn't give her a choice. I'd just take what I wanted. But I'm trying to be better. *She's* made me better. And as much as it fucking destroys me, I have to let her choose her happiness. Even if it doesn't include me." I swallow the lump in my throat, forcing the emotion away. "Because I love her."

She nudges me and chuffs.

I shake my head. "If this is what being good is all about, I fucking hate it."

A soldier walks past, surprising both Belinda and me. But he doesn't stop. His freakishly silent steps continue until he disappears through some hedges. I glance up at the moon. It's still making its journey to fullness, and I'll have to race it if I want to make it to the phylactery before the deadline.

"Okay, enough about feelings. They're dumb. Right, girl? You and I are going to get what we came for. We're going to find that phylactery, and I'm going to get back everything I've lost. We stick to the plan." I give her one more pat and take the reins.

This time when I lead her, she follows.

THE TOWN outside the palace is unlike anything I've ever seen. The buildings are made of stone stacked perfectly, intricate designs created along the walls with various colors of tile. Fae move about much like humans, some of them shopping, others hurrying past as if they're late. For being the realm of the Lord of Death and Darkness, it's a lively place. Shops are open despite the hour, and I pass what I'm certain must be a tavern, music floating from it as raucous laughter erupts somewhere inside.

I don't feel much like company, so I cluck my tongue and hurry Belinda along, her hooves sure on the level cobblestones. Nothing this fine exists in my world, at least not that I've ever seen. I'm used to dirt and grime covering everything, including me, but here even the stones beneath Belinda's hooves are neat and orderly. The air is scented with dark flowers that grow along eaves and up the sides of buildings, not sewage and garbage.

"Your fortune?"

Belinda stops and backs up a few paces, her hair bristling.

A woman strides from the shadows, her dark hair piled on her head and large hoop earrings brushing against her thin shoulders. "A mortal like you should know his fate before he falls upon it."

"I already know my fate."

"Do you?" She holds up a black orb, the center swirling in vivid purple. "Look into my crystal. You'll find yourself there." She smiles, two black fangs protruding from her mouth.

My blood goes cold. "I don't need whatever it is you're selling." I shake my head, but then I see movement in the crystal ball, the purple growing lighter and turning into a form. I'd know those hips anywhere.

"Charlie?"

"Yes." The woman is closer now, her hand reaching for the reins. "Keep looking."

I watch as the shadowy figure of Charlie begins to spin, then a male figure appears beside her. I can't see him fully, but I know it's the lord she's supposed to marry. He grips her waist and pulls her closer. I can't look away, not for a moment. If I do, I'll lose her for good. I'll—"Hey!"

Belinda rears, her startled neigh yanking me from my reverie as I hold onto the saddle horn.

The strange woman hisses and backs away, her movements eerily smooth, two golden candelabras clutched in her hand.

"Wait! I stole those. They're mine. Come back here, you—"

But she disappears into the shadows between buildings, taking my ill-gotten goods with her.

"Dammit!" Goosebumps erupt along my skin when I realize the woman had bared her fangs and was about to bury them in my thigh. I'd been too ensnared in the crystal ball. If Belinda hadn't startled ...

"Thank you." I lean down and press my forehead to her mane. "Good girl."

She starts walking again, though her steps are a bit hesitant, as if she's calculating where the next wily fae might pop out from. I don't blame her. It was a slick robbery. I'm beginning to think there's some truth in what Clotho told me—these lands are treacherous, and I need to watch my ass. Paraphrasing, of course.

We keep riding until the buildings become shorter, houses of the same stone rising on either side of the lane. The dark flowers grow here, too, their perfume more intense as a woman sings in a voice as delicate as glass and a group of fae children chase a rabbit from yard to yard.

The world is far bigger than I ever imagined. But it's also empty. I glance behind me for the dozenth time, hoping to see Charlie galloping up, her customary hat on her head and a wry smile on her beautiful face, but she's never there. When I think of her in Lord Twatface's arms, I grip the reins tighter, so much so that Belinda nickers.

"Sorry." I loosen my hold. "Sorry, girl. It was nothing." I pat her neck.

She turns her head and looks at me with one judgmental eye, then turns back to the road ahead.

I have to stop thinking about Charlie, about the way she insulted me in a million clever ways, the way her hair forever tickled my nose, the way she had this sweet smell —I inhale and realize why the dark flowers smell so familiar. Notes of their aroma are in Charlie's scent, her homeland stamped into her skin.

"Everything here reminds me of her," I mumble.

I glance back once more, then force myself to look ahead. Only ahead. The reminders of her are like thorns burrowing into my chest, searching for my heart to twine around the shredded bits that are left.

I have to get out of this village, away from the palace that rises behind me, its upper turrets shining in the velvety darkness. "Let's go, girl." I press my heels into Belinda's sides and pull my cloak closer around my face.

She picks up her pace, carrying me away from Charlie and closer to my destiny, the night devouring us whole.

TWENTY-FOUR

The village is long gone, the road nothing more than two ongoing divots with wild grasses growing between them. I've passed a few travelers, one in a large cart with whimsical music playing, another riding like all the devils in hell were on his tail. I kept staring toward the direction he'd come from, expecting something horrible to appear on the horizon, but nothing ever did.

We've been riding for three days, only stopping for short breaks. I know I'm pushing her too hard, but I have no choice. My time is ticking down to nothing, and there's still plenty of distance between me and the phylactery.

I lead Belinda off the road and stop, the morning sun warm on my back as I dismount. "I know you're tired." I pour her some water into a bowl and pull out some fruit from my pack. "Here."

She eats them greedily, then shows me her teeth and demands more.

"Water first." I point her to the bowl I've set on an abandoned anthill.

While she drinks, I stretch and walk around a bit, the high grass full of sounds—insects trilling and something scurrying away through the thatch. I can't see anything but rolling hills ahead and behind. We came to a crossroads when the sun had just risen, but I couldn't read the sign affixed to one corner. Though, to be fair to myself, I don't think it was in any language I've ever known. I just stick to the road and hope Clotho didn't send me astray.

"I'll let you sleep tonight." I return to Belinda who's munching on some of the high grass. "I promise. But tomorrow night, we'll have to ride through it again. I don't have long before the Fallen Moon. Once I get the Phylactery, we'll both be due for a long rest, all right?"

She presses against me in a brief hug, then goes back to munching. I let her eat for a while longer as I snack on some grapes and pull out the map Clotho gave me. It also has writing I don't understand along with notations for various areas. The road I'm on is marked, and the rolling hills around me are drawn in simple hump shapes with golden grass atop them. Then after this is what must be a swamp, given the water and the clumps of vegetation. It's labeled, but I've been thinking of it as the Lumpy Swamp, so I'll keep with that.

Then there's a plain, this one orange and somehow dusty looking. And after another expanse of rolling hills is a forest at the edge of the map. White fog is clearly drawn seeping through the trees. The Wood of Mist. I stare at that patch of trees for a while, my mind envisioning the lady from the water waiting there, watching to see if I can make it before my time is up. Once I have the phylactery, will she reward me immediately? Will I finally be whole again right then and there? Because if I am, I know where I'm going next—even if it's foolish, even if it's too late. I'm returning to the palace, to Charlie.

Maybe when she sees me as an entire man, not a broken thing, she'll change her mind. She took pity on me before. It's the only reason she agreed to come with me in the first place, the only reason she's agreed to stay with me. She's too kind to say anything about the hard truth of my appearance, but I know what I look like. No matter how many times I tell myself I don't care, I fucking do. I have to. I know I'm a monster. But what if I can prove to her I'm someone she can be proud of? Then I won't have to let her go. Hope still lives in my breast, the thinnest flame of it dancing and glowing despite the dark.

I stow the map, confident I'm headed the right way, and lead Belinda back to the track before mounting her. "Let's go. We're burning daylight."

She's still chewing and moves at a leisurely pace, grabbing tufts of grass here and there instead of concentrating on the road.

"Don't make me smack your behind." I run my fingers along her mane and pull a little.

She nickers, but not angrily. It sort of reminds me of—*No*!

I refuse.

Every fucking thought leads me back to the same place. I can't think of her except in wishes and hopes. It's too raw otherwise. Too goddamn horrible. But it's too late. Blue eyes and a devilish smile come into my mind's eye, then golden hair, then more of her—all of her. My broken heart bleeds more, but I can't stop it. Not my longing for the part of me that's missing, or the ache it causes.

I pull my cloak tightly around my shoulders as if a cold wind blows, though the air doesn't stir, and I can't protect myself from what's inside my head.

At least I've stopped looking back for her. That's progress. I'm still weak and pathetic, but at least I have a shred of dignity. Just a tiny shred that I cling to with all the might left in my body. But if I look back again, it'll be gone.

Iᴛ's late before I finally relent and make camp. We're at the edge of the swamp, the scent of muck already in the air. Belinda needs a real rest, and it's best we bed here before the ground turns to squelchy shit.

She's lying behind me, snores already rumbling through her nose as she slumbers. I stoke the fire, then lie back and stare up at the sky. The night air is cool, but not uncomfortable, and my stomach is full of food from the palace and a hare I took as I was riding. The moon looms overhead, only one side of it missing. I sigh and glance toward the bog, then take a swig of the fae wine I'd nabbed from the palace.

The euphoria sets up in my blood, erasing some of the pain. Not enough, though. I don't know if it will ever be enough. So I take another drink, the warmth tracing a warm path down my throat and to my belly. It makes everything so much better. I've been sipping it here and there along the road. Not too much, of course. I need my wits about me in these strange lands. But enough. Enough so that I don't feel the blade in my back, the one that's pierced my heart. Enough so that I don't hold her in my mind's eye, just watching her and looking at nothing else. The fae wine could never get rid of her all the way, but at least it keeps her on the edges, her mischievous eyes watching me, not judging me.

A toad lets out a croak, then a belch from the swamp, interrupting the frog songs for only a moment before they start up again. The swamp has its own music, I suppose. I don't look forward to navigating its boggy path, but it's the only way to make it to the Wood of Mist. Even if it seemed impossible, I'd still give it a go. I'm so close now that anticipation makes me restless, unsettled. Sleep doesn't come, not when I can't tear my thoughts away from the phylactery ... and from Charlie. She stands there at the edge of my mind, her form like smoke. I can't grasp her, can't hold her close, no matter how badly I want to.

I'm still peering at the shadowy, scraggly trees when a light appears between the ones closest to me.

"Whoa." I sit up and stare at the orb that floats high off the ground. Maybe it's a fairy? Now that would be something to see. Something scratches at the back of my mind, a memory I suppose, but it doesn't come to me.

I stand and venture toward it, pulling my cloak tighter around my shoulders to stave off the night wind.

"Hello?" I call to it.

It seems to vibrate at my voice, then floats backwards, moving away from me.

"Wait!" I move faster, trying to get a better look at it.

It floats farther away, dancing between the gnarled limbs and floating over the scrubby bushes. I follow it, then stop. More lights dance through the trees, orbs lighting deeper in the bog, all of them somehow dancing to the same tune. I have to catch one. Or maybe they're leading me somewhere important? I don't know.

I change directions, going after first one, then another. I almost lose a boot in a particularly muddy spot but wrench it from the ground and find a dryer area to continue my search.

The more I chase, the farther they seem. Eventually, I stop and turn around. Where's the fire? Fuck. When I look again, the lights have disappeared.

"Hey, wait!" I spin again, though I see nothing save the moon and stars overhead. No more lights dance in the trees.

The scratching in the back of my mind turns into more. Into a memory of the witch of Sac à Puces saying "*Don't follow voices or lights in the trees.*" I take a deep breath and feel a compelling urge to kick myself. Why did I follow it in the first place? Did the orb hex me or something? I refuse to blame the wine, because if I did, then I couldn't drink it anymore. And I *really* need that wine.

The wind blows the stinking smell of fetid mud to my nostrils, and I spin again, this time more slowly. Belinda has to be nearby. I wasn't walking for that long, was I? Maybe if I whistle for her—

"Lost, young man?"

I startle. Ahead of me, sitting atop a stump, is a woman.

"Where did you ..."

She crosses her legs at the knee, her long red dress puddling beneath her, and her red hair curling around her face. "Lost?" she asks again with a beguiling smile.

"No." I reach for my sword. It's not there. I'd been lying down to sleep when the light charmed me into following it. Now I'm defenseless in the bog with a strange woman. "I'm fine. Just leave me alone."

"Why so hostile?" She pouts, her eyes glinting in the moonlight.

"Not hostile, but I already had a run-in with a mysterious lady. One with fangs she tried to use on me. Do you have fangs?"

She laughs and opens her mouth, showing me her white teeth. Her *normal* white teeth.

"Satisfied?"

"If you could just tell me which way my camp is."

"Your camp?" She leans forward, her dress gaping at the front. "Are there more mortals?"

"See, the way you said that ..." I back up a few steps, one of my boots sinking into the mud again. "It doesn't give me any reason to trust you, you know? It was a bit too—"

"Friendly?" she asks.

"No, I was going to say bloodthirsty." I yank my boot from the muck and realize I'm on an island with this creature—for I have no illusions that she's a young woman as she appears—surrounded by watery swamp.

She sighs. "I simply noticed you were lost and wanted to offer my assistance." She bats her lashes.

The wine is telling me this is great, that she'll help me. But I'm not so sure. The wine, if I'm being honest, is the reason I'm here in the first place. "What are you doing out here?"

"I like to go on moonlight strolls, and I followed the lights through the trees. They led me here, and I thought all was lost. But now I'm saved. I've found a gallant young man to help me out of this perilous plight."

"Where did you come from?" I edge around the lopsided island, searching for an escape. "I haven't seen a single village or farm for quite a while along the road."

"I live on the far side of the swamp in a little cottage," she replies smoothly. So smoothly that I get the distinct impression she's had this very same conversation several times. Just not with me.

"Alone?"

"Yes. My poor father passed away some time ago. Eaten by a wolf." She grins. "And now I live all alone." The grin turns back into a pout. "No man to warm my bed. It's quite lonely out here. You're a strapping young fellow, though. Wouldn't you like to come to my cottage?"

I hold up a hand. "Now listen, lady, I'm not warming anyone's bed. If you must know, I'm quite wicked. A really bad character, as they say. So, you don't want to mess with me. I gesture toward the scarred half of my face. "Insides match the outsides."

"I'll be on my guard." She smiles, and her eyes grow a bit wider. "My cottage is warm and dry, though now I'm not sure if I should invite you in. Bad men scare me." She puts a demure hand to her chest. "I wouldn't want to lose my innocence or be forced. How very dreadful." Her vicious grin reappears, then fades.

She's toying with me. I know it. By the gleam in her eye, she knows I know it.

"Still, you seem like the honorable sort. Come to my cottage." Her eyes glow, reflecting back the light just like a cat's.

Despite my efforts, I've yet to find a dry path away from the stump and the lunatic perched on it. "I need to get through the swamp and out the other side."

"Why?" She turns with me, her gaze never leaving me.

"I'm on a quest."

"Well, doesn't that sound exciting? What sort of quest?"

"One that has nothing to do with you," I say pointedly.

"If you'd only come to my cottage, I could help you. I have maps that show the safest paths through the swamp."

"I'm not going to your cottage."

"But my cottage—"

I groan. "Listen, have you met the Eater? Are you two related? Friends, maybe? In on this together somehow? Because the Eater had the same persistent, annoying tone, and I'm certain you're both on the same level of bad."

At this she sits up and hisses, the sound sending a chill down my spine.

"The Eater?" She scoffs. "He is nothing to me. How dare you compare us!" Her voice changes, no longer high and sweet. It's lower, rougher.

"So, I take it you know each other?"

She crosses her arms over her chest, where I notice black hair is beginning to sprout. "Yes, I know him. He's an amateur. One of my *many* admirers. He rolled through here long ago seeking more souls to add to his purse." She makes a disgusted face. "Thought to come upon me and ask me my name. The audacity!" She spits an impressive distance, then wipes her mouth with the back of her hand.

I grimace, but recover and say, "I'm glad you escaped unscathed."

She stands, the dress shredding along the hemline and sticking to the stump. "He posed no threat to me, the fool. He's lucky I let him live, let him continue his artless assault on the world with his incessant question. No artistry in it. A monstrous, foolish killer with no flair. Reprobate. Nothing clever about him."

"Then it will please you to know I ended him."

"What?" She spins, her gaze cutting through me. The dress melts away and remains on the stump as the creature grows bigger, dropping its false skin as if it's nothing more than a cloak. Taller than me, and covered with a thick thatch of dark brown hair, she rises like one of the twisted trees, muck coating her legs up to her knees and her black hair hanging in filthy strings around her head. "You, a filthy human, killed the Eater?" She leans over, her black eyes peering at me as all her pretense falls away.

"I did. He came to the mortal world and tried to get my name."

"You didn't give it?"

"No." I shrug. "I couldn't. I don't know it."

She stomps around the stump, which I realize isn't covered in a tattered red dress. It's blood, the syrupy red liquid soaking the stump and the ground around it.

"The Hag of the Bloody Stump," I mumble, remembering Clotho's warning.

"You know what they call me, do you?" She moves away a few paces, her spine protruding in lumpy waves all the way down to her hair-covered ass.

"I mean no offense. I heard it from a servant at the palace." This monster is massive, and I have no weapon to defend myself. Maybe I can talk my way out of this? I can hear Charlie laughing at the thought of it, a new wound when I need it least.

The hag whirls fiercely, her hair slinging out and pelting me with foul water. "*You've* been to the palace? To King Finnraven?"

"Yes. That's where I came from." I hitch a thumb over my shoulder, though I haven't a clue which way the palace lies.

She points at me with a long, bony finger. "What business does a mortal have with the Unseelie King?"

"I didn't have any business with him at all. I'm simply here for my quest."

She watches me for a while, all manner of wickedness brewing behind her eyes. Every second I spend here is a second that's leading to doom. I have to escape, but I still haven't found a single viable path away from the hag. It's as if the ground behind me turned to mush the moment I stepped from it.

She plops down on the stump, her wretched gaze turning something akin to amiable. "Anyone on a quest needs help. What can I offer you?"

"Nothing." I shake my head. "I'm just going to head back to camp."

"And you're alone?"

I try to weigh if the truth or a lie is more dangerous. Given her similarities to the Eater, I have to assume she intends to devour me and would delight in devouring anyone else in my party.

"Out here, yes. But back at camp, I have two squires. They're sleeping now."

Her eyes narrow. "Why did it take you so long to answer?"

"I couldn't quite hear you." I tap the ear on the ruined side of my face. "Doesn't work so well anymore."

"Oh." She clacks her teeth and speaks louder. "Tell me what you desire, young mortal. Let us make a bargain."

"I could use some help, now that I think about it. But I'm a bit out of sorts here in the swamp. If you could return me to my camp, I might be able—"

She clucks her tongue. "A trick. I can smell it." She taps her bulbous nose, the tip of it covered in dark purple veins. "Are you trying to be clever?"

"I'm not known for being clever, no."

"Then what are you known for?"

I turn the ugly side of my face to her once again. "This, mostly."

"That's nothing." She scoffs and waves a clawed hand, as if batting away a pesky fly. "Humans and fae are alike in that regard—too concerned with the outside, not enough with the inside." She cackles, and the floating orbs light all around us at the sound. The bastards have been hanging here this whole time, watching. "Appearances." She sighs and runs her nails across the stump, blood welling from it. She wipes it along her fur, and in only moments, has become the beautiful young woman in the red gown. "I'm just as vicious like this, young mortal." She laughs. "Perhaps more so. Just as this pretty skin doesn't change my nature, neither do your scars."

"My nature was already wicked. I wasn't lying about that."

"Wicked?" She stands and advances on me, her dark eyes flashing. "I know my own kind. The true creatures of the Unseelie Realm. Ones created by the evil that lurks in the darkest creases of the world or those monsters made by the royal bloodline. You are neither."

She stands only a few paces away, her shrewd gaze devouring me.

"In the mortal world, I was a monster."

Her grin reappears. "Why, what horrors did you commit? Drink the blood of innocents? Crush their bones and use it for face paint?" She drags her long fingers across her cheek. "I've done that many a time."

"I don't remember."

She blinks.

"Look, it's a long story, but I almost drowned in a river, got half my face destroyed, badly injured, lost my memory, and then I heard a voice that told me I needed to come here to get my memories and my face back."

Her fingers have turned into claws again, and she taps one on her chin. "What did the voice say?"

I shouldn't be telling her this. I should be running, even if it means going half speed because of the damn mud. Instead, I say "*If you would recover what you've lost, you will travel to the Wood of Mist and find the Graven Phylactery before the end of the Fallen Moon. Fail in this task and you will live a long life, forever cursed with what you lack.*"

She cackles and spins away, her arms out wide. "A riddle! I *love* riddles!"

I cock my head to the side. "No, it's not a riddle."

"Of *course* it's a riddle." She returns to her stump and draws her legs beneath her, giving her the appearance of a perching gargoyle like the ones I saw in Paris. "Oh, it's a clever one. So apt to many meanings."

I scoff. "The meaning is clear. If I can get this phylactery thing, then I will get my memory back and my face will be fixed. Then I can undo whatever wicked life I used to lead and—"

"Oh?" She cackles. "You know it down to the very letter, do you?" She shakes her head, the stringy hair reappearing. "You are a fool to take it at face value."

"Then what do you think?"

She grins. "You wish to make a bargain, then?"

"I'd prefer to not be eaten."

Her pout returns, though it is decidedly ineffective now that she's back in her hideous form. Then her face brightens. "How about we make a deal for your squires?"

I pull back and do my best to look aggrieved. "I couldn't give them up like this. That would be horrible."

"For one who claims to be wicked, you certainly go green at the thought of slaughter," she goads.

"It's just that they are very kind boys. Orphans. I brought them along to help me on my quest, and they've since become very close to my heart."

"Closer than the quest that may spell your doom?"

I wring my hands. "No. But they're so young, and they trust me."

She runs a claw through the matted hair on her chest. "Best give them to me before the world turns them ugly and bitter. It would be a mercy. You'd be doing something good. No more wickedness for you."

I sigh heavily and pace for a while. "Would it hurt?"

She ponders for a while. "I prefer to hear them squeal and beg. I like to kill them on my stump, their blood a treat for many years to come." She drags a knuckle across

THE BOOK OF G

the welling blood and licks it away. "But only after the bargain is struck. The bargain is key. The give and take. The offer and rejection, and then, *then*—" She sighs dreamily. "—the acceptance. When I reach that peak of offering someone something they can't live without. Then they offer me something precious to them in return, oftentimes their lives." She shivers, a rapturous look on her terrible face. "They think they can cheat me, can escape the fate they've chosen for themselves. Oh, how I adore the look in their eyes when I have them in my claws, and they realize—*I see it when they realize it*— that I've had them there all along. Right here." She holds out her hands. "Right here, their life suspended in these glorious fingers from the time we met until the time they die. That is the art, the beauty. That is what separates me from creatures like the Eater who have no finesse, no code."

I clear my throat. "So, will my squires suffer or what?"

She cuts me a fierce glare and grumbles under her breath, then says, "For this deal, I'd make it quick. If they're asleep as you say, they'd never even see me, just be gone in their dreams."

I let my head fall back and consider the moon overhead for a long while. Though I'm not considering the deaths of my imaginary companions, I *am* considering what will happen when the hag realizes I'm lying. I have to hope I can make it to my sword before her claws make it to me. Unless she's right and I'm already clutched between them, their sharp tips digging into my skin. *Fuck.* This whole thing is a huge risk. Charlie would say I'm being an oaf. But my oafishness has gotten me this far, so why stop now?

"Are they young and meaty like you?" She licks her lips with a green tongue.

"To be honest, one is quite thin—" She grimaces "—but the other is constantly teased for his plumpness. With his shirt fully buttoned, he looks like too much sausage in a thin casing."

Her eyes brighten at that. "That would keep me fed for quite some time." She rises. "Let us go to your camp and continue our negotiations there."

I hold up a hand. "Hang on."

"What?"

"I'd be a fool to take you to them without having made our deal first. What's to stop you from eating them and reneging?"

She gives me a sly look. "I wouldn't turn such a trick."

I stare back at her for long moments.

"Ack, fine." She huffs and plops onto the stump again, sending bits of blood squirting from it. "What do you wish for your part of the bargain?"

"Figure out the riddle and explain it to me." The lady in the water's instructions seem clear, but Charlie remarked on several occasions that it might not mean what I think it does. If the hag can give me more insight, I'd be a fool not to take it.

"That's all you wish?" she asks, leaning forward and putting her hands on her bony knees.

If I could wish Charlie back to me, I would, but this creature doesn't have that kind of power. More than that, I want Charlie to come to me because she loves me as I love her, not because of some spell or silly magic trick.

"Hmm?" she asks. She seems particularly eager to eat my squires, especially the plump one, poor lad.

"Yes. We have a deal."

She cackles loudly, all pretense gone. The glowing orbs light again, mocking me from their positions all around us.

She holds up a crooked finger. "The first piece 'if you would recover what you've lost'—that's as vague as prophecy."

"I've lost my memory, my—"

"Shh!" she snaps, her gray teeth bared. "You've lost what I can only assume are your good looks, some of your strength from injuries, and your memory, as you say. But have you lost more?"

"Huh?"

"What have you lost on your journey, and what have you yet to lose?"

There's so much. Not the least of which was Charlie.

"Think on it." She holds up a second crooked finger. "The second part *'Fail in this task and you will live a long life, forever cursed with what you lack'* is even more interesting. If you fail your task, you will live a long life." Her eyes bore into me. "So what do you think happens if you succeed?"

I see where she's going, but that can't be right. I shake my head at the hag's implication. "No. That's not possi—"

"The Graven Phylactery is no easy quest, especially not for a mortal. The Wood of Mist is home to many foul creatures." She smiles wistfully. "Each one of them hungry for your bones. And the phylactery contains the soul of an ancient dark sorcerer, one who created the Wood of Mist to shroud his evil magic and profane necromancy. You think retrieving it is a task that will leave you alive?" She cackles. "The riddle is clearer than the purest water. To succeed is your death. It is better for you to live with what you lack than to endure certain death to retrieve it."

"That's …" I don't accept it. I can't. "The lady in the water wouldn't have set me on an impossible quest. That's not—"

"Aren't you the one who said you were *wicked*? So very, very vile in the life you don't recall?" She clacks her teeth. "The wicked deserve punishment. Perhaps this is yours."

I wipe a hand down my face, my skin suddenly clammy. "You don't know that. You're just reading into what she said. But that doesn't have to be what it means." I step toward her. "Right? That's not final."

"I've held up my end of the bargain." Cruelty coats her voice as she holds her hand up and twirls her finger. "Now it's your turn."

The orbs glow, all of them flying away and forming a straight line. In the distance, at the end of the row of asshole fairy orbs, I see the flicker of firelight.

The hag stands, her bones cracking and popping as she lumbers toward my camp—the one without a single squire in it, chubby or otherwise. "To your friends, young mortal. The hour grows late, and my stomach rumbles."

I hurry to keep up with her, the ground sturdy beneath my boots when it was nothing but putrid muck only moments ago. "Listen, the sun will be up soon. How about you let me give my squires one more good day. A final meal. Fatten them up for you. How does that sound?"

She doesn't even slow down. "It sounds like you're trying to make another bargain, one that doesn't bode well for you."

"I was only thinking that you've been so kind to interpret the quest for me that I could return the favor with the squires. The skinny one especially, he could do with a full stomach before you eat him."

She laughs. "I'll use his thin bones to pick the gristle from my teeth. Don't worry. Nothing will go to waste."

The firelight grows brighter, and I can just make out Belinda's faint snores. We're almost there, the hag barreling ahead, her claws out at her sides.

"I can hear the plump one." She cackles, then cuts off the sound, perhaps remembering not to wake them.

Belinda heard her though, because she rises to her hooves and whinnies.

"Wait!" I hiss at the hag.

"No waiting." She jumps into the firelight, her claws high in the air.

Belinda bolts, taking off down the road and away from the swamp. I dart into camp and draw my sword from my pack.

"No squires." The hag roars and turns to me, her eyes a matte black as she bares her teeth—now I see the fangs—and roars at me again. "Deceiver!" She slashes at me.

I stumble backwards and raise my sword, swinging to ward off her blows. She screeches and comes for me as I swing again, catching her in the arm. Black blood spurts from her, but she isn't deterred.

"You think you can trick Belmordrid, Hag of the Bloody Stump?" She charges me, knocking me back with the force of her impact.

My sword goes flying as she pins me to the ground, her claws digging into the dirt on either side of my throat.

Looming over me, she hisses, her black eyes like pits of tar. "I told you this quest would end in your death, did I not?" She clacks her teeth, spittle flowing in strings and dribbling along my cheek.

I reach for something, anything, but the ground is barren. No weapons, not even a rock is within my grasp.

"There it is." She grins. "That look. You thought you could beat our bargain. You're just another meal. You've been in my claws the entire time." She leans closer, opening her mouth wide to show me a row of fangs behind her front teeth.

I yell and kick at her legs, but she isn't deterred. The gaping maw expands, her jaw disjointing like a huge snake as I try to fight her off.

She doesn't budge. I turn my head to the side and feel her tongue slither along my ear. The stench of her breath washes over me, and I know this is it.

With another hard kick, I try to force her away. It doesn't work. Her teeth press against my head, the fangs cutting my scalp as I bang on her arm that holds me captive on the ground.

Her jaws start to close, pain ripping through my scalp, but still I fight. I won't give up until I'm dead, that much I know for certain.

My vision goes dark, swallowed by the void of her mouth, the world nothing but rows of sharp teeth, serrated pain, and looming death.

TWENTY-FIVE

The hag jolts, and then I hear the sound of a bow string singing.

"Get off him!" My heart swells at the sound of that voice.

The hag jerks again, and the vicious pain of her fangs retreats. Light returns.

"He's mine!" the hag roars and turns, hissing as Charlie rides up on Belinda.

Charlie fires a torrent of arrows onto the hag, sending her stumbling back.

I roll away and search for my sword as the hag shrieks, the floating orbs darting away, retreating into the swamp. When I find my sword, I turn to the hag. Her claws are raised as she charges Charlie.

"No!" I barrel toward her as Belinda takes off, galloping out of the hag's reach. Arrows stick out from her back, black blood dripping down the shafts as she chases after Charlie.

Charlie is still shooting, twisting her torso so she can let the arrows fly behind her. She looks like a warrior queen, her hair blowing in the wind as she lets out a war cry. But the hag is fast, her feet sure as she thunders after Belinda.

"Go! Don't stop!" I yell at Belinda as I follow them away from the swamp, the hag illuminated by the fading moon and rising sun. Her black form is even more massive, the gangly limbs and sharp claws the stuff of nightmares.

She hasn't slowed down, no matter how many arrows Charlie fires into her, she still runs in that horrible, deliberate fashion, as if assured she'll catch her prey. I won't let that happen.

"Let us make a bargain, pretty one!" she calls, taunting Charlie. "A bargain for your head. I shall wear it as a hat then place it on my stump."

Anger wells inside me at the hag's words, but Charlie's laugh is carried on the wind.

"As a hat, truly?" She taunts over the pounding of Belinda's hooves. They're making a wide arc now, Charlie leading Belinda back toward my camp, closer to the swamp.

"Truly!" the hag bellows. "Something pretty for when I feel fancy."

Charlie's laugh, utterly unafraid, warms me in ways I can't even explain. "I'm glad you think it worthy of fancy dress. I should be honored."

"You can tell me how honored you feel while I devour your tasty flesh." The hag lunges, her claws coming far too close to Charlie.

She should've ridden away, gotten safely out of the hag's reach.

"Almost," Charlie spurs Belinda to run faster, skirting the fire and making the circle again. "Perhaps you've lost some of your strength over the years since my father created you."

That's when I realize she's herding the hag. Bringing her in closer to me as she goes.

Charlie's words cause the hag to stumble, though she doesn't stop chasing. I don't think she can. It's her predatory instinct, stamped into her soul. To hunt, to kill, to devour.

"You are Princess Charlieta?"

"I am."

The hag cackles. "Do you expect me to bow? I'm afraid I've forgotten how to curtsy."

"Unnecessary. However, if you give up my man there and stop your hunt, I'll allow you to return to your swamp."

The hag snaps her teeth, her eyes finally finding me again. "And if I don't?"

"I'm afraid I'll have to tell my father I slew one of his favorites." Charlie nocks another set of arrows. She'll have to teach me that trick. Four arrows at once? Unheard of.

"A favorite, am I?" The hag's tone changes, becoming the sultry voice of the young woman on the stump, and she runs her claws along a strand of wet hair, toying with it as she slows. "He told you this himself?"

"Everyone knows he favors his oldest creations," Charlie says.

My eyebrows rise. My manners may not be on point, but even I know to *never* mention a woman's age.

"Oldest." The hag seethes. "Oldest, you say?"

Charlie smirks, knowing exactly what she's doing. "You were made before he even became king of the Unseelie. So old that the books in the palace library concerning your creation have long since crumbled."

The hag drops her piece of hair and raises her claws, splaying them wide. "I'm certain your royal bones will taste just like everyone else's." She attacks, rushing full force at Charlie.

But Charlie anticipated it, already moving Belinda to change direction and come racing back toward me, the hag on her heels. I raise my sword and charge to meet the creature.

The hag howls with triumph as she lunges for Belinda and brings herself right to me. I bend my knees then push, jumping into the air and shoving my sword into the hag's chest. The blade doesn't pierce her fully, the bones covering her heart thicker than the roots of a swamp elm. I hang onto my sword as she falls back, her claws scraping at my blade as she tries to pull it free.

I land on top of her, then with a mighty heave, shove the blade downward, cutting through her breastplate and sinking into her foul heart.

She lets out a bloodcurdling shriek, her black eyes focused on mine as I twist the blade for good measure.

"Wicked," she mutters, a blood bubble popping on her dark green lips. "You told me you were wicked. You were right." Her claws twitch and weakly scrape against my sword. Then she stills, a death rattle quaking from her lungs as she lies still.

Charlie jumps from Belinda and hits the ground beside me, her bow drawn, an arrow trained on the hag's forehead.

I climb off her, leaving my sword, and wipe the blood and muck off my face.

"Is she dead?"

"Yeah." I stare at Charlie. I can't look anywhere else.

She glances at me. "Are you okay?"

"Yeah." The sun rises behind her, giving her hair the golden halo effect I love so much. She hasn't even broken a sweat, her white tunic without a spot of blood on it.

Slowly, she lowers her bow, her gaze meeting mine.

I can't speak. All I can do is look at her.

"You left me." She yanks back on her bow and looses another arrow into the hag's face. "You left me without saying a *word*." She throws down her bow and stomps to me. "What the fuck were you thinking?" She puts her hands on her hips, the shallow wrinkle—the one that says she's pissed—forming between her eyes.

She's here. Right in front of me. I catch her sweet scent.

"I went back to my rooms, and you were gone. Are you even listening to me? I had to ride Binsaro half to death to catch up with you, and you—"

I yank her into my arms and kiss her fiercely, violently, passionately—in the only language I know when it comes to her. All my hurt, all my anger, it's in this one kiss. She grips my shirt, her fingernails digging in as I crush her against me. It's like breathing air for the first time, as if I'm surfacing from the dark, cold water and sucking in a lungful of freedom. That's what Charlie is to me. My freedom. My future.

A moan rises from her throat, and I swallow it greedily, trying to get every last bit of her. She's everything to me, and I may not have the words or the smarts to say it to her in poetry, but I can sure as fuck show her with my tongue. She sinks her nails in deeper and angles her head, fighting back against me, giving what she gets as our mouths war, our souls twisting and twining together. We're wrapped up in each other, a mess of teeth and nails and raw wounds that can only be healed by *this*. By being together. By knowing each other in ways no one else ever could.

We kiss and war until we can't breathe, can't think. When we finally pull apart, she takes in a deep breath, her lust-hazed eyes on me.

"I didn't just leave." I glare at her, my anger stirring right along with my need for her. "I *saw* you."

"What?"

"At dinner. With *him*. I saw you."

She shoves at my chest, but I don't let her go. "Are you spying on me now?"

"What else was I supposed to do? I wasn't invited to dinner."

"You were passed out drunk from wine!" She bares her teeth.

"You let him feed you," I growl, gripping her more tightly.

Her eyes flash. "I played the part my father wanted. That's all."

"The part where you marry an absolute twat?" I eye her mouth. Even now, I want more of her. *All* of her. "How far are you going to take this? Are you going to play the part all the way to the altar? Is that it?"

"You have no idea what you're talking about." She pushes me harder.

"Because I'm too dumb to understand, right?" I snap.

"No, because I don't want Tristan Martant!" she snaps right back. "I've never wanted him."

"It certainly didn't look that way when you were cozying up to him at the table," I sneer.

"Because you saw what I wanted everyone to see, what I wanted my father to see."

"Yes, you were very convincing." I slide my hand to her hair and grip it, wrenching her head back as I press my lips to her throat. "So convincing I thought about murdering Lord Twatty right there at the fucking table."

She moans, her hands no longer pushing me away as I whisper my lips across her ear. "But I didn't, because I wanted you to be happy."

Goosebumps erupt along her skin. "I'd never be happy with him."

"Why is that? He not wicked enough for you?"

"No." She shoves me again, fire in her eyes when I meet her gaze. "Because I'm in love with you."

I stop. *Everything* stops. I'd imagined those words from her lips more times than I could count, but actually hearing them is ... It's something else, something I never could've conjured in my wildest dreams. I may not remember my past, but I know without a doubt that I've never felt this before, because it's something more powerful than memory. Something unforgettable.

"Didn't you know?" Her voice is softer now.

"No." I swallow the lump of emotion in my throat. Can this be true? How can she love me when I look like this, when I'm so fucking broken inside and out?

"God, that look." She presses her palms to my cheeks, her voice soft now. "You, G. Not you with a different face or you with a past you can remember. I'm in love with *you*." She gets on her tiptoes and kisses me, her lips tender against mine. "Never doubt it."

My mind wants to doubt, to tell her that she couldn't possibly love me. Not like this. Not when she's the most beautiful creature I've ever beheld. But my wicked streak is still here, still branded beneath my skin, because I don't care if I don't deserve her. I want her, and I'll gut anyone who comes between us.

"There he is." She kisses me again. "I can tell when you decide to do the wrong thing."

I bite her bottom lip. "How's that?"

"You get this vicious look in your eye." She kisses one corner of my lips. "And you smirk."

"You love me?"

"I do." She kisses me again. "I've tried not to."

"Why would you do something silly like that?" I grab her waist and lift her until she wraps her legs around me.

"I've managed to avoid love for a long time." She shrugs, her fingers still grazing along my skin.

"Yeah, when you said you were older than me, I didn't know you meant ancient."

Her eyes narrow. "I'm not that old for a fae."

She feels so right in my arms. I can finally breathe again, my mind soothed from her presence alone. She fits me, not like a puzzle piece, more like a broken shard that can either cut me or make me whole.

"I could've handled the hag, you know."

She gives me an amused look. "Oh, sure, you looked like you had her well in hand, especially when she was about to devour your entire head in one bite." She feels along the side of my scalp.

I wince. "She got a little taste. That's all."

Her fingers come away bloody. "Come on, let's get you fixed up." She turns her head and lets out a high whistle. Wriggling from my hold, she slides to the ground.

Belinda nickers, her ears lying back as a black horse appears down the road. He's much larger than her, his bearing almost regal as he walks over.

"Belinda, this is Binsaro. Binny for short. He's a friend." She takes his reins and leads him over to a suspicious Belinda. But when Charlie puts her hand on each horse, Belinda's ears pop back up. "See? You already like each other."

Charlie drops back, and the horses nuzzle each other, sniffing and rubbing like a pair of old friends.

I should've seen it before. I mean, I always realized Charlie was good with animals, but it never occurred to me she had a magic fae power of communication. It explains plenty—from the pigs taking over Sac à Puces when we made our escape to the Beast of Gevaudon. She's been using her ability in plain sight the entire time.

"What?"

I realize I'm gawking at her. "Nothing."

She pulls a bag from Binny's back and sinks to my bedroll. "Come here. I need to tend those wounds."

"I'm fine." I sit beside her and pull her into my lap.

"G." She wrinkles her nose. "You need healing."

"I only need you." I lay her down, covering her with my body as I kiss her.

She protests and tries to sit up again. I don't let her, pinning her hands above her as I plunder her mouth. I need her far more than some fae salve. I kiss her until neither of us can breathe, the world falling away now that she's back in my arms.

When I kiss to her throat and bite down, she whimpers. It sets a fire in my blood, and I yank up her shirt to find her breasts, the nipples hard as I suck first one into my mouth and then the other. I give them ample attention, laving them with my tongue as I move my other hand between her legs. When I cup her sex, I feel her heat through her pants.

"Fuck." I get on my knees and yank at her belt, then unfasten her pants and rip them down her legs. I don't even finish pulling them off before I lean down and press my tongue between her folds.

She jolts. "G!"

I keep pressing my tongue against her slit, licking her clit until she's writhing beneath me and trying to open her legs. She can't, not with her pants still on, and I enjoy torturing her, teasing her clit again and again but not giving her enough to come.

When I get her close again, I stop and lick up her stomach. She lets out an enraged cry and smacks my shoulders.

"What?" I smirk and kiss her mouth again, sharing her taste as she threads her fingers behind my neck.

"I know you want to come." I nibble her bottom lip then kiss along her jaw. "But right now, Charlie?" I bite beneath her ear, feeling her shiver as I do it. "Right now, I want you in the dirt on your fucking knees for me."

She moans, the sound pure sex, and I finish yanking off her pants, pulling her boots along with them. Then I grab her hips and flip her over. Her skin almost glows in the early morning sun, the gold in her hair reflecting the light. I lean down and bite her ass as I free my cock. Then I move lower, licking between her thighs.

She moans when I touch her clit with the tip of my tongue. Then I drag it through her folds and back, circling her tight asshole. Her breath catches as I press against the hole, easing my tongue inside the slightest bit.

"G!" Her tone is tinged with alarm and lust.

"I'll have this soon enough." I lick her hole again, then higher, kissing her lower back then up along her spine.

I grip her hips and pull her back to my hard cock. Her cry is throaty and perfect, her back arching as she spreads her knees more for me. I slide my head along her slick folds, then align myself at her entrance. When I push inside, she cries out, and when I shove all the way with a grunt, she curls her toes.

I lean over her back, reaching beneath her and cupping one of her soft breasts. She pushes back against me, embedding me even deeper.

"Don't hold back." She turns and looks at me with one blue eye. "Never hold back."

I grip her shoulder with my other hand, then pull out and shove inside her. She clamps down on my cock, giving me perfect pressure as I start up a hard rhythm, our bodies in sync as we rut like animals beneath a watching sun.

"This is mine." I bite her shoulder. "Tell me, Charlie."

She jerks as I stroke her clit, my fingers circling it again and again.

"Yours," she chokes out, her breath coming in pants.

"Always mine. Forever." I grab her hair and pull her face around to me, then claim her lips. I tongue her, our bodies moving against each other as we chase our shared pleasure. Sitting back, I pull her up and thrust upward inside her, her legs still spread around me.

"G!" She reaches back and wraps her hands behind my head as I keep stroking her clit. Bouncing on my cock, she moans louder, her sexy noises rolling through me like lightning, my pounding heart the thunder.

I keep thrusting, nothing more than an animal who needs to claim his mate in the most primal of ways. I grunt and bite her neck, and when she moans, I almost come from the sound of it. We're both feral, both lost in each other. My knees burn from the hard ground, and blood drips down my shoulder from the hag's bite. I care about none of it. Only her.

When her hips seize, her breath catching in her throat, my balls draw up and my cock grows even harder. Her orgasm rolls through her, squeezing me in an irresistible rhythm. I can't hold out, my cock already kicking and spending inside her, my fucking vision going black as pure euphoria washes over me.

I yell her name, a guttural prayer ripped from me as I give her everything, emptying myself as I keep rolling my hips and stroking her clit. She shudders, her head falling back onto my shoulder as she takes in deep gulps of air. Bringing my fingers to my lips, I lick them clean.

"*Unf,*" she says.

I smirk and drag my fingers along her slit again, just so I can get more of her taste.

"Wicked." She kisses my throat, then slides forward and onto her knees.

"Where do you think you're going?" I crawl forward then stretch out by the fire.

When I pull her against me, she tries to resist. "I need to see about your head."

"My head's fine." I swipe the sweaty hair from her forehead and kiss her, then pull her on top of me. "Lie here with me for a while. Belinda needs more rest before we go. And I need more of your tight cunt." I lift a thigh, pressing it against her swollen sex.

She bites my shoulder, and I love the sting. "You're so filthy, G."

"But you love me." Fuck, that warms my black heart in ways I can't fathom.

"I do." She gives in and goes limp, draping herself over me.

We lie in the sun for a while, the swamp finally quiet as the bugs in the tall grass around us begin their morning songs. Belinda and Binny are lying together, back-to-back, and Belinda's usual snore lofts to us on a light breeze.

I sigh with utter contentment and run a hand down Charlie's back. "We still have to talk about it. About how you were at the palace."

She groans.

"I just want to understand you, that's all. Can you please help me?"

She props her chin on my chest, meeting my eye. "You've never asked for anything as nicely as you just asked for that."

"What can I say?" I shrug. "You bring out the best in me."

She snorts, then traces her finger around my nipple a few times.

My cock tries to come back from the dead at the sensation. "Are you trying to distract me? Because it's working."

"Maybe." She keeps tracing it, then moves to the center of my chest and runs her fingers through the dark hair that grows there. She takes a deep breath, holds it for a moment, then says, "I thought—I don't know—I thought maybe I could play along again. The way I used to. If I could simply sit through dinner and pretend to like it—to like Tristan—then maybe something would snap into place for me. All the parts of me that I felt were broken and shattered when I left—maybe they'd come back if I simply did what my father wanted."

"And did they?"

She sighs, her breath tickling along my chest. "No."

I drag my fingers up and down her bare back, greedy for the touch of her skin. "You felt broken and you left because of what you did to end the war, right?"

She tenses.

"It's all right, Charlie. Clotho gave me a decent overview of what happened." I kiss her crown, and she relaxes a little. "Though I suspect your recollection of it is a bit different from his."

"From everyone's. The entire realm thinks I did this great thing, but I don't. I know what I did. I've had to live with it every day since." She's silent for a little while, and her voice is sadder when she says, "They don't understand why I had to leave. My father, especially."

"I do." I press my palm flat against her lower back, holding her tightly to me. "You saved the realm, protected your father, kept the people in the palace safe —that's what Clotho sees. Everyone sees that, really. You're a hero."

She looks up at me, firelight playing in her watery eyes.

"But you don't see yourself that way, do you?" I stroke my thumb across her falling tear, swiping it away. "You think you're the villain, the most wicked of all because of the destruction you rained down on the Seelie that day, and you don't understand why no one else sees it."

Her chest quivers, her breath shaking. "I killed so many, G. So many. Ripped apart by the beasts at my command. I can still hear their wails, their cries for mercy. I gave none. The darkness in me—the same as my father's—used me as a conduit. Took my gift, my way with animals, and turned it into something terrible." She shudders. "We won the war, but the cost was too high."

"You did what you had to do."

"No, I made a choice." Her tone turns bitter. "A coward's choice. I sat with my father the entire night before the battle. He was dying, his wound too great to heal with the limited supplies we had left in the palace. The siege was killing him. My thoughts weren't for his life or for the lives of my people—they were for *me*. I didn't want to rule. Even if it was over the ashes of the Unseelie Realm, it was still too much for me to carry. I wasn't ready. I wasn't *him*. My father—I don't know how to explain it— he's more than just a fae. He's a god. The power he wields, the mantle he carries. It's as if he were made to be king. I could never stand in his stead."

"I don't believe that for a second. You're so strong, so brave."

She laughs harshly. "I wasn't even much of a princess. I shirked my duties, ignored protocol, did anything and everything to avoid the weight of my position." Resting her cheek against my chest, she continues, "So I had to make a decision that night. Either gather my courage and take my father's place or make a deal with the darkness that would save his life. And mine. I chose the latter. It worked. We won." A heavy sigh. "But the victory crushed me. The weight of my cowardice, of my refusal to lead the realm—it was like a poison in my gut, rotting me slowly. No one could see it. Every bit of praise, every grateful word stung me. They still do in a way, but the pain has faded in the years I've been gone. The memories are still there, though. I can still hear the Seelie I killed, still smell their blood. I made a choice, and I couldn't live with it. At least, not here. That's why I left. It's why you found me in Sac à Puces, a humble stable boy with a way with horses."

"A stable boy, yes. But 'humble' might be a stretch."

She snorts a laugh, the tension in her shoulders receding a bit.

I pull the blanket over us, the fire warm at our sides. We needed this. In fact, I think she needed her confession more than I did. Sharing pain doesn't make it hurt less, but it soothes the frayed ties between two souls.

"What, no words of wisdom?" she asks.

"From me? Absolutely not. Besides, you already know what I think."

"I do?"

"Yes."

She snuggles closer, her eyelashes fluttering against my throat. "Let me guess. I could rip apart a dozen orphans with my bare hands, and you wouldn't think any less of me. Something like that?"

I smirk. "You could drink their blood, too. I wouldn't care. I'd still love you, even if I might sleep with one eye open after that."

"What if I made a herd of goats attack a blind beggar?"

I shrug. "At least he wouldn't see them coming."

She snickers. "Awful."

I press my cheek to her hair. "Don't start calling me names, Charlie. I was just starting to get sleepy."

She stays quiet for a few beats. "Oaf."

"Charlie, I'm warning you." I reach down and grip her ass.

"Okay, okay. Let's go to sleep. We have a long way to go before we reach the Wood of Mist." She settles down.

I close my eyes, my entire world set to rights now that Charlie is here, and she *loves* me. That makes me smile.

She fidgets a little, then scoots up my body, her mouth at my ear. "Dolt."

"That's it." I pull her on top of me.

She yelps as I thrust against her.

"You brought this on yourself." I grab the nape of her neck and pull her down to me, kissing her senseless before making her moan.

TWENTY-SIX

It seems the only perilous thing about the swamp was the hag. Despite the smells and the bubbling mud, we follow the road through the depths of the bog and out the other side. Still, it eats into our time to navigate the wide expanse of it, and it's late into the night by the time the ground begins to slant upward and turns more solid.

Up ahead are outcrops of stone, grasses growing around them and leading to the orange plains marked on the map. A few nights more and we'll be at the Wood of Mist.

"I haven't been through here in ages." Charlie is astride Belinda while Binny carries me easily.

"I'm not a fan of this riding separate thing," I complain for the third time.

"You already miss me?" She looks over her shoulder.

"I miss grinding my cock against you and pretending it's just the motion of the horse."

"Oh, you thought you fooled me with that?" She laughs. "You're hilarious."

I grumble as fireflies begin to glow around us, fading in and out with their yellow light. "I'm not following you anywhere. So don't even try it." I glare at one as it flits past my nose.

"What?" Charlie rides beside me, her eyebrows up.

"Nothing." I swat one of them away. "Their cousins in the swamp were assholes, so I don't trust anything that glows."

"The wisps? They're not related. You don't have to worry about the fireflies."

I grunt my agreement, but I still keep an eye on the flying menaces. They aren't fooling me a second time.

"You know you should never follow the wisps," she chides.

"I know."

"Then why did you?" She glances at my saddle bag where the bottle of fae wine resides.

"Did Belinda rat me out about the wine?" I ask.

She snorts. "No. It doesn't work like that. But it makes more sense now. You were drunk."

"I had to do something about my heartache, now didn't I?" I shoot back.

She reaches across and grabs my hand, squeezing it in hers.

That's enough to melt me. I think she knows it. I'm weak for her.

"Tell me more about your animal magic." I gasp. "Wait! Have you been using it on *me*?"

She laughs, the sound full and loud. The fireflies seem to gather closer to hear it.

"No! It doesn't work on fae or humans. Only animals."

I sit back in my saddle. "That's a relief."

"You always do what you want." She gestures toward the road ahead. "We're going on your quest, aren't we? The one I'm still not certain of. I tried to talk you out of it, but it didn't work. You tried to talk me into it, and it did. You're far more persuasive than my power could ever be."

I flick some dried mud from my cloak. "I suppose you're right. I *am* very convincing."

"Don't let it go to your head."

"Too late." I smirk.

"Ugh. You're the worst."

"And you're only here to read the map." I dig around and pull out the one I got from Clotho, then hand it to her. "I'm confident we're going the right way, but just in case..."

She takes it. "We're definitely going the right way, but the map will come in handy all the same."

"The Lumpy Swamp is behind us, so what's ahead?"

"The Lumpy Swamp?" She shoots me a sideways look. "You mean Barren Bog?"

"Same." I point ahead. "What's this? The Hairy Hills?"

"What?"

"The tufts of grass. They look like hair. Seems like a good name."

"Try Raven's End."

"What sort of name is that?"

"At the heart of it, it's a graveyard for the Raven line of Unseelie kings and queens. I've ridden through here on my father's progresses. He tours the realm fully every ten years, and he always makes it a point to visit these lands and the cairns of our ancestors."

"Honestly, the Hairy Hills seems like a much more welcoming name, now that you've explained it."

"Afraid of some long-dead regents?"

"As long as they stay dead, I don't have a problem with them." I glance at the sky. Clouds are rolling in from our left, moving quickly from the looks of them. "But all this magic talk is making me wonder."

"They stay dead. Fae can have a wide range of natural gifts—"

"Magic, you mean."

She rolls her eyes. "Yes, as humans call it—*magic*. But I've yet to meet one who can beat death. Even the great necromancer, the one whose phylactery we're after—he couldn't do it. That's why his soul is trapped in some stupid bauble."

"What's the point of that?"

Belinda whinnies as a deer startles from the high grass and bolts. I grab my bow and load an arrow, tracing the deer's path with ease.

"Don't." Charlie reaches over and lowers my arrow. "She has young ones hiding deeper in the hills."

I let the string go lax. "I'm glad you didn't do stuff like this when we were starving on the road. I don't need the rabbit's back story."

She smacks my arm. "I didn't stop you then, did I? Most of the time, it's fine. Just this once, though, I asked for mercy. Besides, I brought plenty with me. We don't need fresh meat."

"Of course we do." I stow my bow. "Puts hair on your chest."

"You don't need any more of that." She grins. "You're full up."

"But what about you?" I let my gaze slide to the open neck of her tunic. "You could use a bit more."

She laughs. "You prefer the Hag of the Bloody Stump? She had plenty, as I remember it. She almost had your head, too, if I remember correctly."

The hag. Her words have been coming back to haunt me here and there. Was she right about what the woman in the water told me? Was it all a riddle that leads to my death?

"Oh, damn." Charlie stares at me. "What is it?"

"Huh?"

"Your face just went all gloom and doom."

I really need to work on a poker face, but with Charlie I can't seem to hide anything. She always knows somehow. Maybe it's because I'm more creature than man and she can sense things with her wild animal magic. "It's probably not important."

"Out with it." She rides closer.

"I made a deal with the hag—" I hold up a hand to stop Charlie from interrupting. "I know it was a bad idea, but actually it turned out to be a good idea because I got her to give her end, and then—"

"I didn't let her kill you."

"She was after my squires." I shake my head in dismay.

"You have squires now?" She looks around at the empty landscape.

"I did, one was particularly plump, but that's neither here nor there. Anyway, the hag gave me her interpretation of what the lady in the water said."

"And?"

"She thinks that if I get the phylactery, I'll die."

Charlie simply nods.

I expected a bit more concern, maybe some sort of dramatic 'oh no!', but she has her usual placid expression. "You ... you don't find that troubling?"

She shrugs. "Sure, but I already told you cryptic words from a lady in the water probably lead to ruin. You can't trust it. Come on, G. What the hag said isn't so far off from what I've been saying this whole time."

Shit. I suppose she has a point.

She reaches out and touches my arm. "Hey, we're going to get the phylactery, all right? I know how important this is to you, and I'm not going to try to talk you out of it. Besides, I won't let you die. You have your uses."

"I'm handy with a bow," I agree.

"You do plenty of other things. Mainly with your tongue."

"Just you wait, Charlie. When we have time, and I've got you in a proper bed—let's just say I've been making a list."

She laughs. "You can't be serious."

"I mean, it's not a written list. But I have been imagining quite a lot." Just the memory of her skin against mine sends heat sizzling through my veins.

"How have you had time to do all that?"

"I started the list the moment I saw those perfect tits."

"Just because I had breasts—"

"No. It wasn't *just* the perfect tits. I liked you, even before you were *you*. I can't explain it, but I feel like I've never truly cared for *anyone* the way I do for you. Like that part of me was covered in dust and forgotten. I don't know who I used to be, but I'm pretty sure I was a lonely, miserable asshole."

"And now you're just an asshole?" She smirks.

"Worse. I'm an asshole in love."

She shakes her head. "And I'm in love with an asshole."

"A perfect pair, Princess."

"Ugh, don't call me that."

"But you're a *princess*. Oh, your royal majestyness."

"Not a thing." She sighs.

"Wait." I reach out and grab her wrist. "Holy shit. Does this mean I can be a prince?"

"Have I mentioned you're the *worst*?" She yanks her arm back.

"I'm just saying. I mean, I would make an excellent —Hey!"

She smacks me hard on the thigh. "Oaf!"

"Don't start." I snatch her wrist again and bring her fingers to my mouth, biting down gently. Belinda glances back at us.

"Charlie started it." I kiss her knuckles one by one.

"No, you started it." Charlie bites her bottom lip.

Fuck, I love when she does that. "Maybe we could stop for just a—"

Thunder rumbles, cutting me off, and lightning pierces the billowing black clouds overhead.

"It's about to get rough." She pulls her hand back and grabs Belinda's reins. "We need to hunker down somewhere."

She's right, but stopping for the storm comes with its own danger. We're running out of time, the weather slowing us down even more. It feels like every time I advance a few paces in this journey, something knocks me on my ass. Maybe it's cursed. Maybe *I'm* cursed and will remain that way forever, just like the lady in the water said.

"We'll make it." Charlie pats Belinda's rear end. "Let's pick up the pace. If we can get to the funeral grounds before the rain, we'll find decent shelter. Then we can wait for the weather to pass. If we keep a good pace, we should reach the Wood of Mist sometime on the day of the Fallen Moon. Just in time."

"Hours. We'll have only hours to find the phylactery." I scratch the scruff on my cheek. "Cutting it close."

"Less talking, more riding." She takes off, her gray cloak flowing out behind her as Belinda obeys Charlie's intent without a single word spoken.

Binny takes a little more encouraging, mainly a hard smack on his haunches, but he quickly out strides the smaller Belinda. We race across the plain, the storm bearing down on us and growing in intensity. Underneath the thunder, I imagine a clock, the ticking growing louder and louder until it drowns out even the storm, the hands rotating until they stop on either my doom or my salvation. But which is it to be?

TWENTY-SEVEN

"Your dead relatives live better than most people." I stare up at the high marble ceilings as the storm rages just outside.

"They're all royalty." Charlie dumps more wood onto the fire, making a nice blaze on the floor of one of her ancestor's sepulchers. "It's the same for monarchs all over—they get overdone tombs."

"This is beyond overdone." I walk past statue after statue of fae, an entire assembly of them weeping, tears carved on their upturned faces. "They have their own wailing entourages here."

"This is the tomb of my great-great-grandfather. He lived for thousands of years before he married. All these women—" She points a stick at the statues. "—they're supposedly his lovers weeping at his death."

"I mean, I don't want to say this lightly, but I'm in awe. He knew how to live." I stop in front of two carved doors that lead to what I have to assume is his crypt.

"Don't be so enamored. He was killed by one of his jilted lovers, though the histories say he died of old age."

I whistle. "He must've broken all those hearts."

Thunder rumbles through the air, but nothing stirs the wide expanse of marble and stone in here. It's as if the place is static, the eye of a storm that never seems to move or change.

"How long has he been dead?"

"Long enough that we don't have to worry about him haunting us." She sits beside the fire, and I join her, pulling her into my lap.

Belinda and Binny sniff around at the doors leading outside. I can't tell if they're apprehensive about the tomb or the storm—either way, they aren't at ease in here. I suppose there's no way they could be. Everything is marble or gold, and not a thing in here is alive —save us.

"What?" Charlie scoots down and lies on her back, her head propped on my thigh.

"Are you going to have one of these someday?" I ask and stroke her hair from her forehead.

"Morose."

"Is that an insult?" I ask.

She laughs, the sound echoing around us, the white marble refusing to grab hold of it. "No. I was just saying your question was dark. But yes, I suppose this is where I'd end up if I stayed." She fidgets. "Not a fan, to be honest. The colors don't suit."

"Not a fan of stark white and tons of gold?"

"No." She takes my hand in hers and stares at my palm. "I prefer it when it's messy. A room piled with books and maps and a mind full of memories—that's what I want. Freedom. Adventure. A life of my own."

"And if your father says it's time for you to take the throne?" I ask.

She traces the lines on my palm with her index finger. "He wouldn't. The fae succession only happens when the monarch dies. In times past, the child of the king or queen would slay their parent and take the throne. It was tradition."

"A death match? That sounds exciting."

She wrinkles her nose. "My father would crush me easily. The things he can do—the things I've seen him do." She shudders. "No one could face him one-on-one and live. And when he dies, that power comes to me. I don't want it. I already tasted it, felt it flow through me. I'm not strong enough to wield it."

"I don't know. I've heard you can be pretty powerful. Calling creatures like me to be your minions."

"Creatures like you?" She glances up at me.

"Obviously. You've lured me into this love trap. Dragged me kicking and screaming, really. I tried to escape you many times. But your power overcame me, and—"

She tosses my hand away with a snort. "You're ridiculous."

"Sometimes." I rest my hand on her thigh.

Rain pelts the top of the structure, and somewhere deeper inside a steady *drip-drip-drip* begins.

Something creaks to my right, and I stare into the darkness. "What was that?"

"The storm." Charlie peers into the gloom, too.

"You sure?"

The firelight makes the statues look fluid, as if they're moving.

"This entire valley is full of these tombs. Nothing lives here." Still, she looks in the direction of the sound.

I pull my sword closer to my side, then relax against the pillar at my back.

She eases back onto my thigh, her tension fading. The storm isn't letting up, the dripping coming faster. It seems more violent than the storms I'm used to, or perhaps that's just because the sound amplifies in all this stone.

My mind wanders back to how we got here in the first place—the hill that looked like a squashed funeral cairn. "You know, I've never asked you where we are."

"Hmm?"

"We went through Finnraven Hill, I guess. But to where? Are we, I don't know, across a sea somewhere?"

"Oh, I see what you mean. No, the fae world is separate from the human world, but still part of it. Sort of like a mirror image. To the fae, our world is the one on top, the true one, not the reflection. To humans, their world is the actual one, ours simply a reflection."

"That's confusing."

"The worlds used to be joined, but long ago magic was cut off from your world. It now belongs to the fae alone, though there are cracks between worlds where magic sometimes seeps through. Those cracks are likely how the Beast of Gevaudon and the Eater arrived."

I'm still back on the mirror thing. How does anyone know which image is the real one? My mind fizzes at the concept. "How do you know all this?"

"I'm the Unseelie princess." She shrugs. "I was educated by the finest fae tutors and lived in a palace with the largest library in our world."

Not for the first time, and certainly not for the last, I wonder at how such a remarkable creature could ever love someone like me.

"I think you're more qualified to lead than you think you are."

She gives me a skeptical look. "Where did that come from?"

I shrug. "And I also think that what you told me about why you used your power to defeat the Seelie—it wasn't entirely true."

Her eyebrows lower. "You weren't there, G."

"I don't have to be. You may think you acted like a coward, but you saved your people. And I know you, Charlie. I know the you that lives in here." I tap her chest over her heart.

She opens her mouth—no doubt to deny it—then closes it again.

I cover her hand with mine. "You did what you needed to do, no matter what reason you attach to it. You did the right thing. A *good* thing. Look, I hate to be the one to tell you this, but you sorely lack a wicked streak. There's nothing stained in there, no mark on you. Lucky for you, I have enough for the both of us."

She gives me a wry smile. "At least you know yourself." She laughs lightly. "How ironic."

"Once we're done with the phylactery and you fall in love with me all over again since I'll be irresistibly handsome, how about we head back to Paris? You can get a job at one of those fancy chateaus like you planned. I can find something to do. I'm good at hunting. Maybe I could be a smithy? I wouldn't mind learning how to make things out of metal. All that hammering would be great for my muscles. Just a thought."

She sits up, her eyes round. "Really? You mean it?"

"Yeah, of course." I tip her chin up. "Whatever you want. I know your father isn't going to accept me right away. Maybe never, honestly. But I'll work on it. If you'd rather stay here, we—"

She kisses me, throwing herself at me and wrapping her arms tightly around my neck. I answer, kissing her back as she practically lights me up with her happiness. I can feel it in the way she smiles while she kisses, the way she clings to me. She has to know I'd do anything to make her happy.

The creak comes again, this time along with some scratching.

Charlie and I are on our feet in a moment, and I draw my sword.

"Stay back." I hold a hand out in front of her.

She smacks it away and draws her bow.

The scratching draws closer, and we both peer into the dark. The wind howls outside, the rain pounding as the drip grows faster, the scratches getting louder and louder.

I turn, tracing the sound until I see movement in the flicker of orange flames. Charlie draws her bow.

The wind whistles outside, the rain growing heavier as lightning flashes between the gap of the doorway. Belinda nickers and Binny paws at the door, preferring the storm to whatever is creeping closer to us from the dark tomb.

The scratching grows louder, setting my hair on end.

I creep toward it, my sword ready to strike.

The shadowy shape ambles toward me.

I raise my sword.

It steps into the light.

Then it screams.

I stop mid-swing.

"What in the seven bloody harpies are you doing here?" A short man, hunched with a patch of gray hair on the top of his head and large, bulging eyes, shrinks away from me.

Charlie lowers her bow and puts one hand over her heart. "You scared us shitless!"

I waver, my sword still at the ready. "Are we fighting or not?"

"No." Charlie waves me away. "No, it's okay. It's just a goblin."

"I scared *you*?" He comes closer and shakes his head. "I almost lost one of my lives."

"*Just* a goblin?" I stare at the creature, his body like that of a decrepit old man, and his skin a light green. He's almost like a walking, talking corpse.

"Harmless." Charlie slides her arrow back into her quiver. "What are you doing in here?"

He steps closer to the fire and holds his gnarled hands out for warmth, his gaze bouncing between us. "Got caught in the storm. My little cart wouldn't have made it out there, so I rolled it in here for a moment. Then I heard noises, saw the fire, and almost got murdered." He shoots me a glare.

I slide my sword back into its scabbard.

"What are you doing at Raven's End?" Charlie sits by the fire again, at total ease despite the stranger in our midst.

"I could ask you the same thing," he snaps back.

"We're on our way to the Wood of Mist." She shrugs.

He sniffles and wipes his bulbous nose with the back of his hand. "I'm here to sell my wares to the pilgrims who visit the crypts to pay tribute. Can I interest you in some blessing salve or a few bones of the elders?"

Charlie's eyes narrow. "You mean you're a grave robber?"

His already lopsided face gives a lopsided smile. "That would be a nice profession if it weren't for the curses placed on the tombs. I won't be the one to bring them down on my head."

"Then how do you get bones of the elders?" She gives him an apprehensive look.

"You aren't going to buy any then?" he hedges.

"No."

He sighs. "Chicken bones, mostly."

Not a bad racket. "How much do you get for them?"

He gives me a sideways glance. "Enough. I don't need any competition, if that's what you're thinking."

"Your business is safe." I sit beside Charlie, though I keep an eye on the goblin.

His eyes glint. "Perhaps you're interested in more exotic goods? A pretty lady like you would enjoy a necklace touched by the goddess of beauty. Or a tincture to keep the bloom on your cheeks no matter your years?"

Charlie looks up. "The rain is starting to die down. We can be on our way soon."

"Wait." The goblin backs away. "Just wait a moment." He shuffles into the gloom, then the scratching sounds starts up again. When he comes back into the light, he's pulling a cart behind him. It's covered with a tatty gray blanket that he whips away to show an array of goods. The bones he talked about are front and center, but there are also vials and bottles, necklaces and sachets. A pile of multicolored crystals weighs down the back of the cart, and he turns a crank that raises a curved piece of wood overhead, several chimes and baubles hanging from it.

He plucks a round insignia from one of the trays. "The Raven crest. Wear it upon your person to bring good fortune."

"Or an arrow from the Seelie who like to roam nearby." Charlie looks over his treasures. "No, thanks."

"How about a jeweled talon?" He grabs a claw coated in gems. "Said to ward off boggans and hags."

"No."

I could've used that a few days ago. Then again, I doubt anything in the goblin's cart actually does what's advertised.

Charlie leans down to peer at the potions. "Do you have anything that's actually useful? A beggar's boon mixture or maybe some ravenweed?"

"I'm not a healer." He grumbles and shuffles to the back of his cart where he digs around for a while.

"The rain's almost gone. We should head out." Charlie turns toward the horses.

"Wait." The goblin stands straight and holds up a vial.

"What's that?" I ask. Whatever's inside has a sparkle to it, flecks of gold flashing in the firelight.

"A rare potion. One that can save a life. Vitae eluvia." He hands it to Charlie. "Careful now. You break it, you buy it." He taps a sign on the side of his cart.

"Vitae eluvia?" Charlie peers at the liquid, apprehension in her eyes. "This could be piss for all I know."

The goblin scoffs. "This was mixed by one of the king's own healers. I've had it in my possession for many years. I traded a very rare pixie relic for this vial, and I've kept it untouched."

"What does it do?" I watch as the gold flecks seem to dance around, moving on their own.

"*Real* vitae eluvia can heal even the deepest wounds. But this isn't real. The last healer capable of creating it died in the war." Charlie hands it back.

A tingle of warning runs down my spine, and I reach for my sword.

"You seem to know a lot about it." The goblin's eyes narrow as he watches Charlie. "*Your majesty.*"

I have my blade at his throat before he can say another word.

Charlie strides to him, coming so close they're nearly nose to nose, her face a hard mask. "State your business with me, goblin, or I'll have G cut you down."

"I-I meant no offense." He swallows hard then backs up a step and bows. "None, my princess. Forgive me."

I keep my sword on him. "Shall I?" I ask her.

She looks at his bent form for a moment before shaking her head. "What gave me away?"

"I've seen you before, your majesty. On the last progress you attended with your father. Here, at Raven's End. That's when I traded for the *vitae eluvia*."

She sighs and pinches the bridge of her nose. "Stand up."

He obeys, his nose quivering as he wipes it again. "If you'll pardon me saying so, you shouldn't be venturing to the Wood of Mist. As you said, there are Seelie about, and plenty who'd like to capture the Unseelie princess. Or worse."

Fuck, he has a point. I realized we were riding into trouble, but I thought Charlie's disguise would be enough to keep her safe—or at least as safe as we can be when surrounded by enemy fae. But if this old goblin recognized her easily, she's in even more danger than I thought.

He holds out the vial. "Take it."

"What?"

"Take it, your majesty. I was saving it for a special occasion. I think meeting the princess is special enough, don't you?"

"I couldn't." She shakes her head. "It's far too precious for you to just give it away."

He grunts. "I admit it does hurt my old heart." A gleam lights in his eyes. "Perhaps you've something to trade?"

She gives a half-smile. "Nothing so valuable as *vitae eluvia*."

"Try me." He juts his chin toward the horses. "Let's see what you've got."

Charlie glances at me.

I lower my sword. "I had some nice candlesticks, but those got lifted from me. Other than that ..."

"I left the palace in a hurry." Charlie looks inside the pack on Binny's back but gives up quickly. "I didn't think to bring much, only food and a few small poultices just in case."

The goblin shakes his head.

"Let's see." I walk to Belinda and pull off my pack.

The goblin hovers at my elbow, watching closely as I dig through my bag.

"Do you mind?" I ask.

"Not at all." He leans closer.

Charlie smirks.

I keep digging, then offer him some fruit.

He shakes his head again.

"How about bread and cheese?" I offer those despite being particularly reluctant to part with them.

"No." He wrinkles his round nose. "What else?"

I show him a few pieces of clothes and baubles I got at the palace, then my maps—though I'm glad he turns his nose up at them. Finally, I dig through the stuff Madge gave me. It feels like a lifetime since I set off from her tiny hut.

"That's all I've got." I touch something hard and pull on it, then remember it's just the old spoon Madge threw in.

"Wait." The goblin stares. "What's that?"

I reach in and grab it, then pull it out. "Just a rusty spoon."

The goblin's eyes light. "A spoon."

"Yeah." I glance at Charlie. She shrugs.

"May I?" He reaches for it.

I let him have it. He brings it close to his face as he stares. Then he puts it in his mouth and bites down.

"You break it, you buy it," I say.

He nods. "Give me this, and the *vitae eluvia* is yours."

"Seriously?"

Charlie pinches my side and gives me a 'don't be dense' glare.

"I mean, yes, you've got a deal." I hold out my hand for the vial.

He gives it to me almost carelessly, his gaze still on the spoon. "Pleasure doing business." Then he tears himself away from his prize and bows to Charlie. "Majesty."

"We need to be on our way." She climbs onto Belinda.

I tower over the goblin and point my finger at his nose. "You never saw us. Got it? If I find out you've told anyone about the princess, I'll come back here and leave with your head."

He nods. "I would never betray a Raven. You have my word." He touches the tip of his forehead, then his heart, a small sizzle going through the air.

"He's bound to it. Come on, let's go. We need to ride hard." Charlie pockets the vial, and I pull open the huge doors, letting moonlight in along with the smell of fresh rain.

Once I'm astride Binny, I follow Charlie from the tomb and onto the road that runs between each of the huge monuments. The goblin has already disappeared into the darkness as we ride away, our steps echoing eerily.

"Why the spoon?" I finally ask as we leave the immense stone graveyard behind.

"It must've been made of pure iron." She pulls up next to me, her eyes scanning ahead of us.

"Iron? It's that valuable?"

"Here, yes. Gold and silver are rare, but pure iron doesn't exist. It comes only from the human world."

"So you're saying I could bring a load of useless scrap iron to the fae lands and make a fortune?"

She nods. "Sure. Your head would end up on a pike, but you'd make a fortune before they caught you."

I could sell it all here, take the gold back to— "Wait. Who'd catch me?"

"The Seelie and the Unseelie don't agree on much, but there is a ban on iron imports throughout both realms. It's the worst form of contraband."

I think of all the bits of busted iron we passed on our journey—broken wagon wheels, barrel bands—any number of rusted nuts and bolts. "Are we talking about the same thing?"

"Yes, G. Iron."

"But why?"

"It's the deadliest element for fae. We can survive plenty of wounds, but a sword made of pure iron will kill us faster than any other instrument. It doesn't even have to strike true." She taps her chest over her heart. "We can't withstand it. If even a sliver is embedded under our skin, it can kill us."

"But our swords—" I point out. "We've had iron this entire time."

"The swords aren't pure iron. They're mixed with other metals when they're forged to make the blade sharp and resistant to rust. Same with horseshoes and all manner of human tools. It's still dangerous, but nothing like the pure iron of the spoon."

I scrub a hand down my face. "So I just gave away a fortune in contraband for that tiny vial? Is that what you're saying?"

She laughs. "It was a good trade. Goblins are known for their business sense but also their loyalty. He won't use it against us, so it's probably in pretty good hands. And the *vitae eluvia* is certainly worth it."

"I have a lot to learn about your world." If I weren't already on a quest given to me by a magical lady in the water, I'd probably need to have a sit down to figure out if I've lost my mind. As it is, we press on ahead, the Wood of Mist lurking somewhere out beyond the horizon.

The moon peeks through the dusky clouds overhead, glowing serenely despite the ever-ticking clock. It's nearly full.

Charlie follows the direction of my gaze. "We'll make it."

We splash through a puddle, mud kicking up behind us as the horses go at a trot.

I finally voice the thought that's been eating at me. "The goblin recognized you."

She pulls up the hood of her cloak. "Only because he'd seen me before."

I dig in my pocket and pull out a gold coin, then flip it to her. She catches it in the air and looks at it, at her own image staring back at her.

Reaching out, I grab Belinda's reins and slow both horses down. "Your face is everywhere, Charlie. It's not safe for you to keep going. I didn't realize—"

"It's not safe for you either." She shoves the coin in her pocket, her eyes flashing. "It's a miracle you've made it this far. You're only a human, G. A strong, brave, rather wicked one, but human all the same. My realm doesn't offer mercy to anyone, not even its own kind."

"Which is why you should stay back. Wait for me with the goblin. I can—"

"No." Her tone is vehement. "You will *not* leave me behind."

"That's not what I'm trying to do. I'm trying to keep you safe." I reach up and drop her cloak from her head. "They'll know your face, and we both know they'll stop at nothing to get their hands on you. I won't let that happen."

"G, we made a deal." She pulls Belinda's reins from my grip. "And the fae take bargains very seriously."

"I release you from it."

She shakes her head. "Not a chance. You and I are going to finish this. We're going to find the phylactery before the end of the Fallen Moon."

"Stay. You never wanted to come this far anyway, remember?"

"That was before."

"Exactly, before you knew how deeply, unbelievably in love with me you are—" She gives me a glare. "—and before I knew you were a famous princess. You shouldn't risk yourself. Not for me. Just stay back and wait for me. You know this is the best plan, Charlie."

"I'm going, and that's the end of it." She clucks her tongue, and Belinda side eyes me as she starts trotting again.

"Come on, Binny." I press my heels into him as frustration roils inside me. "Why are you so damn stubborn?"

"*Me*?" She scoffs. "You're joking."

"No, I'm not. I'm trying to be reasonable and—"

"That's where you're going wrong. Stick to your strengths, G," she simpers. Maddeningly.

"Charlie," I growl and swipe for her reins again.

She whispers something to Belinda, and they take off, sprinting into the dark and splattering mud onto Binny and me.

I grit my teeth and urge him onward, racing after my stubborn, beautiful princess who is no doubt leading us both to ruin.

Too bad I'll follow her anywhere.

TWENTY-EIGHT

"How many are there?" I peek over the top of the ridge where Charlie and I are hiding. Up ahead, the Wood of Mist beckons, the white fog swirling around it even in the sunlight.

"I can't tell. But they're watching the road." She slides down next to me on her back. "A traveler just came through, and they took him off his horse and searched him. If my father knew about this, he'd send a legion here to wipe them out."

"Why are they here in the first place? Don't they have their own realm?"

"Yes, but we've always disputed the borders of our realms. They claim the Wood of Mist and the hills leading to Raven's End as their own. We disagree and claim the mountains and plains farther into their side of the border, though we haven't actively pursued it in centuries. The fae massing here aren't directly sanctioned by the Seelie court. Instead, they're rebels seeking a return to the old ways of war between the realms."

"The war you ended?"

She winces. "Yes."

"Sorry." I squeeze her wrist.

"It's all right." She glances over the ridge for a moment, then settles back down. "The rebels are mostly warriors who survived that day, ones who can't put down their swords—or won't."

It goes without saying they'd do anything to get their hands on Charlie, the reason their realm lost the war. Shit, this grows more dangerous by the second.

"We can't wait for nightfall."

"Is there some other way to get into the forest? Another road?" I dig around in my pack for the map.

"We could enter the Wood at any point along its edge, but traveling too far from the main road isn't a good idea. Every bit of extra distance is time lost. The sorcerer's tower is at the center of the forest and shrouded in the thickest mist." She chews her bottom lip. "The only sure way to it is along the road. It'll give us the most time to search."

"If they stop us and recognize you, we'll have to fight our way out. That's if we even get the chance." I take her hand. "It's not safe, and I won't risk you."

She meets my gaze. "I'm not letting you go alone."

"You have to. You and Belinda can wait here."

"No." She has that stubborn set to her jaw again, the sun playing in her golden hair and her eyes shining. "I already told you I'm not doing that. Besides, what makes you think you'll get past the Seelie?"

"They've no reason to bother with me. I'm just a human, remember?"

"A human alone and entering the Wood of Mist? They'll probably cut you down on principle." She sits up. "We're both going, and we're taking the main road."

"This isn't going to work."

"It has to." She fishes in her bag and pulls out her old, worn cap, then snugs it down on her head. "I fooled you for ages. I can do the same for the Seelie on the road." With a yank, she pulls half her shirt from where it had been tucked in her pants. Then she rubs her fingers in the dirt and marks it along her face and neck.

This is a bad idea, but Charlie isn't going to sit back and wait. I knew that before I asked her, but I had to try.

"Okay, we need backstories. We are wanted criminals in the Unseelie realm for agitating against the king. You are a farm hand, and I am a stable boy—both of us on the run from a great lord's estate. Got it?"

441

"Sounds as good as anything." I climb astride Binny and follow Charlie back onto the road. As soon as we crest this ridge and start into the valley that leads to the forest, we'll be spotted. After that, we'll be locked into this course. My gut churns as we ride, getting closer to the Seelie who'd stop at nothing to get their hands on Charlie. She's charging into danger for me when all I want to do is keep her safe.

The sun rides lower on the horizon, kissing the tops of the tall trees as we finally reach the swirling mists that eddy and flow from the forest.

"I can't see a damn thing." I look behind us, but the mist obscures even that vantage.

"Just stay on the road." She leans forward a bit, hunching her shoulders in a way that doesn't suit her. It suits a stable boy, though.

The moon is already on the rise, glowing in the blue sky as it peeks above the horizon. I'm out of time. If we can't get past the Seelie, all will be lost.

We enter the trees, the forest closing around us like a curtain, and keep a clipped pace.

I keep scanning the woods, looking for fae, but no Seelie jump out at us. There's only the mist and the hooting of an owl somewhere in the distance.

"Where are they?" Charlie's voice is barely above a whisper.

I keep my head on a swivel as a sense of foreboding sets up in my chest. "Change of the watch?"

"They should've stopped us by now. Something's not right."

"Maybe it's a stroke of luck for once?" I suggest.

That's met with an apprehensive *mmph*.

Binny stops hard, his ears flattening as mist flows in front of us. I catch the hint of a sound, like a tapping noise.

"What is it?" I pull my sword and stare at the milky whiteness. "What's in there?"

"G." Charlie pulls up to my side, her gaze on the mist as well.

"What?"

A body drops in front of us. Binny rears, and I hold on tight as he almost throws me.

"Calm!" Charlie cries.

When he drops back to all fours, I look down at the body on the road. It's one of the Seelie fae, his body wrapped in white, his face sunken. "It looks like—"

"Above us!" Charlie yells.

I look up in time to see massive black legs skittering down a tree trunk. A huge spider, its body like velvet, quiet as it moves despite its size. Swinging my sword overhead, I catch one trying to lower itself on me, hanging by its thread. It screeches as I slice into its face, one of its fangs falling to the ground in front of me.

"Ride!" I yell.

Charlie takes off, Binny and I following as more spiders appear, their eyes glinting in the moonlight as they descend from the trees overhead. Dozens of them, maybe more, and all of them following us. They disappear into bands of mist, then swing into view, moving from tree to tree with frightening ease. We have to outrun them. There's too many to fight.

"Faster!" I lean down, keeping my head low as I follow Charlie, racing through the woods.

The horses seem to sense the danger, because they don't slow, their hooves pounding along the forest road as the spiders finally begin to fall back. We're outpacing them.

"Whoa!" Charlie yells, and I turn just in time to see the web stretched across the way ahead. Belinda runs into it, tearing some of it from the trees, but most of it holds.

Binny stops so fast I'm thrown forward and land against the web with a thud. My sword lies several feet away.

"Are you all right?" I ask.

"Fine, just fucking stuck!" Charlie fights the web, hacking at it with her short sword as Belinda nickers. "Stop moving, girl. You're making it worse."

I try to stand, but the web is glued to my back. "Fuck." I throw myself forward, but the web holds. The clicking noises grow louder, and I look up to see the spiders we outran catching up to us. "Faster, Charlie!" I grip the front of my cloak and yank it apart, leaving it stuck to the web as I grab my sword.

"I'm trying!"

I swing, severing the silk where it's attached to a tree at the roadside, then I run to the other tree and do the same. "Go!" I smack Belinda's butt, and she takes off as I climb onto Binny.

Movement in my peripheral has me ducking as a spider swings past, its front legs outstretched. Pain sears through my back as it scratches me, cutting through my shirt as its fangs barely miss my head. The impact throws me from the horse, and I roll off the road, my sword clutched in my hand.

"Stay!" I yell and get back to my feet.

A spider lands in front of me, its front legs reaching for me. I swing, cutting them at the joint, green blood spurting from them as it shrieks. They surround me, all of them trying to grab me, their fangs glistening as they snap and click.

Binny nickers, and a spider flies past me and crunches onto a tree trunk above me. Binny kicks again, sending another spider sailing through the trees.

I take the distraction and swing my sword in a wide arc, making contact with several of the beasts at once, slicing through their faces and legs as I take lunging steps toward Binny.

He snorts as one tries to drop onto his back, then kicks again, sending two more crashing into the woods.

"Go!" I run to him and leap, barely hanging on as he takes off at a jump, his hooves pounding as we race away from the oncoming mass of black legs and glittering eyes. I pull myself all the way up, grunting as I seat myself in the saddle.

I can't see Charlie through the mist, but I'm more focused on what's behind. The spiders are still coming, swinging closer. I heave my sword back and cleave one of them in two, its torso falling and its legs curling up as another takes its place.

They're gaining, jumping from tree to tree and closing the gap between us. I keep swinging my sword, cutting any threads they shoot toward Binny and severing limbs of those who get too close. They keep coming, hissing and clicking as they throw themselves at me. Until suddenly, they stop. It's as if an invisible wall has gone up, and they don't dare move past it. Their glittering eyes fade as I turn back around and peer through the trees.

"Charlie!" I call.

"Slower." I pull back on the reins lightly. "Slower now, boy."

Binny snorts but obeys, his pace lessening as he turns his head to look behind us.

"They're gone. Something spooked them." That thought alone sends a prickle of worry through me. Where is Charlie?

I catch the moon through the trees. It's higher now, gloating at me between the leaves as it shines. The tick-tock is louder now, hammering like the beat of my heart.

"G!"

Binny skids to a halt as Charlie waves from between the trees.

"This way!" She turns Belinda and crashes through the underbrush.

I follow, keeping close behind as she pushes through the fog, picks up speed, and jumps a low, crumbling wall. Binny makes the jump with ease, his hooves clacking on stone as he comes down.

The fog clears, and I look up at a spiraling tower, the top jutting out far above the tops of the trees.

Binny's ears flatten again, and he snorts as he scoots closer to Belinda. "It's all right." I pat his neck. "Calm down."

"I feel it too, boy." Charlie slides off Belinda and comes over to me. "Like a sickness."

I climb down. "Are you hurt?" I look her over.

"No." She moves to my side and inspects my back.

"It's nothing."

"It's not nothing." She opens her pack and pulls out a green vial. "The spiders have venom in their claws. It's bleeding you. Here." She dabs some of the liquid on my back. "Shit, these are deep."

I hiss at the sting. Ravens call from their perches on wizened trees and the tower stones above us.

"This will close the wounds." She keeps going, covering each of the scratches with the salve.

Something shrieks in the trees. I turn toward it and reach for my sword.

"Stay still. Nothing will come any closer to the tower."

"How do you know?" A chill goes through me, goose-bumps breaking out all over my skin. "And the ravens?"

"Like I said, I can sense it. It's oily. Like a stain on the world. This place is steeped in evil. Not even the creatures of the forest venture here. The birds, though, they belonged to the sorcerer. They watch." She finishes and closes the vial. "Let it sit for a moment."

I look up at the full moon. "I don't have a moment."

You'll never be good enough. "Who said that?" I glance around.

"What?" Charlie's brows draw together.

"Nothing." I wipe the cold sweat from my forehead.

She shivers. "This power, it's not natural. Not magic like my father's or mine." Staring at the black tower, she shakes her head. "It's like a disease." Her eyes return to mine. "Don't you feel it?"

"I feel …" I swallow past the lump in my throat. "It doesn't matter how I feel. The phylactery is in there. All I have to do is find it."

She opens her mouth, then closes it again. With a nod, she grabs her pack from Belinda. I get mine, slinging it across my aching back, then head for the tower. I'm so close, right on the edge of being whole again. I can be the man Charlie needs, one her father can accept. All I have to do is reach out and take it.

Charlie, bow in hand, stays at my elbow as we circle the tower. A set of double doors is hewn into the stone, vines growing up around them. I yank them away and push the door open. It whines and creaks on its hinges, giving way to an even darker area within. The scent of damp and rot reaches my nose, and Charlie recoils.

"You all right?" I pull a torch from my pack and strike my flint, lighting it and holding it up to combat the gloom.

"Yes." She looks up, a spiral stair twisting away from us that seems to go on forever. "You?"

"Yes, but I feel it. The sensation you were talking about."

She squeezes my elbow, her touch grounding me. "Let's get in and out as quick as we can."

The sensation of being watched curdles in my gut, but I can't stop. No matter what lies ahead, I'm not leaving without the Graven Phylactery.

You'll always be empty. Never whole again. The voice is closer now. Inside my head. A queasiness rushes through me, my stomach churning.

I venture farther in, holding up the torch. The base of the tower is open, busted furniture and broken glass strewn all over the floor. Papers litter the ground, all of them covered in tiny script with images and diagrams. A threadbare rug is in the center, its edges rolled and frayed. Along the walls are chains with metal cuffs attached, and the black stains beneath them don't leave much to the imagination. This is a place of horrors.

Dust filters down from somewhere above, and the chains that hang in the center of the spiral stair jingle against each other.

"There's something there." Charlie aims her bow upward. "Moving in the shadows. I can't get a bead on it."

I can't see anything except the dark. "We have to climb. There's nothing down here." I wield my sword with my free hand. "Stay close."

She nods.

Hefting the torch, I find the bottom of the staircase and begin to climb. Charlie follows, her gaze fixed on the gloom above us. The stone steps are uneven and filled in at intervals with rotten wood. Without a railing, each step is more precarious than the last.

"Keep one hand on the wall." I glance back at her.

"Just keep going." She still has her arrow pointed above us.

At least I can test the steps before she puts her weight onto them. The sick feeling increases as we go up, my stomach cramping and sweat dripping along my temples.

She's a princess. You'll never make her happy. I try to ignore it, the slithering voice that worms its way into my ears.

The chains shake again, and Charlie gasps.

"What?" I raise the torch.

"It's ... It's big. A creature." Her voice trembles.

"Are you all right?"

She takes in a deep breath. "Don't stop."

I take the next step, the wood giving way beneath my foot. I catch myself on the wall, scraping the skin off my hand as I try to stay upright.

"G!" She grabs the back of my tattered shirt as I fall onto a higher set of stone steps. Thankfully, they take my weight, and I pull myself across the broken spot.

"Careful." I hold out my hand, and she takes it, jumping the distance as more bits of rotten wood fall and clatter to the floor below. "We're almost at the middle landing." I press my lips to her hair in a stolen kiss, then steady her against the wall as I keep climbing.

Above is a wooden ring around the wall of the tower, a narrow walk that must serve as a midway point. Once we reach it, I peer out of one of the tall, narrow windows.

My blood runs cold. "Shit."

"What?" Charlie leans out. "Oh, no."

The moon is still bright, but the bottom edge is obscured by darkness. The Fallen Moon has begun. I have to reach the phylactery before it's completely engulfed in shadow.

"Faster." I take her hand. "We can make it."

"Let's go."

The landing has more scattered papers, but I don't trust the wood enough to search it. Somehow, I know what I seek is at the top.

There was a reason you were cast into the river like garbage. You weren't a victim. You chose your fate with your wicked deeds.

"G." Charlie grips my arm. "G!"

I shake my head, trying to dislodge the voice.

"I hear it, too," she whispers. "Telling me horrible things. It lies, G. Don't listen."

I take the next steps, then stop. "Are we ..." I look down and find the floor spreading out around me, scattered papers and the blood stains in the same locations. "Shit. We're back at the bottom."

Charlie whirls, her bow at the ready. "An enchantment."

Above us, the chains shake lightly.

"So we can't get to the top?" I can't see the moon, but there's an itch at the back of my mind, one telling me to *hurry*.

"I don't know. Let's try again." She gestures for me to climb.

I go faster this time, making the short jumps and turning to catch her before she leaps. When we're almost to the middle level, I slow down.

"If we go through again, will we end up at the bottom?"

"Hang on." She closes her eyes and holds out her hand.

"You want to hold my hand?" I reach out.

"Knock it off." She smacks my hand away and resumes her position.

The flutter of wings echoes around the tower, and one of the ravens flies up and lands on the step in front of the doorway to the middle level.

"That's kind of amazing." I stare at the bird. It stares back.

Charlie motions toward the bird. "Go."

It hops and makes an angry sound that scratches from its throat.

"It's loyal to the sorcerer, but it can't refuse my call." Charlie points a finger at it. "Go, now."

It clucks at us, then hops through the doorway. Only a moment later, I hear it clucking down below.

"Fuck." I stare through the doorway and past it to where the stairs continue ascending. "How do we get past it?" I glance at the chains. "Can we climb up?"

"Not unless we want to be completely at the mercy of whatever is up there. We'd need both hands on the chains, not to mention all our concentration. The floor is a long way down." She chews her lip, then looks down. "If up takes us right back to the bottom, maybe there's a way down."

"Huh?"

"Come on." She pushes me into the doorway, and I stumble and find myself at the bottom again.

"Whoa, what was that?"

"Look for something. Some sort of secret way." She peers at the wall, at the few tattered hangings that remain. "There has to be a trick to it."

"Or we could climb the chains." I point up.

"G, just look!" Her exasperation matches my own as she yanks down a tapestry, dust filling the air.

I edge around the bloodstains and yank on a pair of the shackles bolted to the wall. They're solid. So I keep going until I bump into her. "Nothing here. We need to go back up."

"Wait." She turns, her eyes going to the rug that lies beneath a busted desk, the wood splintered and worn. "There!" She hurries to it, then grabs one end and starts to pull. It falls apart, the threads puffing to dust in her hands.

I pull her back, then kick the remnants of the desk away. With a rough sweep of my boot, the rug disintegrates and reveals a wooden hatch. "Look!"

"That's it." She points to a circular metal pull at the side of the wooden trap door.

I grab it and pull. The small door opens with an angry creak.

"What the ..." My brain goes fuzzy as I stare down at the opening. Through it, I see the same thing I see when I get to the doorway at the middle of the tower. The room with the wooden floor, but I'm somehow looking straight on through the door though I'm looking *down*.

"I'll make sure it's safe." Charlie closes her eyes and gets that look of concentration again. The flap of wings sound from outside the tower.

"No time." I get to the edge of the hatch. It's not like there's a ladder, so I shrug and jump.

"G!" Charlie yells as I land hard. In the middle tier of the tower.

"Holy shit." I look around, then reach up for her. Vertigo hits again as I realize she's looking down at me while I'm looking straight ahead at her. "It's fine. I'm okay."

Then she jumps, falling through the doorway. I catch her before she drops onto her ass.

"Don't do things like that!"

"I'm out of time." I squeeze her hand.

She shakes her head, then gets her bearings. "Well, we're here. Let's go."

We cleave to the edge of the wall, avoiding the moldy wood at the center, and edge around until we get to the staircase.

"Looks like the stairs lead straight to the top." I peer up into the gloom.

Charlie nocks her arrow again. "Let's keep moving."

I step through the doorway.

TWENTY-NINE

"Are you done? We're going to be late." Charlie rushes past me, her dress flowing out behind her as she grabs a necklace from her dresser.

I look down at the plate of food in front of me, the cheese and bread almost gone. "I ..."

"My father's going to have a conniption." She looks at herself in the mirror and tries to fasten the necklace.

I stand and wipe my hands, then approach her, taking the clasp from her small fingers. "Let me."

"He's just so snappy when it comes to tradition." She sighs.

With a gentle touch, I fasten her necklace, then turn it so it's perfectly centered on her delicate neck. "He can wait a little while longer." I lean down and kiss her bare shoulder, her pale ivory dress falling in a deep V down her back. "You look amazing, by the way. Taste even better." I nibble her skin.

"G." She giggles as I grab her waist and pull her against me. "We have to go."

I sigh and kiss her more before standing straight.

She smiles at me in the mirror, the crown atop her head sparkling in the lights that glimmer along the ceiling of her bedroom. Her hair shines like spun gold, the strands longer now, trailing down her back.

For a moment, my heart stops as I look at us. At the exquisite beauty of it all. And for that moment, I can't figure out why it feels so *strange*.

She cocks her head to the side. "What is it?"

"Hmm?"

"You just got the strangest look on your face." She stares at my reflection, her sky-blue eyes tinged with worry.

"I don't know ..." I look at myself, at my smooth skin. I'd shaved earlier, doing my best to get rid of the 5 o'clock shadow that appears every day around nine in the morning. Reaching up, I run my fingers along my cheeks, feeling both sides of my face as the oddest sensation tingles down my spine. My face is ... handsome. High cheekbones, strong chin, a fine, straight nose. My hair is cut short on the sides, longer on top, and falling across the side of my forehead in a dark wave. There's nothing amiss.

"It's all there." I blink. It's as if the reflection shimmers the slightest bit, the two of us frozen there, locked in by beauty, held captive by the near touch of perfection.

"All there? What does that mean?" Charlie turns in my arms and looks up at me. "You've always been full of yourself, but I think this is the first time I've seen you fall in love with your own reflection." She presses her palms to my cheeks. "You've never shaved so close before. Did you nick yourself?" she asks.

"No, I don't think so." I lean down and kiss her, her mouth warm against mine as I pull her closer, the gossamer fabric of her dress rustling in my fingers.

She lets out a slight moan, her hands gripping the front of my jacket. Then she pulls back. "We have to go. You're going to be a prince soon." She smooths her hands down my coat, the deep purple fabric the perfect complement to her gown. "You'll need to be on time, or your subjects might think you've forgotten about them."

"We can't have that." I drop one more kiss on her plump lips, then straighten. "I intend to be the best prince they've ever had—or, at the very least, the best-looking one."

She snorts a laugh, then raises her chin, getting that regal air to her. It's amazing how I didn't notice it before. When she was pretending to be a stable boy, it should've been obvious to me then. It wasn't. I suppose people only look at what's on the outside, at what's obvious—looking deeper is dangerous.

A light knock sounds at the doors.

"Come in."

Clotho enters, then gives a deep bow. "My apologies for interrupting. The king awaits your arrival."

"Are the nobles all here?" Charlie asks.

"They line the great hall to greet the both of you and give you best wishes on your upcoming wedding." He bows deeply again.

Charlie gives me a winning smile. "Ready to watch them all bow and scrape before you, even though they secretly can't stand the thought of a human royal?"

"I can think of nothing better." I grin.

"There's that swagger."

"*G!*" A shout, as if someone is yelling at me from a great distance.

I turn and look out the windows that show the sunny palace grounds. "What was that?"

"What?" Charlie takes my hand.

"I thought I heard—"

"My lord, they're waiting." Clotho steps out the doors and waits, head bowed.

"Let's get this over with, and then we can come back and spend the rest of the day in bed." Charlie squeezes my fingers.

"That sounds wonderful." I turn back toward the doors and walk alongside Charlie down the main staircase. The entire palace is glowing with daylight, and swaths of light blue fabric are draped along the walls and blowing in a light breeze.

"*G! Where are you?*" The voice again, this time colored with panic. It sounds almost like Charlie. As if she's calling to me from far away. But that can't be. I look down at her, at the tilt of her chin and the fluid way she moves. "*G!*"

I stop.

She looks up at me, her eyes narrowing the slightest bit. "What are you doing? We're late."

"I keep hearing something." I glance around at the green-clad servants, all their eyes downcast. "Someone's calling for me."

"Yes, my father is probably screaming in his head that we're ruining his big event by failing to be on time." She squeezes my fingers more tightly. "Maybe you can hear it."

"I think he'd much rather scream in my face." I let her pull me the rest of the way down the stairs and into the wide hallway that leads to the throne room.

More servants are arranged at intervals, and some fae nobles mass along the sides, chatting amongst themselves as they move toward the throne room. When they realize we're walking along the same corridor, they separate, leaving a wide path for us, and bow.

"A guy could get used to this," I whisper to Charlie.

"You'll have to. Being a prince gets you all the deference you've ever dreamed of."

"*G, I'm here!*"

I spin and search the crowd. The nobles at the back have walked behind us, closing us in. "I heard it again."

"It's nothing." Charlie's mouth forms a tight line as she pulls on my hand. "Come on."

"No." I stop and look at her. "There's something wrong." Something foggy and nebulous floats around in my mind, like a whisper I can't quite make out. What is it?

"Nothing is wrong. Do you want to be a prince or not?" Her tone turns curt in a way that seems ... unnatural.

I focus on her, on her face, the scent of her perfume, the way her hand feels in mine. "Charlie, don't you feel it?"

"No," she snaps. Then her face softens. "Are you nervous about the ceremony? Is that it?"

"Maybe." I nod. "I just have a strange feeling. Remember when we were in Sac à Puces and Maggie sang that song about the prince and the princess who got lost in the woods?"

She crinkles her nose. "Yes, but I don't see what that has to do with this."

I smile. "I guess you're right. I'm just being nervous."

She reaches up and runs her fingertips down my smooth cheek. "There's nothing to worry about."

We begin walking again, the courtiers parting for us.

I stop again.

She lets out a huff under her breath. "What is it?"

I pull my hand from hers. "Maggie couldn't carry a tune in a bucket. She never sang more than a few notes before the village dogs began howling, and she certainly never sang about a prince and a princess."

The nobles around us lift their heads, a hiss oozing from them as Charlie snaps her teeth.

"*G! Run!*" The voice is clearer now. It's Charlie, the *real* Charlie.

The woman in front of me changes, her skin bubbling as it turns a rotted green.

"*G!*"

I spin toward the voice, but I can't see Charlie. The nobles are rushing at me, their skin changing and falling away as their skeletal hands reach for me. I have to move or I'll be trapped.

With a yell, I throw myself at the skeletal creatures behind me, bowling them over and snapping some of their bones as I push away from their grasp. They tear at my clothes, ripping into my skin with claws and teeth as I swing and kick, fighting them off. The palace fades, the gilded walls becoming the dark gray of the sorcerer's tower—the *tower*! That's where I am—where I was. I went through the doorway, and that's the last real thing I remember.

"Hold him!" Not-Charlie screeches behind me, her voice deep and full of phlegm.

I keep swinging, fighting my way through the skeletons that continue to throw themselves at me.

"*Come on*!" Charlie's voice is louder now, and when two of the skeletons fall in front of me, I catch a glimpse of her. She's reaching for me through a window, her hand outstretched.

A yell rips from me as a searing pain lights up my back. One of the skeletons has slashed me deeply. I whirl and kick it away, shattering its skull as more grab for me.

"Get off!" I grab the nearest skeleton and sling it into the crowd, knocking down more of them and clearing a path. I step on them, their bones crunching beneath my boots as they scratch and claw, drawing blood as I fight toward the window.

"Behind you!" Charlie cries.

I turn as the moldy green not-Charlie slashes my chest, its claws digging deeply as I topple backwards.

"No!" Charlie screams, then two arrows fly past, embedding in the creature's torso. It simply swipes them away, then reaches for me again.

I kick out hard, my heel smashing into its hand. It screams, the sound shaking the ground around me as I get to my hands and knees and crawl toward the window.

I'm almost there when I feel something grip my ankle and yank me back, my nails breaking against the grimy stone floor as I try to hold my ground. The claws rake my back again, and I scream at the searing pain, then turn and swing hard, smashing my fists into the creature's front. Puffs of green waft from it, and I keep punching.

"Get the fuck off!" I yell and drive my fist right into its chest, the crack of brittle bone sharp in my ears as my fist burns.

The creature screams, the sound high and piercing. I take the opening and turn, getting to my feet and running. When I'm almost to the window again, Charlie leans out farther, her hand reaching for mine.

I lunge forward and grab it, my momentum carrying me through the window and tumbling into a heap on the stone stairs. My legs swing off the edge, and I start to fall.

"No!" Charlie grabs what's left of my shredded shirt and pulls, stopping my momentum so I can swing my legs back onto the stairs.

Then I collapse back, my breathing heavy as blood trickles along my skin. Staring up at the dark spire overhead, I gulp in air. "What—" Gasp. "—the fuck—" Gasp. "—was that?"

"A trap." Charlie pushes me onto my side, the edge of the steps digging into me. "Shit, this is bad."

"It's all right." I feel lightheaded, but I force myself to sit up.

She reaches into her bag and pulls out the small vial of *vitae eluvia*.

"It can't be that bad."

"It's bad." She grimaces.

I wipe a hand down my face, noticing how it's gone back to its usual ruin. "I saw myself. Did you see it?"

"What?" She bites her lip, then stows the *vitae eluvia* and pulls out some of her other supplies. Moving my torn shirt aside, she begins to patch me up. "The other cuts didn't even have a chance to heal." She sighs.

"In the trap, or the dream, or whatever it was—I saw myself." I touch the scarred side of my face. "I was whole. I was ... Did you see me?"

I wince as she takes my hand and inspects it. "I saw *you*. The enchantment didn't change anything for me. I think once you triggered it, I was able to pass through without getting caught in it."

"I saw myself. We were at the palace, and we were ..." I can still see us looking in the mirror, her staring at me as I'm meant to be, love in her gaze. "I was—" Fuck, my eyes sting and emotion forms a lump in my throat.

"It was a trick, G. That's all. Like a maze for your mind. You could've been trapped there, but you saw through it." She rubs some salve on my knuckles. "I'm pretty sure you've broken some of these."

The chains in the middle rattle again, and we both hold our breath and look up. Nothing emerges from the darkness, but I can *feel* something. Goosebumps rise along my arms and the back of my neck. The movement stops, but bits of dust filter down through the tendrils of mist that float through the air. It's above us, and not far at all.

"We have to get moving." I get to my knees, then my feet.

"I'm not finished. You need—"

"We can't wait." I can still see my face, the way I'm *supposed* to look. If Charlie could only see me like that— the thought gives me renewed vigor, and I begin to climb.

She grumbles under her breath, then follows, her bow at the ready as I increase my pace and ignore all the aching parts of me. Time is like a third companion, climbing along at my side but dwindling with each step, its form fading into the mist that swirls and eddies as I move through it.

The chains clank more, the tower narrowing as we circle around and around, climbing ever higher. Some stairs up here are completely gone, and we have to jump the gaps.

"Almost there."

A square of moonlight shines from above. It has to be a trap door that leads to the room at the top of the tower—unless it's another trick that sends us to the bottom level or another trap. *Fuck*. There are no more windows along the stone walls, so I can only guess how quickly the moon is turning dark. As long as that square of moonlight remains, though, it means I still have a chance.

"Where is it?" She aims her arrow at the top of the spire. "It couldn't have gotten past us." She looks down, then leans back against the wall, her breath a harsh gasp. "I shouldn't have looked down. It's so far."

"We're all right." I take her hand. "A few more steps."

She swallows hard and squeezes my fingers. "Go."

I lead her up the last steps until we're both illuminated in the square of light. "Here, a ladder." I hand her the torch and climb, the wood groaning under my weight as I move as deftly as I can. When I reach the upper landing,

I get on my stomach and reach down. "Take my hand. I'll pull you up."

She grabs my forearm, and I pull—the wounds on my back burning—until she's through the opening and into the wide room at the top of the tower. The center is still open, the chains suspended from the roof high over our heads. It's cold in here, far colder than the rest of the tower, and the mist swirls in through the open windows.

"It's worse here. The sickness." She raises the torch, lighting a room with rows of books along the walls and jars stacked along low shelves surrounding the open center.

Two wide stone tables are on either side of the room, and more dark stains mar the floors and walls here. The scent of death is everywhere—rot that seems to float in the air just like the mist. It's heavier here, weighing down from every angle despite the fact we're at the very top of the Wood of Mist.

"Stay away from the center. It's rotted wood around the open shaft." I stride to the nearest bookcase to begin my search, though I keep casting glances to the blackness above our heads. The mist there is so thick it forms a wall, hiding whatever has been shaking the chains.

The first tome I touch turns to dust and mold in my hands. The others, too. Everything here is in some state of decay. I swipe my arm along the bookcase, the entire row of books falling apart at my touch. It's all slipping through my fingers.

You should've died in the water, your meager brains dashed on the rocks. A fitting punishment for your crimes.

"Shut up!" I bring my fist down on the wooden shelf, crushing it into splinters. "It has to be here. I'm not leaving without it!" I go the next bookcase, then the next.

"Don't listen to it." Charlie takes the opposite side, searching in cabinets and even feeling along the walls for any hint of a secret compartment.

When the entire room is nothing but dust, I turn to her. "It's not here."

She looks out the window. I follow her gaze to the moon where only a sliver of its light remains.

My time is up.

If it was ever ticking to begin with.

I wipe my arm across my sweaty brow. "It was all a lie, wasn't it." It's not a question. Not anymore.

Charlie comes to my side, her hands finding my face. "G, I'm so sorry."

"I wanted to believe so badly." The sickness in my stomach increases until I feel like retching. I turn away from her, my guts heaving. "So badly that I put you in danger, that I made wrong choice after wrong choice to get us here. And there's nothing! There never was. I'm not going to get back what I've lost. I'm trapped like this. Forever. Because of the things I've done, the things I can't remember."

"G, it's not—" Her scream cuts through me like a blade.

I whirl as she's thrown across the room, her body hitting the wall hard. "Charlie!"

A creature climbs down the center chains. Three different heads atop the body of some sort of grisly lion, its tail that of a scorpion with a metal spike. One of the heads is fae, its skin rotten as it stares at me with white eyes. One is a bird with black feathers and serrated beak, and the third is a serpent with long golden fangs. All three heads are roughly sewn onto trunks that extend from the body like some sort of monstrous doll.

It jumps to the floor in front of me, shaking the tower and cutting me off from Charlie. I draw my sword, my skin suddenly on fire as my insides twist and turn. The sickness, it's coming from this hideous creation.

"Your evil deeds have led you here." The same voice from my head comes from the dead fae's cracked lips. "A feast for me." Something glints beneath its chin. A red gem, huge and dark, framed with gold and strung on a thick chain. The Graven Phylactery. It has to be.

The creature circles me, its tail dragging along the stone with a screeching whine.

Charlie gets to her feet and reaches for her bow.

I need to keep the monster's attention on me. "You're the sorcerer, I take it?"

The fae grins, its teeth green and rotted. "You've come for my soul." It cackles, the sound bringing bile to the back of my throat. "Thinking you could somehow regain your own?"

I dodge back as the serpent head strikes at me, its fangs coming close as I swing my sword. I barely miss it, and it hisses as it retreats.

The fae's head snaps to the side, its gaze on Charlie who is standing still, one hand out toward the monster. "Your power won't work here, *your highness*. This is no mindless beast for you to puppet. I control the chimera. Not you."

"You'll die all the same." Charlie backs away and nocks an arrow.

The head whips back to me. "You've been sent on a fool's errand. I'll never let you take my phylactery. It's my most precious jewel." He grins. "But at least you've brought me a royal snack."

"You won't touch her." Keeping my sword forward, I advance on the monster.

"I'll feast on her entrails." He smacks his lips, and the bird's head caws.

I swing hard, aiming for the fae's head. The creature jumps back, then digs its claws into the stone and jumps to the wall beside me, holding on as its tail whips out and almost impales me with its metal tip.

Charlie lets her arrows fly, embedding them in the creature's thick hide. The fae screams, and the entire beast jumps onto the chains and skitters up them, disappearing into the blackness overhead.

I run to Charlie's side. "Are you hurt?"

"No." She fires more arrows, sending them into the dark.

"Can you see it?"

Two of her arrows drop, their shafts broken.

"No."

"The phylactery is around the sorcerer's neck." I glance at the chains when they rattle again.

With a roar, the creature comes flying from overhead, its massive claws swiping at us. I push Charlie out of the way and take a hit on the shoulder, my skin flaying open to the bone as one of its claws catches me.

I yell and swing my sword, slicing into its leg as it screeches and jumps away. It's tail drags across the wooden boards at the center, their rotten pieces falling away to the floor far below.

Without warning, it charges me, throwing all its weight at me as I back to the wall. Dropping to my knees, I swing upward, stabbing the bird's neck and opening it with a hard yank, spilling thick black blood onto the floor as the creature lurches backwards.

I press my advantage, rushing it and hacking away at the bird's head. The sorcerer screams as I cut it away, the feathered mess falling at my feet as blood spurts from its trunk.

The snake darts out, and I swing at it, but it's too late. Its fangs embed in my leg, the burn from it like a lit torch inside my skin.

I yell and swing, severing the serpent's head, but its fangs remain inside me, pumping their venom into my veins.

Charlie fires a barrage of arrows into the creature's body, her bolts focused on its heart. Then she grabs my arm and tries to pull me away from it.

"Get back!" I yell and shove her as the creature strikes out with its claws. They barely miss her, and she loads more arrows and lets them fly at the fae's face.

I grip the serpent's head and pull with all my strength. It releases its hold, its eyes still moving as I throw it down the center hole. My leg is going numb, but I still manage to get it under me as I rise and swing my sword at the monster.

It barrels forward, knocking me off my feet, my sword clattering away on the stones. A sharp caw draws my attention to the head I severed. There, on top of the bloody stump, more black feathers sprout as the bird regrows.

The monster turns and puts its hind paw on top of me, crushing me against the floor as it looks at Charlie.

"No!" I yell and reach for my sword, but it's just out of my grip.

"Princess. This is an honor I dreamt not of. How your father will wail when he discovers I've taken you from him." The fae head cackles, its paw crushing me with steady pressure. I can't breathe, can barely feel, but I still try to grab my sword. I won't let it hurt Charlie.

"He'll be pleased when I tell him I've ridded our realm of you." She lets more arrows fly, but the creature knocks them down easily. She backs away until she's against the wall, and the creature follows.

I shove myself out of its grip when it takes a step, then roll away and grab my sword.

"I see you learned arrogance from your father." The sorcerer taunts. "I'll cut that out of you, too." The snake hisses its agreement.

I try to find an opening, a spot to strike that will end it. But there's nothing, its hide too thick and its heads able to regenerate. Its scorpion tail brushes against the hanging chains, the wood floor beneath it flaking away even more at the slight contact.

Charlie is out of arrows, her back against the wall. She won't survive this. Not unless I act.

I make a decision.

"Hey, get away from her!" I throw myself at the monster, slashing at it. "She's the only one who can read the map!" I hack a chunk of its matted hair and decaying flesh away.

It roars and wheels on me.

With all the strength I have left, I launch myself at the fae's head, my hand outstretched. The regrown serpent bites my side, its fangs sinking deep as I reach as far as I can. Agony sears through me, but I keep trying, keep grasping. The serpent retreats and readies itself to bite again. I grip the new feathers on the bird's head and pull myself forward. It shrieks as the sorcerer turns its white eyes on me. "No!"

I grab the phylactery and pull, breaking the chain around the fae's neck and ripping it away.

The fae screams as I hit the stones and run. It follows, fury in its steps.

"You want it? Come and get it!" I hold the phylactery out and back away. My body is numb, my words slurred.

The monster charges.

"G!" Charlie screams as I turn and leap, my body crashing into the chains as I try to grip them with my free hand.

I turn my head, catching sight of her as the monster follows me, its focus on the phylactery as it steps onto the rotten wood that gives way beneath it. With a roar, it loses its footing and falls. I slip down the chains. I can't feel my grip, and the blood on my hands prevents me from stopping my momentum.

"G!" Charlie calls from where she's stretched out on the stone and holds her hand out to me. "Grab on!"

But I can't. I'm still slipping, still losing what little grip I have. The beast roars again, and the chains whip around me as more wood splinters—the monster crashing through the middle level.

"Please, come on!" She strains farther, desperately trying to reach me.

I can only look at her as I lose my grip completely, my numb hand letting go of the chain.

Her scream follows me down into the darkness, all the way to the cold stone floor so far below.

THIRTY

I stand on a windswept roof, a storm raging all around me as I whirl. Several gables rise and fall, as if I've climbed to the top of some huge mansion. Up here, the wind cuts and the rain feels like small stones that try to gouge my skin.

Shielding my eyes from the rain, I hear shouts and the sounds of battle.

What am I doing here?

I lean over the edge closest to me. Down below is a dark gorge, the water white-capped and angry. Behind me, something inhuman growls.

"G!" Someone shakes me. "G!"

Bitterness coats my tongue, and I gasp in a breath, my eyes opening.

Charlie stares down at me, her face pale as she puts her palms against my cheeks. "G?"

I sputter and cough, then wipe my mouth. "What is that?"

Her eyes widen. "You're alive!" She throws her arms around me, hugging me tight to her, so tight I'm having trouble getting my breath.

"Charlie," I grunt.

"You were dead. You were …" She lets go and yanks my shirt up. "The bite. It's gone." Then she moves to my leg.

I look around, then remember. "Oh, fuck!" I sit up.

"Whoa!" She puts her hands on my shoulders. "Go slow."

"Is it dead?" I feel around for my sword as I stare at the monster lying beside me, its body broken, bones poking out here and there, and black blood flowing in a pool beneath it. The fae's head is crushed, and only the bird remains intact, though it doesn't move.

"It's dead. You killed it." She wraps her arms around my neck again. "You stupid, oafish, doltish, idiot!"

"Charlie, now's not the time for foreplay." I kiss the top of her head.

"Why would you do that? Why would you …" She pulls back, her eyes swimming with tears. "Why?"

I press my forehead to hers. "You know why."

She sniffles. "Don't ever do anything like that again. If I hadn't had the *vitae eluvia*—"

"Oh, that's what that was." I wipe my mouth again. "Tastes like ass."

She laughs and sits back. "It saved your life."

"*You* saved my life." I grip the nape of her neck and pull her back to me. "From the moment I met you." I kiss her hard and she answers, her breath mixing with mine as we share parts of our souls.

When we finally part, she sits back on her knees and reaches for something in the rubble.

"What—" My heart lurches when I see the huge red gem in her hands. She hands it to me.

It's heavy, far more than it should truly weigh. The sorcerer's soul must be like lead.

"I was too late." I stare at the phylactery, silently willing the lady from the water to appear. She doesn't. That foolish flame of hope that's burned inside me this entire time finally goes out, leaving a dark wisp of smoke behind. I lost my chance. I'll never be whole again.

"G, don't give up just yet. There might have been enough time. I don't think the moon was—" She makes a sound. A horrible sound.

I drop the phylactery and catch her as she falls forward.

"Charlie!" Something hard strikes me in the chest. When I look down, I see the metal glint of the scorpion's tail. It's impaled Charlie, punching through her with its metal barb.

I grab my sword and swing at the monster's corpse, severing the tail. When it clangs to the floor, I realize then what it's made of. Iron.

"Charlie!" I drop my sword and pick her up, carrying her out of the tower and lying her gently on the stones.

Her eyes are closed, her body unmoving as I pull open her cloak. Blood seeps through her shirt, pooling beneath her as I try to put pressure on the wound. But it's too much, too big.

"Charlie!" I pull her into my arms and hold her tight. No breath stirs in her. There's nothing. *Nothing.* "Charlie!" I yell and press my bloody hand to her cheek. "Charlie, please. Charlie."

She doesn't wake. Her beautiful skin has gone pale. "Charlie." I clutch her to my chest and scream until my throat shreds, and then I scream again. Agony, I thought I knew it well. I didn't. We've never met. Not until right now. Not until this moment as I scream and scream and scream, yet Charlie doesn't wake. She won't wake.

I rock her, keeping her tightly against me as Belinda and Binny come over, their heads down as they stand beside us.

All I can do is hold her. "I'll keep you safe," I whisper to her and kiss her cold forehead. "I'll keep you safe. I'll hold you while you sleep. Don't worry. I'm here. I'll always be here."

I let my tears fall, not for one moment letting her go. I'll hold her until she comes back. She *has* to come back. I'll hold her until then.

"When we get to Paris." I press my cheek against her hair. "When we get there, you can pick out our rooms. Maybe something with a view? At the top of a hill, perhaps. Somewhere close to some stables where Belinda could stay. I know you'd like that."

She doesn't answer.

"Not by the Seine, though. You deserve better. You deserve the best." My voice breaks, and I have to take a deep breath. "Whatever you want, Charlie. I'll make it happen. Just, please—" I can't speak past the lump in my throat, past the tears that choke me.

Instead, I hold her. I keep her close, sharing my warmth with her so she'll be comfortable when she wakes up. I should build her a fire, but I'd have to let her go to do that. I can't. So I sit, her in my arms, and wait for her to come back to me.

THE SOUND OF WATER. Not dripping. Flowing. I hear it, as if a river moves between the trees, flowing over rocks and beneath downed trunks.

I peer into the dark, looking for the source of it. Charlie still rests in my arms, her body so cold. I tuck her cloak in tighter around her, the fabric wet and frigid.

The sound grows louder, rushing over rocks and through crevices, splashing and roiling like the base of a waterfall.

Then a light appears between the trees, blinding in its intensity.

"The Graven Phylactery." The voice from the water is in my ear. "You've found it."

I blink against the intense light and catch the image of a woman, her dress white and flowing as she floats above the ground.

"I set you this task, and you have completed it." She reaches down and takes the phylactery, then closes it in her palm.

A blast emanates from it, blowing me back as I keep my grip on Charlie. The shards of red glass turn to sand between the woman's fingers and fall to the stone, and suddenly the heavy, oily feeling lifts.

"Now, I shall make good on my end of the bargain and return to you—"

"Her." I get my feet under me and stand, Charlie in my arms. "Please. Please, save her."

The woman floats closer and reaches out a glowing hand to Charlie. "She's gone."

"Save her!" I yell.

"That was not our bargain." She backs away, her eyes on me.

"It was." I step toward her. "You said 'If you would recover what you've lost'—this is what I've lost! Her! I've lost her. Give her back to me!"

"You would give up your past? Your face?"

"I would give up everything if it meant she would live." I step even closer, her light hurting my eyes. "Please, take anything from me you wish, just bring her back."

"You would give me your life, then?"

"Yes! Take it!" I lift my head, offering her my throat.

She looks at me, her pale blue eyes seeing me, but also seeing through me. Hearing my thoughts, reading my soul.

I don't care if I'm rotten on the inside and vile on the outside. I'll stay that way forever. I'll accept it. I'll accept *me*. I look down at Charlie and realize she already did. She loved me like this. Loved me as I am, not as I wished to be. Loved me even though I'm wicked and scarred. Loved me as I love her.

The woman reaches to her side and pulls out a long, thin blade. "Your life for hers? Very well then."

"Gladly." I give Charlie one last kiss, then lift my chin again and close my eyes. "Do it."

She hovers closer, her blade warm at my throat. "Very well. Our bargain is at an end."

THIRTY-ONE

"Charlie?" I wake with a start.

"Eh?" Someone asks.

"Charlie!" Disoriented, I sit up, my body aching. "Charlie!"

"You're awake." The goblin from the tombs sits by a fire, Belinda and Binny tied up behind him.

"Where is she? Where's Charlie?"

He gestures toward me. "That cut on your neck needs more time to heal. You should lie down and—"

I toss off the blanket over me and stand. "Charlie!" I'm in the hills around Raven's end, the grass waving in a light breeze as the sun sets. "Where is she?" I run to the goblin and grab him by his shirt, lifting him and dangling him. "Where is Charlie?"

"I don't know of no Charlie." He shakes his head, his eyes wide. "You were sleeping here, and I … I had my cart and thought you might be a customer so I—I—"

I drop him and whirl, dashing to Belinda. "Come on, girl. We have to go back for her."

She nickers and shies away.

"Hey!" I grab her reins and put one foot in her stirrups.

"Where are you off to, G?"

That voice.

I freeze, everything in me going still as I put my feet back on the ground. When I turn, I catch the entire world in my gaze. "Charlie?"

She runs into my arms.

I catch her and lift her, crushing her to me. "It's you."

She peppers kisses on my cheek. "G!"

I put her down, then yank open her cloak.

"Hey!" she smacks at my hands, but I ignore it. I spread my palm over her chest. "It's gone. The wound is gone." I meet her eyes, the blue of them the same shade as the sky.

"You made a good deal." She shrugs, her eyes swimming with tears.

I grip her shoulders and kiss her, tasting her, knowing her. She's real. This is real. I grab her ass and lift her, and she wraps her legs around me.

"I'll just, er, I'll be goin—" the goblin mumbles.

I kiss her until I can't breathe, then pull back and stare at her, almost disbelieving this is real. "What happened?"

"The lady in the water took your bargain. Apparently, the hag was right. There was some wiggle room in the terms. She needed some of your blood to seal the deal—well, your blood and your agreement to let it go, to sacrifice it."

"Sacrifice what?" I ask.

"The life you thought you needed. The one we've been chasing." She looks away. "I understand if you're upset about—"

"No." My voice comes out strong and loud. "I'll never regret doing anything that keeps you with me, that keeps you alive. You're my life. *You.* I can't lose you, Charlie. I can't." My voice breaks and I kiss her, our tears mingling as I carry her to the bedroll and lay her down.

"You won't lose me." She cups my face and kisses me softly. "I'm not going anywhere. After all, I'm the only one who can read the map." Her smile sends heat all the way to my toes. With rough, grasping hands, I take her shirt and yank it right down the middle.

She yelps.

"It's gone." I run my fingertips over her smooth skin. When I close my eyes, I can still see the barb, still see the metal coated in her blood.

She grabs my wrist, holding me steady. "It's gone, G. I'm all right."

I lean down and kiss her right over her heart, covering her skin with my lips and saying silent thank yous over and over again to the lady in the water. "When I thought you were—" I can't say it, can't think it. Not again. Never again.

"G. I'm here." She runs her fingertips along my brow, then down the scarred side of my face. "I'm not going anywhere."

I kiss her chest again, marveling at the smooth, healthy skin. When my cheek brushes against her hard nipple, she jolts. And when I wrap my lips around it, her back arches as she runs her fingers through my hair.

"G," she says breathily as I kiss one breast, then the other, giving them ample attention as my hands rove lower.

"I couldn't let you go." I return to her face and stare down at her, looking at every freckle, every color in her iris, the curve of her lips.

Her eyes water again, and I kiss away the tears that escape. "I love you, G." She leans up and captures my mouth, her tongue sweeping inside and pulling a groan of need from me.

I unbutton her pants, then in a blur of yanking and tugging, we strip until we're naked under the fading sun, our bodies pressed together.

"I love you, Charlie. I'll never let you go." I slide inside her and swallow her cry, drinking her down as I thrust slow and sure. She hooks her ankles behind my back, urging me deeper and harder as I revel in her, worship her.

I give her what she needs. She's so fucking sexy beneath me, her nails digging into my shoulders as I hold her hips in place. I drive into her, pulling my name from her as I make her come, her body coiling and releasing around my cock. She's everything to me.

I claim her again and again, making her mine the way she was always meant to be.

Who I was doesn't matter. It's who I am now that defines my life, my legacy.

I thought the quest was meant to give my life back. Instead, it gave my life meaning. It gave me the one person who sees all of me and loves all of me, no matter what I lack. For that, I'll be forever grateful to whatever circumstance put me in that river. It led me to my destiny. It led me to *her*.

EPILOGUE

"This prince guy looks like a twat. Does he realize that?" I stare down at the gilded carriage as it passes by.

Charlie elbows me. "Shh, G! You're so loud. He can probably hear you."

"Maybe he should." I snort a laugh. "Look at that long hair and those big, round googly eyes. Chin like the back of a foot. How the hell did he ever convince anyone to marry him?" I scratch the scruff on my scarred cheek. "Defies logic."

Charlie looks up at me and rolls her eyes. "Perhaps he was more attractive when they met. There's probably a story there."

"I bet he can't even grow a beard." I wrinkle my nose as the carriage passes by, the prince and princess waving at the Parisians on the road or in the windows. "And prince of what? It doesn't make sense."

She shrugs. "I'm not entirely sure. They're from some far province, just touring the city. The brunette's got her nose in a book—seems like a good sign."

I scoff. "They should see what real royalty looks like. You put them to shame."

She glances down at her mud-splattered riding pants. "I hardly look like a princess at the moment."

"You always look like a princess." I lean over and kiss her.

She smiles against me. "You're just trying to get into my pants."

"Always." I cup one of her breasts and squeeze.

"G." She smacks my hand. "We don't have time. I've got to change so we can make it to Finnraven Hill by sundown." She holds up a finger and backs away.

"Your father won't care if we're a little bit late." I follow her.

"You know he most certainly will." She smirks. "Well, he won't mind if *you're* late. It's me he wants to see—Oh!"

I snatch her into my arms and throw her onto the bed.

"G!"

I jump on her before she can get up and claim her mouth with a kiss. "You know he'll love me eventually."

She laughs and kicks against the bed, rolling us so she's on top. "It's been what, two years? He still refers to you as 'that human pet of yours'."

"I don't mind." I take her hand and press it against my trousers. "I could use more petting though."

"You're wicked." She sighs.

"That's what I hear." I lean up and press my lips to her throat. "I'd like to do wicked things to you."

"We can't." She pushes me down onto the bed. "We still haven't bought a baby gift for Vivian and Luc, and we're visiting them when we're done at my father's."

"We'll pick one up on the way. Plenty of stores here in Paris." I unbutton her pants.

She giggles as I flip her onto her back again, kissing her, then pulling her pants and panties off.

"There's my favorite little Parisian hideaway." I inhale her scent then lick her from entrance to clit.

Her laugh turns to a moan as she spreads wider for me, giving me all the access I need to feast on her.

"See? We have plenty of time, don't we?" I tongue her. "Don't we?"

"Yes." She looks down at me.

"That's what I thought." I press two fingers inside her and suck her flesh until her thighs begin to shake.

When I crawl up her body, she yanks me to her, kissing me with a need that turns my already fiery blood to lava. Positioning myself, I slide inside her, groaning at the way she envelopes me so perfectly.

"So fucking tight." I pull back and slam home, rocking the bed as we kiss and move with each other, doing the dance I love the best.

Her body, so soft and strong, is built to ride mine. So I roll her on top. She strips her shirt away, giving me a view of her tits as she rolls her hips, chasing her pleasure as I surge up to meet her. Cupping her breasts, I squeeze them and pinch her nipples.

When she piles her hair on her head, her hips mesmerizing in their rhythm, I almost come from the sight of her. She's too much. Always has been. But I've always wanted more than I deserved, so I take her, thrusting into her again and again as she grinds against me.

Licking my thumb, I press it to her clit and stroke her.

Her moans grow louder, her body trembling as I grunt with each push of my hips, each stroke of my cock inside her. I can't stop myself, not when she's on top of me. I stroke her faster, bringing her to climax. When she reaches it, her hips lock, and she throws her head back as my name passes her lips.

"That's it. Come on my cock." I yank her hips tight to me and grit my teeth as I come, my cock kicking, filling her with me as I worship her with every bit of my soul.

My vision swims with the pure pleasure of it, the deliciousness of claiming her as mine, marking her with my seed as she milks me.

When she finally takes a breath, I pull her to me, tasting her again and tonguing her deeply. She relaxes on top of me, her body warm and languid.

She bites my chest, her even teeth no doubt leaving marks. "Now we're definitely going to be late."

I smack her ass. "Worth it."

She laughs and bites me again. "We'll have to hurry to make it before the shops close."

"It's just a baby. How much stuff could it need?" I sigh contentedly and run my hands up and down her back.

She props her chin on my chest, her eyes sparkling in the golden light of sunset. "I think you'll find babies need plenty of things."

"Hm?" I stare at her.

The slightest smirk plays at the corner of her lips. "Clothes, nappies, a crib, all manner of toys—babies are a lot of work." She glances around our apartment. "More space for certain. I was thinking something a bit farther out, perhaps with a yard and some chickens."

My heart stutter steps, as if tripping over itself. Surely, I'm misunderstanding her. I am, after all, an oaf. With shaking hands, I cup her face. "Are you ... are you saying ..."

She scoots up my body and presses her lips to mine. "Yes."

I wrap my arms around her, my entire body trembling as I kiss her. "I thought you couldn't, I thought ..." My words won't form.

"It's rare." She kisses my cheek. "And it won't be without difficulty."

I gently roll to the side and lay her next to me, then run my hand along her stomach. "A child, really?"

"Really." She grins. "*Our* child."

I move down and kiss her stomach. "Beautiful like you, smart like me."

She laughs and runs her fingers through my hair. "We can only hope."

I kiss back to her mouth and pull her into my arms, holding her there for long moments.

She sighs against me, her lips pressed to my throat. "Are you happy?"

I smile, tears trying to well in my eyes. "You already made me happier than I ever had any right to be. And now? Now you've given us a family." I kiss her hair. "I already worshipped you, Charlie. Now what's a man like me to do?"

She snickers, her hands roving my chest. "I rather enjoy that thing you do with your tongue, if you're looking for suggestions."

I smirk and lay her on her back, then move down her body once more, licking her between her thighs until she comes so loudly the neighbors bang on the walls. Then I do it again.

When I finally let her breathe, I pull her into my arms. The sun has long since set, the fluid Parisian night rushing around us like a river. One that will carry us to our destiny. I don't care if I wind up on a riverbank again, as long as it's with Charlie. With the memory of our lives together, and with our love as my only identifier, the truth of it stitched into my soul.

HAPPILY EVER AFTER

Acknowledgments

I've had this story bumbling around in my head for a few years now. The villains are always my favorite, and I can always get behind The Bad Guy no matter what their twisted hearts lead them to do. My dearest reader, I get the feeling you're similar in that respect, so thank you for being a kindred spirit.

Thank you, Mr. Archer, for telling me to "just do it" when it came to this story. I know you wanted something a bit more mainstream, something that would help you with your goal of becoming a "kept man," so I appreciate you encouraging me to follow my heart on this book instead. You're a keeper.

Huge thank you to Mel. This cover would've never been created if it weren't for your dogged efforts with the talented Perfect Pear. You two are a dream team when it comes to graphics. It was a delight for me to sit back and watch you two squabble and then, as always, come up with something absolutely gorgeous.

Zakuga, you are the most talented person I know. I feel like I'm talent-adjacent just being near you. I'm so glad I can call you a friend. You are a warrior for what you believe in, and I know that your true artistry can never be replaced. It's fucking brilliant. You always blow my mind with the beauty you create, and I can't thank you enough for working with me on the images for this novel. You're the art GOAT, my friend. Don't ever doubt it.

NSFW ART

Fancy a look at some NSFW art of G and Charlie? If you're 18+, click below. If you aren't, what are you even doing here? You should be reading *The Hunger Games* or something with more suitable levels of gory violence and zero sex, because god forbid you read about love. Wait, where was I? Oh yes, if you are of age and want to see some juicy bits, you're in luck!

(https://www.lilyarcherauthor.com/bookofgnsfw.html)The password is: **dinner**

.

ALSO BY LILY ARCHER

Fae's Captive

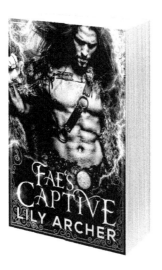

My college roommate is the worst. Cecile steals my food, brings guys over at all hours, and parties instead of studying. But those quirks pale in comparison to what she does next. She drugs me, and I wake up imprisoned in an alternate universe full of terrifying creatures.

Now, the biggest and scariest creature of all--*a fae king*-- believes I'm his mate. He's freed me from the dungeon but keeps me close. So close, in fact, that I'm beginning to like his wintery gaze and ice-chiseled body. But secrets and villains lurk throughout this new world, and I don't know if I'll survive long enough to figure out how to get back home.

Fae's Consort

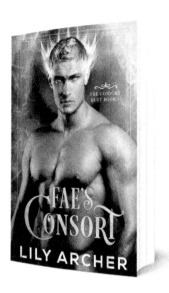

They call me the village spinster. I rather enjoy it. Single and free to dance with the witches under the moonlight whenever I please—what could be better than that?

When the day king shows up to take ten changelings as his consorts, I'm happy those selection days are behind me. At least I thought they were. But instead of ten young females, King Solano chooses only one. Me. Emma Druzy, sock darner and 28-year-old spinster of Moonhollow.

He takes me to the day realm, a world of sun and beauty the likes of which I've never imagined. Solano is far more than he seems, his wit and his warmth breaking down my walls.

But there's danger here, too, the sort that creeps up on you despite the bright light of day. And if I'm not careful, I'll lose my heart to the day king or my life to his enemies.

Omega Academy

Drawing, my online clan, and planning my escape from my mother--these are priorities. Or, at least they were, until three huge alien Alphas came to abduct me and take me to their planet. But it's not just a simple process of probing and then releasing me back to Earth. All those movies are lies. These three males keep me. And I'm suddenly a cadet at an Omega Academy where I'm supposed to learn how to serve the Gretar Fleet.

None of this makes any sense to begin with, nevermind the three Alphas I can't seem to avoid. But they say we have a connection, that we're a circle, whatever that means. And my body seems to agree, because anytime they're near, I can't seem to think of anything except Kyte's horns, Jeren's smirk, and Ceredes's long, hard ... sword. Focusing on class is almost impossible, and the Omega Academy isn't for the faint of heart.

I have to learn who my enemies are, how to make friends, and how I fit with the three males I can't stop thinking about. All doable, right? No. Not right, especially when I discover the fleet has other plans for me. The bond with my three Alphas may be the only thing that can keep me safe, but that means we need to consummate our circle. Yeah, you read that right, consummate. Deep. Breaths.

A Land of Never and Night

Peter Pan is just a story passed down from my batty ancestor Wendy about a boy who never wanted to grow up. And that's all it is to me until I'm kidnapped by a man with a twinkle in his eye and a shadow that does his dirty work.

Peter Pan.

But he's not a kid anymore. He says he wants to protect me from Captain Hook, that together we can save Neverland from endless night. All I have to do is tell him stories. Tale after tale. Night after night.

I do as he asks, and slowly, he becomes more than just a muddled myth from long ago. He's a man, one who no longer accepts acorns when what he truly wants is a kiss.

I know it's a delusion, one that might claim my life. Even so, I begin to put my faith in Peter and his Lost Boys.

But danger lurks around every corner of Neverland, and it's *always* closer than you think.

About the Author

Lily Archer believes in fairies, mermaids, and fierce fae warriors. Armed with nothing more than her imagination and a well-worn MacBook, she intends to slay the darkest beasts of the fantasy worlds and create true love where none seemed possible.

Be sure to sign up for new release alerts at lilyarcher.com!

SIGNED books are available exclusively on my website.

Printed in Great Britain
by Amazon